CROATOAN, EARTH: THE SAGA BEGINS

WRITTEN BY: M.V. JOHNSON

EDITED BY: COLTON J. CARPENTER

Trinary

Copyright © 2022 Michael Johnson

All rights reserved. No part of this publication may be reproduced, distributed, or transmitted in any form or by any means, including photocopying, recording, or other electronic or mechanical methods, without the prior written consent of the copyright owner, except in the case of brief quotations embodied in critical reviews and certain other noncommercial uses permitted by copyright law. For permission requests, contact the publisher, Trinary Press.

This is a work of fiction. Names, characters, businesses, places, events, and incidents are the products of the author's imagination or used in a fictitious manner. Any resemblance to actual persons, living or dead, or actual events is purely coincidental.

Published by Trinary Press

Paperback ISBN: 9798414618584

Direct all inquiries to:

TrinaryPress@gmail.com

Chapter 1: Contact

I remember well the day the saucers came. It was chaos as one might expect.

Governments panicked. People rioted. It took less than three days for the governments of the world to declare martial law. The saucers hung over every landmass. We did not need telescopes to see them either. The saucers were that big. Their arrival was the biggest news event in the history of mankind. The question "Are we alone in the universe?" had finally been answered, and that answer was a resounding "No, we are not."

Scientists with blogs and Twitter accounts, conspiracy theorists, and theists from nearly every known religion in the world flocked to social media to voice their fears and share their theories. Politicians stampeded CNN, FOX News, Al Jazeera, and all the other major news networks with the intent of calming the people, and even though their voices were calm and collected, we could see the fear in their eyes. They were just as scared as us. Experts shared their conjectures as to why they thought the aliens had come, tossing them around like a football to anyone who would listen. They clung to their theories like toddlers to their security blankets. All the theories Hollywood made famous were out there in full force.

The saucers had come to plunder Earth for our minerals and steal our resources. They were slavers here to take us into bondage. They were peaceful explorers in search of life on other planets. The ships were part of a scientific expedition, and they were here to study us. They were scouts here to test our defenses. The only thing that was apparent was that no one knew why they were here, but everyone had a theory. They had a theory because the saucers never landed. They never descended to make their intentions known. They did not attack.

They refused to communicate. Other than knocking a few weather satellites out of orbit by accident, they did nothing at all. They were like moths crowding a streetlamp. The saucers came, and they did absolutely nothing. At least, they did nothing in the beginning.

While the saucers did nothing, we sure were busy. The riots lasted for three months, and when the saucers never landed, our fear turned to curiosity, fermenting like grapes into wine. They could have destroyed us at any time. We had no hope of standing up to so many. Each ship was the size of Iowa, and when NORAD finally managed to count them all, it found that there were a whopping one hundred and six of them. NASA confirmed the count two days later. Each ship was given a target designation by the military. Warheads were prepped, launchers positioned, alliances formed, and it was all done in the name of defending humanity from the alien horde. We stood no chance against what was up there. I knew it, and so did our world leaders. If we fought, it was not going to be a fight for Earth's survival. It was going to be an obstinate attempt to go down swinging. Thankfully, the call to fire never came and the ships blocking our view of the stars never descended. Five months after their arrival, a threshold concern was raised requiring that a decision be made. There were still cosmonauts on the ISS. They were evidently running low on Tang and powdered ribeye or whatever it is our astronauts eat. At least, that is what I took away from the President's broadcast. The cosmonauts needed to be rescued or resupplied if they were to survive. I remember watching the debates over whether we should launch a space shuttle to resupply them, or whether we should task Space X with the mission to rescue them. In the end, they went with rescue. I think the government just did not want to risk losing their only means of space flight should the worst happen. So, Space X got the job.

Even though we risked starting a war with the aliens, we still chose to save our people. I think that says a lot about humanity. Though, I suspect it had less to do with saving their lives and everything to do with wanting to debrief the people who had the closest vantage point to the ships for the longest. A Dragon class rocket of Space X design was selected to make the journey. A day was chosen. A launch window was selected. Nobody watched SpongeBob that day. Every channel on every station aired the same damn thing, a ship with a big red "X" painted on the side tensely awaiting it's launch window.

Newscaster after newscaster showed the same dozen retired astronauts—now consultants—explaining what the people were about to see. I watched with bated breath. This would either be a boring taxi ride for a bunch of Russian scientists, or it was the one deliberate act by the people of this world that was going to doom us all.

It was believed by many who watched that these were our last moments, this would be the extinction of man.

But, as many had hoped and even more had feared, the launch happened as planned. I started drinking. I drank faster when the newscasters announced that the Dragon shuttle was passing within one mile of two of the saucers. When they successfully docked with the ISS, the satellite imagery of the coupling left humanity breathless and dazed. The ISS was like a ladybug on the windshield of an 18-wheeler compared to the saucers in the background. I stopped drinking when they made their second trip past the two saucers while on their return voyage. I had to stop drinking because I drunkenly passed out.

When I did finally awake, I was laying on my couch soaked with my own disgusting mixture of piss and stale beer, but despite this, the news kept repeating that all was well. Mankind would live. The visiting space craft was apparently uninterested and unthreatened by our trip up among them. The politicians who made the call to go were praised by those who chickened out and other armchair warriors. The cosmonauts were healthy and even appeared briefly at a press conference, though their responses were heavily censored. Debriefing those who had floated amongst The Arrived, as they were called, was paramount. They had surely seen much more than we had from the ground. Whether that was different than what we experienced was never revealed to the public. As I sat there, hungover and praying for death, I realized that this was a victory of sorts. Perseus had saved Andromeda, but this time, the Kraken did not care.

All went back to a post-arrival state of normalcy. People worked with an ominous dread pressing down on them. People boarded planes fearing they would never arrive at their destination. All was calm until the week before the anniversary of their arrival. The governments tried to play it down before the public, but I was one of them. They could not hide the truth from me. I knew what was coming because somehow, in my mind, The Arrived had shown me.

The visitors had finally made first contact.

It started on a Friday. Pilots from all over the world had reported the same phenomenon. A mysterious magnetic field was intermittently interfering with their navigation systems. Planes were constantly forced to correct their headings. On Saturday, the period of interferences got longer, and planes veered even further off course. By Sunday morning, the call went out that planes all over the world were being grounded. The skies of Earth were declared no fly zones. The skies had not been this empty since Kitty Hawk. By Sunday, the magnetic field was starting to interfere with telecommunications. Cell phones would not work. Television was fuzzy and radios the world over crackled with dead air. Everyone sensed it. Something was about to happen, and on Wednesday, something did.

All the TV stations came back in, clear and undisturbed. Radios worked again. The magnetic interference was gone as if it had never existed. It was anti-climactic to say the least. I was so convinced that this was the end that I almost spent my entire life savings on vice and entertainment. This had become a thing now for some of us. The fear of total annihilation will lower some inhibitions. People were hooking up like never before. I'm not sure what it is with the prospect of death, but when faced with it, people get horny. They develop this sudden desire to copulate and reproduce. Maybe, it is a survival instinct: a biological arc response. If we are probably going to die, let's all get pregnant. If one of us survives, at least mankind will go on. Living in the first world like I did, this sounded ludicrous, but then again, when have the multitudes ever been on the cusp of extinction as they were right at that moment? There was the Holocaust and a bucket full of other genocidal events, but till now, I had never realized that this could be the end of all things. There may be no Lazarus Rising awaiting us. I thought that the last pages of humanity's story might at this moment be receiving its last few lines.

But Wednesday arrived, and I did not have to spend my life savings to have sex with a stranger. The interference stopped, and I did not need to eat that sinful fruit.

I was glued to CNN after that. The governments still called for a moratorium on flying, but there was talk of an easing up of the restrictions if nothing new presented itself in the interim of the next few days. It seemed a prudent precaution. It turned out to be a good decision on their part, because on Thursday, all Hell broke loose.

Chapter 2: Psychic

There had always been a debate as to whether psychic ability was real or not. There were psychics who sold their wares on television. There were mediums in places like New Orleans and Vegas. I had always dismissed these things as coincidence because science was my mistress.

On Thursday, the argument was settled once and for all. Frauds were revealed and real psychics were discovered. It started as a dull ache near my temples that slipped down the back of my skull. It felt like a pent-up pressure like when you have blocked sinuses only worse, and it kept getting even worse. By the end of the first day, we were screaming the world over. Every psychic on the planet was being contacted by them. It had to be them. It was like someone was pressing a dull rounded rod into my skull right between my eyes and with it came an image. It was a strange collection of glyphs arranged in row.

They were just shapes, but the pain was real. I screamed like I had never screamed before. It hurt horribly, but those shapes would not go away. They would not stop. Through the pain I managed to wonder why they were doing this. Why were they attacking me? What did the word mean? That was when the pain ended for me. I was into my third day of the psychic attack when it occurred to me. It was not just a string of shapes. It was a word. The pain was less severe now and knowing that it was a word got me to thinking about what that word was. What was the word they wanted us to know? And like that, the shapes changed and became letters. I knew the word. I knew it and understood it. I had even seen it before. They taught that word in school. It was a word American's feared, because it was the only word left behind when the colonists in Roanoke, Virginia disappeared in 1595.

As it turned out, I was not the only one who had been given the word. It was given to all the psychics. Some suffered only a short time, merely hours. Others suffered longer, days like I had. When the pain was linked to the understanding of the word, the call went out, and the word was whispered to the rest of those like me. In the news reports, the psychics all stopped screaming when they heard the word whispered into their ears. Nobody knew why they wanted us to know this word. What did it mean? What was "croatoan"? I did not know. Understanding of the meaning was not required, only that we know the word.

The EMP blast came the moment the last psychic uttered the word. People with pacemakers dropped dead. People on life support died. There were traffic accidents, and a few key industrial facilities suffered explosions and accidents as equipment went offline in a cataclysmic chain of events. Six planes who'd ignored the flying ban—two of them smugglers—crashed as a result of power loss. The power worldwide was off. The planet was dark for the first time in my life. I saw more stars that night than ever before, but that was not a lot. The saucers blocked our view of the universe, but what I saw was beautiful.

When the power returned, so did the televisions. With it came the news of all the deaths. Tens of thousands died. A call to attack the saucers went up. It seemed this was the first volley fired, but then another newscast aired. In the darkness of the power outage, a solitary saucer had descended and come to land. It was not one of the Iowa-sized saucers. This seemed more a shuttle or a skiff. It was a little over two football fields in diameter, and it was sitting in a field outside a small town in southern Kansas. Aliens had landed in Cherryville. The moment they said the little town's name, I rushed outside to see; I lived in Cherryville. I could not see the ship from where I lived, but I knew the field from the newscast. I knew where it was and so did the military. Their trucks started arriving in town about the same time I decided to go see the saucer firsthand.

The military was quickly establishing a perimeter around the craft. Several helicopters could be heard in the distance, coming to survey the situation. The field that the saucer had descended upon was large. Just last year there had been a local fair in this field very field, and I distinctly remembered a Ferris wheel in the exact spot that the saucer now occupied. I am sure I was not the only observer to note that coincidence.

It was not what I expected. The ship was metal like our own. There were dents in the hull and scorch marks on the side but no door that I could see. Though, I did not walk all the way around it to verify the fact. I kind of felt like I was looking at the Millennium Falcon. I expected Han Solo to pop out with Chewy in tow, but no dice. The ship just sat there silent with birds perched on top and cattle grazing beneath it. This was not the ET event I imagined it to be. CDC trucks arrived an hour after the landing. The entire population of the town was gathered off to the side to watch. Homeland Security and the FBI showed up. Politicians arrived by the end of the day. A consortium of scientists came and conferred with the alphabet groups. The worst of all who came were the theists.

The church goers and dooms day cults converged on Cherryville, filling the streets and preaching their contradictory messages. Their followers came with them. For three days, the ship sat there doing nothing. Vendors of various goods descended on the field. Hot dogs, burgers, funnel cakes, beer, and cheesy alien souvenirs were sold by the thousands. Small tents popped up only to be replaced by bigger tents mere hours later.

People picnicked on the grass like it was a Saturday in the park. Half of those in attendance were tense and scared. They alternated between anxiously staring at the saucer and whispering to one another in hushed tones as if the saucer may hear them. The other half were thrilled and exhilarated. I was neither. I was in pain. I was having another psychic episode. Luckily, I realized that the symbols I saw in my head were words and avoided the worst of the pain. The word was a simple one this time: "Meet." No other word accompanied it, but there was a compulsion to act. I resisted this and instead bought a funnel cake from a vendor.

A murmur went up from the crowd as I spooned blueberry sauce onto my cake. I could not see what was happening, and I climbed up on a truck's bumper to see. The truck's driver glared at me for a moment, but his eyes were drawn to the same place mine were: the saucer. A group of five men and two women were striding out into the field between the perimeter of armed soldiers and the ship. The ambassadors of humanity had been selected.

There was no huge ramp that descended or door of white light that opened from the saucer. There was a small port on the bottom of the ship, a long ladder, and a middle-aged white man in peculiar dress. The man climbed down. He caught a brown case that was dropped to him from someone unseen within. The murmuring in the crowd grew louder as people laid eyes on the first alien they had ever seen.

I bought another funnel cake.

I watched the man from the ship take a moment to compose himself before beginning his march to those who awaited him. A gasp of disbelief went up when the pilot suddenly stopped and raised a foot. He had discovered a Kansas landmine. He studied the bottom of his boot for a moment then spent the next few moments trying to wipe the cow poop off on the grass. When he was satisfied that his boot was clean enough, he covered the last little bit to the seven ambassadors of man. He set his brown case down on the ground and pulled from it a tray. He spent a few moments unfolding legs so that a small table stood before them. Then, from the bag, he pulled what looked like an iPad. It was a small handheld tablet which he set before the group. I could see him touching it then looking expectantly at the seven. I felt a pain in my head again. The word "meet" came to me once more followed by that compulsion to walk.

I tried strawberry sauce on my funnel cake this time. It was delicious.

As I continued watching the events unfold, it became clear that whatever the pilot was trying to convey to the seven was not coming across. My head suddenly hurt. A new word formed: "Wait." I found another truck parked nearby and climbed up to sit on the edge of the bed so I could see and still eat. I did not realize anything was up until I noticed that the people around me were backing away quickly. I looked around for the cause and saw the seven ambassadors walking across the field toward the funnel cake vendor. The pilot of the ship walked beside them. I did not want to be here directly in their path. I tried to find a place to set my cake so I could hop down, but the truck bed had rails and there just was not a good place to set it. I decided to jump for it and slowly slid off. My rotund belly bouncing as I landed. With my hands full of cake, I did not have one to spare to catch myself as I tumbled forward to the ground. My funnel cake flipped off my plate, strawberry sauce and all, and landed on the pilot's boots. A groan went up from the ambassadors. The pilot looked at the mess on his shoes then at me and pointed his finger in my face.

"Him? You want him?" a tall blonde in the middle asked, studying me in disbelief.

"What?" I asked, struggling to rise. One of the male ambassadors, a neatly coiffed man with a red tie offered me a hand. My head suddenly hurt.

Croatoan. The pilot looked at me with raised brows and jerked his head toward the seven.

"What's he want with you?" another ambassador asked. This man had gold rimmed glasses and a cheap dress shirt from Target.

"He . . ." I looked at the faces of the seven, suddenly feeling very exposed. "He says 'Croatoan.'"

"What's that mean?" the blonde asked, as if I would know. The pilot answered for him. He stepped forward and extended his hand. In my head the word formed again.

"Croatoan," I said, as the blonde nervously took the alien's hand. They shook. The pilot moved to the man in the red tie. The word was there again. "Croatoan." The word appeared every time he extended his hand to shake, and I realized what he was saying. "It means hello."

"He said 'hello?'" Gold-rims asked.

"I think he's been saying it all along. I think that's what 'Croatoan' means. It's them saying hello." I glanced over at the pilot as another word formed. "He says 'yes.'"

The ambassadors were suddenly very excited. They could finally express themselves. They could get the answers they craved.

"Ask him why he's here," the blonde instructed. I shrugged and turned to the man.

"Why are you here?" I asked out loud, repeating the question. He smirked at the absurdity.

"I could have done that," the blonde declared angrily.

"Then you do it," I said, turning to walk away. "He understands you just fine, but I don't think you have the ability to understand him."

"Why not?" Gold-rims asked.

"They're psychic," I said. That should have been obvious, and I was beginning to question the wisdom of whoever put these people in charge of representing Earth.

Funny, the pilot observed.

"I know," I told the visitor. "That's what this world is like sometimes. People talking above others or talking below them. No one ever talks to them."

Good? It was a question from the pilot.

"Sometimes. No. I don't know these people personally. They're big wigs," he frowned. "Er . . . they are important," I said, sweeping away the euphemism.

Ah, he responded inside my mind, understanding.

"So, why are you here?" I asked again.

Time for the Harvest, he seemed very none threatening, but I took a step away anyway.

"Hey, Gomer," the blonde snapped, "we're the ambassadors. Not you. Just ask the questions and translate."

"Screw you Cactus Kathy," I snapped back. "I don't work for you. I don't know you. This don't concern me."

"Today, it does," the man in the red tie declared, motioning to a couple of soldiers. I turned to walk away, and they stepped before me with rifles in their hands. They did not point them, but I got the message.

"Fuck you," I said, pointing to the first soldier. "Fuck you," I said to the next. "Fuck you and you and you," I told the others, pointing to each in turn. "Fuck all of you. This don't concern me," I declared. I was too pissed to check my privilege. One of the silent four ambassadors, suddenly stepped forward. It was the second woman in the entourage. She wore red-rimmed glasses, and a dress that came just below her knees.

"Hi. I'm Mercy Mangrove. I'm with the State Department. I'm speaking for the president here." She gestured to red tie. "This is Aaron McDonald with Homeland. The man in the gold-rimmed glasses is Peter Sang." I could not help smirking at this. "He's our everything dealing with space attaché. Your adversary there," Mercy told me, gesturing to the blonde, "is Tessa Barnes—NSA. The other three men back there are Richard Weaver, Michael Sommers, and Eric Whitehall. They're FBI, CIA, and my UN counterpart respectfully. We don't really need you to serve as translator. We could find another. There were thousands of psychics contacted, but we're here now. We could obviously make you, but we'd rather you just . . . cooperate. This is a little too important for petty squabbles. Don't you think? We don't want any misunderstandings between us and them." She paused and stuck out her hand. "I'm sorry, I didn't catch your name."

"Albus," I lied. "Albus Dumbledore."

"Well, Albus. Would you help us?" I looked at the seven ambassadors and wondered how they missed a reference like that.

"We need to know why they came," Mercy said. "Could you ask them that?"

"I did already," I grumbled, glancing toward the smirking pilot.

"Has it responded?" the blonde prodded.

"Yes. He has. He said it's time for the Harvest." There was a low moan of fear from the civilians close enough to hear. The pilot looked around, even as the seven ambassadors conferred together. It only took a look from each to the others to relay their thoughts. It was not telepathy. It was a military intuition. I was beginning to fear they had a contingency in place if this all went sideways. I decided to cooperate. I was hoping I was wrong, but I was doubtful. Scared men do stupid things and there was not one ambassador among them with an unclenched sphincter.

"They came here to harvest us?" Aaron from Homeland Security asked in disbelief. I swallowed hard.

"I suppose." I replied. Aaron adjusted his red tie. He studied the pilot more closely, trying to determine the creature's strength and weakness. I did not wait for the question to come. I knew what they wanted to know, because I did too. "What do you mean by Harvest?" I asked of the pilot. He motioned us back toward the little table and the tablet they had left behind.

Explain, the pilot smiled disarmingly. I shrugged.

"He says he'll explain if we follow." It was getting easier to covert the words into English. The pain was lessening each time a new word came. I was realizing that with the word came a sense of connotation with it. Another word formed and I was confused by it. It was their symbols that changed to the letter A. No connotation. Then it happened again with for different shapes and the letter that formed was E. I began to suspect what this was. I relaxed and let the shapes come to my mind. It hurt but only at first. Pretty soon, all the vowels and shapes represented in the alien alphabet streamed into my head like cable television. There was a pause followed by a stream of common things like combs and coffee cups and apples and so on. With each picture came a set of symbols. I was getting a crash course in the alien language.

"Are you okay?" Mercy asked.

"What?" The stream in my head was distracting.

"You look like you're in pain," she said, falling in beside me.

"Yeah. He's . . . teaching me his language, I think." The pilot glanced back and nodded once. Mercy caught this and smiled back politely.

"What do you think he means by Harvest?" she asked.

"Not sure," I grunted. "There's a connotation that accompanies the words he gives me. I-I don't think it's bad."

"He doesn't think it's bad or you don't think it's bad?" she asked, and I realized there was a difference. If the pilot had come to Earth to harvest humanity for food or slavery, then of course, he would not think it bad whereas mankind would. There was much to consider in this. Not everything may be as it seems.

"Good question," I applauded. "Guess we'll find out."

The moment I saw the pad on the little table he had set up, I recognized what was written on the front. It was a formula. The pilot touched the screen. A border of symbols appeared around the edges. He seemed to touch these at random. It took me a moment longer to recognize these. They were numbers. Suddenly, a new screen appeared. In the center of the screen was a rust-colored planet. A moon circled it. In the distance was a sun. The pain in my head flared as the stream of images and symbols sped up. I could feel my heart beating with my eyes. The steady thrum of my heartbeat blurred my vision momentarily, and I staggered. I probably would have fallen if not for Red Tie. Aaron caught me by the elbow and helped prop me up.

"He's still fiddling with your head?" Aaron asked, shooting a glance toward Gold-rims. Peter was studying me, and I could see the wheels turning in his mind. It was like I could see the itch in his brain. That man wanted to dissect me.

"Come on, Albus. Don't give up now. We still need you," Aaron declared playfully. "What is he showing us?"

"Ask him," I gasped. "You ask, I'll translate his answer," I said. I was really regretting dropping that funnel cake. It might be my last.

"What is—" Aaron began, but Mercy put a hand on his arm to quiet him.

"Before we begin, may we know with whom we speak?" The ambassadors had already introduced themselves when first they met, but due to their inability to understand their visitor, they never received a name in reply or a station. They did not know if it was a janitor to whom they spoke or an emperor.

The alien stepped back from the table and smiled, eyes twinkling with mirth and pleasure.

Of course, he thought.

"Of course," I relayed. An image leapt into my mind. It was a strand of DNA. Several of the spots on the strand stood out brightly. I looked at him and accidentally sent my thought back.

That's your name? I asked telepathically.

That is who I am, he replied conversationally.

Do you have a name? Do you have a symbol identifier that translates to our language? He seemed confused then shrugged. It was a very human reaction.

"Well," Mercy asked.

"His name doesn't translate. It's a strand of DNA. Give me a moment," I pleaded, then went back into the alien's mind.

May we give you a name? It is our custom. He smiled plaintively and shrugged again, gesturing for me to proceed. I thought of a name, smirked, and threw it into his brain. He considered it and shrugged again but followed it with a quick nod.

"His name is Luke," I announced.

"That's a very terrestrial name," Tessa observed disapprovingly.

"Yeah. He allowed me to pick a name for him. They don't name like we do," I explained peevishly. I did not like the NSA chick. She was rude and aggressive.

"Does he have a rank or station or are you going to pick one of those for him too?" Tessa fired back. I did not comment. A look from Mercy gave me pause. It was a warning to stay on point.

Do you have a position or rank among your people? I inquired to Luke's mind. Luke seemed insulted and irritated by this question. I tried to put his mind at rest. *It is a peculiarity of custom. They need to know in order to understand what level of respect to afford you. Leaders of the people receive more respect than tradesmen.* I sent an image of a chess board into his mind and quickly identified the pieces and their importance overall. He sent back the image of a bishop. I relayed this to them.

Mercy stepped forward then and bowed respectfully. "On behalf of the United States of America and its territories, I welcome Luke to Earth." It was a formal greeting and Luke bowed in return, taking his cue from Mercy.

This is tedious, I whispered into his brain. I saw the corner of his mouth twitch with mirth.

Indeed, he replied. *It's like this every time we stop. Go. Stop. Bow. Kowtow. Dance. Eat. Hug. It's the job though. What about you? What's your story?* he asked, bowing to each of the ambassadors in turn.

Just a guy. I eat. I sleep. I hunt and fish and drink too much. I sent images of me working at a quarry and driving a front-end loader into his mind. He shook his head sadly as if he was sorry for my plight.

Sorry, he responded. A connotation of great empathy accompanied it.

What are you sorry for? I enjoy my life. No word came back in reply, but a sudden sense of relief flooded my mind. It came from him.

We didn't mean for this. We didn't mean to take this long. The Harvest is harder on the colonists if the population grows too big. We like to come when the colony is smaller and collect you. We were delayed.

"What is this?" Aaron asked unaware of the conversation between me and the alien. He crowded the table so he could see the tablet.

Here, Luke replied, *before we arrived.* A feeling of countless centuries sifting by flooded my mind, shrinking it.

"It's Earth before they made things grow on it," I explained in awe.

"You mean before they terraformed it?" Gold-rims inquired. Peter adjusted his glasses and shouldered one of the silent ambassadors out of his way. "Are you saying they created Earth?"

Yes. We terraformed it. We populated it. We are you, Luke revealed silently. I felt weak. This was heavy reality. I did not relay what was said immediately. I was too dazed and needed time to process it.

"Albus," Peter called irritably. "Is—"

"Yea-Yes," I blurted. "It's all them. They terra-whatevered the planet. They made everything grow. They populated it. They put it all here. They put us here. He says we're them. Earth was one of their colonies."

"This is astounding," Mercy murmured in disbelief. "How do we know he's telling the tru—"

"How do we know he isn't lying?" Tessa demanded, giving the alien a scathing look. There was sudden wrenching in my mind, like I was being pushed aside.

"You don't," I fired back hotly, "and what does it matter? There's more of us than you. Do you think we care if you don't trust us? You don't get to feel safe. Not now. As far as you're concerned, we're a deity with a fist full of lighting posed and ready to jam it up your ass anytime we feel like it." The pressure eased and I found myself suddenly sliding back into the driver's seat. I looked at Luke for an explanation, and he simply shrugged in apology.

Meet my sister. Another image of DNA popped into my head. I knew it was different than Luke's, but I could not tell how I knew it. Luke turned back to the ship. *Oh, sorry in advance.*

"Explain yourself, Gomer," Tessa barked, storming over to stand before me. "I can snap my fingers and have your ass on a C130 to black site in Mogadishu getting fuc—"

"Shut up," I snapped at her. "It wasn't me. Evidently, they can use me as a megaphone when it suits them." I followed Luke's gaze—we all did—back to the ladder beneath the ship. "It was her."

All eyes turned to the ship just in time to watch a lithe figure drop the thirty-five feet from the ship to the ground. She did not touch the ladder on the way down but managed to land softly as a cat upon the grass. That was fifty feet away, and I heard no sound as she landed. She was different than her brother. She sported a long ponytail that flowed through loops fastened to her top. The loops followed her spine down the center of her back. She was not dressed like her brother with his bizarre jacket and tunic. She wore a weird form of armor made of small polished grey plates and small twinkling links. She wore some form of holstered weapon on her right hip, and a sheathed blade on her back with a stubby three-inch hilt. I didn't need to ask for her rank among the alien horde, but Luke supplied an image any way of a knight. He planted the chess piece in my head.

This was a warrior. I had seen lots of soldiers growing up. Looking around the perimeter of the clearing, it was easy to see that she belonged among them. I was in love with her and terrified of her at the same time.

All around the perimeter, the sound of soldiers clicking their rifle safeties could be heard. If Luke's sister heard it, she did not show it. She never spared a look for the men in green. Her focus was Tessa. If the sound of her breath catching in her throat was any indication, Tessa realized this.

"Meet Leia everyone," I announced flippantly, using humor to manage my fear, "Luke's sister." It was a reference they all got. Seven sour-faced government officials fixed me with a look of undiluted animosity. They did not find it as funny as I did.

Leia was not her brother. She was no diplomat. She was oil thrown on a spark. She would either cause things to flare or snuff them out. I could see that Tessa was intimidated, but the soft mechanical whine of an Abram's tank turret swiveling in the background bolstered her diminished courage. An Abrams backing you will do that.

I would like to think that as a people, we were above this. Sure, we had a history of conquering less advanced peoples, but this was different. We were on the losing end this time. There were one hundred six Iowa-sized flying saucers flitting around in space like an iron knuckled juggernaut posed to attack. It was my deepest desire that this would temper diplomatic relations. It was not a matter of whose junk was the biggest. We were standing under an alien armada the likes of which no Earthling could conceive. They had clearly won the contest. I just hopped Tessa was not going to be a sore loser about it.

Enough, Luke patiently declared, drawing a malice-filled look from his sister. *We're diplomats, sister mine. Act like it.*

Diplomats? she sneered. *We're here to do our jobs. This isn't a negotiation. We've been here for 371 rotations. We have waited seventy-one rotations longer than that the council demands of us. We need to harvest and move on. You know what's coming. We wait, and they'll catch up and this colony is lost. We'll all be lost. We've lost too many already.*

Leia stopped berating her brother and fixed Tessa with a look of challenge. *She hinders the process.* His sister's hand slid up to the sword on her back, the hilt suddenly elongated in anticipation of being drawn. Luke's calmness broke as he saw the first couple inches of bared steel slip from her scabbard.

Enough! Luke bellowed. It wasn't like the back-and-forth Luke and I had been enjoying. His command was like a fist. His sister was blasted backwards and sprawled on her back.

"Enough!" I roared in concert with him. I was dizzy from my sudden ejection from the driver seat. Everyone was looking at me. I must have been a sight. My eyes were wild with fear. I had not merely been pushed to the side. I had been hurled like a stone into the furthest corners of my mind. I had just shouted down some alien Amazon. Well, I did, but I did not. I looked to Luke, my hands quivering in fear.

I'm sorry, he said simply.

"What's going on?" someone asked. I was not sure who had asked so I ignored them.

Who did that? I asked, feeling naked. I felt like some serial killer had skinned me and walked around in my flesh.

I did, Luke answered. *I don't like dominating colonists, but you were too close. If I hadn't taken over, I would have broken you.* I looked to Leia, still dazed by what had happened.

I don't wear a weapon because I don't need one, he explained. *Again, I'm sorry. Give me a moment to tend to this, and then I will return to talk. Please extend my apologies to the rest. This will only take a moment.* He turned to his sister and marched over to tend her.

"A challenge, brother?" she gasped, struggling to rise.

You know better than to— There was suddenly a curtain of white noise blocking out the conversation. Truth be told, it was a relief. I did not want to be privy to an alien sibling rivalry.

"Albus," Tessa barked. "What's going on? Answer me or—"

"Or nothing," I snapped back. "Stop threatening me. You're always threatening me and bullying me. Stop it. I'm here because I'm the only person you have handy who can converse with them. Show me some respect." I rubbed my temples. The white noise was straining on my senses. I would have a migraine later. Tessa was indignant, but a restraining hand from Mercy was a . . . well, it was a mercy. "They're arguing," I explained. "Leia is angry at you. She says you are a hindrance. They don't have time for negotiations. It's a harvest and they should get on with it so they can leave. I think they're being pursued, and they're wanting to finish business and be gone so as not to draw attention to us. They're trying to protect us from someone or something. It's been following them. They were only supposed to give us three hundred rotations—I'm guessing that's a day— to do this meet and greet. They're seventy-one days behind schedule."

"What just happened to her?" Aaron asked, gesturing to Leia.

"Never mind that. What's the Harvest?" Mercy pressed. I shrugged. I honestly did not know.

"I don't know. Luke claims they were delayed and that they should have been here years ago. They say the Harvest is supposed to happen when the colony is smaller because harvesting large colonies terrifies the colonists. We're the colonists. I can see where he's coming from because I'm about to drop a deuce in my pants right about now."

What's a deuce? Luke asked. I sent him a mental image and his eyebrow shot up in surprise.

You asked, I told him dryly, *what about your Leia?*

Leia? he laughed. He evidently got the reference. *Funny.* He stepped aside and made room for his sister at the table. *She's been managed.* Leia gave him a bitingly bitter look but kept silent. *Let them ask their questions. She's impulsive, but my sister isn't wrong. We haven't' much time.*

What follows you? I asked, deeply interested in the answer. I felt a finger of dread trace my spine and dread had cold fingers.

Luke shrugged and shook his head. There was an apology there, as if he feared to say too much. *What follows is what follows us all.* His answer was cryptic and unhelpful to say the least. I waited but he would say no more on it. My eyes strayed to the sky and to the pale grey disk beyond the blue. I was afraid. What hovered above was more power than man had ever dreamed of, and with a stray thought, these beings could obliterate us and destroy us all, yet they were running. I couldn't help but wonder what terrible terror was out there that could so completely humble this armada. Then it occurred to me. We have always had our gods, but even our gods had their devils. The free world had the Nazis. The Olympians had the Titans. I looked to Luke. He had whatever followed him. I guess making enemies was a hereditary trait.

Chapter 3: Conversation

Luke was frustrated. I could sense it now. The telepathy was getting easier. *Really though, we need to recommence. I'm due to our council of nations soon to schedule and coordinate the Harvest. Please, ask them to continue. I'll answer all their questions. The Harvest is where we allow part of the population of the colony to return home with us. It is strictly voluntary. We harvest to keep the colonies from growing so large they damage themselves. This colony is rapidly approaching a threshold limit. If you grow much larger, population controls programmed into your strands will enact. These are highly volatile control methods. Millions will die when that threshold limit is exceeded. Please, convey this.*

I glanced at Leia's bottom and an image leaped into my head without me meaning it to. I quickly smothered it, but not before that thought carried over to her. The look she gave me was not friendly and a little confused. I hurriedly did as Luke bid me.

"It's strictly voluntary?" the UN dignitary asked, seeking clarification.

"That's what he said. They were supposed to come long before this. I don't think they'd normally reveal themselves in this fashion otherwise. We're way over capacity so they figured they'd make a more direct approach," I said, receiving a nod of confirmation from alien ambassador.

"Were they responsible for the disappearance of the Lost Colony?" Richard asked. I tried to recall which alphabet he was with. I was pretty sure it was the FBI. I knew the story of the Lost Colony, and I was not sure why he cared if it was them. They were the colonists from Roanoke who had mysteriously disappeared leaving behind only the word "Croatoan" carved into a palisade. I quickly relayed this question to Luke.

How long ago? he asked, irritated with the question. He thought it frivolous. The look on Leia's face showed she was finally in agreeance with her brother.

"I don't know," I replied, looking to Gold-rims for the answer. The scientist gave me an inquisitive look. "The colony at Roanoke, when was it abandoned?"

"Late 1500's," Mercy supplied. She shrugged when I gave her my surprised face. Her answer had been automatic. I was impressed. "I like history," she said it without apology. I liked her. She was short and feisty. I looked back to the alien ambassador and quickly calculated the number of years.

It would have been about four hundred years ago. I said, approximating it. He seemed confused by this, and I realized he was unfamiliar without units and measure. *One revolution of our planet around our star is a year. It takes 365 rotations to equal a year.* I expected his conversions to take time, but he had the answer instantly. His eyes only flickered once, and he responded.

It wasn't these countries, but it might have been a drift that broke off and proceeded us. There have been several through the years. Why do you ask of this one? he inquired.

"The word 'Croatoan' was carved into a tree or something when the colony was revisited. You've been saying Croatoan a lot since you arrived," I said this out loud for the benefit of the seven ambassadors.

Croatoan is our word of greeting. It is like your aloha. It means hello and goodbye depending on how it's being used. I revealed this to the ambassadors. When they asked what I meant about drifts, I had no reply. I asked, and he laid out the structure of their society. It dawned on me as he described the structure of their governments how it was all arranged, and the significance of a drift became apparent. I hurriedly explained this to the ambassadors.

"Each saucer is a different country in their society. Each saucer has its own government. A drift is when some of the countries break off and go their own way. He's suggesting that maybe one of these drifts beat them here back when the colony was small and took the Roanoke colonists with them. He doesn't know for sure though, but he acknowledges that Croatoan is their word and their word alone. The short answer is yes. It was them." My head was starting to throb horribly. I needed an Aspirin or Tylenol.

"How is the Harvest conducted?" Peter inquired. He was keenly interested in this act.

Your leaders explain it to your people and give them the choice to go or stay. They decide. A tour of the ships is provided for any leaders or functionaries who care to visit. We will explain all. We will dispense all knowledge as to the inner workings of our government and even provide one-on-one testimonials from our citizenry. Those who wish to return home will rally in locations around the planet. We'll send skiffs to ferry them to our ships. This is full disclosure. We will provide representatives if you provide translators. We identified all of your translators for you ahead of time. Luke gave his sister an irritated look, and I realized she had been sidling off to the side. His look was enough to freeze her in place.

Is that why you forced that word into our heads? I exclaimed. *That hurt.*

It was necessary, Leia interjected callously. *Don't be so weak.*

I relayed all that was said to the seven, and they spent a few moments murmuring amongst themselves. The man I knew as Aaron McDonald was not relieved by the open-air discussion.

Evidently, he had been elected by the seven to voice their concerns.

"I appreciate your candidness. What you propose is interesting and would solve a problem that has become an increasingly troubling thought in the minds of our world leaders. We had thought to spread to beyond the stars ourselves. It seemed the only real solution to the problem we're facing. We'd planned on doing it ourselves though," he said, smoothing his tie.

"Why reinvent the coobla?" I loudly exclaimed, irked that Leia had seized control of me again. *Get out.* I sensed hostility, but she vacated the driver's seat readily.

"What?" Aaron blurted in confusion.

"She took control again," I replied, "and it's getting really freaking old." I snapped, giving her dagger eyes. She sniffed disdainfully and looked away. I wanted her so bad.

"Okay," Aaron said, dismissing me. He turned his attention back to Luke. "That being said, we have a few concerns and a couple troubling questions that need to be addressed."

"What are they?" I said, repeating Luke yet again.

"We were attacked. You attacked us twice," the Director of Homeland Security revealed. "And not just us. You attacked every nation on this planet. You killed tens of thousands. That is a declaration of war." Luke was taken aback and confused by this.

"You don't want us for enemies," I told the seven ambassadors. Leia and Luke turned on me in confusion. They had not forced me to say that. The seven ambassadors paled so cold was my delivery of the threat. I was winging it. There was no way I was going to let this dingleberry start a war with me at the helm.

"That wasn't us," Leia announced, taking control of me again. She surrendered control as quickly as she took it, but it was all the time she needed to undo what I had tried to do.

Don't do that, she admonished before going silent once more. The dignitaries all eyed me caustically.

"What attack?" I asked, knowing that was the question Luke would ask.

"You hit us with a massive electromagnetic pulse that wiped out our electronics worldwide," the science guy accused. "It killed almost twenty thousand people."

How? It was Leia who asked this. She was genuinely troubled by the accusation.

Many of the people killed wore pacemakers. They're electronic devices that help individuals with bad hearts. They looked confused. I considered my words. *With bad cardiac muscles. The pacemakers regulate heart beats. I shot an image and position of the organ into her head. Your EMP overcame their shielding and killed thousands of them. It also shut off the life support systems for many injured patients. That was tens of thousands. A few air transports fell out of the sky and a few industrial facilities were destroyed killing workers and civilians. It wasn't a very good way to say hello,* I confessed. Luke and Leia look crestfallen.

We warned you ahead of time, Luke quailed. *The magnetic interference we caused first was so you would know to prepare for the EMP burst. We gave you time to prepare.*

"How is that time to prepare?" I asked incredulously.

"What's he saying?" Tessa barked.

"He said that was what the interference was for. They were giving us warning to prepare for the EMP burst. I think they expected you to take precautions to protect our EMP vulnerable electronics."

"Four days?" Aaron grumbled. "You gave us four days to prepare?"

"We gave you four days. You grounded all air traffic. We assumed you'd understood the reason for that interference. Then we greeted you verbally by way of your telepaths. We cleaned our feet and knocked," I said. Leia was gesturing her disbelief while hijacking my voice box. I farted and she departed, throwing me a disgusted look. "It was her," I explained yet again. "Well, the speech was her. The gas was me."

Bring us their bodies, Luke entreated.

"How can they think that makes it alright?" Tessa complained.

"You had weapons trained on us. We couldn't descend safely while you could see us. An EMP should have blinded you temporarily so we could land and have this meet and greet," I told them with Leia's voice. I did not fight her this time, but I really did not like her taking control without permission. It was rude.

"Whether accidental or on purpose, it was you who killed our people. This needs to be addressed before we go any further."

"Bring us those who've died," I said with Leia at the helm once more.

"Why?" Mercy asked.

"We can return them to you. We can make them whole," I whispered, stunned by what I was hearing. Stunned that this was possible. There was silence all around. I roused my mind and tried to force her out. She did the mental equivalent of kung fu kicking my brain into my stomach.

"We'll need to confer," Mercy said.

"We will meet one week hence," I told them as Leia. She spilled out of my mind like water warm water from an ear canal. It was pleasant and creepy.

Please convey my apologies, Luke said, guiding his sister back toward the ship with one hand. She went without resistance. Luke stayed behind and extended his hand to each of the ambassadors. *I must address our council and apprise them of all that has happened. And any of those who died as a result of our EMP, have them present when we return, and we will make them whole. We must make them whole. We did not mean for this to happen. We will reprint them for you, then proceed with the Harvest. Please, convey my apologies and tell them we will make this right.*

I mumbled, "Croatoan," each time he shook their hands, but I was not paying attention. He had finally said something that lived up to expectations. Finally, he had said something that was hardcore sci-fi. He was going to print new humans. I had no idea what that meant, but it made me want to rush home and plunder my Netflix account for everything sci-fi. Luke and Leia boarded their ship, climbing the impossibly long ladder. I studied Leia's body intently. I could not keep the thoughts out of my mind. More than once, I caught her returning those looks. Each time she was irritated and confused. I was beginning to wonder just what the limit on this telepathy thing was. How far away was too far? Then I remembered they had put the word

"Croatoan" in the brains of over a thousand telepaths . . . from orbit. I let a thought leap into my head of me and Leia naked in a pool of lime Jell-O. There were no words. The response was just a mental backhand that left my eyes unfocused and my head buzzing. She could still hear my thoughts. This made me smile through the blurriness.

I quickly conveyed Luke's apologies to the ambassadors and delivered his message concerning the dead. With my obligations met, I headed toward the funnel cake cart and hoped they had not run out of stock. Behind me, the gigantic shuttle in the midst of the field began to hum and whine as its engines came online. I felt the hair all over my body stand on end as whatever form of engine they used powered up. Several cows were tossed and tumbled beneath the ship when it took off, and watching it take off was impressive to see. There was no hesitant pause before a slow acceleration. One moment 40,000 tons of ship was sitting in a field, then it was gone. It rose so fast that people were drawn forward into its wake. Unfortunately for me, the funnel cake cart was among them.

"Shit," I exclaimed, pulling my cap from my back pocket where I had kept it holstered. I unfolded the bill and pulled it on my head then headed for home. I made it nearly thirty feet before a group of soldiers descended upon me. Two of them grabbed me—one under each arm—and dragged me back to the ambassadors. I tried to struggle, but they were Marines, and I played a lot of Xbox. I was not going anywhere, so I relaxed and let my heels drag.

"Mr. Dumbledore, would you kindly follow us?" Tessa asked. She was not really asking. The Marines had not let me go.

"Where?" I asked, suddenly nervous.

"Washington to brief the President, and then to New York to address the United Nations," Aaron answered.

"Why?" I whined, confused.

"To debrief. To face charges of interfering with a presidential dignitary. Sedition. Treason. Hell, you're going to come with me because it pleases me," Tessa told me snidely. "I don't really care the reason. You're coming and that's final. You were in their heads, and they were in yours. You're a threat to national security just now. You won't be leaving my side anytime soon."

"Fine," I declared strenuously. "But I have one condition. Otherwise, I'm . . . I'm . . . otherwise, I'm biting this Marine."

"You don't want to do that," Mercy warned. The Marines bringing up the rear grinned and shook their heads. I suddenly missed warm cuddly Leia. The mental back hand left me dazed and seeing double. Dammit! How freaking far was far enough?

"What is your condition?" Mercy asked.

"Funnel cake." Tessa drilled holes in my head with her fiery gaze. "Extra powdered sugar," I added, looking pointedly at the up turned cart.

"You're kidding, right?" Tessa snapped, marching around the Marines to face me down. I smiled, she groaned, and the funnel cake was delicious.

Chapter 4: Washington

The helicopter ride was tense. Tessa was convinced I could read her mind and got agitated any time I made eye contact. Aaron refused to engage in any conversation. If I did not know better, I would have thought he was deaf. My one saving grace from crushing boredom was Mercy. Mercy was congenial and engaged me in conversation during our ride to Tulsa.

I learned that her father had been a Colonel in the Air Force before taking a consultant position with an independent security firm that contracted to the CIA. She had followed him into the Air Force, but after six years, had decided it was not for her and followed in her mom's footsteps by going into politics. Despite the differences in our social and professional statuses, she seemed keenly interested in my life. She had made the same jokes they all made about a fat man working in a quarry. Fred Flintstone's name came up. I rolled with it. I dreaded the jokes, but they were not horrid, and I knew she meant no harm. I told her about fishing in the evenings and pheasant hunting in the fall. I regaled her with stories of the work I did for the farmers around town sometimes. She seemed entranced by my description of the sunsets and panicked by my descriptions of the tornados. At least she spared me the Wizard of Oz jokes. That was something. Maybe it was less than classy but at least considerate.

Can you hear me? I asked, throwing my thoughts toward the sky and Luke's sister. I smiled sardonically when no answer came in return and went back into my conversation with Mercy.

The pilot of the helicopter was unhappy when we piled out of his helicopter. Extra powdered sugar was a nice idea, but very messy when the doors were opened upon landing. The circulation of the rotors overhead scattered the sugar, coating everyone. Tessa and Aaron were rightfully pissed. They looked like a Colombian cartel boss had sneezed on them. Mercy was a little more laissez faire about the whole thing. I did apologize, but they were not having it.

The moment we landed, dark suited men with shoulder holsters and no sense of humor took me in hand and ushered me to a black suburban with blacked out windows. The rest of the ambassadorial delegation was already inside waiting for us. Their helicopter landed first. Aaron took shotgun, though I clearly called it first. I was put in the back seat and sandwiched between FBI and Science Guy. CIA and UN took the middle seats with Mercy sandwiched between them. Secret Service was driving. Tessa rode in a different SUV with her own security detail. No doubt, she was trying to put distance between me and her so I could not violate her mind like Leia had done to mine.

You hear that? I asked, slinging my thoughts into the heavens. *Mind raping is bad. No means no. I'm not a piece of meat.* She did not reply. I did not expect her to.

The SUVs took us from the hangar where the helicopters had landed to a different hangar on the other side of the Tulsa Airport where we boarded a private jet for Washington. I wasn't sure which agency was picking up the tab, but I considered it taxpayer money. I drank when drinks were offered. As a taxpayer, I was paying for the drinks. It was about time I sampled what I was paying for. The Secret Service may have carried me on the plane against my will, but by the time we touched down, carrying me off the plane was a matter of necessity. As a taxpayer, I can assure the people of the United States of America that their money has bought their politicians the best scotch money can buy. I sampled it myself and know what I'm talking about. In fact, I sampled all they had, repeatedly.

Frankly, Washington was somewhat of a blur to me that first night. I remember lots of laughing (by me), lots of sexually charged innuendo being thrown around (by me), and I think someone pretended to hump a bomb-sniffing dog at the airport (probably me too). After that, it was lights out. The hotel they put me up in was swanky and filled with men in black. Tessa gave them instructions and blew me a kiss, I think. I might have imagined that. In my room, a meal was provided. I ate it. I wore the robe provided and tried to watch scrambled porn, but my heart was not in it.

My thoughts kept drifting back to my morning with Luke. I liked him. He seemed down to Earth and genuine. As far as alien ambassadors go, he was my favorite. I did not want to think about her because I did not want her to bitch slap my brain again, but inevitably, my mind went back to Leia.

She was a hot head, impulsive, fiery, feisty, and all the things a man like me did not deserve, which might be why I did not entertain the idea of pursuing her. She was an alien. I braced for her reprimand at my thoughts of her, but nothing came. I was emboldened. Maybe there was a limit to how far we could communicate telepathically. I tested that theory and imagined myself seducing her. At first it was the scotch, but then as I relaxed, my thoughts became sincere. I really imagined myself with her and the thought made me happy. In the theater of my mind, we lay entwined in sheets, naked, and still. I imagined her hands on my chest, and my hands tracing the smoothness of her thigh. The scotch had been raining round houses on me all day. Now that it had me on my back, it sensed victory and began curb stomping my brain. *Goodnight*, I told her. I know I dreamed, but I could not tell you what I dreamed of. The scotch had Edward Nortoned me. I was dead to the world.

Chapter 5: Preparations

Luke gave instructions to his second in command and sent him down to Deck 30 to audit the Harvest preparations. The tallies from the other saucers had not all arrived. This really bothered Luke. He had made first contact already. The asteroid was turning on this. The other representatives had one week to hammer out the rest of the details on this Harvest. It should have been done a hundred rotations ago.

"I think I need a few rotations of rest and relaxation on Deck 131," he announced to the empty corridor, referencing a different ship famed for its luxurious resorts.

It was quite by accident that he sighted his sister seated in an arboretum beyond the passage he currently stood in. He had not expected to find her here, and he started to hail her, but he sensed something amiss. She was a warrior to her core, and her mind was usually unnaturally alert. She should have already sensed him and greeted him. It was strange that she had not. Something was distracting her, and it intrigued him.

He walked quietly down the hall toward the large arboretum and took a seat on a bench behind a low wall of hedges some hundred feet off. It was considered rude to eavesdrop on another's private thoughts. Still, he softly pushed his mind out toward her to see what so distracted her. She was his sibling. That allowed him the occasional egregious moments of trespass exempt of reprisal. He just had to be careful, or she would tell their mom on him. He tiptoed toward her mind with his own.

He glanced about the park to see if anyone else was about who might betray the fact that he was spying on his sister. There were a few campers a quarter mile off, but that was all he saw. He was alone for the most part surrounded by 50-foot-tall trees and the numerous human sculpture that dotted the arboretum. Sometimes, he would flinch with guilt mistaking one of the thousands of statues populating the park as a real person. He realized this was just a trick of a guilty conscience.

    He began spying out the statues in his vicinity and wondered at their makers. Each was an heirloom brought along by a colonist harvested from other worlds. They were a sentimental sort. Luke had found that the most interesting characteristic of all in the colonists he had met. They formed the most peculiar attachments to the things they owned. It was allowed, of course. Luke, however, had been trying for decades to replicate this level of intimacy with something he owned. He had a sock he liked more than the rest, but he doubted that was the same as what the colonists had.

    He looked about the park and breathed deeply the scents of the soil and plant life. Somewhere off to his left an artificial breeze had been kicked up to rustle the leaves and flex the trees to keep them strong. This arboretum was the closest one to the Hall of Khans—a name given it by one of the first colonists ever reaped. He had seen a lot of the other parks on the ship, and he had always thought this one to be the nicest.

    He glanced toward the Hall of Khans. The name was a little fancy for Luke's taste. It was just the auditorium where the ambassadors and political dignitaries met to commune with one another in private. The room was shielded to block the probing thoughts of those not privy to the discussions within. He liked to go there when it was not in use and sit so he could relax and be absolutely alone. Privacy: an oddity in his world.

    A wall of white noise flared to life, drawing him back to the present and pressing his mind away. *I'm telling mom*, Leia threatened suddenly. He smirked.

You seemed distracted. I was curious. He felt a flush of guilt and embarrassment from her—even through the white noise. That made him even more curious.

How was the council meeting? she asked.

As you would expect. They're all promising results and few are delivering. A third of the ships have yet to audit their resources and report back their projected tallies. It's a pain in the . . . he left off the graphic for her benefit. *Until they get me those numbers, I don't know how many of the colonists we can take on.*

How many do you think we can manage? she asked absently. She was still distracted.

With the numbers tallied so far—about two thirds of the nations—we can comfortably handle 1.2 billion of them, he replied, shamefacedly.

I wish we could take them all, Leia whispered. *It seems wrong to leave them behind.*

We could have once, but the last drift changed all that. We can only take what we can take, he said. *We're not responsible for this. The Drifters are. They fled. The blood of the colonists we leave behind isn't on our hands. It's on the hands of those who broke away. The Drifters killed these people. Not us.*

Maybe they'll be passed over, Leia suggested hopefully.

They would be the first colony to manage that. The conversation had grown somber and dark. Luke did not like talking about what was coming—what was following. It was like a blade hanging over his neck, waiting to drop. *Maybe those we leave behind will get lucky. There has to be a first time for everything.* He did not sound convinced.

Yeah, Leia whispered, not believing it for a moment.

Sorry for the thought sniffing. It won't happen again. He got up to leave.

I'm still telling mom, Leia said, flooding his mind with mirth. He chuckled softly and walked off, leaving her to her thoughts.

She followed him with her mind and lost him when he returned to the empty Hall of Khans. His mind vanished behind the shielding built into the walls and ceiling of the chamber. She scanned the park and determined that she was unobserved. She was wrong.

Like a child spying on its parents, she crept stealthily from the ship. She let her mind fall back into the atmosphere of the world below. She did not have to search for him. The trail of his thoughts was easy to follow, and she sniffed them out like a hound. He was like a freaking child with his thoughts. There was no control or reservation. Everything he thought was there to see. He was the most open person she had ever met.

She was furious the first time he imagined her. She had almost lobotomized him on the spot. The second time, she knew he was playing with his newfound ability. The moment she decided to leave though, his thoughts changed. Even though they did not know one another, he was sorry to see her go. With his sorrow, came his true thoughts. The sincerity of his admiration struck her. No one up here was ever that honest with her. Everything was politics and guarded thoughts. No one was ever privy to another's entire mind. Those she lived among greedily hid themselves behind walls of white noise and revealed only what they wanted others to see. He was not like that. Yes, he was vulgar, crude, smelly, not very handsome, uncultured, and not all that bright, but he was sincere. That blinded her to most of the rest.

She was getting close and slowed her mind. She did not want him to know she was mentally sniffing him. She was a hypocrite. She knew it. With the colonials, she felt free to plunder their minds. It was like searching out lost and abandoned living quarters when you're young for exploration. It was the adventure of children, and she felt the same way with the colonists. Their minds were open and unlocked. It is not breaking in if they leave them open, she told herself.

She slowly pushed herself into his mind. He was asleep and he was dreaming now. Before her brother had distracted her, she had been watching in amazement as this colonist imagined her and him entwined one with the other sharing a moment of intimacy. What the colonist did not realize was that she had taken the place of the construct he had created. She had felt his fingers on her skin, and she had liked it. He had been so gentle. Her brother's intrusion had really pissed her off more than she would have ever admitted to her brother or herself.

She did not know what to make of his dreams though. They were not what she had expected. She wanted to see more of him being gentle, more of him and her being intimate. What she saw was not what she expected. I was so not what she had expected and to such an extent, all her discipline went out the window and she blurted out the only thing she could think to say.

What the fuck?

She had not meant to let that thought sift into the mind of the colonist. She had just wanted to watch unobserved. Leia quickly retreated off a short distance, keeping herself small and hoping he would not see her. A flush of embarrassment colored her cheeks a hundred miles away.

The man upon which she mentally spied did not seem to notice her presence. His thoughts were fuzzier than before and scattered, which made his dream seem that much more bizarre. What had surprised her were the rotting men in the dream. A flood of rotting men was breaking into a decrepit woodland domicile. The colonist dreaming about them was eagerly cutting off their heads and shooting lead projectiles through their chests.

Beside him, glittering like starlight with her sword in her hand, was his dream version of her. She was fighting the rotting people with him at his side. It was the warrior in Leia, but she could not help being critical of her dream incarnation. His version of her was clumsy with a sword. Many of her strikes left her exposed after. There was no way the real Leia would ever make mistakes so blatant. The real Leia felt irked by the colonist's inaccurate representation of her, but the more she watched, the more interesting it all became. She thought the guy sick for fantasizing like this, but the longer she observed the pair in combat, the more excited she became. She was not sure why, but it looked fun, and she felt an overwhelming desire to join the fight.

Hey, she called, pushing into his mind then suddenly retreating. She felt embarrassed and even nervous, like a child breaking a parental rule on a dare.

He looked over at her, his left hand cutting down rotting man while his rifle rested on his shoulder. He raised the gun and wagged it at her in greeting, then absently shot another rotting man stumbling toward him.

You'llerrr misssen all da frun, he told her, slurring his thoughts. He pointed toward a boarded-up window behind her. She turned just in time to see rotting men suddenly knock the boards away. The maimed men tumbled through and awkwardly rose. She studied them curiously. They were not very fast and had little tactile dexterity. The men were clumsy.

The closest one lunged at her unexpectedly, grappling with her while it tried to tear out her throat with its rotten putrid teeth.

It took her by surprise. Watching him and his version of her, they had never let the rotting men get that close. She understood the threat they posed and why he was fighting them. A moment later, she understood what this dream was. She did not know who the rotting men were, but she understood the purpose of the dream. It was an endless wave attack where one could unremorsefully destroy an army of aberrations deserving of death. It was a guiltless festival of carnage and death.

With the realization came action. She deftly twisted the wrist of the rotting man grappling with her and pulled his arm out wide, then delivered a hard uppercut with the heel of her free hand. Her opponent's head snapped up and its jaw broke with a satisfying crack. She let go its wrist in that moment so she could seize its head in one hand and chin in the other. She snapped its neck with a quick twist then faded back so she had room to draw her sword. She knew it was not actually there, but in the dream it felt right. She smiled at the familiar feel of its hilt in her palm. She ripped the sword free and brought it out wide in a hissing whistle before slashing across then back and up. The next rotting man approaching her literally flew apart as a result.

She started to rush the next of the rotting men when something soft touched her mind. She knew the touch. Someone was trying to sniff her thoughts. She turned and fled back to her body, drawing her mind back as quickly as she could, cursing herself for a fool. Two times in under an hour. The colonist was proving a dangerous distraction.

She sat absolutely still upon returning to herself and scanned the area with her mind. There were campers a long way off but no one close. Yet, she knew that feel. Someone had been scanning the park, and they were trying to be stealthy about it. That only ever boded ill in her experience. She found no one near at hand in the arboretum and rose to her feet to see if her eyes could find what her mind had missed.

There was no one, and her thoughts went back to her brother and wondered if he had tried again. Her top lip drew back into an irritated sneer. If he had pulled her away again just to irritate her, she would do more than tell their mom. She had been having fun for once. She sent her thoughts out ahead and down the hall past the Hall of Khans. There was nobody there. She drew her sword as a precaution and looked at the door. She wanted to confront him about sniffing her thoughts again, but she was not sure if she should.

On one hand, she was afraid of adding to her brother's level of distress. The success of the Harvest rested firmly on him. Its success or failure would be his as well. This could ruin him if it all went wrong. And on the other hand, if he was not the one sniffing her thoughts, then she would be admitting that once again she had allowed someone to take her unawares. It was an embarrassing thing to admit. She stood there weighing the pros and cons of confronting him. The final factor to consider though was that if it was not him, then someone else had been spying on her. Despite her concerns about her brother's wellbeing and her own embarrassment, if a threat existed, she needed to know about it and she needed to know immediately.

It was almost as if someone were responding to her need to know as something heavy slammed into the wall from inside the council chamber, rattling the door before her. Her indecision vanished. She kicked open the auditorium door and came in with her side arm drawn and her sword ready, low, and leading.

There was no pause in her entrance. She did not stop to take in the sight with her eyes. Her mind flooded the room in search of targets. She found six minds down below, one of them was her brother. He was grappling with one of the men, trying to keep the man's sword out of his throat.

The moment her eyes touched the charcoal armor, she knew they were all worthy of death. They all had to die. She ran down the steps toward the floor of the auditorium where the orators were supposed to stand, snapping off three quick shots. There was no streak of light like the colonists pretended there to be in their movies. There was a high-pitched ping and a hole laced with fire appeared in the two of the assassins and the podium next to a third. She was lining up another shot on the man she missed when something heavy ricocheted off her armor. It was shank of metal—probably a blade—but it had glanced off her shoulder plate breaking two links of her armor in the process. Her wound was a small harmless laceration.

She slapped the control plate on her chest to activate her armor and threw herself down the stairs, twisting around in mid-air. It saved her life. The blade that had struck her had come from near the doorway she just come through. A sixth assassin was coming to his feet. She realized even as he fired his side arm at her, that he was the heavy thing that had hit the wall a moment before, courtesy of her brother no doubt. Another assassin screamed as he too was hurtled end over end into the wall to her right. Her brother was fighting back.

The sixth man fired two shots at her. One left a burning ring in the steps between her knees, and the other left a trail of burning rings through the backs of the stadium seating to her left. He had missed. She did not. She fired off four shots. Four rings of fire suddenly appeared in the man. Three in his chest and one where his face had been. She rolled backwards as she landed, flipping over and onto her feet with her back to the two men still standing.

She knew one of the remaining two had broken off his attack on her brother in hopes of taking her unawares, but she sensed him. She did not bother turning to face him. Instead, she touched a button on the hilt of her sword, and her sword's blade suddenly shot backward into the hilt and out the other side. With the sword reversed in her grip, she held firm and locked her elbow to her side to brace for the impact as the assassin behind her impaled himself on her blade. She did not savor the kill. She hit the button again and her grip reversed yet again and just in time for her to blade to bear once more. She brought it down on the neck of the mortally wounded man, taking his head.

The assassin struggling with Luke had her brother on the floor with his blade in the air. She brought her sidearm up to end the man, but a ring of fire appeared in its side, severing the barrel and breech.

She threw herself sidelong and to her right, rolling as she landed. She pressed another button her hilt and held it. Six inches of her sword hilt, split off and raced to the other end of her blade, stopping nine inches shy of the end. She released the button as she came out of her roll and the short section of hilt and exposed blade dropped from the end of the blade. She caught the freshly crafted dagger it as it fell free from the rest of the blade.

The assassin struggling with her brother was between her and the assassin who had shot her side arm. Burning rings were appearing in the furnishings around her. She dodged left and right to avoid being hit and when he stopped to reload, she charged. Flipping the dagger in her hand so that she gripped the blade. She waited until she was a short leap from her brother's attacker and flung the knife at him. She was aiming for the man's stomach. That was the only reason he was able to avoid it.

He broke from his grapple with her brother, twisted away from the path of the blade into a graceful pirouette and fell upon her brother anew with his blade posed to plunge through her brother's chest. She could not stop him. He gripped the hilt in both hands to put all his weight behind it the strike. There was no way to stop him.

She had missed the man grappling with Luke, but he had not been her target. She had expected him to dive away to avoid the thrown dagger. His dodge had been expected, but his recovery not so much. Her dagger was meant for the other man; the one who had destroyed her side arm and was even now frantically struggling to reload his weapon. This man had not expected the throw. He was genuinely surprised when nine inches of nanite steel sprouted from his chest.

He was even more surprised when the nanites broke loose inside him, abandoning the hilt of the knife. They spread through his blood stream, repairing the damage to his chest while simultaneously attacking his nervous system. He toppled over sideways, paralyzed. The hilt of the dagger fell away. The nanites hit his brain before he had even managed to crash to the floor. It would be up to Leia to decide if he ever got up again. For now, he was her captive. She would retrieve him when she was done with his companion.

Leia knew she could not reach her brother before the assassin's blade pierced his heart. Luke must have known that as well, and just moments before, all would have been lost. His attackers had been attacking his mind as a group. They were smothering his thoughts to keep him from focusing the force of his will. With one thrown knife, his sister had remedied this, removing the last obstacle in Luke's way. As the swordsman's blade dived for his heart, Luke's will exploded forth unchallenged.

Off! he roared into the assassin's head. The force of his will flinging the man straight up.

Leia smirked, and raced forward, intending to meet the falling body of the assassin with an upward slice of her blade that would have cut the man in half. The falling man was not incapacitated as she had hoped though. He flicked his sword out wide, deflecting hers away.

Luke was already rolling, even as the man landed. His sister would need room to work. Luke kept rolling and Leia inserted herself between him and his attacker.

Who are you? Leia demanded of the man. The man did not respond. *I hope you for your sake, you fight better than your friends.* The man's only reply was a menacing smile.

His skin had been brushed with a film to camouflage its color. She made a study of his face taking note of his long aquiline nose with its broken ridge, his thin lips, and high cheek bones. He had a long neck, narrow shoulders, and dark brown almond eyes. He had traced his eyes with some dark pigmenting pencil and hid his hair beneath a dark wrap of cloth.

He rushed her as she rushed him. Their swords met once, twice, and again. They twisted away from each other, and Leia came back in slashing horizontal, left to right, letting that strike flow into an upward slice that would have split the man from groin to grin if he had held still.

He had not. He fell back before her first strike, rolled left to miss the powerful upper cut, and stabbed out at her with his left. She deflected his blade with a palm strike to the flat of it, ripping her blade sideways in its wake.

The man got his blade back in position to stop her strike, catching it just below his guard. She ripped her blade back the other way, spinning with it into a crouch while holding her blade at the ready should he press his counter. She gripped the hilt of her sword in both hands, tip up and angled out toward him. He had retreated a step and held his blade reversed with the hilt up in front of him and his blade down in a guarded position. They stood like that for several long tense moments. Each was trying to anticipate the other's next move.

You're better than they were, she admitted grudgingly. The man dipped is head slowly to acknowledge her compliment. He said nothing, however. Leia watched the man's left foot slowly shift back and out. She lowered the tip of her blade slowly and raised the hilt and her left elbow in preparation for the attack, but he was not shifting to attack as she had thought. The man's sword never moved, but his free hand did. It quickly darted inside a loose pocket on his battle skirt. When it came out, it was clutching a short, elongated piece of metal as thick as her hand. She did not recognize it, but she knew it could be almost anything. She was ready to deflect it if he threw it at her, and even attempted to attack the man as her brother had done. She summoned her will and put it behind a word.

Die! she commanded. The man flinched then smiled and flicked the metal object away. She brought her blade back before her at the ready, but it was not necessary. The man was not throwing it at her. He had thrown it off to her right. She heard it landed and bounce a couple of times before coming to a rest. She did not look to see what purpose it had served. Not with him. He had probably expected her to look, throwing the device as distraction. She was not taking the bait if that was his ploy. Instead, Leia attacked, rushing him with her sword tip leading.

The man sidestepped her attack and retreated two steps. From the direction of the thrown object, a new sound began. It was the hiss of small machines accompanied by the click and clack of small metallic legs. She had never seen that type of object before, but she had heard of them and cursed. She attacked again, stabbing for the man's heart. Again, he sidestepped and retreated. She repeated the attack, and he repeated his dodge and withdraw.

You think you can make it to the door before I kill you? she asked, thinking this his plan. The assassin smiled. Leia scowled and attacked, but her opponent simply lowered his blade ready to receive her strike. This gave her pause and a moment of doubt, but it did not stop her from seizing the opportunity to end it.

Luke's wail of distress followed her, but too late. *No!* Luke called, throwing his thought at her in a bid to stop her. The assassin's plan revealed itself a moment later as he released his will in a single focused blast meant to burst her heart.

Her brother was strong, but when he brought his will to bear, it was like being punched. The man she faced was far more disciplined. The force of his will came to bear like a blade. It was narrow and focused. He did not even use a word to focus it. He said nothing. He just threw his entire mind at her and waited for her to die, and she might have if not for her armor. She was not a low-level Watchman. She was an Imperial Knight and was afforded the articles of protection that came with that position. The nanite sword she held and the psionic armor she wore were standard for all Imperial Knights.

She had been trained to ignore the hum of the armor as it sought to match the wavelength of the assassin's psychic assault. It was disorienting but not disabling to her. The plates of armor flexed to deflect the bulk of the blast, splitting the focus and scattering the blast in ambient waves that dissipated into the room. Her head was uncovered, so even with the armor, she felt a wave of force inside her head. It hurt, but it was not debilitating. The pain was worth it though just to see the smug look of satisfaction on the assassin's face slide away as the tip of her blade punched through his armor, heart, and scapula.

Leia smiled back for his benefit and hoped he would live long enough to see it.

No, Luke moaned again.

You can relax. I'm fine, she told him, trying to put his mind at ease.

I'm not—I wasn't warning you, he snapped, looking off into the corner of the room where the assassin she had disabled lay. The man was a bloody mess. Small spidery bots dragging scorpion looking tails crawled all over him, slicing through arteries, and carving off gobbets of meat. Her eyes went to the elongated device. It was just a skeleton now. A frame to which the crab-legged machines had clung. She understood then why her brother had told her no. He was trying to stop her from killing the only man left they could interrogate. She shook her head turned back to Luke.

Oh, she said simply, secretly pleased with her handiwork but disappointed with the outcome. *If it makes you feel better, he never would have talked. He was too disciplined to talk. Maybe next time, we'll get lucky.*

Luke gave her a flat unfriendly look, but he realized that there would be a next time. There had been a lot of next times since the Drifters left. Next time, she might not be there to save him. Next time, they might succeed.

She strolled over to the mutilated corpse and quickly cleared the biggest of the bots with her sword, stomping on the smaller of them. She turned her armor off and reached down to retrieve the hilt of the dagger she had flung. The blade was missing, having broken up to incapacitate the man. She considered it for a moment, then pressed the end of the hilt against the dead man's chest and pressed the recall switch. The body twitched and spasmed then lay still. When she pulled the hilt away, nine inches of nanite steel slid out behind it, leaving an open wound behind. She reconnected it to her sword and wiped away the blood. The hilt of the dagger reconnected with the sword hilt all on its own. With the blade whole once more, she re-sheathed it and began to search the bodies as her brother called the local security node for assistance.

They sent six this time. She observed, crouching near the last man she had killed. A search of his pockets revealed little. She went body to body discovering nothing to help in identifying who these people worked for or where they came from. She returned to the first body she searched and rubbed at the dark eyeliner, smelling what wiped off. She smeared it on a film and tucked the film away for later investigation.

They're trying to derail the Harvest and slow us down so the others can catch up. They'll send more next time, Luke warned. Leia rose before him, wiping the rest of the assassin's eye liner on her pants.

They send more, then I kill more, she told him defiantly. He did not doubt it. What he doubted was his survival.

Chapter 6: Captivity

Morning came, and with morning came last night's revenge. My head throbbed and ached. My stomach was turning somersaults, and there was a taste in my mouth like I had been sucking on copper pennies since midnight.

Tessa's goons showed up around 7 a.m. to drag me from bed. With much pushing and prodding and not smiling, they got me in the shower. I stayed in there for nearly an hour. Coming out, I found my clothes gone. A query with the secret service resulted in me finding that my clothes had been thrown out. Mercy's assistant had sent her assistant out to shop for me. I found several changes of clothes laid out on the sofa. They all required that I wear a tie, but I did not wear ties. I informed the secret service agents guarding my room of this fact, and they surprised me by knowing me better than myself. After only a few moments of discussion, they had managed to correct my memory. I did in fact wear ties . . . now.

The shoes were tight, but they fit. I did not much care for the dress socks. When I was done, I asked my prison guards what they thought. Evidently, getting their opinion required a higher security clearance than I presently enjoyed. They said nothing.

If I said anything embarrassing last night or untoward, please know I'm sorry. It was the liquor talking. Just . . . don't get pissed, okay? I apologized so let's just let bygones be bygones. I threw my thought at the ceiling. The Secret Service agents followed my gaze to the ceiling then looked back at me like I had lost my mind. Maybe I had.

So, where are you from? Is it nice? I asked, trying to make conversation. There was no answer. A knock at the door let me know it was time to leave. *I used to live near West Plains, Missouri. It's a nice place. A lot more rural than some people like, but I enjoyed it. There was good hunting in that area. Do you hunt? What about fishing? I really don't know anything about you. I don't know if you grew up on a planet or if you just live on that flying saucer thing of yours. You're kind of an enigma to me.*

Would you shut up? It was only four words, but it made me smile.

I followed the Secret Service agents down the hall, loaded into the elevator with them, and took it to the lobby. There were two more agents waiting. They led the way outside where a black limo waited. A younger version of the security detail opened the rear door for me. I tried to tip him. He dumped my tip on the drive. The three quarters bounced and rolled under the car. I considered retrieving them, then figured that might look strange considering the car and how I was dressed. I pantomimed a message of "blow me" to the man. He ignored me for the most part, though he did close the door a tad quicker than was necessary, pushing me forward into the car and nearly making me sprawl in some stranger's lap.

There were other people in the back already. I recognized Aaron from Homeland Security and Mercy from the White House, but the other person whom I had nearly sprawled on was a mystery to me. Her hair was drawn back in a tight ponytail, her skirt hugged her hips, stopping at her knees, and a pair of dark-framed glasses perched on her nose. She sat up painfully straight with her knees together and an open planner in her lap. A pen posed ready to record if necessary. I figured she was the personal assistant to one of the other two.

There was only one place for me to sit, and I took it. It was beside the woman with the planner. She gave me a cursory glance and returned to her attentive state, dismissing me out of hand. Our seat faced backwards so that we could face Aaron and Mercy. It was uncomfortable.

"Sleep well?" Mercy asked politely.

"Possibly," I replied back. "Thanks for the clothes," I told her plucking awkwardly at the suit jacket wearing me. Mercy nodded toward her assistant.

"Thank her," Mercy said. "She's the one who picked them out."

"My assistant picked them out," the woman corrected.

"They fit pretty good. How'd she know what size I wore?" I asked conversationally.

"She probably just guessed. Her father's fat as well. Probably looked in the fat section of wherever she got them," she replied callously. To Mercy, she asked, "Roger Wiiat wants to meet to discuss setting up a time to meet with the President. His stated purpose is that he wants to discuss the White House's response to the alien attack. How is Thursday for a possible sit down, after your meeting with Hammond, but before your meeting with Senator Maccs?" Mercy seemed to consider it and nodded her approval.

I looked from Aaron to Mercy to the assistant. They were pretty much all ignoring me. I did not much care for not being the center of attention. It was my weakness and flaw.

"Why the suit?" I asked, plucking at the jacket.

"You're meeting with the President," Mercy's assistant supplied with indifference. She was penciling down Roger Wiiat for 9 a.m. Thursday. "This is respectful. What you were wearing was—"

"Comfortable," I supplied helpfully.

"Not respectful," she finished.

"I'm kind of a prisoner," I told her. "I'm not really big on showing respect after being kidnapped."

She went on as if I had not spoken. "The Oval Office doesn't have a boot scraper. There's no mini fridge filled with Coors Lite. They won't be serving you nachos or pigs in a blanket or whatever the hell you eat. It is the center of the free world. It deserves respect even from the likes of you. So, you wear a suit," she snapped waspishly.

"You're kind of a bitch," I told her bluntly. Evidently, she knew it. This was the first thing I said that made her smile and it was a smile of pride. Mercy turned her head away and tried to hide her amusement behind her hand. It was a wasted effort. I could see it reflected in the limo glass of her door.

"I'm afraid we still don't know your name," Aaron announced suddenly, breaking the silence, and turning serious. "You're obviously not the snowy-haired leader of Hogwarts, so who the hell are you?" I glanced toward Mercy. She had turned back and was curious as well.

"Names are overrated," I told him philosophically.

"Well, you're about to meet the President. With a name, you get to do that in person and with dignity. Without a name, you get to do it in another room via video while wearing handcuffs, and I won't guarantee the chains will ever come off once they're on. The choice is entirely yours though. Either way, we'll still run your prints and know your name before the day is out." Aaron crossed his legs with confidence, rested one arm on the door, and the other in his lap.

What do you think I should do? Should I give them my real name? I asked of Leia. She did not respond.

"What's it going to be? Option A or option B?" the man asked.

I gave Mercy an apologetic shrug. "I'll take option B." Aaron was not amused.

The assistant gave me a look of disgust. "You're an idiot." I shrugged and said nothing. I was not altogether sure she was wrong.

"I'm an idiot?" I asked indignantly. "You bought me a suit so I could sit in a jail cell. I look like a freaking senator."

"Oh please," she scoffed. "You hardly look like a senator. A used car salesman perhaps. Maybe an insurance salesman. You definitely don't look like anything remotely resembling a senator."

"Why? Do I look honest?" I quipped.

Mercy turned her head again. She needed to hide another smile. I grinned and wagged my eyebrows at her. This was a woman used to smiling.

When we arrived, it was not the entrance I expected. We did not arrive outside like it was a hotel. Instead, we passed through a few layers of security to reach an underground garage. Here we disembarked, and I was cuffed. Mercy was not pleased by this judging by the look of disapproval she gave Aaron. I was allowed to follow them into the building proper. Inside the metal door, I found myself in a cold cement-walled passage with frequent turns. I was with them for the first half-dozen turns, but then Aaron, Mercy, and their retinue stepped into an elevator and disappeared leaving me alone with the Secret Service.

I was led by three agents to a conference room. Before each seat was a camera, mic, and monitor. Three men in grey suits sat around it. The first was reclining comfortably with his legs stretched out and his ankles crossed. He was chewing on an ink pen and looking bored. The second man was turned sideways in his seat, leaning back with one arm laid on the table. A coffee cup filled that hand. The other man was set up with a laptop, which he was feverishly typing on. He wore a headset with a mic on it.

When I entered, there was a blue splash screen on every monitor, but as I took the seat the Secret Service pushed me into, an image of a long conference table populated with suited men and women appeared. There were a few men in uniform with very formidable looking medals and pins of rank. One wore oak leaves. I did not know what their ranks were, but I figured it high if they had a seat at the President's table. I had never served so I did not know.

I studied the three men in grey. They had a maverick look about them—bored and filled with unjustified self-importance. The lanyards around their neck sported security passes, but I could not make out who they were here to represent.

The one with the coffee leaned forward and came to his feet. He circled around behind me and took my hand in his. He splayed my fingers wide and pressed my palm to a digital scanner beside the laptop. A blue light moved from the bottom of the scanner to the top then back again. I struggled to retrieve my hand, but he held it there until the man with the laptop nodded.

The other man who had been lounging came around the other two. He carried a strange looking camera with him. The man who had scanned my hand turned my chair sideways and gripped my chin in one hand, pushing it up so the other man could take my picture. A green grid suddenly appeared on my face, projected by a light below the camera lens. I could not see the laptop screen, but I guessed it was a digital camera meant to aid in facial recognition.

They were there to determine my identity I surmised. I was curious to see if I was in their system. Judging by the cocky air of self-importance and the smug sense of entitlement, I figured them to be three of Tessa's goons. The NSA seemed the fastest way to identify someone out of all the alphabet agencies. I was curious what name it would find for me.

"So, what's your deal?" the photographer asked, fiddling with the buttons on the camera. He walked over to the laptop guy. That guy plugged a cable into the camera. "You some terrorist or what? What'd you do?" He set the camera down and went back to his seat.

"Shut up, Richie," the scanner guy snapped. "You know better than to ask. Do your shit and zip it." Richie grinned and flipped his buddy off, bobbing his head as he complied.

"Him?" the laptop guy quipped. "He came in with Barnes," the wooly man seated behind the laptop announced, grinning. I studied him. He seemed more down to Earth. His beard was neatly trimmed, but thick and full. He wore square specs, no jacket, and wrinkled jeans. A tweed jacket hung from the back of his chair. This allowed me to notice that the holster on his hip was empty. They were guests in the White House.

"Woah," Richie declared, doubly interested in my story. "You were out there for that ET shit? Come on. Spill. What was it like? Did you see them? Were they covered in tentacles? Were they Ridley Scott style aliens or Jody Foster-looks-like-your-dead-dad type of alien?"

"Cut the shit, Richie," the second grey man snapped.

"You're not curious?" Richie asked of his companion. "They're going to conference upstairs, then they will spin this shit and tell us what they always tell us. This is our chance to get it firsthand. I mean," he turned back to me, "you were there, right?" I kept quiet. I had been warned in the car to keep my mouth shut and speak when cued by Mercy's assistant.

"Hey, tubby," he barked testily. "Answer the question. You were out there, right?" I stayed silent. "Did they touch you? Were you probed?" His grin was mocking. I had seen his type before. He was a jock showing off for the team. He was an untouchable. I tried to melt his face with my mind. He tried to bully me with small stinging slaps to the face. "Did they do things to you? Is that why you're quiet?" I tried to hit him in the head with my brain powers. He was unmolested by my efforts.

Why can't I move things like your brother? I demanded, sending my thoughts out to her. I accompanied it with my short-term memory of what was happening. I did not expect an answer, and at first there was not one.

You have to find something to focus it. Like a word, Leia replied haltingly. *Focus on it, then use the word like a battering ram. It's hard to do. You have to practice.* I was surprised she deigned to answer me.

How . . . How are you? When this is all done and stuff do you want to get— She didn't let me finish the thought.

Shut up! she snapped, sending a stinging little slap with the command. It smarted, but my vision was not blurry. She had held back. I smiled.

"How long until they're ready?" Richie asked of the bearded one. There was some typing behind me.

"Five minutes, maybe," the bearded one announced.

"Five minutes. You hear that? We want to know what happened out there in Kansas. Did you see the aliens?" he slapped me. I was generally jolly, but this was starting to get serious. "Answer me."

"I'm not supposed to talk about it," I replied, breaking my silence. "They said I'd be charged with treason if I did."

"Fine," Richie announced. "Don't say anything, but you know something?" He motioned to him and his two colleagues. "You don't want us as enemies. Do you have any idea what we could do to you? Do you know what we could do to the people you love? We just want a taste of what you're going to tell them upstairs. Did you see the aliens? Why are they here? Do they come in peace?"

I tried to push my mind into his. It was like trying to push wet spaghetti through a cement wall. I strained harder.

"I think he's going to shit himself," Richie told the others. He slapped my cheek again tauntingly. The other guys laughed. I had endured enough. I imagined that my mind was a hammer and his face was a nail. I threw everything I had into the image.

Suck it! I shouted silently, pushing at the words like they were a dam. At first there was nothing, no movement at all, then something slipped. In the next moment, the damn burst and a huge surge of will exploded forth aimed at his stupid grinning face. I felt weak watching what happened.

The force of my mind felt like a hurricane as it left me. It was now a force unto itself. I waited for him to fly backwards like Luke had done to Leia. He did not even blink, but three chairs back on the table, his empty Styrofoam coffee cup slid an inch and toppled. I gasped from the amount of strength it took to do even that. I mean, it was something to build on.

"Hey. Cut it out," the bearded one told them. "They're almost ready upstairs." He must have been right. Mercy's hateful assistant arrived just a moments later with her own assistants in tow. She looked at the three NSA agents, determined there were two too many and sent everyone but the bearded one from the room. They did not bother to protest. They were on loan. The moment they were out, she turned to me.

"Name," she demanded. I looked over at the bearded one. She followed my gaze. He looked up in confusion, first at me then her and shrugged.

"We don't know yet. I put his prints in AFIS and I'm running his head shot through our facial recognition system. I'm also running them through the NSA database. It could take a while. There's no hits yet." She turned back to me.

"Have you tried contacting his employer?" she asked. "He works in a quarry near . . ." she looked at me. "What was the name of that town you lived in?"

"Cherryville," I replied politely. She did not thank me. I was not sure she understood the concept. "See if you can find the quarry. Fax them a headshot and see if anyone knows him."

The bearded one went to work on the laptop. A few moments later, he pulled a cell phone and made a call. He got up and drifted toward the far end of the room for privacy.

"Name," she demanded again, as if her stern manner could sway me. I shrugged as if in defeat.

"My names Andre Cassanges," I relented. "I'm a recluse." She looked to the bearded one, snapping her fingers to get his attention.

"Andre Cassanges?" She gestured to the laptop, and he hurried back, putting the person on the other end on hold. He typed the name into his laptop and waited for a hit. A moment later, he was chuckling.

"What an honor," he told her dryly. "This man invented the Etch-a-sketch." She gave me a disgusted look of impotent rage.

"I recall the day the idea of the Etch-a-sketch came to me. Of course, back then I didn't call it an Etch-a-sketch. I just referred to it as the shaky box. The idea was more a philosophical foray into the human psyche. Think about it as I did. There you are, and your life is shit. Don't you wish you could just take life by the edges and shake out a new start. Well, I had these thoughts too, and I must tell you, I wish I had thought of this as a kid. Then it hit me. Boom! What if there was a toy children could play with that would let them—"

"Name," she demanded. She wasn't buying it.

"Fine, you unfriendly wench. My names Ayn Rand. I'm something of a nomad—a gypsy really," I told her facetiously. She looked to the bearded one. He was surprised by this. He didn't even have to type it in.

"It's an author. Ayn Rand wrote Atlas Shrugged," he told her in a bored sounding voice with a slight look of amusement.

"I don't have time for this," she demanded, checking her watch. "Give me a name that isn't tied to some book or invention. I don't care who you are. I just don't want you to embarrass me in front of this group," she told me in exasperation, pointing to the monitors. "Please?" she added plaintively. "You don't like the system. I get it. But this? It's my career you're messing with." I empathized with her.

"It's not my name, but you can call me Daniel—Daniel Sojourner," I said, grimacing. It was not my name, but it was a name I had used before. She looked to the bearded one. He typed it in. No hits came back. The bearded one shook his head and gave her a thumbs up, then picked up the call he had put on hold.

"Good enough," she declared. She turned me toward the camera and took her cue from the bearded one. Her assistants swarmed my person, adjusting my collar, smoothing my suit, straightening my tie, applying powder to the shiny parts of my face. When the bearded one declared my appearance good on screen, I was instructed to keep my cuffed hands in my lap for the duration of the interview. I fell back in my seat. Washington sucked, and I was tired of the whole ordeal.

When all was done, Mercy's assistant shooed the other assistants from the room, she collapsed into the seat next to me and swiveled so she could study me. Her lips were pursed in contemplation of my person. I could feel her eyes tickling me all over. There was a curiosity there, but it was not for me. I think she was curious why they wanted me to speak to them.

"Why you?" she blurted suddenly.

Nailed it, I gloated to no one in particular.

Nailed what? a voice replied without warning. The question startled me, but not as much as the speaker. I did not know them, but they felt close at hand.

Woah! Who the hell is this? I asked excitedly of the voice I had just heard. It was not Leia.

Shit! the voice exclaimed in fear, going silent.

CHAPTER 7: BLOODHOUND

Who are you? I queried, asking it over and over. She never responded. There was another psychic in the building. Whoever it was, was gone now. I was not even sure it was a girl, but it felt like one. I do not know how I knew that. Whoever it was, they did not want to be found.

I sent my mind out searching, trying to find an open mind like a phone searching for an unlocked Wi-Fi router. I did not know how to use the ability well enough to find them though. I changed tactics. When Luke had tried to hide his conversation with Leia, he had put up a wall of white noise to block my ability to hear them. I started searching for a wall like that. After a few moments of searching, I gave up in frustration. I could not even pick the thoughts from the people in the room, though judging by the looks the bearded one was throwing the assistant, I could guess his.

. . . if she has a boyfriend . . . The voice just popped into my head. I turned and looked at the man in surprise. He looked up and away. That was him. I was certain of it. I tried to do it again, concentrating hard. His mind was silent and unreadable. How did I do that? I wondered. I looked to the assistant and wondered if it was her doing. Was she the mysterious voice I had heard before? I studied her eyes for some indication that she knew that I knew that she was psychic. She studied me back.

"Well?" she snapped.

"Well, what?" I snapped back, wondering if this was her admitting to being the girl.

"Why you? Why'd they pick you?" she asked. I only saw the brief flash of jealousy because I was trying to read her at that moment. That flash said it all. I understood her now. She was not the mysterious voice I had heard. She was the assistant to the mouthpiece of the President of the United States.

It was not a glamorous position, but she was proud of it. She had probably fought her way up the ladder for years to reach her present station. And here I was, I had just been eating a funnel cake in the right place at the right time, and now I was the chosen mouthpiece of an alien nation, and I was about to meet the leader of the free world.

. . . me. It should have been me. I blinked in surprise. I had heard that. I had heard that, and it was her. Her face even stressed and moved in time with the thought. It was her thoughts. I had heard her thoughts. I tried to eavesdrop on her inner thoughts to see if I could, but it was a repeat of the bearded one. Her mind was closed. It was getting very frustrating. There was a system to this. I knew it. I just could not pick out what the trigger was.

"Hey! Don't ignore me. You don't ignore me," she told me tartly.

"Look, I get it. You fought and clawed your way up to become the assistant to the assistant of the President. You've probably heard what happened out there in Kansas, and now you see me, seemingly a nobody who is now the megaphone through which two worlds are shouting. I didn't work for this. It was just thrust upon me. To you, it's not fair. How could it be. You are invested. This," I gestured to the monitors and surrounding buildings, "is the monument you spend your life building. The sculpture of your efforts. You deserve this, but I don't because it was free for me. In your eyes, you've climbed above all others. You are the oligarch in your world, but then I came along and found a winning lottery ticket and now you don't feel so special. Is that right?"

You're freaking right it isn't fair, you stupid blue collar inbred piece of trailer trash. I heard that clear as day. *What was it like? What was it like standing out there? Did they adore you? She likes you more than me now. She . . . I just want her approval. I just want her respect.* My brow furrowed in confusion, and it dawned on me who she was referencing. I wondered if Mercy knew. I looked at the stern impassive features of the assistant, and tried to pluck another thought, but it was gone again.

"I've never lived in a trailer park in my life," I told her indignantly. The bearded one gave me a look of confusion, but the assistant's eyes went wide with shock and surprise.

"You?" she asked, coming forward in her chair. She glanced at the bearded one then back at me. She pointed at me then at herself. "Me?" The bearded one was frowning even more, but there was a twinkle of interest. I had screwed up.

"Calm yourself, girl. Have some dignity. You're way to uptight for that to ever happen. Well, I mean if there was enough alcohol, maybe. And, if my choices were slim. I'm not saying there's a good concrete yes in this, but maybe. Probably not though." I turned back to the camera. She suddenly flushed red with embarrassment, realizing how her inquiry had been delivered. She gave the bearded one a look and he turned away, striving to avoid eye contact. His mustache was riding a little higher on each side of his face.

"That's not what—I would never—I " It was kind of amusing. I had made her speechless. I wondered how many senators could boast that accomplishment regarding her.

"We're live," the bearded one announced, putting a finger to his lips to quiet the red-faced assistant.

The next two hours were very boring. I was very cooperative. Sure, I am not a fan of the government on its best days, which were few and far between, but Margaret—turns out that's what the Mercy's hateful assistant's name was—was right about the Oval Office and the President. They were deserving of a modicum of respect. So, I kept my hands in my lap as ordered, and I paid attention. I honestly answered the man's questions and the frustrating and tedious questions of his cabinet. They reacted poorly to the news that something unknown pursued the aliens hovering above. It was going to be one of the key talking points when their ambassador returned.

The decorated military men wanted to know if I had gleaned any information that might manifest as a weakness to their biology. I was a little snarky here, since I do not like the idea that their first instinct was to find a way to kill them. However, I understood prudence. I suggested jokingly that maybe they could steal a saucer and upload a computer virus to their mother ship to disable the fleet above. I was being facetious, but they still wrote it down. I guess you do not get to be the decorated military Christmas tree they got to be by sitting around watching Jeff Goldblum cash in on his ability to work a verbal pause repeatedly into every line of dialogue he speaks. I forgave them their naïve nature. They were only human after all.

Mercy was surprisingly on point throughout. She worked the discussion from a humanitarian perspective. She pointed out that the world really was overpopulated, and in less than a hundred years, hard decisions would have to be made. She referenced China's one child rule and explained that it would be considered humane by comparison to what would come. When she pointed out that the wars were not killing off enough of the population to offset the effects of overpopulation like they had hoped, I was astounded.

This opened up a whole lot of questions for me that I could not answer. Were the governments of the world actively provoking armed conflicts to thin the world population? The implications were staggering. Had they been proactive this entire time in dealing with the issue of overpopulation. If so, they were doing it in the only publicly acceptable way possible to them. It was not a pleasant thought.

I had to put things in context. The context was that I was talking about the United States of America. There was no way they could pull off a worldwide manipulation like that. It was always about the oil with them. Money was always their motivator, or was it? I was suddenly not so sure.

The questions of which gods the aliens worshipped came up. It was quickly shelved for later discussion. The gist of the meeting was to find out what precautions the U.S. government should take in all of this. All in attendance agreed that they should at least hear Luke's proposal before passing judgment.

The most interesting of these discussions occurred when the subject of the alien attack was broached. The aliens had offered to repair the dead and restore them. This got into a lot of conjecture on what exactly their medical technology was and the merits of a possible technology exchange as an apology for the pain and suffering they had caused the people of Earth. It was decided that a dozen or so bodies would be provided expressly for the purpose of seeing the process of reanimation in action. No one was really interested in having them reanimate all of those who had died. The damage was done, and most of those who had died were on their way out anyway. The families were already grieving.

Tessa was present for the meeting as were the other six ambassadors. She admitted what each of them knew. Even if the dead were brought back by the visitors, there was no way they could trust those revived individuals not to be some kind of pre-programmed puppet solider working for the ETs. The security risk was too great. Twenty-thousand mind-controlled reanimated bodies would be one hell of an army. It was the one thing everybody agreed on unanimously.

There was one significant breakthrough during the meeting. The wall of white noise I had been searching for was located and quite by accident. Well, that's not exactly true. I found the white noise, just not the person putting it up. I could not be sure if it was the woman I had heard earlier or someone else, because I could not determine which one of the people sitting with the President was putting up the wall.

I spent the last hour of the conference studying each of the women in attendance. I tried to push my mind into the room repeatedly, but it was a fantastic failure. It was like trying to pick up a penny with crooked tweezers while looking in a mirror at a monitor being fed a video stream on a time delay of the penny in question. Everything was backwards and discombobulated to me.

I made it into the room a few times with my mind. It was hard, but doable. I discovered the wall on my second foray. After that, it got harder.

The telepathy is not easy. It is not an out of body experience. It is not me drifting effortlessly through the halls. I am still keenly aware of what is happening in my body. I can even get up and walk around and write while broadcasting my thoughts, but it is like flexing a muscle. The longer you do it the more exhausted you grow. University kids often claim to be mentally exhausted after their finals. It is a real thing to be mentally exhausted. Constantly projecting one's mind is like doing sit-ups with your grey matter. This analogy, led me to realize that if it is like flexing a muscle, flexing muscles makes them stronger. I resolved myself to practice in my spare time.

It really is the little breakthroughs that matter.

Discovery of the white noise presented a new problem. It was a problem because it meant that there was a spy among the President's staff. One of the people I had been staring at was false. The fact they knew how to erect a wall of white noise to block out my intrusion demonstrated their telepathic ability was more advanced than mine. It also meant that they were aware there was another telepath around. Why flex a muscle you do not have to? This led me back to the voice of the mysterious female I had startled earlier. She was the only psychic other than Leia who knew I was in the White House. My problem became determining who to tell about the spy. Maybe it was Tessa? Everyone I knew was in that room with the spy. Who could I trust? I was not sure what to do. I did the one thing that made any sense at all. In confided in the one person in Washington that despised me most.

"There's a spy in the White House."

Margaret just blinked in mute stupefaction.

The meeting had been adjourned with many key talking points determined, conditions for action put in place, and a list of potential trade initiatives earmarked for later refinement.

"There's a spy in that room," I told her again. The bearded one's eyes went wide with surprise.

"And, you know this how?" he asked, turning in his chair to face me. I looked back at Margaret. Her eyes narrowed, her lips pursed, and I realized she was doing the same thing I had just done. She was weighing the pros and cons of acting on the knowledge. On one hand, I was an undeserving git. On the other, it was a blatant breach of security. Her decision was revolving around whether she wanted to help the individual she considered competition.

"You know how I know," I replied, holding her gaze. "I know this the same way I know you're in love with your boss; the same way I know you live only for her approval." Her mouth dropped open in surprise.

"W-What? You and Mercy Mangrove?" the bearded one asked, falling back into his chair in disbelief.

"Wait here," Margaret ordered, rising, and quickly leaving room.

Being left alone with the bearded one quickly became awkward. We did not talk. He pretended to be busy with his laptop, and I pretended he was not wanting to ask me about the encounter with the alien ambassador. After twenty minutes of avoiding the pasty pachyderm in the room, he could not take it anymore.

"I have to know, man. The aliens, you really met them," he gushed. "Just give me something. Anything. Nothing vital. I'm a huge sci-fi nut. I need to know this. I have to know. How many did you meet?" He had me at sci-fi nut.

"Fine," I told him, leaning in so as not to be overheard by the security outside. "I'll give you this. I met two of them. They were brother and sister."

"Two?" He bit his knuckle in his excitement. "That's so cool." He considered this and frowned, adopting a shrewd look. "Now, when you say brother and sister, are we talking siblings by blood?"

"By blood," I said in a total deadpan.

"Okay. Yeah. Awesome. Did they have tentacles or . . ." He left it hanging.

"That's one of those things I'd get in trouble for answering," I said, leaning back.

"Their names. Do they have cool names?" he asked, grasping for anything I would give.

"Many would think so. Their names were Luke and Leia," I replied soberly. He sat very still, no expression on his face, and slowly closed his eyes as if realizing the joke. I thought he would be excited and even find it funny considering his being a sci-fi nut.

"You're a real asshole," he told me hotly.

"No really, that's their names," I protested. "I'm serious." He gave me the finger and went back to his laptop.

"I just wanted something. You couldn't even give me that. Something small. That's all I was asking for," he groused.

After that, silence reined. So, it was a great relief when Margaret at last returned—hateful, malicious, cold-hearted, ice queen Margaret. A man who I had never seen before was with her. He wore a suit much like the Secret Service agents, except his jacket was unbuttoned, there were three phones on his belt, a shoulder holster clearly visible, and a walkie in his hand.

The man followed her into the room, took in me and the bearded one, and jerked his thumb toward the door. "Out." The bearded one nodded, closed his laptop, stowed the scanner, and camera in two black cases along with his laptop, and left.

"Daniel, this is Michael Ross. He's the Secret Service section chief overseeing White House security. He wasn't present at the meeting, and we can trust him," Margaret said, vouching for the man.

"Ms. Barton says you have knowledge of a possible spy on the grounds; you believe it is someone close to the President?" He glanced at the cuffs I was wearing, and I saw my credibility sifting away. "Who do you suspect. Which government?"

"It'll sound weird, but I don't know. I'd need to be closer. I can't tell from here." It clearly sounded like an excuse to see the President.

"You want me to put you closer to whom?" Michael asked shrewdly, eyes narrowed with suspicion.

"Well," I looked to Margaret for support. She gave me nothing and just stood there shaking her head and waving me off. "Well, everyone who was at that meeting."

"Wait? You want me to put you in a room with the most powerful man in the free world, and his staff?" The Secret Service section chief asked in amazement. "You want me to parade you in there seated on a unicorn while I'm at it? People don't just get to see the President."

"Okay. Yeah. I was being stupid. Just forget about it," I told him in embarrassment.

"But there's a spy, Daniel," Michael argued. "Don't you want to catch the spy?"

"Well, yeah, but you made it sound like . . . like I was . . ." I was confused.

"Like you were crazy. Yeah, you sound crazy. You're here in cuffs in the basement of the White House conferencing in on a Top-Secret meeting because they didn't trust you to be in the same room as the President of the United States of America." The section chief shrugged. "It kind of makes you sound desperate and exceedingly crazy."

"Yeah. I see your point."

"You vouch for him?" Michael asked of Margaret.

"Not enough to bet my car," she replied, giving me an apologetic look. She had trouble pulling off the look.

"That's what I thought," he remarked, turning to go.

"Unless," Margaret called out unexpectedly, coming forward. Michael turned, curious. I looked to her, curious myself.

"Unless what?" he asked, indulging her. She looked to me for support now. She was sticking her neck out for me. I gave her two thumbs up.

"Unless, keeping him away had nothing to do with the president. What if it was to keep him from identifying the spy?" she ventured. We both had the gist of her thinking.

"What if that's why I'm being kept away. What if it wasn't to keep me from the President all, but rather—" Margaret took over, giving me an irritated look. It was her theory and her glory if she was right. I gave up the reins of conjecture to her.

"But rather, he's being kept away because he'll out the spy?" she finished her supposition and fixed the section chief with a look of challenge. She must have spent years perfecting it. He caved.

"Would you have been able to identify the spy if you'd been in that room?" Michael asked.

"Now that I know what I'm looking for, yeah. I'd know." I was confident this would be the case.

"And what would you be looking for?" Michael asked. I did not know how to answer that without sounding retarded.

"Static," I told him. "There's a sound when they try to hide." I pointed toward the ceiling. "When they try blocking their thoughts. I can hear it." The section chief looked at the ceiling in confusion, then realized the "they" I was referring to was hovering in saucers above the world.

"You mean one of them is posing as us?" Michael asked, raising his walkie.

"Don't do that. Not yet," I warned.

"Give me a reason not to?" he replied, his radio hovering, ready to broadcast the call.

"Whoever it is, they're better at this than I am. You know why I'm here, right?" He nodded. "You understand why I'm important?" He nodded again.

"I'm privy to it all," he confirmed.

"If you let security know, the spy will be able to pluck it out of one of your agent's head and know they're being hunted. They'll disappear, and we'll never see them again," Margaret said.

"Fine," he remarked, conceding to their wishes. "We'll do it your way." He stepped forward and removed my cuffs. "Most of them should still be up there." He led the way, motioning for the two secret service agents guarding the room to bring up the rear. He gave them a vague non-specific warning of a potential imminent threat. He left the threat ambiguous in case the spy they hunted tried to pluck it from their head. They could not reveal information they did not know.

It occurred to me that there was a reason why the spy put up that wall of static. Without it there, anyone could tip toe into their mind and eavesdrop on their thoughts. I did not know how it was done, so I just imagined an old television set without a signal. I imagined the snow, and the hissing crackle of dead air and hung that thought like a curtain about me.

Michael led me down a corridor and into the same elevator the rest of ambassadors took earlier. He punched in a security code, hit a button, and me, him, and Margaret were spirited away to higher floors. The door opened. We walked a short distance, made a couple of turns, and entered the conference room. I strode in behind the section chief and opened my mind to the people in the room. The spy stood out to me like she was wearing a sandwich board. The moment my mind touched her wall, she flinched and dropped the pot of tea she was holding. Michael looked to me, and I nodded, leveling an accusing finger her way.

"It's her," I said. The wall of white noise was deafening. Michael drew his weapon, receiving a cacophony of startled exclamations from the ambassadors and aides in attendance. She did not look dangerous.

Michael did not have to call out instructions to his men. This was drilled into them. The young woman serving tea to those seated was quaking with fear, but she did as she was instructed. She followed their instructions to kneel, cross her ankles, and interlace her fingers behind her head.

She looked at me as if I'd betrayed her, and I felt empathy for her, but wasn't sure why. The two agents that had accompanied us into the room took the woman into custody and led her away. She held my gaze the entire time.

Why? she asked pleadingly, as if the answer was not blaringly apparent.

You're a spy, I replied in the theater of our minds. I do not know what I expected as her response, but confusion was not it. I listened to the receding sound of the white noise as they took her away. I could sense it growing fainter. Now that I had her scent, I could follow her with ease, which only confused me.

"What is the meaning of this?" Tessa Barnes barked angrily. The NSA Director made as if to rise.

"Stay seated, Madam Director," Michael commanded. "There's intel she may have been working for an outside entity." He moved to put his gun away, but I placed a hand on his shoulder and started scanning the faces of the seated men and women. He gave me a questioning look and brought his sidearm up to a ready position.

The white noise was still present. It was greatly reduced but still there. A quick survey of those in the room showed me the other spy. I did not even have to push my mind out to know it was her. I could see the disappointment and resignation written on her face. I felt something inside me break.

"Not you," I moaned, gesturing reluctantly to the end of the table. She had been the only one to show me any kindness in Washington. Now that I was here, I wondered how I had missed it before. I realized then that I had come a long way with my telepathic ability since Kansas.

Mercy did not wait to be called out. She rose from her seat and came around the table and stopped before the section chief who studied her in mute disbelief. She turned and presented her wrist to him. Michael reluctantly pulled his cuffs and hooked her up.

"We left you alone, like you wanted," she told me sadly. "Why would you betray us after all this time?"

I don't know what I found more disturbing, the fact that she thought we had a history predating the alien landing, or that she was inferring that we had some secret arrangement as well.

I wanted to ask more, but everyone in the room was jabbering and conferring and hitting me with queries. I felt terrible. Something significant had just happened, and I had no clue as to what.

More of Michael's agents arrived. Michael passed Mercy off to two of those agents and told them to keep her separate from the other prisoner. I was not sure how effective that tactic was going to be considering they did not need to be in the same room to communicate. The other men and women in the room were demanding answers, but Michael quieted them with a look and a call for silence.

He motioned me forward. I threw my mind out, searching each of the people in the room. There were no others. The room was clear of spies, probably.

Over the next six hours, I was used like a bloodhound to clear the rest of the White House. Tessa had insisted that I be transferred to her custody for holding, but Aaron McDonald had claimed me under the authority of Homeland Security. I was debriefed and allowed to return to my hotel room. My security detail was doubled. U.S. Marshals had been brought in to guarantee my safety. Homeland bolstered their detail with agents guaranteed to prevent my escape. The only bright point in my sequester this time was that they felt I now rated special treatment. The porn channels were unlocked.

I collapsed on the bed, remote in hand, and surfed the channels. I had ferreted out two spies in the White House. I was a hero of sorts. I should be thrilled, but I was not. I felt lousy. I felt worse than lousy. I just wanted to go to bed and pretend it never happened. I did not want to be the mouthpiece for two worlds. I decided then and there, I was not going to cooperate with any of them again. I was no dancing chicken.

I need your help, Leia announced, falling like an angel into my head.

My heart was suddenly racing. *Name it,* I declared excitedly. My reservations forgotten.

Chapter 8: Commitment

You're sure of their origin? the man asked.

Yes, Daimyo, Luke replied, using the man's formal title.

Daimyo? the man repeated, chuckling mirthfully to himself.

It is your inherited title, my Lord, Luke said, reminding him of the fact and silently wondering where the man's mind was wandering.

In this, I envy the colonists. They had a simple way of labeling. Each name their own. You can build an identity around a name. A title, not so much. He strolled through the arcade enjoying the feel of the artificial breeze. The endless lane of arches was a nice colonial affectation adopted into the design of the ship. It was one affectation he enjoyed greatly. The sprawling lawns to either side and their babbling fountains with the flower wreathed shores had always been his secret retreat after the rigors of the day.

He slipped off to dine among the fronds when the ship's rotation brought it broad side to the Earthling sun. He had been the sole voice of opposition the last three times the council governing this particular level of the ship attempted their aesthetic upgrades. It was only that archaic title he had inherited that had kept the arcade intact and serviced each time. A title did have some use, it would seem.

I heard a colonial finally gave you a title. He smiled and Luke allowed an embarrassed smirk to bend his lips.

It's just a name, not a title, and the man in question was being mirthful when he did. The name was given in jest, though I'm unsure whether the ambassadors of his planet were aware of this. He has called me Luke.

Luke? A deific apostle? A prominent figure in one of the dominate religions of this world as I understand it. This may taint relations with the colonists of the other belief systems. It might be prudent to abandon this and request another less controversial label. Luke shook his head in response.

They recycle their labels and award them with whimsy. While I do not doubt your wisdom or disregard your council, I saw the jest in this man's mind. The Luke for which I was named was an iconic theatrical character who traveled the universe righting wrongs. It is somewhat fitting considering who I am. Unless you demand it, I'd like to keep the label. I'm growing fond of it. The colonist meant no insult when he gave it. I saw that right off. Luke hurried forward and opened the door for the man he considered his surrogate father. The man nodded his thanks and strode through, stepping aside to allow Luke to rejoin with him.

"Keep it," the Daimyo told him, speaking aloud for the first time since the Sub-prior's arrival. "If it pleases you, it pleases me." He smiled to show he meant it.

The gallery in which they found themselves was long and narrow with a low ceiling. Witchfire canisters secured to the columns along the wall lit the room. The faint green light combined with the white artificial ion lighting pouring from cans in the ceiling gave the chamber a warm cozy feel. An overstuffed and richly upholstered set of sofas filled recessed sitting area in the center of the chamber. It was sunk into the floor so that one's head, when in recline, rested slightly above floor level.

A guest-master arrived as they took their seats, kneeling so that he could remove their slippers—a custom on this particular level of the ship for those settling in for their later hour repose.

My good Lord Merrik, Daimyo, Luke murmured softly. He paused to consider how best to proceed.

"Come, we've known each other far too long to stand on ceremony. Unburden yourself. What bothers you?" Merrik asked, accepting a small bulbous glass of amber-colored drink.

Luke raised his hand, three fingers extended. A gesture familiar to the guest-master. It announced that the man flashing the sign was a member of a popular monastic order. The guest-master bowed silently and hurried off to prepare an appropriate beverage for the man. Luke gave a shallow bow and took a seat opposite his friend.

Lord Merrik, the attacks are growing more frequent. A chancellor was executed in front of his family on the Isle of Wren. I've survived nine assassination attempts myself since donning the mantle of Grand Reaper. I'm only a Sub-Prior, and I've had the position less than four hundred rotations.

Six congressmen have been ambushed since reaching this colony alone. We've lost senators, abbots, barons, and a governess. We're dying in our beds all so this Harvest can be realized. Luke lost himself in the play of the Witchfire for a moment. *When is it going to end?* he asked pleadingly. Beseeching him to be earnest in his response.

It ends when it ends, Luke. We have our directive. We make the Empire whole again. Nothing else matters. The man sipped his drink and selected a morsel from a small white platter the guest-master had provided.

How are we supposed to do that? We're fractured, Luke asked.

We fix what was broken, Lord Merrik replied as if the answer was obvious.

It was at that moment that the guest-master returned with a simple unadorned cup filled with water for Luke.

Luke accepted a cup of water from the guest-master and set it aside. The Daimyo spoke with confidence and certainty. "We bring the Drifters back into the fold, we destroy the insurgency, and we reap the colonists. This is how we fix it. This is why we're here."

And you think the First Colony will allow this? They'd rather see us dead, my Lord.

"They'd rather see us turned, Luke, but that is unworthy of consideration or reflection. Our directive is clear. We mend what is broken. Men and women may die along the road as we rush to see our mission realized. These are good deaths. These are necessary deaths. They say that the last time the Empire fractured, the Emperor ordered that the severed heads of the Drifters be rained down on the capital city non-stop till the insurrection was ended. It rained heads non-stop for twenty-six rotations. On the twenty-seventh day, the dissident leader capitulated, no longer able to stand the slaughter of his followers. In the end, he begged the Emperor to punish him." He studied Luke closely.

Call off the Harvest. Let us move on before all is lost. We can afford to lose one colony, Luke begged. He flushed red with shame, but he remained adamant. The look of disappointment in the Daimyo's eyes was crippling.

The Daimyo's response was firm and wrathful. *We. Mend. What is broken. These people, we call them colonists and that's our fault. That's our injury. That's our sin. Calling them colonists has made us see them as outsiders and foreigners. They, like us, are Cojokarueen.* Lord Merrick leaned across and laid a hand on the hand of the man he considered a son before speaking aloud. "We are the Cojokarueen, and if we are strong, the Empire is strong." He sat his cup down on the crescent table between them and allowed the guest-master to assist them in re-donning their slippers.

Switching back into the mental communications Luke was so accustomed to as part of his order, Merrik beckoned Luke. *Come. Let me show you something.*

He crossed to an oval portal between two columns adjacent to the door they had entered by. It hissed as it shot into the wall to expose a room beyond. The next chamber was small, square, and filled with soft pale light and warmly varnished tables.

Monks sat at these taking their repast. The pair passed through the chamber and into the corridor beyond. Following the corridor led them to a low balcony that swelled from the walkway only to overhang a circular courtyard. This courtyard gave way to another courtyard on lower deck below.

The first courtyard was filled with strolling couples and people visiting. Children crowded around the rail at the edge because the lower courtyard was not empty. That courtyard was populated with men and women in a familiar grey plate armor interspersed with link mail. These men and women marched four abreast, turning smartly each time the chip horn was sounded. The small quick quacks of the horn were always followed by the stamp of many feet. Lord Merrik gestured toward the stairs and waited for Luke to descend. He followed after and led the way to the rail. The children who saw the Daimyo approaching parted making way for him and the Grand Reaper. The courtyard was a parade ground where colonials trained to become Grey Guardsmen: the constabulary patrolmen for every country in the Empire.

Look upon them, Luke. These are your brothers and sister, and they were colonists not too long ago. These are the colonials from the last Harvest. They're already Grey Guardsmen. Less than half of them will qualify for soldier training and get to wear the ebony class armor of an Imperial Guard. Of those, less than a quarter will be chosen to squire for an Imperial Knight. Only a handful will ever get to become knights. He went silent and turned to the man he mastered. *Do you know why the Empire has survived, my son?*

We make good soldiers, Luke guessed.

We have survived, because those men and women down there volunteer. We survive because the Empire didn't forget them. We survive because they know we value life. They all want to be heroes. Those men and women on the planet below are our family. We're all children of the Empire. We don't leave our children for the twilight hounds, or the marsh cats or the First Colony to claim and devour.

Luke closed his eyes, keenly feeling his shame and his cowardice. Merrik turned to take his leave, convinced he had made his point, but decided a dose of hard reality was still in order. "We are Cojokarueen, Luke, and those are our brothers and sisters as I have said and that should be all the reason you need to reap a good Harvest. But if that isn't enough motivation to do your job, then understand this, every colonist you leave behind will be claimed by the First Colony. They will swell the ranks of our enemies, and we can't have that. The First will either leave this planet flush with new recruits or leave a bloody mess. This is not just about patriotism. It's also about survival. Reap well, my son."

Luke fell back into the railing, feeling his world swirl and quake. He could not do this. They had picked the wrong man to serve as Grand Reaper. He could not do this. He fled the courtyard, uncertain as to where he should go. He was afraid. He was so very afraid. And that realization gave him pause, but more importantly, it gave him a plan. He suddenly knew what to do.

He had to find his sister.

Chapter 9: Friends & Enemies

"Where to?" the liftman asked, stepping aside so that Leia could enter. There were others onboard but not enough to make the ride uncomfortable. She strolled through the doors with a swagger that the citizenry associated with the knighthood. It was a walk filled with confidence and challenge.

Do you like spaghetti? I like spaghetti. More accurately, I like cold spaghetti. I think it has better flavor, Daniel said, barging into her thoughts. She sighed with exasperation. The man never shut up. Always talking, talking, talking. He prattled on, so she pushed him to the back of her mind. It was like having music playing softly in the background. She would be lying if she said she hated it. It was kind of comforting listening to him talk about unimportant things.

"Madam Knight?" the liftman called again. The fact that the man preferred to speak verbally spoke louder than words to her as to this man's origins. Most of the colonials harvested, even after they learned how to use telepathy, preferred to speak.

Level 12. Quad 3. The Hope Fall District, she supplied. She waited for her seat assignment. It had been a tiring day. Killing assassins was fun, but the inquisitions that followed were tedious and trying. Three boards of Inquisitors asking the same questions six different ways in an attempt to trip her up combined with having to submit her after-action report to her battle commander really strained her patience.

A fight was simple. Why not keep it simple? She fiddled with the film in her pocket. She should have volunteered it up with the other evidence at the scene, but she had not. There was something familiar about it. The other assassins had not been wearing any, but she was sure she had encountered it before somewhere. It was a long time ago, but for the life of her she could not remember where. Her hope was that if she kept it with her at some point, she would remember its origins.

"Seat 38, if you please," the liftman replied with her seat assignment. It was the number he would call when her destination was reached. It would be a while. Level 12 was forty floors down and Quad 3 was near the center of that level. The battalion commander's headquarters were near the hull of the ship on level 52. Her ride home was easily a hundred leagues by lift. In colonist time, it would be at least an hour-long ride.

She sauntered deeper into the lift ignoring most of the passengers. Occasionally, a child would reach out to touch her armor, and she would smile and shake the young one's finger or make a goofy face to make them laugh. When she finally found the seat the liftman had assigned her, she found that someone had gotten sick and vomited on it.

Instead of seeking a new seat assignment, she just took one of the empty ones. She could remember the number. She shrugged her shoulders to settle her sword and reached back to pull her hair from the spinal rings. If her swordmeister ever found out she was running shag while in armor, she would spend a full rotation doing PT in full gear as punishment. He was touchy when it came to the public image of the knighthood. She removed the keeper from her hair and let her brown hair spill across her shoulder plates.

You ever do something you regret? I did. I did it today actually. I discovered two of your spies and reported them. Why were you spying on us? And, for how long. I mean, she'd been the President's aide for his entire term. How long ago did you people arrive? She still had him tuned out for most of what he was saying. She just assumed he was trying to entice her into conversation again. They did not have any spies on the ground. She thought of the way he touched her and sighed, shaking away the thought. He was a distraction. Messing around with him had embarrassed her and almost gotten her brother killed. However, something he had just said struck a chord. They had caught two spies. Why did they think the spies were theirs?

She almost responded, but she changed her mind and tucked this information away for later. Her duty had ended for the day. She did not want to think about the colonists or the Harvest or assassins. She wanted to relax. She leaned back in a corner, not bothering to grasp the rings hanging from the ceiling. She had perfect balance and the jostling of the lift would not affect her much. She looked around the lift, taking in all the people. Some were happy and merry and talking in that animated way civilians do. An old woman in a shawl sat a few seats away from where she leaned. A box of office supplies was on her lap and a defeated expression on her face. Leia figured she had just lost her job.

There was a ping and a tone as the lift rumbled to life, followed by a sudden drop that made her feel like her stomach was in her mouth. Evidently, the first drop off was many decks below. The lift would be traveling at this speed for some time. She looked to the mess on her seat again and suddenly sympathized with the unknown rider responsible. She adjusted her sword so she could lean and stretch out her legs in a bid to get comfortable. The armor made it tough.

One of the first things the army had taught her during her stint was to remain alert even in sleep. The moment his hand touched her arm, she was awake and moving. She seized the offending hand, twisted the wrist, and laid hands upon the tunic of the man brazen enough to touch an Imperial Knight uninvited. The moment she saw his face, her anger drained, and she released him, mumbling an apology. It was just the liftman.

"My apologies, Madam Knight," he told her, massaging away the pain in the wrist she'd bent. "It is your stop." She rubbed at her eyes and yawned, nodding and mumbling another apology, which he was too professional to refuse.

She stepped from the lift into a bustling byway filled with hundreds of people going about their daily lives. The time on the saucer was determined by its rotation and the time was a little after mid-rotation, which was called evening by the colonists.

Her duty was over for the day. It was over for most of the people in the lane. Like them, she was on her way home. She felt the tingling probes of telepaths, searching the crowds for their friends and loved ones. They were all polite and courteous and made no attempt to probe her mind. She had no fear here. This was home.

She headed left off the lift, moving away from the central hub. She traveled the byway glancing at the shop windows and the lit placards jutting out above the doors that advertised the products within. Normally, she ignored these, but one of them caught her eye, and she changed her mind about her direction. It was an impulse, and she crossed the byway like she owned it. The citizens did not refute her claim. They flowed around her like she was a pillar supporting the roof.

She looked at the sign one last time before entering, tapping the Network Interface Device on the back of her hand. The NID woke to her touch. She entered her security code and stared at the glyphs displayed. She brought up a regional scanner and studied the moving glyphs, expanding the screen with a touch. The NID gave her a holographic interface showing the region around her in greater detail. The holographic interface hovered a few inches above the NID. She found her tracking center and touched several of the glyphs in the immediate vicinity, then dismissed the interface. With it gone and her targets picked, she quickly typed in the name of the bar and sent her friends an invitation to join her.

The NID chimed five times as her friends responded. She smiled and went inside.

Her fifth friend was in the area on business but could not get away. The other four had agreed to join her for drinks though. This cheered her some, and so she plunged into the depths of the bar. This was not one of the social establishments filled with youthful revelers half-dressed and dancing to loud music. This was for the enlisted; this was for Grey Guard commanders, Imperial soldiers, Air Corp pilots, and Imperial Knights.

She saw a few familiar faces upon entering—regulars here—and returned their waves and greetings, mumbling pleasantries with those who stopped her and politely refusing offers for her to join in with those already deep in their cups. She spied a table in the back that was unoccupied, but a dour-faced man with one eye, thick meaty hands, and arms that could tear a man's head off stopped her and motioned her to the bar. She did not refuse him since he was the bartender and owner. Instead, she smiled big at the sight him and hurried over to share words with him.

"You still on duty?" he asked in a dark unfriendly voice. His voice sounded like someone was using a cybernetic gauntlet to crush rocks. It was grating and rough and unpleasant.

Nope. I just finished my shift. He pointed to her sidearm and sword.

"Then lock 'em," he commanded. She sighed in exasperation but reached back to do as he commanded. It was the rules. No drinking on duty, and if armed, you peace lock your weapons. It prevented unnecessary blood shed should a night of carousing turn hostile. It was also the law. She reached over her shoulder to lock her sword and did the same thing for her holstered sidearm. She knew the bartender had a wand behind the bar that could unlock them when the night was over. She had a wand at home that could do the same. Every soldier did.

Sorry, Uncle. I forgot. The one-eyed man grinned broadly and shrugged, and like that the dour-faced expression was gone.

"It happens, and speak for crying out loud," he told her crossly. "Your brother's the freaking monk. Not you." He was gruff, but she did not hold it against him. He was always gruff. He had been like this since she was little.

"Be nice," she admonished, kissing his cheek.

He gave her a quick smirk, hiding it away quickly before the other patrons could see it, and poured her a flute of Colonial 9. It was a popular beverage brought on board when the ninth colony was harvested. It was the preferred drink of the enlisted because you never suffered lingering effects the following morning, and it could be tweaked with ultrasonics to alter the flavor. All the tables had ultrasonic coasters here.

She leaned across and kissed his bristly unshaved cheek.

"Be good," he told her sweetly. Another smiling patron bellied up to the bar beside her. "Whadda you want?" her uncle snapped hatefully.

"Uh . . . " The man quavered, suddenly unsure of himself. The man looked at Leia and back to her bartending uncle. "I was just wondering if she'd like a . . ."

"She already has a drink," her uncle declared, drilling holes in the man's courage with his gaze.

"Uncle, be nice," she chided gently. "He thinks I'm attractive and has just come trolling for a tryst. Few men would be so bold. Let me at least see what he's bringing to the table." Her uncle grunted and turned to pour the man a drink. Leia turned to the man. "Well, go on. Show me what your idea of romance is?" The man smiled and projected his amorous thoughts into her head. "Really?" she asked candidly. "That's what you think a woman wants? You walked into my mind like you were wearing muddy shoes in your grandma's cell then showed me a formula interlude with censored intercourse. You censored your fantasy to keep from offending me. Have you even killed a man?" she asked harshly. The man wilted before her and turned away embarrassed. Leia gave her uncle a playful wink and walked away, flute in hand.

"Where do you think you're going? I poured you a drink," her uncle growled at the wilting man.

"I don't want it," the man murmured weakly. The bartender shrugged and downed the drink himself.

"That'll be five cron," he announced menacingly. Leia smiled as the man nervously doled out the five credits for the drink he did not order. She was still smiling when she found that the table near the back was still available. She sat, putting her back to the wall and waited for her friends to show. She did not have long to wait.

The first of her friends to arrive was Ailig only moments after Leia sat down. Ailig Tuiin was a colonial harvested from the 36th colony of the Empire. He had been an elite soldier in his colony, and upon rejoining with the Empire, he easily managed to master the requirements of the Grey Guard. He became an Imperial soldier in his second year aboard the Kye O'Ren, and he was chosen after his second petition to become a squire. That was where Leia had met him.

Leia had been a legacy. Her stint in the Grey Guard and as a soldier had been strictly a formality. Her father and uncle had been knights as had their father. For her, becoming a knight was a matter of choice not merit. Ailig had not had an inside byway into the knighthood. He had to fight his way all the way up. He had to squire three years before finally ascending to full knighthood. That was one year longer than most squires had to do. He had been like a brother to her since. She greeted him with a kiss on the cheek, which he returned.

Her other three friends arrived as a group a short time later. Two of them were knights like Leia and Ailig. The other was a soldier who had made that his life goal.

Borbala Rowden never talked about how he became a knight. Leia had seen the ink branding on his arm and had looked it up. He had been a pilot with the Air Corp at some time in his life. His mannerisms and habits had been those of a soldier, and he showed nothing but contempt for the Grey Guard of which he attested never to have been a member. This made his past something of a mystery. Every knight was required to serve as a Grey Guard and a soldier before squiring, even the legacies. If he had managed to bypass the Grey Guard, then someone in the knighthood or above had some serious pull.

Milintart, like Borbala had been named by colonial. Milintart was a child of mixed heritage born to a colonial father and a mother of first blood citizenship. Her mother had never suffered the hardship of a Harvest. She had been born in the capital city where the heart of the Empire used to beat before the first fracture. Milintart suffered some teasing as a soldier, but after she showed her fellow soldiers the teeth she had knocked out and collected from the other men foolish enough to mock her, the teasing would quickly die. Only the people sitting at the table knew her father was a dentist and that was the source of the jar of teeth she carried.

The soldier, and final friend at the table, was Xi Pich, but the others called him "The Pig" due to how his name was enunciated. He was a former colonist. He was a most unremarkable kind of man except for the peculiar condition that afflicted him. The man knew no fear. It was not that he was brave by choice. His brain just didn't register fear. Of the five seated, he had been the only one invited to be a squire.

The meet up at the bar was business as usual for the five friends. They were disappointed to hear that Magnus would not be joining them—the friend who had to work—but were still thrilled to see that Leia had come back to the neighborhood. They knew her brother had requested her to head his security detail during the Harvest. This was where the conversation eventually went, and the moment they learned that she had saved her brother from First Colony insurgents, that's all they wanted to hear about.

They wanted her to describe every punch and sword slash. The quizzed her on her thought process of why she used one move and not another. They talked strategy, and like she, they were keenly interested in the last assassin. When she had told them that he had been stronger than her brother with his telepathic ability, they seemed doubtful. Her brother was Pre-Prior. There were only two classes of monks stronger. If the assassin had been able to best him, then this was something new. The insurgents were typically cowards, attacking from cover. Most did not even have telepathic ability.

Xi did not have much to offer in this conversation of tactics. He spent most of his days training on all the military equipment he had to learn or cleaning it. He was the one who turned the subject back to the colonists. There was a tradition among the group to see who could take lovers with the new colonists first. Leia and Milintart had an unfair advantage over the men, but there were a few colonies harvested where the men had won out. The subject of the new colonists left Leia suspiciously quite on the topic.

They tried to get her to contribute, but she refused repeatedly. The conversation had made her think of the colonist that kept pestering her. With the thought came curiosity and embarrassment. She let her mind go soaring back to him, trusting her friends to guard her while she was gone. She found him in his room. His mood was surly, and she realized he had probably had a bad day too. She thought about saying hello, but quickly changed her mind and withdrew her consciousness, coming back to herself. She did so only to discover four quiet friends leaning in close as if to listen in on her thoughts. So startled was she by their rapt attention, she could only blink and start with surprise. She was already leaning back in her chair, so her little flinch ended with her wind-milling her arms in an attempt not to fall over. She fell over anyway. They had caught her off guard.

Dammit! she cursed.

It was the third time this colonist had made her drop her guard. Her friends exploded with laughter. This drew the attention of the other patrons who joined in with it. They teased her outrageously and wanted to know who he was. She was nervous and thought they had actually sniffed her thoughts while she was away but then realized they were accurately guessing that it was a guy that had distracted her. She knew none of them would be so rude as to sniff her thoughts. It was considered the pinnacle of rudeness and on par with shoving your hand down someone's leggings. It still made her angry. It was an irrational anger to be sure.

Embarrassed and angry at with herself, she made an excuse to leave. They begged her not to, but it was more serious to her than she cared to admit. She was in such a rush to be away, she failed to stop by the bar to have her uncle lift her peace lock from her weapons.

Outside, the byways had thinned of people. She headed home, taking a corridor off the main byway. It was a narrow thoroughfare designated for foot traffic only. She turned off twice more, entering the section of residential cells she knew as her neighborhood.

All the doors she passed were familiar to her. Each had been colored or painted or tiled by the owner who dwelled within. Each door was an extension of the homeowner's taste, and it was with relief to see the one belonging to her mom. She was mocked by the other knights for still living at home, but she ignored it, considering it the cost of having friends. She loved her mom and had loved her dad during his life. Their cell was her place of peace. It was where she felt safe.

It was also where they attacked her.

She felt the bite of the drug in the palm of her hand. They had coated the handle with it. It stung her hand like acid, sizzling for a second, before taking effect. The moment her vision began to swim, she realized what had happened. The effects were not instantaneous, so when the men rushed her, she was still able to fight. She reached over her shoulder for her sword, staggering with the motion. The hilt did not extend like it was supposed to, and she cursed.

She went for her sidearm, but the holster would not release. With no other choice, she decided to fight them bare handed. They came with weapons, but when she did not draw her own, they changed tactics and barreled in to knock her down. The drug made her head swim and for most of the struggle, she was fighting with no idea where they were or what they were doing. She tried to send her mind out to her friends that she was in trouble, but she was having trouble focusing. She knew she could not find her brother or a watch commander in her condition. With no other recourse, she followed the only path she knew by heart and hoped he was still awake.

Chapter 10: Reaching Out

I need your help! Leia screamed into my mind.

To me, she entered my mind like an angel. There when I needed her, her words arrived, which made her words ironic. My heart was suddenly racing.

Name it, I declared excitedly, sending the thought back.

Find my brother. Tell him. I'm . . . taken. Kidnapped. My uncle . . . She fell silent. She was gone. There was a note of desperation in her voice and trace of fear. I sat there blinking in stupefied shock. How was I supposed to do all of that? I was essentially a high-class prisoner still.

Getting out of the room was not nearly as hard as I thought it would be. It seemed I had bought some goodwill with my spy revelation. If only I had kept that knowledge to myself, this might be easier. I needed help, and there were only two people I knew of who could help me with that.

My problem was that the two people I suspected could help me would not be very receptive to the idea. What I needed was a way in. The rest could be worked out. Besides, I had a suspicion based on something Mercy had said to me that might help grease the wheels. I just needed to convince my security detail to contact Aaron McDonald so he could convince Tessa Barnes to put me in the same room—or vicinity—as Mercy. I was pretty sure I knew how to make it happen.

Can you hear me? I'm coming to get you. Be strong. It was probably a little melodramatic and cliché, but that seemed to be working for me lately. After all, she called me for help. She did not call her brother or superiors. She called me. I was not going to let her down. Well, I probably would not let her down. I am a realist.

It had taken me six tries to convince the Marshals and the Homeland security agents to contact Aaron. It only took me twenty minutes to score a late-night meeting with him. Then, it took almost two hours to line up transportation and a mobile security detail to take me to Aaron's office. Turns out, he's a workaholic night owl type. We were pushing nine o'clock by the time we arrived at the Office of Homeland Security.

After getting my visitor pass, it was up the elevator and down the hall to the suite offices reserved for Aaron and his people. I found him nursing a glass of scotch, sleeves rolled up and tie loosened. His jacket hung on a coat rack near the door. He motioned for me to sit and told the security detail to wait outside.

"I'm listening," Aaron announced, taking a seat on the edge of his desk. "You said it was urgent and couldn't wait till morning."

"It is urgent. I just realized that I need to be in the same room with the spies," I blurted. I was not really good at subterfuge. "They can still relay their information to their handlers up there." I pointed toward the sky.

"How? They were searched . . . and well. They have no radios or communication devices." The old man shrugged and took a sip of his scotch.

"They don't need devices. They have this." I pointed at my head like I was holding a gun to it. "You remember the psychic episode when everyone started babbling the word 'Croatoan?'"

He frowned and nodded, suddenly troubled. "Distance isn't a problem to them."

"How can you be sure?" Aaron inquired, getting up to walk.

"You remember how I found them? I was looking for the sound of that mental wall they put up. I realized there was another sound overlaying that. It's the sound they make when they communicate with one another. I can block it." Of course, this was a complete fabrication, but that's the deal with psychics, no matter how stupid it sounds, it is next to impossible to prove. "You've got to trust me. If Tessa is the NSA's version of you, then you know what she's probably doing about now. She doesn't strike me as the gentle type. If they're able to communicate with their people up there, then what Tessa is doing may just create a diplomatic incident this world won't survive."

"Tessa knows what she's doing. If all the security agent directors were siblings, then Tessa is our much smarter spoiled know-it-all sister, and daddy buys her the expensive toys. The NSA is our brain trust, son. I know you mean well, but this is out of your hands. You did a good job finding them for us. Trust your government to do the right thing and take care of them." I was not sure if he was making a joke, so I kept quiet.

"Fine. But what happens next is on you. I warned you. All our blood is on your hands." I got up to leave, my stomach cramped with stress. He let me get as far as the door.

"Whose blood?" he asked.

"No blood," I replied, shaking my head as if I changed my mind. My eyes flicked toward the ceiling, but I pretended to try and hide it. "I was just talking out my ass, sir. I'm going to do what you said. I'm going to let you handle it. I do trust my government. I just don't trust Tessa. She's going to ask them hard."

"Actually, she is asking them hard. They refuse to talk. We don't have any other choice. They infiltrated the top tier of our government. We were prepared to negotiate with them, but this is not how negotiations work. You don't spike the wheel before the negotiations have even begun. This is espionage. This is their doing. If there is blood to be had, they started it."

"Unless it was not them." I let my eyes flicker toward the ceiling, trying to make it look like I knew more than I did. I was not sure where I learned it, but I knew that if you wanted someone to do what you wanted them to do, then you had to make them think it was their idea in the first place. Aaron watched me. I kept my eyes lowered, looking at his socks. I turned to go. I did not want to be too obvious about my manipulations. I was willing to walk away.

"Sorry I bothered you so late, sir. I guess I was just high from having found the spies. I'll find another way to help if there is still time." I paused a moment and adopted a distracted look, holding perfectly still, and put a faraway look in my eyes. I started to nod as if I was receiving a message and hurried out, my security leading the way. I made it as far as the elevator.

"Bring him back here," Aaron called, as we were all piling into the lift. I allowed myself a small triumphant smile.

"I know you are manipulating me, but I don't know what your angle is, so get your ass back in here and tell me the damn truth. No more lies." I smiled inside, though I was still quailing with fear. This could go all kinds of wrong.

I was marched back to his office, and security closed the door behind me. He gestured toward the seat again, but I shook my head.

"Spill it, son," he told me, setting his glass down and taking his seat.

"The truth, sir. They've contacted me and told me to have you release the prisoners or else. The images of what they're going to do to us is bad. There are not words, sir. If we care about our planet, about our survival, then we have to free them," I told him in earnest. He did not even blink. He sat there chewing the inside of his lip, patiently waiting. On what, I was not sure. No, I did, but I was really hoping I was wrong.

"You get one more chance to be honest. I am not your parent. I am not a schoolteacher or a principle or a cop or the gas station clerk you are trying to buy booze from. I am the Director of Homeland Security. Spotting liars is what I do best. In fact, it is a job prerequisite. I know something has you bent out of shape over this detention. I saw it in your eyes when Mike arrested her. You did not want to out Mercy as a spy, but you actually care about this country, this government, and this world. So, you outed her because you had a duty to do so. You genuinely want to help. I can see it. So, help me understand. Why is this so important to you?" I was caught and there was no way to manipulate the man. I had only one recourse, and it was to tell the truth. I hoped it worked.

"I was not lying about them being able to communicate with us from up there. I have been talking with the ambassador's sister since they left," I explained, understanding that this made me a spy technically.

"This entire time? Even when you were in the meeting with the President?" he asked. I saw his hand inch toward the phone.

"Yes. I know it makes me look like a spy too, but I am not. We don't talk about the government or the meetings or the things me and you talk about. I talk to her about fishing and hunting and how good cold spaghetti taste. We just talk about life, and we are trying to get to know each other. Well, I do all the talking. Sometimes she tells me to shut up."

"You have a crush on the alien chick?" he asked in disbelief.

"Did you see that ass?" I responded, giving him the look all men understand. "I like her. She is gruff and stuff, but she is not a monster."

"So, why are we here then?" he asked, leaning forward.

"You remember in Kansas, I told you and the other suits that I overheard them talking about the fact that something out there was pursuing them? The ambassador's sister has just been kidnapped. She called out to me to contact her brother." Aaron seemed skeptical but interested. I quickly relayed the message Leia had sent me word for word as it was given to me, complete with inflections. "I think she was drugged, and she needed my help to notify her brother. The problem is I can't."

"And you need the spies to communicate that message to her brother?" he guessed. I shrugged helplessly and nodded.

"I can't find him. With Leia, I think the only reason my thoughts found her was because she was thinking about me too. During the briefing with the President, I tried repeatedly to find my way into the conference room, but it was extremely hard. It was by luck that I managed to do it the three times I did. That's how we found the spies and using that as a segue into a separate topic, I need to tell you that I don't believe they are spies for the people upstairs." Aaron frowned.

"It was you who said they were spies," the Director pointed out.

"They're telepaths, like me, but with greater ability. The woman serving tea, we talked briefly when she was taken into custody. She asked why I had outed her, and I said because you're a spy. I expected her to refute this. The guilty always do, but her response was a feeling of confusion. Then, Mercy said something to me. She asked what happened to me." Aaron nodded, having been there to hear it. "In here," I said, pointing to my temple, "she said that they left me alone like I wanted." I don't know what she was talking about, but in both cases, I did not get the feeling that they were tied in with the guys upstairs, but I think they can relay the message to the ambassador for us."

"There is a lot of interpretation of facts in your theories and a lot of supposition. My problem is that if they are spies, then letting them communicate with the others would be a major breach of security. You're asking me to go out on a limb for you. I need more than this, son. A lot more."

"What if I can get them to talk?" I asked candidly. "I can tell if they are lying. If they put up a wall, we know they are being dishonest. Let me have a shot at it. That's all I'm asking. If we get the intelligence you want, then you and the rest of the alphabets can brief the president and find out if we can relay the message or not. On one hand, you risk revealing talking points for a boring ass meeting since she could have revealed everything about our government prior to that meeting. That meeting is the only thing that they have potentially failed to reveal to their handlers. On the other hand, you are helping the ambassador for an alien armada save his sister from kidnappers and most certainly death."

I continued, "Maybe it's a test. I don't know, but right now, you know what I know and there is a lot of gain in helping find her. All I need is an hour with them. This is an hour that could potentially grease the way for this technology you have been wanting to trade for. What would you do if it was the Russian ambassador's sister? You would help find her and leverage that act into some kind of concession. Be the used car salesman the American people have come to rely on. Get out there and sell that Pinto." I sat back, keyed up by my speech, and waited for him to react. He leaned back in his chair for several long moments, and I began to worry when I saw him reach for the phone. Either he believed me and that was the phone call that was going to save my future girlfriend, or it was him calling Tessa Barnes to report that he had caught another spy. He hit a button on the phone.

"Cassidy, get me Tessa Barnes on the line." I held my breath and prayed this man could sell a Pinto.

Honestly, I had expected that a lot of things might happen when he pressed that intercom button and mumbled that dreaded greeting.

"Hello, Tessa," Aaron called. His voice was light and bubbly. His eyes were not. They were fixed squarely on me.

"What is it, Aaron? I'm busy just now." There was the sound of voices conversing in the background. A printer squawked as it printed out some unknown document. Phones rang. She sounded like she was in a call center in India.

"I need a favor," he said, and like that, my wish was granted.

I was bustled from the building, sandwiched between two U.S. Marshals, hooded, and transported to an old warehouse. I could smell the musty smell of soured earth and wet rusted iron. It had a smell. I could smell the aromatic bouquet of the wild grasses and the stalky weeds long before they took my hood off.

The Marshals drove away, leaving me at the mercy of Tessa's goons. There were six of them. One wiped a wand over me, presumably to check for weapons or bugs. Then a new bag was yanked down over my head and cinched. This bag was nicer. Aaron was right. The NSA really does get the nicer toys. I think it was coated with lanolin or something.

"Hey?" I called, after being sandwiched in the back of another SUV for the trip to see Tessa.

"How much further?" I asked, pushing my mind out toward the man who I had directed my question toward. I had learned something about reading another person's mind. It was easier if you had some idea as to the gist of what they were thinking. I had a long time to consider how I was able to overhear the bearded one and Mercy's assistant's thoughts. I could overhear their thoughts because I knew approximately what they were thinking already. So, I pushed my mind toward the NSA agent holding me to see what he was thinking.

The thought was more a feeling that a hard number. The man did not think that it was much further, and an image of a transmission shop came to me. The mental picture had a sign that read "Jagger and Son's Affordable Transmission Repair." And like that, I knew where we were going. I could even see the address on the building and the street sign beside it.

"Not much farther," the man replied.

"So, is Tessa waiting for me there or am I to receive . . . special treatment?" I pushed my mind out toward the men around me.

There was a scattering of images from the men around me. I saw the suburban we were in drive into an open bay of the transmission shop. I saw their plan to lead me into the front office, then behind the counter, then down a hall, into another office. There was a false wall covered in rims. Steps would take us down. One of them was thinking about the septic smell of the wet concrete in the basement area. There were many rooms. The one thought they all had was of Tessa standing with other suits outside a series of rooms with glass windows. Inside of these rooms were prisoners.

More than one of them thought of me sitting at an interview table with my hands cuffed to it. Someone important would be sitting opposite me. Only one of them thought I would be tortured. His thoughts were of me being water-boarded and burned with cigarettes. He saw acid being dripped on my arm. He saw hammers being used on my feet. His mind went to silver trays covered with shiny tools like you would see on a surgeon's cart or a dentist's office. This man enjoyed his job. It was not so much that he saw these as a possibility. This man was just hoping to use these things on me. I marked him in my mind. He was dangerous.

"Shut up," the man who had spoken commanded.

When the suburban slowed, then stopped, I realized we had arrived. I could hear the bay door opening then heard it close again after we pulled through. Even through the bag, I could smell the old oil and transmission fluid. They pushed me in the direction they wanted me to walk. I stumbled over cords and lifts, but two of the NSA agents held me by the elbow to keep me from falling. A door opened, and the sound of the echoes changed. We were in a smaller room with a lower ceiling. I bumped into the walls several times, scratched my arm on something jutting from one of them, and cracked a knee on the end of a counter.

"Jesus! You can take the bag off." Their reply was me being pulled around the end of the counter. I walked hard into the edge of a low wall.

"Shut up," one of the other men commanded.

"Jagger and Son's Affordable Transmission Repair at 3028 W. Market Street," I announced in exasperation. "That's where we're at, right? Take off the bag so I can walk, you sadistic fucks." I was wheeled around and pushed against the wall. There was some whispering, and the bag was yanked off. I looked around. The lights were off, but it was most definitely a transmission shop.

"How did you know that?" the man holding me demanded.

"I just do. So, would you prefer to drag me into the office at the end of the hall and through the hidden door into the basement, or would it be easier to just let me lead the way?" I asked, snidely.

"How do you know of this place?" the man demanded again, slamming me hard into the wall again.

"I know the same way that I know you and them," I gestured too the two men on my right, "think of him as a monster. That man loves to hurt people." We all looked to the man I had marked. He was smirking.

The three men looked to the fourth member of their group, and I could see the sneer on their faces. They did not like him. I did not need to read their thoughts to know this. The man I had singled out was not fazed by my revelation either. He knew what he was, and he knew the others did not care for him.

He studied me with cold eyes. They were dark and intense like a tiger behind glass watching the young tender children of tourists slap the glass with impunity. They were the eyes of a hunter, a predator, a killer. His greatest desire was that someday the glass would break.

He smirked and reached for me. I felt my skin crawl as he touched me, but all he did was spin me around and push me toward the last office. I took his meaning and led the way. I even twisted the rim hanging on the wall that opened the hidden door. The stairs were dark, but the light from downstairs provided me the light I needed to navigate them.

I sent my mind down into the basement. I could feel others down there, but their minds were closed to me. I found Tessa. She was down there, and for some reason, that made me breathe easier. It meant there was a hand on the leash of the animal behind me. I moved further into the basement, and I discovered the wall of white noise there. It was strong and solid, and I instinctively knew it to be Mercy. I looked around for the other wall of white noise and was surprised to find it blinking on and off like a television with a loose connection. I pushed at the mind hoping to put her mind at ease, but the moment the wall blinked off and I touched her thoughts, I recoiled. She was screaming.

I quickly descended the stairs, startling the men leading me, and I hurried down the hall with them trotting to keep up. My hands were not tied, so it was easy to out distance them. I pushed past a plastic curtain and into an area lit bright with fluorescent lighting. Tessa looked up in surprise at my sudden entry. I ignored her and pushed past the other suits in the room and made my way to the cells beyond.

Mercy was seated in a room in a grey jump suit under the glare of blinding lights. Her hair was wet as was the top half of her jumpsuit, and her head lolled from side to side with apparent exhaustion. I tried to call to her, but it was no use. The room was soundproof. I could hear the faintest of noises from the other side of the glass and realized they were blasting her with some kind of loud noise.

I moved on to the other woman I had outed. She was in worse shape. She sat huddling naked in the corner of her room, while a man sprayed her face and body with a water hose. I sent my thoughts into the room with Mercy and tried chipping at her wall of noise, but she refused to drop it.

"What are you doing to them?" I demanded, though I knew the answer.

"Getting answers," Tessa replied when the men finally dragged me back to stand before her.

"This is inhumane," I accused.

"Possibly. But, then again, they are alien," She responded.

"This will go bad for you. This will go very bad for you," I threatened.

"Hardly. Aaron said you could make them talk. How?" she demanded.

"This ability," I said, gesturing to my head. "It gets easier the more you use it," I told her. "I can get them to talk."

"What? Like compelling them?" she asked.

"No. I can convince them to cooperate. I think Mercy has confused me with someone she knows, and I think I can use that to get her to talk." Tessa's eyes flashed with interest. I did not want to get into more detail, so I left it at that. Aaron had told me not to reveal too much to her. In fact, he had advised against this. He told me that he could get Tessa to put me in the same room with the spies, but once I was there, I would be beyond the safety of his agency. If Tessa suspected something was up, then there was no telling what she would do. He used the word "volatile" to describe her.

"We'll see," she replied, gesturing to the men holding me. They let me go, and she led the way toward the room where Mercy was being kept. A technician outside her cell dialed down a knob and flipped a couple of switches. The lights dimmed to a more comfortable wattage, and the faint droning sound coming from within died away.

Tessa unlocked the door and opened it for me. One of her stooges carried a chair into the room for me to sit in. They placed it opposite Mercy. I ignored it and went to her instead, cradling her face in my hands. "Can I get some water in here for her?" I asked, horrified at what I had done to her. This was on me.

You . . . came back for us, she whispered weakly into my mind.

You know me? I asked, accepting the glass of water the agent brought me. I held it to her lips, and she drank greedily from it.

Of course. You spilled your funnel cake . . . on the alien's feet, she replied. Her smile was weak.

No. You know me from somewhere else. You said you left me alone like I wanted. What did you mean? She looked at me now with interest, struggling to overcome the exhaustion.

You don't remember, do you? What happened to you? Why you left? You were gone for so long. I thought that was why he picked you from the crowd. I thought the Grand Reaper knew, but he didn't. You hid your mind from him. He didn't recognize you. He let you go. He let us all go. He doesn't know who you are.

Her eyes closed, and her head nodded forward. This made her smile, but then the exhaustion took her, and she passed out. I got up, confused by her last statement, and exited the room. What did she mean?

Who was I?

Chapter 11:
Interrogation

"Well?" Tessa asked.

"She'll talk. She just needs to rest for a little while first. Her mind is incoherent, and her thoughts are swimming. Let her sleep for a little while. When she's lucid, she'll talk."

I moved to the other spy's cell. The man in there had turned the hose off. "Can we put some clothes on her?" I asked, disgusted with what they had done to her.

"See to it," she told her agents. The man with the tiger eyes was standing at the window leering. I really wanted to put my fist through his face.

A short time later, she was brought out, dressed in a grey jump suit like the one Mercy was wearing. The woman's eyes were wild. I saw The Bearded One from the White House basement seated among the technicians at the end of the corridor. He waved. The other two agents that had accompanied him were there as well. The one who had slapped my face was sitting on the edge of The Bearded One's desk. He smiled cockily and gave me a mocking wave. I was among friends, evidently.

The woman was terrified.

"Did they hurt you?" She sent a sudden flood of images into my head. She had been water-boarded, bombarded with loud noise, and cooked under blinding lights. She pushed an image of Tiger Eyes in my mind. She showed him entering the chamber. He was the one who had stripped her. He was the one who raped her while the suits and technicians watched. Afterwards, he had ordered her sprayed with the hose.

I felt a searing surge of anger toward the man, but the anger vanished with the sound of a scream. I turned to find Tiger Eyes on the floor holding his head. I turned back to stare at the prisoner in shock. She smiled, then they pistol whipped her into unconsciousness.

"What the hell?" I demanded.

"She was attacking my man," Tessa explained, motioning for the men to return the prisoner to her cell. I did not respond. I just watched them drag the poor woman away, and I felt guilty. She was not the one the one who had attacked him. I was. I looked down on the horrid man with the tiger eyes. He was unconscious just then, but I knew he would not be the same. I did not know how I did it or what I did, but I knew the man had properly been punished.

"You let that man rape her?" I accused wrathfully.

"I let that man interrogate her. Rape is one of the fastest ways to humiliate a prisoner and rob them of their power. This makes the other interrogation methods faster and more effective," she explained. "It's like marinating a steak before grilling it or soaking beans over night before boiling them. It cuts down on the cooking time." She turned to look at the slumbering Mercy and the room through which the nameless spy had been taken, then turned her attention on me. "It looks like we have a little one on one time while we wait. I've some questions for you."

"You're not going to have him rape me first, are you?" I asked, acidly.

"Depends how cooperative you are," she replied, leading me toward a conference room at the end of the corridor. The frightening thing was that I knew she was serious. It was a white room like the others with a glass wall, but inside this room was a long grey metal table with unbuckled wrist restraints built into it. It was the table I had seen in the minds of the men who had brought me here.

"You're a peculiar individual. We still don't know who you are, Daniel." Walking into the interview room after hearing this filled me with dread. She motioned for me to sit, and she took the seat opposite me.

"Daniel is a good name. Good as any," I replied, on guard.

"But it isn't your name, Daniel. Not your real name. I'm interested in who you really are. I've talked with my agents." She looked out the glass window to the three men I had met at the White House. "My analyst had some interesting information for me. He noticed that every fake name you gave them, had a common component. He is really very good. He says a lie tells us something about who we are. You told us you were the headmaster of a fictitious school of wizardry. Then you told us you invented a children's toy and gave some back story as to its inspiration. This you followed up by telling us you were Ayn Rand. And then, you settled on the name Daniel Sojourner." She looked at me hard. "Why won't you give us your name?" she asked.

"The truth?" I replied. "I don't know it. I don't remember who I am or where I live or if I have a family. All I know is that to live here after 9/11 you must have a name and a verifiable history, and I don't. I know I've lived here my entire life. I know I have friends, but I can't remember them. I know I'm lonely. I'm tired. But most importantly, I think I'm hiding from whoever caused me to forget." I lifted my bangs to show her the nasty scar hidden beneath my hairline. "Anytime I think of the past, I think of wings. I don't know who I am. That's the truth," I declared, putting my cards on the table. Tessa leaned in to look at the scar.

"That's one version of the truth, you mean, and that's a bullet wound," she replied with a fair degree of confidence.

"How could you know that?" I replied. She turned to The Bearded One and crooked a finger. The man entered with a file. He handed it to her, and he withdrew a short distance. She set the file down before me. I opened it. It was a picture of me in a WWII army uniform. I looked the same.

"I told you, my analyst is good. You see, when we lie, we tell things about ourselves. Normally, this would have passed us by. We would have missed this if not for the alien horde floating over our heads, Daniel. You claimed to be the man who invented the Etch-A-Sketch, and my analyst thought that a peculiar thing to claim. But you mentioned new beginnings and starting over as your motivation. So, he started looking for people who vanished and began again."

"Then, you mentioned Ayn Rand and the timelessness that followed that author's literary works. Atlas Shrugged was one of my favorite books growing up. Her views. Wow." She sat there in silence, contemplating me as I read the file. "The analyst looked in a different time for you and found you." She tapped the file with her index finger. "Your name is Thomas Pilgrim. You fought on D-Day at Normandy. That's when you were shot. They dragged you off the sand afterwards, but you were in a coma and stayed that way for five years. That's where all record of you ends. In the report we found, the Corpsman tending your ward wrote that when he made his rounds, your bed was empty, and you were gone. You'd just up and vanished; never to be seen again until now."

I studied the file, shaking my head as if to refute it. "That's impossible," I told her. The picture of me in uniform could not have been me. It was so long ago. "This isn't me," I snapped, shoving the file at her in a huff.

"Oh, that is you," she said, "it most certainly is you." She leaned across and touched the mole on my cheek then pointed to the photograph. I pulled the file back and looked at the age they had down for me and quickly calculated it up.

"You're eighty-eight years old," she supplied, "according to that file, but in this one . . ." I looked at her in confusion.

"That's impossible." The picture she was showing me looked exactly like me. "That would mean I haven't aged a day."

"Peculiar, isn't it?" she replied. She held out her hand to The Bearded One and he put another file in her hand. "In this file, you're much older." The Bearded One was looking at me as if he were seeing a woman naked for the first time. "Imagine how strange I felt when my analyst showed me this," she said, passing over the next file. It was me in uniform again. Only the uniform looked older. It was the uniform worn by WW1 soldiers. "Or this." She accepted another file and laid it down before me.

"We collected DNA from your hotel room and ran it. A historical society donated a large allotment of Civil War paraphernalia—muskets, bugles, journals, cannons, and such—to the Smithsonian. The Smithsonian found viable DNA in the grooves of a bayonet belonging to a man called Silas Gardner and put it in their index. Evidently, you were stabbed once, Silas—or Thomas or Daniel or whatever your name is." She shrugged.

My hand went to the scar on my ribs beneath my shirt out of reflex. I had always wondered where it had come from.

"You're very old. You're psychic like them. Just exactly, who are you really?" she asked. I shook my head helplessly, studying the files. I did not know and told her as much. "I assumed you'd be willing to take a polygraph to confirm your ignorance." I nodded. She rose from her seat as her technicians entered with the polygraph machine. They began hooking me up. "You know, when Aaron called me and said that you could make them talk, I was skeptical, but thrilled that he was surrendering you to me. It was like a gift for God," she declared, joyfully. "I had planned to stick you in a cell of your own and torture the truth from you, but I think this is better. We have traces of you in ever war America has ever fought, except for the Revolutionary War. You were in Korea, Vietnam, both World Wars, Afghanistan, Iraq, and so forth. That, and only that, is why you're not undergoing rendition right now."

"You've fought for this country since it became a country is my guess. I've found nothing to the contrary. Plus, I believe you. The scar on your head and the medical records of you in a coma give credence to your claim that you don't remember. You might very well have some form of retrograde amnesia. Torture just wouldn't work. What I do know, is that you've become my new favorite toy, Daniel, and I plan on playing with you a lot." She got up and went to the door. I was not sure if she meant to throw her thought at me, or if it was an involuntary act, but I heard it clearly.

Get used to this place, Daniel. You won't be leaving it any time soon.

Suddenly, I felt I was the one in danger.

Danger compelled me to act. I sent my mind toward the ships in the sky, searching for Leia. I could sense her. I knew about where she was. It was a dark place filled with musty smells. There was the smell of earth and the stench of sewage. She could smell mold. I could also tell that she was not alone. I squatted in her mind for a little while, trying to offer her comfort. I imagined myself as an angel in her mind radiating warmth.

I could feel the minds of other men and several women nearby. They were tense and silent. I tried to creep from Leia's mind and into the mind of one of the men guarding her. There was a familiarity to this mind. The familiarity was not to this mind but rather to one like it. I had touched a mind like this before. I tried to creep into the man's mind, to go deeper. Suddenly the man's mind was awake. Actually, that was not technically true. The man was still unaware of me. The other mind was a visitor there as well. I saw yellow eyes before me and darkness rushing toward me like smoke from a fire, and I realized I could not flee. I froze before the power of that mind and would have been devoured, but then Mercy was there pulling me away.

Don't, she warned. She wrestled me away before the darkness could reach me. *Don't ever enter their minds. You know this,* she snapped like a mother to a child. She was panicked by what I had almost done. *What has happened to you?* I remembered the file Tessa had shown me.

I think I was shot a long time ago. It put me in a coma and robbed me of my memory. I don't know who I am any more. This felt like the truth. There was a need in me to know the truth, and I think she picked up on it. *Who am I?*

You're the Magpie. You were our leader. You were the one who convinced us all to leave, she revealed, though that meant nothing to me.

Leave where? She showed me a picture of the ships. *Wait, I'm one of them?* I asked in surprise.

We all are. Seventeen hundred years ago, we began to reap the colonies of the Empire. You were a Grand Reaper once, but before that, you were the protégé of the First Reaper, and you took his place when the first reaping went wrong. And you were the one who discovered sickness in the First Colony and spoke out against it. The Daimyo didn't listen, and the sickness spread to the ships. When the Daimyo was converted by the colonists of the first colony, as the new Grand Reaper, you ordered the infected ships disabled and abandoned. You ordered all on board to be set adrift, but they couldn't be deterred. They fixed their ships and pursued. When—

She went suddenly silent. I waited but she did not resume the story. The moments grew long and pained. My nervousness grew. I didn't know what a Reaper was. I recalled my conversations with Luke and deduced that he was a Reaper since he was here to harvest the colony. If she was right, I was an earlier version of him.

Mercy? Mercy? I called to her. She did not respond, and I realized she had passed out again. I waited. I looked out the window and saw that two of the agents were guiding Tiger Eyes from the area. His eyes were open, but they stared into nothingness. I did not feel guilty for what I had done, just confused as to how I had done it. The man had deserved this and worse. He would be lucky if he could use crayons after he recovered. This made me happy.

I sat alone in the room for almost three hours waiting for news of Mercy to wake. At this point, one of the NSA agents brought me a couple of donuts to eat and a bottle of water. I spent my time after, trying to make the bottle move. I made the bottle wiggle several times, but it refused to slide.

I closed my eyes after that grew tiring and thought about the bottle. I do not know how it happened, but I realized why I couldn't make it move. I was thinking of the bottle as being separate from me. I am made of atoms. The bottle is made of atoms. We are connected. I kept trying to push on the atoms in the bottle, when that was not how physics works. I needed to push on all the atoms between me and the bottle, like dropping a quarter into one of those dozer machines so that the sliding sled could push off the quarters in the front. It made more sense than what I was doing.

    I opened my eyes and stared at the bottle, then pushed with all my might. The response was spectacular. The bottle flew across the room like I had shot it from a cannon, shattered the window, and knocked out an NSA agent walking past. I stared at the broken glass in surprise and the surprised faces of the people beyond. Even though they were going tactical, I could not help but be proud of what I had just done.

    "That was awesome."

Chapter 12: Escape

There are some moments in which we find ourselves where we are forced to act. That moment when you are in a restroom and discover that the man beside you had lousy aim at the urinal. No matter how badly you have to piss, you just have to step aside and let the man piss. I found myself in a situation like that. I had just shattered a plate glass security window with an empty plastic bottle and the power of my mind. I could either stand there and let these men piss on my shoes, or I could act to stop it.

Guns were pulled. Safeties were thrown. I heard the rattling clicks of machine gun clips being jacked in and shells being chambered. I was either all in now, or I let them come in here and Hannibal Lector me with straightjackets and loud noise aimed to keep me from concentrating.

They came in a two-by-two cover formation. I focused on the atoms between me and the wall and pushed as hard I could. The wall flew apart like I had detonated an IED behind it. The men in the front took the brunt of it, going down hard. The ones behind them went down dazed. The ones behind them covered to keep from being blinded with dust and splinters. The wall fell short of the third men in the group. I got up and marched forward, hugging the walls to keep from being shot.

"I didn't mean to do that," I shouted down the hall.

"Do you think that really matters now?" Tessa called back from wherever she was hiding. "It's not your fault, Daniel. This is on me. I thought you loved this country." I paused at the window of the nameless spy.

"I love this country just fine, Tessa, but I can love it without loving everyone in it," I said, drawing in my will.

The next two guards in line opened up with their handguns. I pushed on the air in the hall between us. Their bullets splattered into walls around me, but the force of the blast I had just sent their way sent them flipping over backwards.

It gave me time to kick open the door to the room holding the nameless spy. I scooped up a chunk of wood from the hall and threw it like a baseball at the first of the NSA agents to climb back to his feet. I pushed on the knot of wood with my mind, sending it flying like a bullet toward the man's chest." It hit his vest like a bean bag round from a riot gun and hurtled him backward into the legs of the men coming around the corner.

When his partner rose, I had nothing to use as a weapon, so I pushed on him, and used him like a missile. The man cleared a path for me. Agents fell as did the suits ducking for cover. I punched one of the first agents I dropped with the wall and kicked his partner in the face.

The one I punched was out for the count, but the one I kicked rolled over and bawled, holding his broken face in his hands. I felt bad about that. I kicked in the second door where Mercy was being kept and hurried to release her. I had to pat her cheeks to get her to wake. She did, but she did so slowly.

What's . . . What's going on? she asked groggily.

I'm white knighting, apparently. I'm rescuing you, I replied, though I was not sure if that was a fact yet. One of the agents made it to the door and jammed the end of his gun around the corner. I could sense his intentions before he did it and pushed on the section of wall where he hid. The bullets sprayed the wall around us as I flung him across the corridor. I was not fast enough. He managed to hit me with his spray. They felt like dull thuds, kind of an impact without pain. I looked down at my side and forearm and watched the dark thick blood gurgle out on the surface of the wound like Jed Clampett's bubblin' crude. The pain hit a moment later.

The lead was scorching hot, and I felt them inside me burning and boiling the blood around them. I fell over sideways, but I caught myself and came back to Mercy's restraints. They were Velcro and easy to remove. I could not sense the agents coming for me anymore. I could not sense anything through the pain.

"I've called an RRT, Daniel. That's a Rapid Response Team," Tessa revealed. "They'll be here in fifteen minutes. Give it up. You can't win through this." I fell over sideways, holding the wound in my side.

Sorry, I told Mercy. I think she could sense my remorse. *I-I tried to make it right. I thought I was doing the right thing. I'm so sorry.* She smiled sadly and came to her feet. She touched the scar near my hairline then looked me in the eyes.

I thought you betrayed us, she confessed. *I thought you forsook us. We're good now. I didn't know about this,* she said, indicating my scar. She rose to her feet, weakly. The first men to round the corner did so with their guns ready and their fingers on the strained triggers. I felt Mercy's push. It was not a hammer blow like I had been using. It was a feathered pillow and a lullaby, and one word to focus it. "Sleep," she told them, and the men collapsed. I felt her mind expand like the wings of phoenix and beneath those wings was the compulsion to relax and rest. "Sleep," she said again. I could not see the men and women affected, but I knew they were out there. I could feel them collapse and give up.

Mercy disappeared into the room where the nameless prisoner was kept. She returned a moment later with the same woman stumbling beside her. Mercy let the woman lean upon her. "We need to get you out of here," she said, looking at my wound with dread.

"It's just a scratch," I lied. I felt the force of her mind push at the wound. It was a narrow, focused push. I screamed in pain as I felt the bullet begin to move. The moment she was confident she had it, she pushed at it hard, and the bullet blasted through the rest of the flesh and exploded out of my lower back. I nearly passed out from the pain. The bullet ricocheted of the tile floor behind me and disappeared further in the room. She motioned for the nameless spy to help her. They used my shirt as compress for my wound and my belt to tie the compress in place.

"We need to go," she said, lifting me with the help of her fellow spy. We made it as far as the door before my pants fell to my knees. The two women looked down in surprise, Mercy smirked. I had picked a hell of a day to go commando. With Nameless's help, I managed to get them pulled up again and this time I held them up as they helped me out. We found Tessa in a panic room of sorts. She was knocking on the glass to get our attention.

"It's bulletproof," she shouted, sporting a smug little smirk.

I thought about testing that claim, but I knew I did not have the strength to focus. I felt regretful as I studied Tessa's gloating smile. She was a monster. I need not have worried though. Nameless felt the same way as me evidently. The bulletproof glass, as it turned out, was not much of a hurdle to a telepath.

Nameless stopped and faced the Director who had trapped herself behind her bulletproof glass. A rage burned inside her. There was no word to focus the blast and no warning. Nothing exploded. One moment the Director was smirking because she thought she had outsmarted us, the next moment her head was slamming into the wall behind her. She kind of stared at us in shock and slid to the floor like some cartoon villain who had lost a fight. I could feel her mind. She was still alive, just unconscious. That was a relief actually. I was not sure what the punishment was for killing the Director of the NSA, but I was sure it was not good.

N-Nicely done, I complimented. She gave me a fleeting smile laced with sadness. They had done too much to her for her to smile.

"I need your help, Mercy. I need it." I was having a hard time staying lucid.

"It'll have to wait. Their team will be here any moment." I nodded my understanding and tried to move under my power as much as I could. My hip and leg were slick with blood.

"I need you to contact the alien ambassador. His name's Luke," I said, shaking my head to clear the fog. She looked at me like I had lost my mind. "His sister has been taken hostage," I explained.

"Why should that matter to you?" she asked, confused.

"I-I . . . She has a nice ass," I confessed. Nameless actually laughed at this; it was a short burst of mirth that did not last. "Do it for Aaron. He's the one who sent me to help you."

"I don't even know their ambassador. I met him, but I don't know his real name," she confessed. The stairs were difficult to climb as a trio, but we managed to make the top. After that, it was a matter of stealing our captor's suburban. I pushed the memory of Luke's DNA strand into Mercy's head. She looked at me in surprise, then backed out of the garage bay and through the bay door. The switch for it was not easy to find, so we resorted to more direct methods of getting out. I pushed the list of demands Aaron had into her mind.

Nameless was driving. "Where to?" she asked.

I pushed the address and destination into her head. We were going back to the offices of Homeland Security. That had been the plan Aaron and I had cooked up if things went sideways. Things had most certainly gone sideways. Nameless nodded and sped away. Mercy turned to me. They had laid me on my back in the back seat. "Are you sure you want to do this?" she asked. "If the Cojokarueen discover it's you, they will turn this world inside out to find you."

"Tell Luke. Tell him about his sister. Tell him I can find her. He just needs to meet Aaron's request and come get me." I gasped in pain. My arm felt numb. I was pretty sure the bullet had nicked my bone.

"You don't remember what you did to them. They despise us. We're traitors in their eyes." She was clearly not on board with this, but I could see she would do it.

"Do you want to go home?" I asked. She nodded. "They're being pursued, Mercy. There are things coming for them. If they're coming for them, then they're coming for us. We need to know what's happening. We need to tell Luke the truth. Call to him." I felt myself fade. She hesitated.

"They'll kill you." That surprisingly didn't bother me just now, seeing as how I was teetering on the edge anyway.

Mercy focused on the image of DNA and let her mind home in on the individual it belonged to. As she got closer, she got braver.

They have your sister, Mercy declared, barging into Luke's mind.

Who is this? Luke demanded, suddenly on guard. He had been in the process of searching the cell he and his sister shared for her. He needed her help to make the harvest work. She was not there. He was on his way to search an officer's bar nearby when Mercy contacted him.

My name is unimportant. We've met though. I was one of the ambassadors for Earth. You knew me as Mercy, she revealed. Luke stood up straight, suddenly very interested in what this woman had to say. Earthlings for the most part were not psychic. *The translator you picked from the crowd. The one who dumped his dessert on your feet. Your sister has contacted him. She's been taken prisoner.*

By whom? Luke demanded, suddenly scared for his sister.

One moment, I'll ask. Mercy's mind disappeared for a moment, then came back a moment later. Luke knew where he had to go. He headed there at a run. *The translator says she mentioned her uncle. He says that your sister also commanded him not to lose her. He can track her. I know this for a fact.*

How could you possibly know that? Luke asked.

The idiot is in love with her. He was in her mind a little while ago. There were others in the room with her. They're first colonists. I got there just in time to pull him out the kidnapper's mind. Luke came to a stop.

How do you know about the first colonists? Luke demanded, suddenly angry. He was pretty sure he knew the answer. Mercy replied by pushing a list of demands into the Grand Reapers head.

If you want to know that, then you have to agree to meet these demands. This is what the Earthlings want in return for that information, she explained, and he could tell she disapproved.

I can't get the Daimyo to agree to this. We don't arm colonists. Not like this. Not with this kind of weaponry.

Then tell him we have Magpie, she fired back. Luke's mind went silent. Magpie was the most wanted man in the Empire. He was solely responsible for the Empire's current fracture. He was the one who convinced the Drifters to leave. The Daimyo would pay almost anything to get his hands on the man.

Tell them they'll have their weapons, but we want one thing more. We want the man who calls himself Albus Dumbledore, he said, using the name Daniel had given the field in Kansas. *We want the translator or there is no deal. If he can lead me to my sister, then I want him as part of the deal. And let your bosses know we'll tear your planet apart to lay hands on Magpie.* The heat of his vehemence was blistering, and Mercy pulled away in the face of it.

I don't think that'll be a problem, she replied looking into the back seat. *Consider the terms agreeable.* She pushed coordinates of the meet into the Reaper's head. *Also, bring medical assistance. Magpie is injured.* Mercy vanished from Luke's mind and came back to herself. She immediately checked on Daniel. He was weak and barely conscious.

"I set the meet." She pushed the coordinates into his head. "They agreed to the terms and conditions. They'll be here soon."

The office of Homeland Security suddenly came into sight and with that sight came their pursuers. The Rapid Response Team had caught up at last. Nameless put her foot down and Mercy sent her mind flying toward the offices of Aaron McDonald. Even as the NSA suburbans rammed them from behind.

The NSA agents were relentless. Bullets shattered the windows and periodically bounced against the metal frame of the stolen vehicle. The agents tried repeatedly to execute a PIT maneuver. Nameless was not a total novice though. She might have served tea to the president for the past seven years, but before that, she had a history. She swerved left and put the front of one of their pursuers into the back of a taxi that was idling on the shoulder. They did not hit hard, but it was hard enough to deploy their airbags.

There was one benefit to being an experienced telepath and a driver. You always know what the other driver is thinking. Every time the pursuing agents tried to slam into her, Nameless left them kissing air. This went on for several moments before they broke away. She lost them on the side streets. One black SUV pursued. When she found them again, they were sitting crossways in the road, weapons out, and ready to fire. The street was too narrow for her to turn around. There were no alleys to escape through. And the SUV behind her was tight on their tail.

Keep driving, Mercy commanded. Focusing on the vehicle and agents ahead. *Keep driving. Don't even think about stopping.* Nameless dipped her head to let Mercy know she understood the order. Nameless jammed her foot to the floor and the engine lurched in surprise at the sudden flood of fuel. Mercy threw her mind forward, imagining the front of the vehicle in which she rode as a snowplow.

She threw her mind forward shoving the atoms between her and the suburban ahead. She hit it near the top of the cab where the center of gravity was highest, crushing like a beer can. There was a wet sounding spray of automatic rifle fire tearing into the cab. As they rocketed forward, the force of her will combined with the speed of our suburban, sent the NSA suburban barrel rolling down the street. NSA agents dove for the sidewalk to get out of her way. Nameless plowed through the roadblock in the wake of the wreckage dodging on to the sidewalk to get around the toppled SUV. The SUV behind her followed.

From there, we had a straight shot to Homeland. We came in fast, screeching to a halt in front of the doors. Nameless scurried from the vehicle, running around to pull me from the back seat. It was clear she struggled with me, too weak to be much help. I was not sure why Mercy was not helping her.

Help me get him out, she begged, tugging on me. Mercy did not respond, so Nameless went to check on her and gasped in horror. Mercy had her hands pressed to her throat. Blood was bubbling out between her fingers. There were other bullet wounds, but this was the worst of them. Mercy was dying. Nameless put her hands over those of Mercy, fighting to stop the bleeding, but it was futile. She was suffocating on her own blood.

Protect him. No matter what, protect him, she begged of Nameless and Nameless nodded, opening Mercy's door to render her aid. It was a wasted effort though. *Don't cry,* Mercy whispered into her mind. *Please don't cry.* Nameless felt her bottom lip quiver and her eyes water. Mercy gasped one last time, air gurgling from her wound, and choked out on her own blood. She died looking very sad. Nameless fought the tears, but like the blood flowing between Mercy's fingers, the tears seeped through closed eyes. This was not just a woman she had known casually.

There was surge of will inside her that sent a small shockwave out into the world around her. The suburban before her rocked sideways, sliding a few feet away. A No Parking sign lay suddenly horizontal to the ground, bending where it emerged from the concrete. The trees near by flapped in a wind that was not there. Loose trash flew away in a ring around her. The two surviving suburbans screeched to a stop on the far side of the suburban in which I lay.

Those agents flanked left and right with no idea what they faced. How could they. Those poor dumb bastards. They brought their weapons up, seeing only an unarmed girl and two wounded prisoners. She held her will up like a shield around us and focused that will like a blade. She was about to cut some men in half.

"That's enough!" a new voice commanded. This voice was accompanied by the sound of many machine guns being readied. Homeland Security officers swarmed the grasses around the NSA agents and the suburban.

"These are our prisoners now," Aaron declared.

"We can't do that, sir," the NSA captain declared. "These people are escapees from an NSA holding facility. They attacked our director."

"Is your director dead?" he asked, a note of concern in his voice.

"No, sir. She's alive, just injured. They tore the place up pretty bad though. Respectfully, they're coming back with us."

"They're going with me," Aaron declared. "You're in my parking lot and under my jurisdiction, agent."

"They're going with us," the captain argued back.

"We're not going with anyone," I called out weakly from the back seat. "We brokered the deal. They're coming for us." I pointed toward the sky. "They'll be here to get us in a little bit."

"I beg to differ," The captain snapped. "Take them," he commanded, and two of the NSA agents rushed forward, intent on taking us into custody. This was when they encountered Nameless. It was like they had tried to strangle lighting. She did not just hit them. She put the focus of her will inside them and pushed everything in opposite directions. The two men who grabbed for her blew apart like they had swallowed grenades. The rest of the men backed away, suddenly less sure of themselves. Homeland Security agents and NSA agents alike brought their guns up to fire.

"Do you really think . . . she's going to let you . . . pull those triggers?" I asked, bluffing. "She can read your thoughts. The moment you pull those triggers, she'll take control of you and make you shoot each other."

I can't really do that, Nameless admitted.

They don't know that, I replied.

She was my mother, Nameless confessed.

"Who?" I asked aloud. She pushed the image of Mercy into my head. I pulled my thoughts away. I had done this. This was me. I had outed them as spies. I put them in that NSA black site. I got Nameless raped and Mercy killed. I pulled my hands away from my wound and pulled the compress aside. There was too much blood on my hands. Nameless glanced back at me and saw what I had done.

"He's bleeding out," she cried. "Help me!" No one moved. She turned to Aaron. "You don't understand who this man is," she snapped. "He just surrendered to them. If he dies, they will burn your world and let the solar winds scatter what's left. During your entire history, no man has been more important to your planet. They want him at any cost." Her hands were shaking. The NSA captain looked to the Homeland Security Director. Aaron nodded.

"Get an ambulance. Stop that bleeding." The men refused to touch Nameless and with good reason, but she quickly moved aside to give them access.

"Who is he?" Aaron asked, coming up to Nameless.

"His name was Magpie once upon a time. He was a Prior and a Grand Reaper. He broke the Empire apart thinking he was saving it."

"Did he?" Aaron asked.

"I don't know," she confessed. "I really don't know." They watched as the NSA agents pulled me from the back seat and laid me out on the ground. I was vaguely aware of three of them working feverishly to stop the bleeding. Somewhere far above, three twinkling lights entered the atmosphere unannounced and fell like comets toward the ground.

I smiled faintly. The Grand Reaper was coming.

Chapter 13: The Search

Baggam Rain was not the terror his knights purported him to be. Was he rough and vicious? Yes. Was he caustic and hard? Definitely. Was he unforgiving and stern? Absolutely. But he was also fair, just, and wise, and sometimes he even smiled.

Today was not one of those days. He was retraining knights and trying to teach them not to kill unruly colonists when the Harvest commenced. It was always this way. Traditionalists who loved their world would inevitably try to sabotage the Harvest on behalf of the planet, though no one asked them to do so.

Baggam had conducted himself well since taking command of the battle group. They had not lost one knight or colonist during the previous Harvest to weapons fire or sword. Word was circling that this Harvest would fill the ships to capacity. The Daimyo had selected the Grand Reaper personally. It was typically a council selection but not this time. Lord Merrik had selected the man personally on the recommendation of Ayu Morn, the last Grand Reaper. Baggam had decided early on that if the Harvest fell short or failed, it would not be the fault of an Imperial Knight aboard the Kye O'Ren. He was adamant about that.

Baggam was often at the council meetings, and he had prepared the flight group during the meet and greet the day prior. He had seen the man from afar, but never once had he the privilege or leisure to meet the man in person. He was a little underwhelmed. He was nothing like his sister. Then again, Luke was not a warrior. The commander sent his mind out to inspect the newcomer. The man's mind was strong. It still did not change his opinion of the man, but it did encourage Baggam to show the man a tad more respect than he would have another.

"Whadda you want, monk?" Baggam growled upon seeing Luke.

Luke looked the man up and down. He was taller than most men by half a head, wide in the shoulders, thick of body, with a mass of red curly hair that at first glance looked as if his head was on fire. His arms looked as if they could twist juice from a steel bar, and his legs looked as if he had used them to kick asteroids away from the ship on a regular basis.

The man was old—younger than the Daiymo—but older than the rest of the knights. A beard and mustache of the same red hair flowed down his chest like a waterfall of flame. Luke had caught the man mid-meal. A dining apron was tucked into his collar and allowed to drape over his broad gut. His beard had been parted to either side of his belly to limit the number of crumbs it collected.

A word, if you don't mind, Luke said by way of greeting.

"I do mind and speak aloud. I don't want you plundering my brain box. I got important things up there I ain't intent on sharin'," he commanded.

I need to locate one of your knights.

"Begone. I'm busy. It's after mid-rotation and repast time. You got a request, submit it to the ninnies who push the paper. They'll be back in the office in the third tenth of tomorrow's rotation. Come back then." The battle commander, unused to having his commands disobeyed, considered the matter settled and sliced into a jaja fruit. He popped it in his mouth and chewed with a lot of energy. When he swallowed, he noticed that the Grand Reaper was still there.

Her name is . . . he pushed the image of her DNA strand into the battle commander's mind. *The colonists call her Leia. She is my sister.*

"Are you deaf. I'm taking my repast. This is a cruel time to be talking of work. Is this really how you want to put your sister on my radar?" he told Luke threateningly.

"It is important," Luke declared aloud.

Baggam dropped his fork and knife in amazement. If it was important enough for a Pre-Prior to break his vow of silence, then food could wait.

"What do you need," the commander inquired, coming to his feet and tossing his dining apron aside, "and why are we looking for your sister, Reaper?"

She's been taken. He pushed the memory of the message he had received from Earth into the battle commander's head. The battle commander's bushy brows creased in anger as he listened to the message and his faced flushed red in anger. Someone had dared to molest a knight under his command. Some coward had just committed suicide. These were his children. The knights were his hard-knuckled, steely-eyed, battle-hardened sons and daughters.

"I got this," Baggam growled menacingly. He stormed over to the door to his office, ripped it open, and looked the two knights standing guard in the eye. "One of your sisters has been taken. Grab some siblings and bring me some heads."

I need at least one alive, commander. Baggam gave Luke an irritated look but relented.

"Bring one back alive. Kill the rest." He pushed the image of Leia's DNA into the knights' heads. They nodded and raced off to carry out the command.

I also need an escort to the surface, Luke added. He pushed a list of the things they were going to need into the man's head, and then pressed his NID to that of the commanders. The file with the list of equipment was transferred automatically. *This will be a delivery and retrieval. They have two of our people. We need them back. The Daimyo commands it.*

"You can't be serious. You can't give them these. I won't do it," the commander declared.

You will. This is a direct command from Lord Merrik himself. Be ready to leave before this tenth rotation is done, and put the fleet on alert, Luke told him, marching through the door.

"I know she's your sister, but this is too much to pay for the return of a single person," Baggam protested.

We're not trading it for my sister. We're trading it for Magpie. He's here, and he'll know how to find those who drifted. We finally have a chance to mend what was broken. We can make the Empire whole again. Luke searched the commander's face and saw a mix of feelings wash over his gruff craggy face. He didn't say a word. He just nodded and went to work arranging the Reaper's ride, his argument nullified by the news. Magpie changed everything.

Along with arranging Luke's transportation, Baggam sent out general quarters call to the military. When the ship wide call went out that an Imperial Knight had been captured, the military responded just as they had been trained to do. The Grey Guard responded first.

The locator in her NID put her on Level 12, in Quad 3. This was where the Grey Guard went, converging on her locator signal. They found her NID in a bin down the walk from her parents' cell. It had been stripped and tossed.

A priority alert was given to the Imperial Knight substation on Level 12. Their telepaths homed in on her biometrics. This should have ended the hunt quickly, but those who took Leia were familiar with the abilities of the knighthood. Every time they tracked her biometric data, it led them to a smear of her blood.

They found her blood on door handles, lifts seats, and on strangers wandering the byways. It quickly became apparent that her captors had been spreading her blood around like trappers spread the musk of the animals they hunt. It would take forever to find Leia this way. Even as they zeroed in, more hot spots blossomed into existence. The insurgents who had grabbed her were cleverer than the knighthood gave them credit for. If the knighthood was going to find her, then it was going to be because they got lucky.

Baggam Rain's answer to this dilemma was to order more knights from other levels down to Level 12 to aid in the search.

Commander Rain's last update was not an encouraging one. There were a hundred knights scouring Level 12, and there were three times that many Grey Guardsmen. Baggam had authorized up to an additional thousand to be called on if the watch commanders deemed it necessary. The only way the commander could see clear to finding the Grand Reaper's sister was to flood the level with more hunters than foxes.

If they could put out more knights than the kidnappers could put out false leads, then there was a chance they would find her before her captors bled her to death. Everyone involved knew this was a stall tactic meant to distract the Grand Reaper from his job. The First Colonists wanted one of two things, but both really. They wanted the Harvest delayed as long as possible so that the First Colony ships could catch up, and if that failed, they wanted the Grand Reaper's Harvest to go poorly. The more colonists they left behind, the more colonists the First Colony got to sweep up when they finally did arrive at this planet.

While the Grey Guardsmen and knights searched Level 12 for Leia, Baggam and Luke, along with a retinue of knights descended to the planet below. The saucer ride into the atmosphere had been rough. One of the knights had suffered a head wound from the turbulence after he rapped it hard on the bulkhead of the Fast Flight Skiff they were using for this foray.

Those manning the scanners picked up the tracking signals of the planet's defense system. The skiff pilots were veteran Air Corp officers. They were not too worried about the clumsy weapons of the colonists. For the past year, the Imperial Army and Imperial Knights had been working together to catalogue and rate the different class of weapons the colonists used. They watched the fighting on the ground from above and determined that except for a couple weapon systems, the colonial weapons posed no threat.

Of course, it was only a survey of the weapons the colonist dared to use. They knew there were weapons the colonists used as deterrents; weapons so horrible those who had them feared their use. Commander Rain had confidence in the analysis of his subordinates and so stood with his men in the first ship as they couriered Luke to the rendezvous point Mercy had given them. The knights feared nothing. What they lacked for firepower aboard the skiff was more than made up for by the long guns on Kye O'Ren who was covering their excursion from above. The long carbon shells they fired were powerful non-nuclear artillery capable of withstanding the heat of atmospheric entry, and they were powerful enough to destroy entire cities with each shot. The Kye O'Ren never had to fire more than one shot to make its point.

"They're going to kill her, aren't they?" Luke asked of Baggam. Baggam sucked a bit of ja-ja fruit from between his teeth and spit it out, mulling over the question.

"No reason to wonder, monk. They either will or they won't. It doesn't change our response here. We find them. We kill them. If they kill her first, we kill them slower. She's an elite weapon of the Empire. She's an Imperial Knight, Reaper. A knight! Don't insult her by worrying. She died the day she signed up to be a knight. The only reason she's still around," he spit noisily, "is because my knights are too stubborn to lay down and rot. You keep your mind on this. You keep your focus on apprehending Magpie, and I'll keep my mind on finding your sister. If everyone does their job. Everyone gets to go home happy." The ship bucked as they hit the inner atmosphere. The ride only got worse from there.

"We have colonial fliers bearing down on us commander," one of the pilots announced. Baggam moved to the front, took hold of the ring in the ceiling, and raised his chin.

"So?" he rumbled, unfazed by the news.

"What if they fire on us, sir?" the pilot asked. Baggam looked at the pilot who had spoken, making the man feel small.

"Don't get hit," he replied, as if the answer were obvious. The other pilot smirked.

Chapter 14: Retrieval

Luke sent his mind down to the surface. He searched the minds of those on the ground, looking for the man who had called himself Albus Dumbledore. He found the name repeated over and over in every mind he touched. Everyone seemed to know the man.

Who was he? Dammit! he snapped to no one in particular. Baggam shot him a curious glance but said nothing. Luke kept searching, plundering the mind of a youth he found that was currently thinking the name Dumbledore. He delved deep into the kid's mind for an image of the man. What he found was a frail looking old man who supposedly ran a school of wizardry. He delved deeper and found that it was a character in a book. *Dammit!* He cried out in frustration again, realizing the translator had given him a false name.

He tried to find the colonial ambassador instead. He searched for the one who had alerted him to Magpie's presence in the colony, but he could not find her either. He sent his mind back into the city where she had been at the time of first contact. There should have a been a trail to follow. Very few people had the discipline to not think about someone they had just met or talked to. As long as she was thinking about him—even a little—he should have been able to find her. A two-way connection was easy to reconnect under the right conditions. This was why he wanted Albus. If he truly had feelings for his sister, and she reciprocated even a little, he could find her. He could do what the Imperial Knights could not. He could rescue his sister and save her life. As this thought process transpired in Luke's mind, he saw Baggam staring out one of the many windows of their flier at approaching colonial fliers.

The colonial fliers were F-35Cs, naval jets launched to meet the alien incursion. They zeroed in on the three imperial personnel carriers that Baggam's Children—as the Imperial Soldiers aboard the Kye O'Ren called the knights under Baggam's command—were currently riding to the ground. Baggam had no fear of the planes closing in on them. They would be fools to shoot on the ships of an armada capable of eradicating their entire planet. He had never met the people of this colony before, but he was gambling on the chance they were not fools.

The coordinates Luke was given were for a large field near a tall pinnacle of stone outside the capital building in D.C. The Earthlings had a name for the pinnacle of stone. They called it the Washington Monument. It was a holy place as far as Luke could determine. They seemed to worship there judging by the huge crowds that gathered near the stone. The Division of Intelligence aboard the Kye O'Ren were fairly certain this was its purpose. As a result, the pilots of the skiff were given clear instructions not to damage it. The destruction of religious temples would make the Harvest twice as a hard to execute.

The coordinates had been Mercy's choice and not one Aaron would have picked. He had been so invested in Daniel's survival, he had completely forgotten about the alien ships coming to deliver their end of the bargain. Worse, he forgot to notify the White House of their arrival. He suspected the inevitable call from NORAD had probably puckered every butthole over at the Capitol Building.

When he heard the F35Cs coming in, the Director of Homeland Security finally took notice of the three fast flying alien ships headed his way. They were coming fast and did not appear interested in deviating from the path of the five fighter jets bearing down on them. He hoped his call would reach the White House before an intergalactic incident was realized. He dialed the direct line to the White House, but the phone just kept ringing.

"Can he travel?" Aaron asked to his security detail as the phone continued to ring.

"He's in bad shape, but yeah," the NSA Captain called back. "I think the bullet nicked something inside."

The Director swore, and a White House aide chose that moment to answer his call. "This is Aaron McDonald, Director of Homeland Security. I have an urgent call for the President. It has to do with the three alien ships bearing down on Washington. I need him on the phone ten minutes ago." He slapped his hand over the phone and turned to Nameless.

"Can they fix him? Your people, I mean. Can they fix him?"

"You better hope so," she replied, chewing her bottom lip. "For all our sakes, I hope they can."

"How long on the ambulance?" Aaron called out to the armed men around him. One of the men flashed five fingers twice in reply. "Ten minutes? Too damn long." He looked up at the descending ships and tried to calculate their ETA.

"Director, the President is awaiting your call. I'm connecting you now," the aide told him, punching a button on the phone.

"This is the President," a familiar voice on the other end of the phone called.

"Thank you for taking my call, sir. There are three fast moving alien ships descending on Washington, sir. They are friendly. I repeat, they are friendly. You need to call off the Navy jets. Call them off now, sir." Aaron heard the captain curse in frustration. "One moment, Mr. President." Aaron came down the steps, glancing toward the sky nervously. "What is it?" he asked of the captain.

"He's bleeding internally. I-I can't stop it."

"Fuck!" Aaron cursed, pacing off a short distance to gather his thoughts. "Load him up. Load him up and head for the Washington Monument. Redirect the EMTs. Have them ready by the time we arrive. That man does not die. You hear me. He does not die." He remembered he had the president on hold.

"Sir, this is the situation." He informed the President of all that had transpired, stressing the need for them to call off the fighter jets. It took him several minutes of fast talking to convince the President that this was not an attack. It took even longer for him to talk the President out of attending the meeting. As far as Aaron was concerned, the plans to meet with the world leaders was still scheduled for five days.

The President, Aaron believed, should under no circumstances be allowed to speak with the alien ambassador before that scheduled time. They had already brokered a back door deal for alien medical technology and advanced weaponry. If word of this got out, there would be no peace with the other nations. It would be seen as back-channel maneuvering to gain alien technology for the United States, which it was, but the U.N. did not need to know this.

The ambulance was waiting for them by the east entrance to the monument. The SUVs arrived next, with Nameless standing guard over Daniel's pale body. The EMTs tried to put him in their ambulance in preparation for transport, but the NSA and Homeland agents would not allow it.

"You fix him here," the NSA captain commanded, turning to face the bright lights in the sky. The F35Cs veered suddenly, changing direction so that they ran parallel to the alien ships. The captain felt a surge of relief.

"He needs a hospital," the paramedic tending Daniel exclaimed. "His skin is black from blood pooling. He needs to go to the damn ER now or he is going to die."

"He stays here. You stay here. You do what you can for him, but everyone is staying put," Nameless shouted back, drawing in her will. Loose items in the back of the ambulance began to float as a result. The captain studied the floating items for a moment, giving the former prisoner a wary look.

"Do as she says," he snapped, remembering what happened to the two men she blew apart. "You don't wanna make this one angry."

"No. He doesn't," she replied, sending a shiver of fear down the captain's spine.

The paramedic stared at the floating bandages and scissors and just nodded in reply. In the distance, they could hear sirens as the D.C. police responded to the reports of gun shots and car wrecks. Aaron did not have to see them to know that the FBI, Homeland Security, and the NSA were all sending agents to their position. The White House would undoubtedly be sending D.C. police cars to the monument as well.

"I want you on crowd control," Aaron called, noticing that people were beginning to gather. "When the other agents arrive, I want the crowds back so far their pictures of this landing look like bigfoot video. You," he gestured to the NSA Captain, "handle your people. I want the cell towers offline, and internet traffic in and out of D.C. cut." The captain nodded and pulled his men away, pointing out the people gathering across the street.

The men converged on the bystanders, and the people gave ground before them.

"You," he gestured to one of his agents, "coordinate with the FBI. D.C. and the surrounding areas are now a no-fly zone. I don't want a plane within a hundred miles of this city. This goes for drones and hot air balloons. If it flies, ground it, shoot it down, or I don't care. I want this bottled." The man singled out nodded and hurried off to make it happen, dialing as he went. The Director gave several of the other agents missions as well, keeping three agents in reserve to guard Daniel and Nameless.

Keeping the landing secret turned out to be a tougher job than the Director had anticipated. The skiffs came in one at a time. The moment the first skiff hit the ground, an entire squad of Imperial Knights popped out of the drop doors, dropping the ten feet to the ground. The skiff shot back into the air and took an over-watch position to cover the next skiff.

The knights the first skiff dropped raced off in all directions to establish a perimeter. They carried long vertical poles nearly their height before them, and as they came, the poles blossomed large overlapping petals of light. Everything the knights saw through the shields, appeared as if under the full glow of the sun. The shields outlined anything alive in red. The poles ended in a spike on one end. These they jammed into the ground before them and took a knee behind the overlapping petals. They pushed the barrels of their long rifles through the hole in the center of the shield. Aaron looked at the rifles they carried and wondered what it was they did. He wondered if this was how the Mayan's felt when the conquistadors arrived on their shores with their muskets and arquebuses.

The next skiff that swooped in dropped its warriors like the other, but these warriors came armed with heavy guns. Two-man teams raced forward, setting up turrets, and battle screens for them to crouch behind. The luminescent force fields blazed to life, shooting between the armored pylons the knights planted. These knights were armed with long rifles as well and took a knee to steady their aim. Their rifle scopes picked out anything with a heartbeat and zoomed in on it, tracking that beat.

The third skiff came in like the others, but it came in to land. It hovered a few feet off the ground and just long enough to let a handful of knights drop to the ground. These were armored to the teeth, with large broadswords upon their back. They held long poles just like those on the first skiff, only these planted their poles in a wide arch facing the ambulance. The skiff landed and the ramp dropped, followed by the opening of a forward hatch at the top of the ramp. The moment the ramp dropped, knights in mobile turrets poured out onto the grass. The knights manning them stood up in the chariots, reclining at a slight angle as they raced down the ramps. The force fields protected the drivers, formed a semi-circular shield around them. It guarded them from rifle fire forward and on their flanks. The chariot drivers raced through the openings the first two squad of knights left in their ranks.

Aaron looked at the armor and heavily equipped knights and swallowed hard. From the look of what he saw, there was enough aliens and fire power on the field to cut through all the agents on the field ten times over. He desperately hoped he had not made a mistake in bringing them here. He started across the field and was joined by Richard Weaver, the FBI Director, who strolled out on the field to meet him.

"This your doing?" Richard asked, glancing back as the Nameless spy jogged across the green to catch up with the two men.

"You're going to need a translator," she explained. Aaron nodded and turned back to Richard.

"Not entirely," Aaron responded, answering the other director's question. "It's a series of unforeseen events and bad case of being in the wrong place at the wrong time."

"Wait up!" a woman's voice called, frantic and pissed off. Aaron looked back to see Tessa Barnes half-walking, half-jogging to catch up with them. Nameless began drawing in her will. Aaron watched as his tie started to rise of its own accord.

"Shit," Aaron exclaimed in distress. Nameless looked to him, and he just shook his head, cautioning her not to do what she was planning on doing.

"There seems to be some bad blood between you two I'm guessing?" Richard asked, misinterpreting Aaron's exclamation, though Tessa's arrival was not very welcomed.

"No. She's just a hot head, and," he gestured to the three squads of knights arrayed before him, "does this look like the proper venue for a hot head?"

Richard shrugged, giving the man a lopsided smile. "It takes all types. We die doing the right thing, and we die doing everything wrong. In the end, does it matter? Let her come. We'll do damage control afterwards."

Aaron glanced sidelong at Nameless, then stopped and fixed his fellow director with a look of reproach. "Richard, this is damage control." Richard studied his counterpart then nodded. He had no reason to doubt his claim.

Tessa caught up to them fifty feet from the alien front lines. Richard slowed as did Tessa, but Aaron and Nameless kept walking, boldly marching toward the wall of knights. When they reached the front lines, the knights before him stepped back and to the side, opening a passage before him. Tessa and Richard exchanged looks of apprehension, then quick-stepped to rejoin the other two.

Baggam and Luke strolled down the ramp on the back of the ship together. Luke was dressed in white ceremonial monastic armor. It consisted of durable white quilted leggings and a knee length battle dress. A white quilted pad covered his right shoulder. In his hand, he carried what looked like a scepter. Possibly, Aaron thought, it was a symbol of his station.

Baggam did not stand on ceremony. Thick tree trunk-sized legs rose from the ramp and disappeared under a kilt of sorts with small over-lapping fish scale armored plates. He wore a nanite sword on one hip, a battle rifle on his back, and two different side arms. One was small like what his children carried, and the other was long, like the sub machine guns the colonial special forces sometimes used. He carried a utility belt on which were threaded a multitude of pouches. An armband circled is left bicep, and from it, hanging upside down, were two wicked looking daggers with serrated tips.

"And who are you?" Commander Baggam demanded of the foursome. He eyed them contemptuously, letting his eyes linger on Nameless. They all looked to Nameless.

"He wants to know who you are," she told the trio, translating Baggam's words for the ambassadors.

"I am Aaron McDonald, Director of Homeland Security. These are my counterparts, Tessa Barnes with the National Security Agency and Richard Weaver with the Federal Bureau of Investigation," Aaron said, introducing his companions. He turned to Nameless and shrugged. He did not know her name.

"I am called Palasa: Flame of the Forest," Nameless announced proudly, shrugging off her colonial name. Baggam's brow creased deeply and the look he gave Palasa was dangerous and promising pain.

"That's a Drifter's name?" Baggam declared accusingly, drawing the nanite sword on his hip.

"Commander!" Luke called out, gathering his will to stop the man should it prove necessary. Aaron and the others eyed the exchange nervously.

"What was that about?" Tessa asked with a sneer.

"I gave him my true name. He now wants to kill me, but the Grand Reaper has forestalled my execution," Palasa explained. Tessa sighed heavily. She seemed saddened by this news.

"And who do we have the pleasure of addressing?" Aaron asked. Baggam stomped down the ramp, towered over the three, then pushed through them. He came to a stop a few yards further on.

Where is that traitorous bastard? Baggam demanded, sword in hand still.

"He wants to know where Magpie is," Palasa told them, relaying the commander's message.

"Who?" Tessa asked, unfamiliar with the name.

Magpie! Luke demanded, echoing Baggam's call. Palasa repeated what he said for the others. Two of the directors looked at Luke, completely clueless as to the name mentioned. Aaron was not.

"Present him, please," Luke urged, struggling to remain polite. He searched the area around him. "Also, where is Albus Dumbledore? I requested his company as part of this deal."

Palasa repeated what was said and asked. Aaron remembered that Albus was the alias Daniel had given to them that first day in the field. He was surprised that the alien ambassador was ignorant of the fact that Daniel and Magpie were the same person.

"The man you know as Magpie is bleeding out," Aaron announced. He did not miss the small smile that lifted the corners of Tessa's mouth. Aaron motioned for Palasa to relay the message, and its urgency.

Magpie is injured. He is bleeding out and is in dire need of medical attention. Do you have a med chamber on the ship? she inquired of the commander. He grunted in reply.

"Aye," the commander replied scornfully, as if just talking to the Drifter soiled his tongue. "Though I think I'd much prefer the fatherless heathen bleed out."

Then wait two ticks longer and you'll have your wish, Palasa replied indifferently.

What of Albus? Luke asked, urgent in his need for the man's company. His sister was still in the hands of the insurgency.

The man you know as Albus Dumbledore goes by the name Daniel Sojourner on this planet, but elsewhere, he is known as Magpie, Palasa announced, much to Luke's chagrin. *You have met Magpie before, Reaper. If you wish him to find your sister, then you need to act now and save his life.*

Luke studied the woman before him, irritated that he had to save the life of a man he planned to try for murder.

"He dies and we'll destroy this planet," Baggam announced, marching over to Palasa and leaning in until their noses touched. He was trying to intimidate her. She did not react as he expected her to. Instead of looking away, she stood up on her tippy-toes and kissed the tip of the burly man's nose. He spluttered with indignation and swatted at the air before him like a kid who had just been tricked into kissing a toad. "If he dies, you die."

Oh, go blow that threat up someone else's skirt, Commander, she snarled back. *Do you think you intimidate me, sir? Do you?* She marched toward him, putting the big man on his heels. He did not know whether to swat her, spank her, or marry her.

Palasa relayed the Battle Commander's threat.

"That hardly seems fair," Tessa argued.

"Fair? How long has he been here? One hundred years? Two hundred? This world has been harboring a mass murderer responsible for the deaths of five point eight billion colonists," Baggam barked.

Palasa relayed the message. Tessa's face paled, suddenly uncertain of her standing. "How would you treat the person responsible for hiding a killer like that from you?"

Palasa didn't bother to translate that part. Instead, she addressed Luke. *Do you want Magpie alive or don't you?* she asked him hatefully. *If so, offer the use of your med bed. Or do you want to explain to the Daimyo why the one man capable of reuniting the Drifters with the Empire bled to death fifty yards from a med chamber?*

Tell them to bring him to us, Luke commanded.

She did and Aaron motioned for the ambulance to drive out to meet them. His agents drove the ambulance right up to the alien perimeter and helped the paramedics offload the injured man. They collapsed the gurney and backed away.

Four knights hurried forward, grabbed the gurney, and carried the man aboard their ship. A knight returned a moment later, tossing the gurney down the ramp as if it were garbage. The paramedics looked at the destroyed bed then to the trio of directors. Richard waved for them to leave. They did as they were told, hurrying away.

"This deal is done," Baggam declared, marching up the ramp.

Palasa relayed this message, and Aaron cleared his throat and reminded them of their deal. Luke eyed the man and shook his head in disbelief.

Pay that man, he told Baggam. Baggam studied the trio of directors, mulled over the wisdom of the request and shrugged. It was their planet. It was theirs to destroy. He called out commands to the knights in attendance and marched the rest of the way up the ramp, disappearing inside.

The knights closest to the ramp began their orderly exfil. The directors moved aside quickly when the chariot style tanks re-embarked onto the ships. Luke nodded to each of the directors in turn, uttering the world "Croatoan" after each bow. Palasa relayed this word of farewell as Daniel had done in Kansas, then gave Aaron a curt bow, and began following the Grand Reaper up the ramp.

Where do you think you're going? Luke asked her, stopping at the top of the ramp.

Wherever Magpie goes, I go, she replied.

No, you don't, Luke argued.

Are we to battle, cousin? she asked curiously. Luke blinked in surprise. No one but assassins challenged the Grand Reaper. It just was not done.

No. You just can't come, he told her stubbornly.

Try and stop me. She drew her will in. Luke's mind went to his sister's plight, and he realized he did not have time for this, so he capitulated and gave her what she wanted.

Take her into custody, he told the surrounding knights. Palasa grunted in surprise as half a dozen minds smothered her will while a big burly knight marched over and put her in cuffs.

"Bury my mother, please. Do something nice," she called down to Aaron. Aaron nodded that he would, and the three ambassadors for Earth backed away, giving the knights room to maneuver.

The first skiff raised its ramp, closed its door, and zipped off into the night sky. The other two ships lingered, taking turns on the ground to off load the crates of weapons Aaron had been promised. They offloaded med beds and medical scanners. When the last ship was unloaded, the knights filed on and disappeared, shooting into the sky behind the first skiff.

The last skiff followed the example of the first two and with it went the last know alien on planet Earth. That is, unless of course, you counted the other seven billion humans on the planet.

Chapter 15: Revival

I wasn't sure how long I had been unconscious. I appeared to be in a tanning bed of some sort.

I sent my mind out, searching for others. The closest mind was a woman in the other room. I sent my mind out into the night sky in search of Leia and followed her trail to where she was kept. It did not take me long to locate her, but it did take a while to figure why my mind went down instead of up. I pushed the top of the tanning bed off me. My wound felt healed or nearly healed. By the look of the items in the room, I was on one of the ships in the sky.

Help me, Leia whispered weakly.

I'm coming. Just a little longer, I whispered back. There was a feeling of relief from her. I peeked through the doorway and into the other room. The woman in the room was tending another. I glanced around, searching the walls for other exits, and I found that the door out was to my left and far from the distracted woman. I crept out of the room and toward the door. Outside were two men dressed in grey uniforms, with curious black rods hanging from their belts. They were guarding the room so I could not escape most likely.

I gingerly picked up a pan from shelf near the door and stepped out into the lane. The guards looked at me in confusion. It took a moment for them to act. They both went for the metal rods at their waists at the same time. I reacted by slamming the pan in my hand down on the head of the first guard, then swung the pan backwards in a mighty back hand that laid out the other. There was a loud—BONG! BONG! —as the pan connected both times, and the guards fell to the ground unconscious. I was not sure what the long black metal rod was, but judging by their uniforms, they were some form of police, which made the long rod some kind of weapon.

I looked around to see if the altercation was witnessed. One old man shambling by stopped to watch the attack, stood there staring, then smiled and carried on. I smiled back then hurried off to the sound of the physician calling for me to come back. I tossed the pan aside before reaching the connecting lane. This one was wider and far busier. I ducked into it and disappeared among the crowd, zeroing in on the Leia's position. She was far away and far below.

The wand was not heavy, but it was bulky, and the people I passed seemed to take notice of it quickly. I tried to hide it up my sleeve, but the tunic the medical staff put on me fit oddly. The sleeves came to the middle of my forearms. The back came only to my waist, which let the bottom of my belly hang out from beneath it. The leggings I walked out of the medical cell in appeared to be made of some form of biodegradable thread. The more I walked, the more I sweated. The more I sweated, the faster they broke down.

A man-made eye contact from the far side of the byway and watched me with more interest than I thought was polite. He wore a dull yellow jacket, grey pants, ratty shoes, and a turban of sorts. It was made of cloth as wide as my hands, which he had wound around the top of his head twice before pinning it, so that both ends hung down on his right side, straddling his shoulder. He seemed very interested in me and watched me until I passed from view.

Out of sight was out of mind, and I turned back to the path ahead. The byway was crowded with people in many forms of dress, but there seemed to be a predominant fashion trend. Few people wore the turban of the man I had passed. Most wore vests that resembled leather over long sleeved blouses.

For the women, the blouses ended in large, fluted sleeves that drooped like open lilies about their wrist. The men's sleeves billowed across their forearms but cinched tight for the last four inches or so. There was a slight resemblance to the pirate shirts in old Errol Flynn movies.

The women wore knee length earth-toned skirts with tight white leggings beneath. The men wore darker leggings that almost looked indigo in color. The women wore slippers, and the men wore ankle boots. Their hats would be considered silly by the people from Earth. What was I thinking? I was from Earth, and their hats were very silly. Some rode like fins upon their head, others draped off to the side like the caps worn in Venice back in the day. The children ran around between the adults in the byway dressed like miniature replicas of their parents.

A squad of men dressed in grey uniforms like the men I had clubbed outside the doctor's office, came down the byway, laughing and jostling each other. Some held batons like the one I stole, letting them dangle at the end of their arms. They hung to the right of the corridor so that the main stream of traffic could flow around them.

I quickly hid the black wand I stole up under my tunic, and I started to move to the far side of the byway, but I stopped when a stranger's hand cupped my elbow and stopped me.

"You don't want to do that, friend. They're trained to look for that," a voice said from very near to my right ear.

"W-What?" I stammered, looking quickly to my right.

It was the strange unshaven man with the turban I had seen earlier. His coat hung open wide at the bottom and closer at the top. He was not rotund like me. In fact, he looked slightly starved. His fingers were grimy around the tips giving them a purplish hue, and the edges of his nails were caked with a buildup of dirt.

"You see, the trick is to walk down the center of the byway. They don't see the people in the center. These people," he said gesturing to the people before us, "are invisible to the grey men. They only see the people who try to avoid them," the man revealed, looking straight ahead as if we were old friends out for a leisurely walk. I studied the man curiously.

"You were watching me back there," I accused.

"I watched a lot of people back there," he retorted, continuing forward. He kept his chin lifted as if some haughty medieval lord and kept his eyes on those ahead of him. "They also see the people who look around and gawk, like you do, friend. You act like a tourist here. Are you from the colony on the planet below?"

"I-I . . . yes," I replied. It was the truth, technically.

"Ah. So, you've come to walk the levels." He looked around after the Grey Guard had passed, then studied the way I was dressed. "Were you injured?" he asked. My hand betrayed me, going to my side out of reflex. The area was still tender beneath the skin. "Ah," he said, nodding his understanding. "Was it on the shuttle up from the surface? The turbulence did me in when I was harvested," He admitted with a laugh. "It bounced me around like a shroodle ball the entire time." He looked back over my shoulder in confusion, searching the crowd that followed.

"Is there a reason you keep looking back?" I asked.

"I'm looking for your Guilt," he replied, perplexed that he could not spot the man or woman. He did spot a couple of conspicuous men, but after a moment of being watched, they veered into a side corridor and disappeared. The turbaned man clucked his tongue thoughtfully.

"Guilt?" I asked.

"Yes. Yes. It is your chaperone. The man or woman they send to follow you." He gestured quick toward the byway ahead. "They're the ones supposed to save you from people like me. Your Guilt is hard to spot though," he confessed.

"Do I need protection from you?" I asked, arching a brow quizzically. The man did not seem very threatening.

"What happened? Did you wake and wander from a medical cell?" he asked, plucking at my sleeves.

"I woke in some weird bed. There was no one there, so I wandered out into the corridor and kept going." I was bending the truth, but that seemed preferable to being incarcerated by the alien ambassador. I could sense Leia. It was almost like she was beneath me. Far, far beneath me.

"You've gone nomad, I see," the man said with a smirk, smacking his chest proudly. His nose was enormous, with a straight bridge. It came to a straight point, then cut back sharply to join his upper lip. He brushed the tip with one finger as if touching it for luck.

"Nomad? You're a nomad?" I asked.

"Ah, yes. Living rough is the best way to live," he declared proudly. My stomach growled just then. He glanced sidelong at me, raising a brow. "You're an endangered man, my friend. You've wandered out into the wild of the Kye O'Ren with no idea how to fend for yourself." He rapped on the hidden baton suddenly. "Lucky you found this."

"I'll be fine," I told him, unsure if I was telling the truth.

"Where will you go? You have no Guilt to guide you. You wear patch clothe and walk with a rumbling belly. You fear the grey men and conceal one of their weapons beneath your clothes. A weapon I think you did not come by honestly. Tell, me my fellow nomad, do I speak truth."

"There might be some truth to what you say," I hedged. He smirked.

"You're a man like me; a man who picks his words with care and hordes them like the wollywok hordes grim-tree seeds. I think we are kindred." He patted me upon the back heartily. I noticed a placard high upon a column with a strange series of glyphs, and I recognized them. They'd appeared along the border of the tablet Luke had brought to the surface outside Cherryville that first day we met.

"That says we're on Level 319," I blurted, gesturing toward the column. The man glanced at it without seeming interest, but then let his eyes slide back to me as if he were afraid to turn his head.

"You read Cojokarunese?" he asked, suddenly interested for the first time.

"I understand it a little." I ignored him and tried to determine just how far from the top of the ship I was. It was a useless thing to try and determine from below decks. The ship seemed to be composed almost entirely of cubed cells and busy highways.

"My apologies," I said, extending my hand, "I didn't catch your name." The man was genuinely surprised by this. The mysterious man persona he was trying to maintain crumbled for a moment and the proud noble carriage faltered as he considered the proffered hand.

"No one has ever asked me that before," he admitted, searching my face for some clue as to my motives. Then like that, the haughty wise companion returned.

"Well, I'm asking," I told him, leaning in so as to make my hand more inviting.

"They once called me Gorjjen Doricci. They still call me this," he confessed, chin raised, eyes riding the ridge of his nose.

I grasped his hand and pumped it twice. "Daniel. Daniel Sojourner."

"So, who is Gorjjen Doricci?" I asked with a grin. He shrugged and went back to holding his chin aloft.

"I was once a citizen of the thirty-ninth colony: The greatest colony. I came aboard with my sister and her poog." I didn't recognize this word and said so. He made a cradling motion with his arms. "Poog," he repeated as if stating it a second time would make me understand him better.

"Do you mean a baby?" I asked. The man searched through the words of his world and chose the one he thought fit best.

"I believe daughter. Little her," he corrected, "and also, baby."

"And now, you're a nomad?" I remarked in good humor. The man smiled.

"Indeed," he replied proudly. "Though the citizens here don't use this word. It is a word from my home colony. Here they look down on we free and call us things like Fringers, Wraithmen, and my favorite, Lift Lepers."

"Seems like poor titles to carry," I replied, understanding the sentiment. Except for the noble persona he was endeavoring to create, the man was a transient like the homeless people back on Earth. "So, you're homeless?" I asked, thinking this an innocuous inquiry.

"Am I?" The man asked with an edge to his voice, gesturing around him. "Do I not have a roof over my head? Do I not have a place to eat? A place to sleep?" he responded, gesturing to a bench beside the avenue. "Have you not seen the Stacked Courts or camped upon the green in any of the hundred arboretums throughout the ship?" He was smiling. I smiled with him once I realized his mood was not soured by the question but invigorated by it. I did not let him avoid the question though and asked it again.

"Every citizen has a cell," he responded. "The Empire sees to that. They're windowless compartments with wall screens that show whatever you wish them to show. If you want to see a glade with a babbling brook, you may request it. If you want to see the towering city abodes of the Angus 9 colony, it is there for your viewing pleasure. But with these, you never feel the sun upon your cheek or the wind with its pollen and perfumes."

"The Empire provides food for everyone free of cost." He looked up and down the byway, spying an open area ahead. "Ah, come with me, my friend. I will show you. I will let you taste of the fruit the Empire provides."

He took the lead, and I followed in his wake. A short distance ahead, the byway intersected with others in a wide-open area. It was a large hub where traveler's paths converged and crossed. Amid it all were half a hundred vendors hawking their wares. There were some fabulous smells mingling with the crowd and several carts with large crowds gathered around them.

I breathed deep and sighed. "It's a food court?"

"A plaza," he corrected, though I didn't see the difference. Hundreds of people lounged on benches and at tables, eating fabulously scented meals that had either been roasted, baked, fried, or grilled, and I suspected it was done to perfection. Or so it seemed. "Would you like food?" Gorjjen asked suddenly. My stomach growled in reply, and I nodded, stepping up to wait outside one of the carts.

"Ah," he says to me, "so you have many cron in a pocket there about?" Gorjjen asked, patting my pockets. I was not familiar with the word and said so. He dipped his fingers in his pocket and produced a coin with some kind of leafy seal upon one side and some ancient man's face upon the other.

"A cron? No. I have no cron." I looked longingly down on the skewers of glazed sweet meats. "You said the Empire feeds everyone. I just assumed . . ." I left off and shrugged as if it did not bother me. I thought my companion had decided to teach me about the Empire's ruthless injustice. I thought he was showing me the dirty underbelly of the beast. He chuckled with good-natured intent and motioned for me to follow.

"The Empire does provide, my friend." He marched me over to a kiosk in the center of the plaza. There were only a couple of people milling around it. They did not look thrilled having to collect their government cheese as it were. Most of the citizenry seemed to shun the kiosk as if there were something ill about it.

Gorjjen pulled the equivalence of a paper bowl from a tube in the side of the kiosk and placed it in a glass-fronted box. There was a screen above it. He scrolled through it reading off a long list of meals I had never heard of before. I just told him to pick out something he liked. He nodded and quickly scrolled down the menu till he found it. He tapped the screen and a timer counted down from thirty. Inside the box, a long needle-looking protuberance descended from a revolving block that moved back and forth along a track. It moved lightning-quick to and fro, covering the bottom of the bowl with a bizarre secretion that solidified as after each pass. As I watched, a crust began to form. As the needle moved, it rose, and as it rose the crust began to look like a baked roll. The needle left a hollowed-out pit in the center.

When it was done printing the roll, Gorjjen selected another menu item, and the food printer began to print out a purplish gelatinous sauce. The sauce slumped and clumped and pooled in the center of the roll. A moment later, a chime sounded, and Gorjjen pulled the bowl from the chamber. I was hesitant to take it from him, but did so, reaching for it politely so as not to offend. He pulled it away with a smile and shoved it in another box.

"One must wait," he advised. On the front of the box was a large square filled with buttons. There was a sudden flash and another chime. When he retrieved the bowl this time, everything was steaming. I realized then that the second box was some sort of flash microwave.

He procured me a spoon and gestured to a recently vacated table. I went with him, and we sat so I could try the food. It almost tasted like a cinnamon bun filled with French onion soup--almost. It was terrible and had the most nauseating after-taste I had ever encountered. It made my stomach churn.

"That is god-awful," I announced, coughing with laughter. Gorjjen spread his hands wide and dipped his head as if in agreement.

"The Empire feeds us, but it doesn't really feed us," he remarked sagely. I couldn't help chuckling. He smiled expansively, and I broke down laughing. He laughed with me. When we were done laughing, I ate the rest of the roll and gravy. I really was hungry, and terrible food or not, I was not the kind of man to waste a meal. He offered to fetch me something more palatable, but I waved off his offer. I suspected every meal that came out of that kiosk probably came with a horrid aftertaste. I ate what I had, because I did not want to have to try and choke down another dish of government food down anytime soon. Better to choke it down now while the nauseating medicine-tasting food was still on my tongue.

"Gorjjen," I called out conversationally when I was done, "how many levels does this ship have?" He thought about it and held up five fingers on one hand and the thumb on his other.

"Six hundred and six levels," he replied, "if you count the utility decks at the bottom and the aquifer." I could see him mentally inventorying all the decks he knew.

"I need to get to one of the lower levels. Do they have elevators on this ship or some transporter system that can get me down there?"

"We have lifts," he confirmed.

"Do they cost cron?" I asked worriedly. He smirked and shook his head.

"I need to get to one of the lower decks. Is there any way you could point me to where these lifts are?"

"Why would you leave this paradise?" he gestured to the ship around him. "This is my favorite level."

"I'm looking for someone," I replied. "She's in trouble."

"Oh. And what kind of trouble would a friend of Daniel Sojourner find herself in?" he asked. I was not sure I wanted to tell him. I did not want him running off to the grey men to collect whatever reward they were offering for my capture.

"She was kidnapped," I murmured, hoping this would not panic the man. He merely shook his head in disdain, clearly agitated with the nature of the crime.

"Sad this. And too much of it of late." He genuinely looked mournful. "Congressmen are being killed, Senators ambushed, Abbots assassinated, and now this. Kidnapping. This is not the first time I have heard of this, friend. Others have been taken. Why even the lady knight that is sister to the Grand Reaper has been taken." He shook his head again. "Why was your friend taken?"

"To delay the Harvest," I replied. "My friend is this lady knight you just mentioned. I've come from the colony to rescue her."

Gorjjen Doricci rarely broke character, but this time he did. He could not help it. He could not stop laughing.

I sat up straight, startled by his laughter and a little incensed by his rudeness.

"What's the joke?" He did not stop to answer—not right away. "You don't think I can save her?"

"All know this, my friend. All. Many search for her. The knights scour all of the Kye O'Ren in search of her," he said, smiling wickedly. "Pity to those fools who did this. When the knights go looking, the knights be finding, and the wicked fools found all end up dying. This is how it is aboard the Kye O'Ren. Baggam's Children will find your lady knight. Of that, all is certain. But the First are bleeding her dry to hide her. They talk about it in all the tunnels."

"I will save her," I declared. "I will not let them kill her." Gorjjen snorted derisively. "You seem to know something about this. Tell me what they're saying in all the tunnels? Tell me about those who took her."

"The First?" Gorjjen muttered, shrugging. "They're the First; the infected." He looked back toward the mouth of the tunnel we had come down, his eyes narrowing. "You say you have no Guilt?" The change in the line of questioning threw me.

"No. I wasn't exactly released. I was a prisoner. I got lucky and took them by surprise." I studied the man who claimed to be a friend and wondered if there was something more sinister about his motivations. "Why do you ask?"

He shrugged, shooting furtive glances toward the crowd. Those looks were beginning to make my skin crawl.

"You'll want to go down to find her, yes?" he piped up suddenly. I nodded, chewing the last of the printed roll. "You'll need clothes, my friend. These are nearly done for. Come, let us find you a more fitting wardrobe."

The clothing he found me was the common clothing worn by those native to the level. I found a vest and a puffy sleeved blouse and dark indigo leggings. We had a problem finding boots in my size at first, but in the end, Gorjjen came through.

I stared at the voluminous sleeves and shook my head, refusing to go out in public dressed like this. An episode of Seinfeld popped into my head unexpectedly, and I giggled under my breath as I remembered the infamous pirate shirt. When Gorjjen realized I was dead set on doing something about the sleeves, he pulled lacings from a pair of boots and twined them around my forearms to batten down the puffiness.

"Do they have elevators that can take us down to the lower levels?" I asked of my new friend. He seemed to consider the question. He watched as I hid the black wand up my right sleeve. He offered me another lace to lash it in place. I began to wonder if this wand was anything like the trackable police gear on Earth. Gorjjen interrupted my wandering mind.

"We have lifts that can take you up or down as you see fit or left, right, forward, and back," Gorjjen replied.

"I just want to go down. She's down there. Below us."

"How is this known to you?" Gorjjen asked curiously.

"I can feel her," I tapped my temple. I thought about sending my mind down to check on her, but I did not trust Gorjjen enough not to report me while I was spaced out.

"You're an empath?" he asked, interested in me all over again.

"I'm a telepath," I corrected, not realizing that they were basically the same thing. He looked over my shoulder sharply, like a dog catching sight of a squirrel, and quickly grabbed my hand. This he used to pull me along in his wake, urging me to hurry.

"What is it?" I asked, looking back. I could not see what he was fleeing. I started to push my mind out toward the crowd behind us, but it gave me a quick but smart smack across my right cheek. I almost struck him, but he held his hands up hurriedly to stop me.

"I meant no harm. I meant no harm. You must never touch their minds. You must not touch the minds of strangers here or anywhere aboard the Kye O'Ren. It is dangerous," he warned.

"I've been in other people's minds before, Gorjjen. I know what I'm doing." I was a little cocky in this claim and a bit of a liar.

"How do you know one of them isn't a First Colony insurgent?" he asked. "How do you know? You don't know. No one knows till it is too late. Never touch their minds."

"I'm fine with that. I am. Just tell me what the big deal is?" I demanded. "Why is everyone so nervous where these First Colonists are concerned. I've been picking up snippets here and there for days. I know the Grand Reaper fears them. A friend of mine back on the planet warned me to stay out of their minds too. Why is everyone scared of these people?" Gorjjen looked back toward the tunnel we had vacated and hurried me down a side corridor. Here was where we found the lifts. "Why can't you answer a simple question? Why is it such a big secret?"

"Not here. I will tell, but later. After we are on the lifts, I will tell all." He looked back again, cursing under his breath. We did not have long to wait. The lifts went on for as far as I could see and there were lifts arriving and leaving every few minutes. Calling them lifts seemed disingenuous though. They seemed more a cross between a subway car and a ski lift. They were huge on the inside, reminding me of the yellow school bus that came to pick up my neighbor's kids in Cherryville.

"Fine," I said in surrender, as the lift doors opened. The liftman was a frail old man. His skin was wrinkled and shriveled and hanging loose on his frame. He opened the door to let us in and grimaced when he caught sight of Gorjjen.

"Where to, good sirs?" he asked, stressing the word sirs so that it sounded condescending. I looked to my companion.

"Which level did you say the knights were searching for the lady knight?" I asked. Gorjjen made a rude gesture toward the crowd behind us—for no reason I could fathom—and turned to the liftman.

"Take us down to Level 12. Quad 3," Gorjjen said, patting the liftman's cheek insultingly. I frowned, not liking this side of the man, but I said nothing.

"Seats 23 and 25," The liftman replied, turning away in a huff.

Gorjjen hurried through the car and sprawled on a seat in the corner, throwing both legs up on the seat next to him so he could lounge in comfort. He put his back to the wall, crossed his ankles, and studied the door.

The seat he took was not the one assigned. The number on it said seat 40. I was nervous sitting in non-assigned seats, but there were very few people on the lift. I did not understand the significance of the numbers. I did not know that it was these numbers the liftman would call when our destination was reached. I decided to take a seat opposite my new friend so I could keep an eye on him. He pretended to be relaxed, but he kept his eyes on the lift door until the moment they closed. When they finally did close, he blew a blast of air that turned into a sigh of relief.

"You wanted to know about the First?" Gorjjen asked. "Let me tell you about the First Colony."

Outside the lift, two men stood staring at the closed lift doors, then shared a look that spoke volumes to each other. With a tired sigh, the dark-haired man on the right made the call, making use of his NID. He waited for a response. Baggam Rain was not happy his men lost the trail, but he understood that shadowing people on lift was near impossible. He relieved the two and made the call to the lower substations himself, putting each level on alert, and transferring the transmitter identification number in the baton that was with Magpie. Every knight on the lower levels was watching that signal's progress. So, it was a surprise to all when the signal suddenly stopped on the lowest level of the ship and suddenly made its way to a Grey Guard sentry outpost near the aquifer.

A pair of knights converged on the outpost and discovered that their target was not there. The baton was and so was the Guardsmen who found it, but there was no sign of Daniel.

Baggam was less than pleased.

Chapter 16: Captive

Leia could tell they were coming. The water rippled and surged as they waded through it. She tried to keep her breathing shallow, holding it for when the water covered her mouth. Somewhere far overhead, a loud knock sounded, followed by the whining hum of a transfer case and the fluttering chop of fan blades as they struggled to get up to speed.

Leia clenched her teeth, nostrils flaring, and focused like Luke had taught her. She focused on one point far away, keeping her mind just out of reach. She felt their hands on her arms, but she did not resist. It was a futile act to resist. On her best day one of them was a challenge, and when she had been grabbed there had been seven. Although only six of them walked away from that ambush. She was not sure how the fight ended, but she suspected that she might have bit her attacker's throat out. When she came to and the drugs finally left her system, she found she had big chunks of meat in her teeth. Not that it mattered right now. All that mattered was keeping her mind out of reach. What mattered was that she keep her mind focused on that single point; that single thought; that singular refuge. What mattered was that she persevere.

She was laying with Him in her mind again. With Daniel, that is. Once, this fantasy had been his, and she had just been there to watch. She realized when she was watching that Daniel was not the burly, uncouth, uncultured slob he pretended to be. In his mind, he was elegant and graceful, pure, passionate, and almost divine. She was not sure he even knew that about himself. But there it was. This was the Daniel she saw in her mind. It was why she kept going back. He made her want to bask in his radiance. The fantasy she was hiding in used to be his, but now that she needed his radiance to protect her, the fantasy was hers and it was saving her life.

She imagined his fingers tracing the naked flesh again, tickling the skin between her knee and hip. Shivers of excitement ran ringingly through the core of her being. She felt that tingle of excitement pulse and scratch at her with distracting intensity, and she found herself clenching and unclenching her stomach and legs every time one of those aftershocks rolled through her; every time she imagined the feel of his body beneath the sheets, every time she offered him her lips; every time she felt his breath hot and wet upon her neck.

Water splashed her face. For a moment, she spluttered, inhaling some. Their minds fell upon her like wolves upon an injured hare, tearing at her sanity, but she was still strong enough to flee, and she did. She fled back into his arms, throwing up her wall behind her.

The First Colonists raised her from the pool of water where she lay. This was no longer in her mind. They raised her dripping and cold and pulled their knives across her legs and stomach, slicing her open enough for the blood to run red and free. Bowls were thrust beneath the wounds. Blood filled them before it had a chance to mix with the water below.

When they had enough, they let her go, dropping her back into the cold water with a splash. She shivered from blood loss, but they did not care. The weaker she was, the easier she would let them in. The assassins passed their bowls of blood to others in their group and her blood was sopped up with folded rags so that they could stain the lifts, loiterers, and unaware travelers with it to throw off the battalion of knights searching for her.

Are you scared? the Daniel she imagined asked.

No. I'm an Imperial Knight, she snapped hotly, as if that was all the reason she needed to prove her claim.

You're still a person. He raked his fingers lightly through her hair. It felt good.

Knights know no fear, Leia declared stubbornly, lifting her chin with pride so that she could look him in his soft brown eyes.

Weren't you fearful when they told you your father was gone? You were so small back then, hiding beneath your quilts. You were terrified. All you had was Luke, but then he joined the order and went away. He left you behind. They all left you behind, he said, an accusation in his tone.

You shut your mouth! she growled, turning on him.

Don't you fear what waits for you in the dark? Everyone fears the dark, Leia. Everyone. You can't be the child and the monster all time. Sometimes you must pick one or the other. You were a child back then. It was your duty to be afraid. Then, you were the monster, loving the feel of your nanite blade wading through the flesh of your enemies. You're a prisoner in your mind, Leia, locked in behind a wall with monsters waiting without. No one will blame you. No one will blame you if you become that child again. Let me protect you. Let me shield you from the evil things.

She studied him for a moment, and pushed him away, kicking her feet over the side of the bed in which they lay. His words were meant to be comforting, meant to be permission to her, excusing her for this one moment of vulnerability, but they were not. It made her angry instead.

That's shit, she declared. *It's our truth that we are the monsters in the dark, and we are those children hiding in those beds. We are one and both and one, and we've just got really good at hiding in the one till it's our turn to hide in the other. I don't fear the darkness because I am in the darkness. To fear it is to fear myself and that makes no sense. So you ask me, do I fear the dark? No. I fear what happens when I let the darkness out!*

She studied his eyes, yellow and pale, and wondered how he could be so cruel as to want her weak. The yellow eyes were what brought her to her senses. Panic surged within her, and she fled back into herself, strengthening her wall anew. She had almost let it fall. He had almost gotten in, and she had almost opened the door without a fight.

"Get out of my head!" she growled, pushing back against the abyss. The yellow eyes retreated, hissing and spitting in protest. She flung herself back into her fantasy and once again it was only the touch of Daniel's fingers upon her naked flesh.

She did not open her eyes. She could not. If she saw them there, perched like vultures about her, she would stumble in her resolve, and he would come for her again.

She lay still, bringing her breath down to a slow inhale and an even slower exhale. Her breath grew so soft it barely disturbed the surface of the water in which she lay. Soon, it was just the sound of the fan overhead. She did not make a sound and neither did the nine colonials from the First Colony who watched over her. They squatted silently in the water around her, their minds dead, their bodies still, and each unaware. They had stopped fighting Yellow Eyes long ago. They had let the darkness in long ago, and now they watched and waited. He watched and waited. She would drop her guard eventually. He knew this. Everyone dropped their guard in the end. And when she did, he would make her his own.

Everyone gets converted.

Chapter 17: Fine Dining

An Imperial Soldier can be an imposing figure. They are more savage and disciplined than a Grey Guardsman, but they lack the telepathic and equipment sophistication of an Imperial Knight. And in an Empire where almost everything runs like clockwork, Imperial Soldiers have become more of an honor guard for the monastic orders. Sometimes, there are inter-level conflicts aboard one of the ships and the Imperial Soldier is tasked with putting down the uprising.

Each ship and country in the Empire has its own battalions of Imperial Soldiers. Not every ship suffers these inter-level conflicts though. So, Imperial Soldiers watch and stand guard and chaperone and shadow prisoners who are summoned from the prison level. Today, it was a soldier called Empeagrii tasked with the chore of retrieving a prisoner from holding.

Right away, he was smitten with her beauty. She carried herself with regal grace tainted only with a sadness of which she would not speak. Empeagrii was a good soldier and knew not to question her or speak to her. He did puff out his chest and anoint her person with many smiles, and though he tried to put meaning into each look to communicate with her, Empeagrii ultimately knew failure.

She carried herself like a lady of high birth. The soldier tried to discern the reason for her incarceration, but there were no clues about her person. He almost broke the rules, opening his mouth several times to speak to her, but each time, he closed his mouth and looked to his toes for advice. When they at last arrived at their destination, the elegant lady turned to her chaperone and smiled.

"Thank you, sir," she said, dipping her head. "Your nervous fawning was quite amusing, and I will miss it." He stood dumbstruck, unsure how to respond. In the end he closed his mouth and opened the door. This was the only right way to respond, according to his watch commander. He was a little man with little man insecurities. Empeagrii wanted no part of him, and so, he obeyed the rules and said nothing to her. To those within, he clearly announced the prisoner's arrival.

"The prisoner, Palasa," he said aloud, backing away so that she might enter. With his duty done, he retreated to the end of the corridor and served as sentry until those inside consigned her once more to his care. Until then, he had his daydreams in which she figured prominently.

You didn't tell me she would be lovely. I feel betrayed, Lord Merrik teased. She dipped her head in acknowledgement of the compliment. He turned on his companion, playfully remonstrating the man. "Luke, why did you not tell me she was beautiful. I would have received her in a more lavish manner. I'm very put out with you, my son." To the prisoner, he gestured to a seat opposite his. "Please, Lady Palasa, would you join me?"

"Thank you for the kindness, Daimyo." She accepted the seat and took in the room. It was a lavish cell. Rich burgundy carpet, thick and soft, covered the floor. Several priceless paintings covered two of the walls like windows, and like windows, thick curtains framed them. Statues and figurines from every colony decorated the shelves and corners. Canned Witchfire lit the corners, aimed to direct the shadows away from the priceless art they showcased. An intricately carved bookcase stood against the far wall and rare volumes with hand stitched bindings decorated them.

The Daimyo reclined, completely at ease. His shoes were absent, but soft slippers covered his feet. Luke stood behind the Daimyo, staring out a broad portal and down at the dark side of the Earth. Cities glowed on the surface, showing up brightly like some giant hand had embroidered the darkness with gold thread. Palasa looked down on the only home she had known for the last four hundred years.

"It's quite lovely, isn't it?" Lord Merrik remarked, rising to join Luke.

"It's unique," she confirmed. "There's no place would I rather live." This statement seemed to bother the Daimyo. He stayed quite for several moments as if deciding how to broach the conversation he had brought her here for. Luke refused to look at her. This worried her. She did not try to sniff his thoughts. Other than being rude, in his present mood, he might take it as an act of espionage.

"Tell me something, Lady Palasa—It is Lady, yes? You are the Lady Palasa who served as second lieutenant to the second Grand Reaper; to Prior Magpie himself?" The Daimyo gave a little snort of laughter. "We had to go back into the archives to discover this. It was no easy feat."

"Lord, all you need to have done was ask. I have no guilt for what was done. We did it to save you and them and him." She gestured to Luke.

"Perhaps," Lord Merrik mused, distracted. He turned to the Grand Reaper beside him and placed a strong comforting hand on Luke's shoulder. "The Pre-Prior, my friend and surrogate son, wanted to turn you and Magpie over to the Inquisitors. I think he wanted you and the Prior to experience the ministrations of a Grand Inquisition."

Palasa felt an involuntary shudder of fear run down her spine.

"But you thought otherwise?" she asked, licking her lips nervously.

"I did. In the days after that First Harvest, what Prior Magpie did would easily have earned you and him and the rest of your confederates a Grand Inquisition or worse. There was so much anger back then. So much ignorance. Rather than try to wring the story from you and risk you lying, I thought this would be a more pleasant and effective way to get you to open up about what happened." Luke gave her a scathing look but stayed silent. As if on cue, a swarm of guest-masters swept into the room, each carrying a tray of Cojokarueen delicacies. There were dishes among them that Palasa had not tasted since she had settled Earth with her mother.

"Come. Dine with us and tell us your story, sweet Lady Palasa, the Flame in the Forest." She studied the pair and rose, nodding that she would accept his kind overture.

Yes. Tell us of your sins, Luke added. Her eyes narrowed, and she felt a cold trickle of sweat. Luke's animosity rolled off him like smoke off a burning house. Palasa was suddenly very nervous.

They settled in around the circular table, Luke and Lord Merrick dividing the table into thirds with how far they sat from one another. Palasa took her seat, completing the pattern they started. Three guest-masters remained, and they carefully ladled soups and gravies onto the roast meats and vegetables. The Daimyo leaned in and breathed deeply of the food. Eating was one of his guilty pleasures.

"Do they have Fauvian game birds down in the colony?" the Daimyo inquired, making polite conversation.

"They have a variation of the bird. They call it pheasants," she replied.

"Pheasant," he repeated the word as if tasting a sip of a new wine to see if he liked it. It seemed he did. "Pheasant then.

Maybe you weren't missing out quite as badly as I had thought," he said with a smile.

Palasa looked at her plate and shrugged.

"They don't have anything like ja-ja fruit in the colony," she revealed, slicing into one of the purpled fruits. "They don't have Kaden spears either," she told him, brushing the long vegetable in question with her fork tines.

"Then this is quite the treat for you," the Daimyo observed, raising his glass in salute.

"There were things I missed," she confirmed. Luke sighed heavily and all eyes went to him.

"Perhaps, I should start?" she suggested.

"For Luke's sake, I believe maybe you might." Lord Merrik smiled to soften the moment.

Lady Palasa stared out the window, and down onto the planet as she decided where to start her tale. She nodded absently as if confirming that a point had been picked.

"The armada had been tasked by the Emperor to harvest the imperial colonies to help maintain the population densities at a manageable level. Protocols were established and tolerances exacted. Above all else, the colonials were guaranteed certain rights. Foremost among them was the right to freely practice and retain their religious beliefs in the colony and on the ships," she said, informing them of facts they should already know.

"The Emperor is a fair man, and this is known to us," Lord Merrik observed, taking the opportunity to speak highly of his cousin.

"Indeed," she told him in full agreement, "but even a god king can be wrong at times." This made the Daimyo's brow crease with irritation. "With more experience, we might have understood that blindly following this precept of free religious belief carried with it certain consequences. If we had thought to question it, we could have saved billions of lives."

*If you and Prior Magpie hadn't—*Lord Merrik raised a hand to forestall Luke's hateful accusation.

"We have invited her here to tell her side of things, not to lay accusation, my son." Luke fell silent, dipping his head in acknowledgement of the point.

You are, of course, right, great Daimyo, Luke replied in a more respectful tone.

"You do not agree with this freedom of religion?" Merrik asked.

"I agree with it. I'm just saying that there is no universal rule. Every situation is different. We should have questioned this precept before arriving at the Sylar colony. I didn't know what to expect upon arriving any more than anyone else. I suppose we all expected them to be afraid, to be panicked, or at least apprehensive at our unexpected arrival, but they weren't."

You say they were not? Luke asked, joining in on the conversation. There was an edge to his question, but he kept his voice calm and cordial out of respect for the Daimyo.

"They were not. They accepted our arrival as if they'd been waiting centuries for it. They perched like carrion birds everywhere. They perched in windows and the edges of roof tops. They perched like something less than human. And Prior Magpie was the first to question this. He was the first to question the wisdom of blindly following the Emperor's mandates. He sensed something wrong with the Sylar colonists. In that first three hundred rotations that we waited and watched; one thing struck him as odd." Lord Merrik and Luke listened, hanging on every word.

"The Sylar colonists only practiced one religion," she said. The Daimyo and Luke seemed unimpressed with this.

Strange, but not unheard of, Luke remarked.

"True, and this was Magpie's opinion. He did, however, bring it to Abbot Aug Moon's—the First Reaper—attention. I know we're supposed to revere our reapers, but Aug Moon was a vain aristocrat appointed by the Emperor. It was an act of nepotism. He ignored Magpie's warning and reaped the colony anyway. He is the one responsible for what happened that day."

"It only became apparent later, midway through the Harvest, that what Magpie feared was actually coming to pass. There was something terribly wrong with the colonists," she said this in a soft murmur, as if reliving that first Harvest.

Terribly wrong? Luke queried. *You are of course referring to the Sylar virus.*

"I am, though this is what you call it. Magpie doesn't believe it to be a virus. He thinks it's a parasite. It spread like fire at zero gravity through the ships, and Aug Moon was the first infected. People known to worship the gods of the Empire suddenly and quite unexplainably began to worship at the makeshift altars of the harvested colonists. Six ships had become infected before Magpie realized action needed to be taken. Aug Moon and the Daimyo of that time were aboard those vessels, and it was with a heavy heart that the Prior called for their destruction."

You're telling me that he couldn't just quarantine them till a cure was found? Luke snapped. Lady Palasa looked to the Daimyo for an explanation for the outburst.

"Luke's father was aboard Fire Jammer, one of those ships Magpie destroyed. This is more personal for him than it is for us. He holds Prior Magpie personally responsible for the death of his father," Lord Merrik explained. Lady Palasa's first instinct was to apologize for the man's loss but looking into the Pre-Prior's eyes showed her there was no forgiveness to be had from him.

"You say Magpie believes that the sickness is a parasite instead?" Lord Merrik asked, coughing gently.

How could he know such a thing? Luke asked, with a sneer.

"Indeed," Lord Merrik said, lending the support of his voice to that of his surrogate son. He coughed gently, pulling at his collar with one finger.

"Daimyo?" Palasa called out of concern. "Daimyo, are you well?"

Luke who had been sneering throughout the story, suddenly abandoned it out of concern for the man next to him. Lord Daimyo began to turn red, coughing hoarsely. His last mouthful of ja-ja fruit sprayed the spread.

"What's wrong with him?" Lady Palasa demanded, rising to tend the man.

"Poison. He's been poisoned. Help! Guards! Lord Merrik's been poisoned," Luke yelled to no guard in particular.

Lady Palasa came around the table and kneeled next to her host. "What can I do?" she asked frantically.

Don't you think you've done enough? he snarled. She looked at him and realized he was blaming her for this.

"No," she responded, using a table knife to cut a tube from the embroidered edge of the tablecloth.

"Don't touch him," Luke spat, breaking his vow of silence again.

"Don't be stupid. The poison is closing his throat. He's going to suffocate," she declared. Luke began to draw in his will. Palasa ignored him and went to work on the dying man. If the Daimyo was going to die, it was not going to be because she did nothing.

Chapter 18: Identities

"It was a planet of the sick, a virus disguising itself as a religion. They say that during the first Harvest, the First Reaper became infected. He knew what this virus was after and stocked the ships with these diseased . . . perchers. These people who squatted and watched with glistening eyes spread their foulness to the fleet.

They say a Prior took the old Reaper's place and burnt away the colony with fire from the long guns. Some say he used rockets. It was a tragedy for all. Some say he was brutal and cruel, a sadist. They say when he saw that the sickness had spread to those on the ship, he called out to the Harvest Council to determine what could be done. The Council was of two minds. Some wanted to quarantine the infected ships, which I think the Prior would have allowed had the infected stayed put. But, they didn't. They started sending out skiffs to the rest of the fleet, and in this way, the infection began to spread. The Prior—this Magpie—he was able to convince some of the ships, those that hadn't taken on refugees, to separate themselves from the rest of the fleet. The moment he had them separated, he opened fire, destroying the polluted saucers. No one knows how he gained access to the Battle Bridge or how he was able to subdue those within, but he did. Billions died that day. Not thousands. Not millions. Billions. Among those killed was an Abbot and the Daimyo governing over the fleet.

When word of this reached the Emperor, it's said he ordered the Harvest Council to take the Prior into custody. He was to face justice for what he had done. However, the Prior refused to board the ships that'd taken on the infected and the refugees fleeing the destroyed ships. Instead, he fled with the ships he'd convinced to separate from the armada. The hundred or so ships he convinced to leave the main fleet are known now as the Drift. Most just call them Drifters though. This Magpie, this new Reaper, most label him the Butcher of Sylar, but to those like me, to those who have seen this sickness firsthand, he's a hero. He saved us.

Of course, those are just stories. That hardly makes them true. There are some people who tell tales in the plazas and at the mini-shows who actually believe that the Prior will return someday to save us from the First, from the colonists of Sylar."

Gorjjen finished his tale and fished a bottle from his pocket and took a swig from it then passed it to me. I took it hesitantly. It smelled like plums but also like scotch and honey. It was moderately disgusting. I took another swig before passing it back.

The lift bumped and shook as it dropped. How many levels we had passed, I had no idea. From what Gorjjen had said, the ride down to twelve would take a little over a knell. After ten minutes of discussing what a knell was with my companion, I was able to discover it to be approximately an hour. Talk of the First had irked me, especially since I knew that this Magpie he spoke of was me. I found it preposterous that someone would think me a hero, but at the same time, I could not really imagine me killing a billion people either. I was just a dirty redneck with no people skills and a bad credit score.

"You said your sister and poog?" I asked, recalling something he had mentioned earlier.

"What about them?" he asked, surprised by the question.

"You said you came on board with your sister and her infant daughter. Where are they? Surely, they miss you? Don't you miss them?" I asked.

"My friend, of course I miss them, but let's not speak of them now. You will only sadden me, as you have done with all these sad stories you have made me tell." Gorjjen took a pull from the bottle. His eyes grew distant like they were seeing another time.

"Did something happen to them?" I could see the question distressed him, but I was curious about the man. As a newcomer to the ship, I felt it only right that I learn as much as I could about my companion, so I waited for him to summon up the courage to answer me.

"Death. It's what happens to us all. It happened to them," he replied with a mournful sigh.

"An accident?" I guessed, but he was already shaking his head.

"Alas, not, my friend. Alas, not. Old age. They lived a long and happy life, but in the end, the Shadow Man takes us all. This is as it was for them." Gorjjen offered me his bottle again, but I waved it off.

"Old age?" I asked, looking at the man before me. He was barely thirty. "How could they have died of old age? Was your sister that much older than you?"

"Older, no. She was my youngling sister, five years my youth," he said.

"What about your niece? Her daughter? Surely, she needs you." I was not understanding the gist of what he was saying evidently. Even if his sister had died, his niece would surely need him. I began to wonder what type of man Gorjjen was to run out on family as he apparently had. He was smiling, and he spread his arms expansively once more as if to show off his slender frame.

"I look good, no? Yes, my niece as you call her, she too has passed on. The old age took her as well. This left only Gorjjen the Great, wanderer of the realm we call the Kye O'Ren." He could see I was confused, and he turned to face me, putting his feet on the floor. "See my friend. I have the implant. My sister and her poog did not. They said it was wrong and unnatural. Wrong? Perhaps. But who does not want to live forever?" He showed me a scar on his neck. He was smiling, but there was a sadness about him. "They never tell you how lonely it will be." My fingers went unconsciously to the small scar on my own neck. It was a tiny scar, but like Gorjjen's, it was there on me as well.

"This implant lets you live forever?" I asked.

"What is forever? It lets you live long. It throws the switch, my friend. No more growing old. No more happy meals with loved ones. No more watching the little one play after first meal. Forever is a lonely path. Pray you never take the implant. It is better for life to be short. It stays fresh. In this way, each day is a gift. Be a smarter man than me. Okay, my friend?" I nodded and considered his words, understanding for the first time that I really could be this Magpie person everyone thought me to be.

"Your billy," Gorjjen said, holding out his hand. I had no idea what he was talking about.

"What?"

Gorjjen smiled. "It took me some time to figure it out, but if you have no Guilt to follow you, then who could they be?"

I was confused still. "Someone is following me?"

"Two men. I see them since we met. They look like knights, but dress common like us. Since Gorjjen is loved by all, then I think, they must be after you. But who could want my new friend? This makes me think of the grey men you took the billy from. The baton, my friend. They follow the billy." He kept his hand out, and reluctantly, I removed it from my sleeve and laid it in his hand. He looked at it, then looked at me, and for a moment, I was worried he was going to use it to take me prisoner, but instead, he smiled and slipped it behind his seat.

"We let them chase your billy instead for a while, yes?" He grinned, and I couldn't help but grin with him.

We hit Level 12 a few minutes later and disembarked. The liftman seemed happy to see us go. We made it twelve feet before the reality of our situation became apparent. There were Greys everywhere. Standing there in the byway, we watched as three squad of knights passed us, each headed in a different direction.

"Whoa," I whispered in awe.

"Indeed, my friend."

I pushed my mind out in search of Leia. She was not on this level. She was close, but not here. I could feel her, but she still felt like she was down and forward. I pushed gently toward her mind, creeping into her mind. I sensed that dark presence again. I was trying to get into her mind, but so was it—they—Him. The darkness stopped attacking her, and I realized nervously that Yellow Eyes knew I was there.

Yoooou! The darkness cried in sudden recognition. *YOOOOOU!* And he came for me. His anger preceded him like the tip of a sword. I fled, leaving Leia behind . . . again.

"We have to hurry," I said to Gorjjen. "He's trying to get in her head."

"Who, my friend? Who is this you speak of?" He gave me a quizzical look and I shrugged. I had no name for him—for it.

"Yellow Eyes. The thing inside the infected. I sensed it. It's trying to get into her mind." I looked about, helplessly. Gorjjen backed away tracing a circular pattern in the air before him. I had never seen it before, but I recognized the motion. It was his version of tracing the cross to ward off the evil eye. "We need another lift. We need to go down."

"No, my friend. You say you've touched their minds. This is no good. You could be infected now. It's best I go my way. This is best." He started to walk away, but I hurried to get before him.

"Please. I just want to find her. I left the moment it sensed me. Just . . . I have to save her. I don't know why. I just have to. Help me find her." Maybe it was the look in my eyes. Maybe Gorjjen recognized a sadness like his own. I do not know, but the man relented, and motioned for me to follow.

"Come. I know a place. A place where my kind gather. Let us go and find what we can. We cannot find her unless we hunt. And we can't hunt empty handed. What would you do if you found her? They will have many. We are two, and I call you friend, but know, I have no wish to die beside you. The lady knight means nothing to me. People die. People do. But I see it in you. You need her," he told me.

"Need her? No. She's just attractive. I have a weakness for pretty girls," I corrected.

"You need her, my friend. You have a darkness in you: A guilt. I know not from whence it comes, but you have a guilt that shows as sadness in your eyes. Look at me, my friend. Look at these sad noble eyes of mine. They are windows behind which my guilt lives. See them. These eyes are your eyes, my friend. Lie to others, but never lie to yourself. You need this woman. You need her to help you fight your darkness." He held me by the shoulders, and I had to dip my head to acknowledge his words before he would let me go.

Did I need her to help me fight a darkness? A memory I did not remember flashed into my mind. It was me and her fighting zombies. I had absolutely no idea when we would have done something like that, but she was smiling while she fought them.

"Where do we go?" I asked. He smiled and gestured off to the left.

He led me down the byway, strolling straight down the center. The Grey Guard and the patrols of knights ignored us, giving us no mind. They seemed to be more interested in some type of pub on the right side of the byway as we passed, and this made me smirk. Soldiers and cops were the same the universe over. They worked together. They drank together.

The place Gorjjen took us was several corridors off the main byway. I tried to keep track, but it was hard to keep the curving corridors straight. Where we ended up looked like a small park. It was roughly a half-mile wide by twice that long, and my mind shrank as I considered how this wide-open field could be located in the middle of a star ship. Gorjjen must have sensed my amazement.

"This? This is nothing. You should see the arboretums near the outside of the ship. There are massive fields that go on for miles, with trees six and ten times the height of a man. Those parks are astounding. This is just a place where the people bring their children. Where the soft women bring their pets to walk and other things." He wrinkled his nose at other things.

He paused at the entrance to the park and searched the area for signs of life. There were women and young children walking dogs and other strange beasts. There were cat-eared foxes, horrid looking cats with tall-pointed ears and elongated canine muzzles, and lizards with small saddles that some of the little children rode while their parents walked them around a small track. It was by far the strangest thing I had seen so far.

"This way," Gorjjen called, pulling me toward the far edge of the park. It was a long walk, but when we arrived, I discovered it was not for naught. There were people like him lounging beneath a support girder in a small alcove.

I looked out at the park, mesmerized by its size and realized for the first time that I should not be that astounded by it. On the news that first week the ships arrived over Earth, they described the ships as being roughly the size of Iowa. Only Iowa does not have over six hundred levels. The diameter of the ship may be the size of Iowa, but each of these ships was much, much larger than that. If Gorjjen was right, each of the ships was six hundred and six times the size of Iowa. No wonder it took so long to reach Level 12 by lift. I was traveling roughly a hundred miles to reach it.

Gorjjen placed a hand upon my chest and bade me to stay. I did while he headed toward the group to make introductions. When he finally motioned me forward, I did so, warily. They looked less than trustworthy.

There were four of them. There were three women and a man. They reclined on scavenged items. One looked as if the bag he sat upon had come from some college kid's dorm room. It looked every bit the part of a bean bag. Though, I had never seen a bean bag recliner before. Despite the setting, it looked comfortable. The man sitting in it wore a white long-sleeved tunic with a long green coat over it. His hair had not been washed in a while and looked greasy. The white tunic was stained several times over. His leggings had been a dark indigo like mine once, but they had faded out atop the thighs and knees. The right knee had a hole in it that was fraying. His boots looked new though.

The three women were not any more attractive. Two of them were desperately in need of pilates and a Gold Gym membership. Not to say I had a problem with overweight women, because that simply was not the case. But there is an obese person, then there is an *obese* person. These women looked like their flesh was melting off them. I tried not to gawk. They each wore large muumuu type tops made of big multicolored patches. Their leggings looked like brown sweatpants.

The other girl was count-her-ribs skinny like she did not know where the free food kiosk was located. Her thick hair was in bad need of being cut and jutted off in every direction like brown tongues of flame. She wore a satin blue top with a plunging neckline and cream-colored leggings worn thin about the knees. Her eyes were dark circles. She glanced over at me, looking me up and down as if she were looking at a meal. She pulled out a pencil, uncapped it and began to trace a dark line around her eye with it. Gorjjen tried to hide his disgust, but I saw his sneer. The skinny woman disgusted him more than the obese women did. I figured it was because the woman wore no bra and was being embarrassingly obvious in her showcase of her breast. Her top was very loose and with how she was sitting, there was nothing to hide her pink-nippled treats. I tried not to stare. I failed miserably though.

"So, Gorjjen here says you want to know about that there armored piece of ass that was taken by the perchers?" the man on the bean bag announced. I tried not to take offense at his reference to Leia. Gorjjen was not as controlled as me. He stomped hard on the bean bag between the man's splayed legs, causing the bag to throw him forward. Gorjjen grabbed the man by the hair as he came flying forward.

"Be respectful," Gorjjen commanded. The man tried to nod his understanding, but Gorjjen was not interested in his response just his actions. He shoved the man backwards into the chair. I felt a tingling sensation in the air behind me, and I looked to the three women.

"If you're drawing in your will to attack him, don't" I warned heatedly. The big woman in the middle looked up and sneered at me, but the tingling subsided.

"Thank you, my friend," Gorjjen said, giving the big woman the stink eye to let her know he knew it was her. She looked away.

"And yes. I want to hear what they're saying on this level about the Lady Knight's abduction."

Gorjjen stepped forward and gestured to each of the people in kind starting with the man to whom I was speaking and ending with the skinny girl in the blue top. "Roga, Riga, Rime, and Jalequise. Riga and Rime are sisters; twins I believe." I studied the two larger ladies and saw no facial similarities to give evidence of this, but Gorjjen seemed sure of this.

"She was taken from outside her parent's cell. A grey man who questioned us said they coated the door handle with posq oil." Rime looked to Roga over on the bean bag as if seeking his approval. He nodded that it was okay to speak.

"Posq oil," Gorjjen explained, "is a narcotic. It burns the skin and makes you sleep. It's very rare but effective. This would be the best way to take your Lady Knight unawares."

"They didn't take her unawares. Not entirely. She killed one of them perchers," Jalequise blurted, wanting to be in on the telling. "They say your Lady Knight, she bit one of them percher's throats out. Chewed it up like it was a sweet meat from the plaza." I couldn't help but smile at this. This was just how I expected Leia to behave.

"She traveled all the way down here just to visit her mom and dad?" I asked.

"Naw. Not from what they say. This is her neighborhood. She still lives with her parents, but she has others here to see. Like her Unc who owns the bar back on the byway. She also has friends here about. I feel bad for your Lady Knight. No one ever comes back after a percher gets them. They either convert 'em or kill 'em." The skinny girl fell back against the wall, her eyes growing unfocused.

"The bar her uncle owns. Is it that officer bar we passed on the way from the lifts?" I asked.

"Yeah. A real screw that one. He's as hard as long division. Used to be a knight 'imself, before he went and got gimped up. Her pa too. She came from a line of knights. She's a legacy that one." Jalequise signed deeply, running her hands down the inside of her thighs. If she were a cat, she'd be purring. Gorjjen's sneer returned.

"Her friends, are they all knights as well?" Gorjjen asked before I could.

"Not all. The Pig is an Imperial Soldier. He was there with the others drinking with her before she went a missin'," Riga confessed.

"The Pig?" I asked, wondering what kind of man earns the nickname The Pig. My imagination was not much impressed with a man by that name.

"Aye. They also call him Fearless on account of the man knows no fear," Riga added. "Could be a woman needs a man like that about on occasion." Roga flashed her a rude gesture in response and Gorjjen chuckled.

"Where can we find The Pig?" Gorjjen demanded. I looked at the man in confusion. "We need weapons," he replied as if that explained it all.

"They'll know over at the barracks," Riga answered. "Just ask to see The Pig or Fearless. He's kind of famous right now being as he's the Lady Knight's friend and all. Gorjjen pulled a cron from his pocket and flicked it to Riga and gave the big lady a wink. I gave the man a startled look, but he just shrugged as we walked off. "What?"

"You and her?" I asked. He blushed a bright red.

"I've always liked big ladies," he told me firmly.

"Yes," I said, glancing back. "Yes, you do." He blushed even redder.

I glanced back to the four people fighting over the cron Gorjjen had given them and noticed the skinny girl trying to take it from the others. She seemed out of her head and delirious.

"What's her story? The skinny one?" I asked. Gorjjen glanced back and that sneer of his reappeared.

"An addict," he quipped.

"That pencil she used on her eyes?" I guessed.

He nodded before elaborating. "It's a popular drug aboard the ships. The grey men try to stomp it out, but it's easy to make, so it keeps popping up over and over. I have no love for that kind. No love, my friend." He spat in her direction.

As it turned out, the barracks were just off the byway but past the lifts. We walked the center of the byway again, but near the lifts, I caught Gorjjen glancing back over his shoulder as he had done on the upper levels.

"What's wrong?" I asked. He shook his head as if it were nothing. "Come on, don't do that. If we're being followed, then just tell me."

"We're being followed," he announced without hesitation.

"Knights?" I asked.

"I don't think so. Knights usually track in pairs. There are three of them following us, and they look small to be knights." He gestured toward a side corridor, and we ducked into it quickly. "Come, I know a place." The moment we hit the corridor and were out of sight of those who followed, Gorjjen sprinted off ahead. I ran after, struggling to keep up. I glanced back as we reached a bend in the corridor and saw the three he thought were following us. They were in fact following us, and they broke into a run the moment they hit the corridor as well.

"Where are we going?" I huffed.

"Where all of us nomads go when we're being followed," he called back.

"Where's that?" I asked.

"To find a soldier," he declared as if that were obvious. "A nomad likes freedom, but we have an aversion to being killed."

"I thought they were just guardsmen or knights," I declared, suddenly very confused.

"We are only ever followed by one of four people: knights, soldiers, guardsmen, or perchers. They're not knights. A guardsman never would have entered this corridor, since it only goes one place, and they have no jurisdiction here. That means they're either Imperial soldiers, or they're perchers. And since this corridor ends at the back entrance to the barracks, why would they chase us. They know they'd have us trapped. I fear they know you're looking for your Lady Knight, my friend, and we are unarmed. So, we find a soldier." We rounded the bend and crashed into the very soldiers we were looking for.

"Get off me," one burly bloke commanded, throwing me aside. Two of the others latched on to Gorjjen and held him by one arm each. "What's the hurry?" I pointed toward the corridor.

"Perchers," I said. "Three of them." The soldier's eyes narrowed as if was unsure whether to believe us.

"He speaks truth, my friend. Three of the infected follow us," Gorjjen confirmed.

"Watch them," the big soldier commanded. His head seemed a little small for his body and as a result, his helmet did not fit quite right and lolled to the left. He drew a thick iron bar from his back. This he held in both hands, twisting near the end. Three thick blades snapped out the other end to form a very evil looking mace. He stalked forward, with his mace held low. He made it as far as the bend in the corridor.

Here, several things happened. A bunch of small and silvery objects came flashing out of the darkness, whistling as they came. They buried themselves in the soldier's cheek and chest. I could not tell what they were, but I could imagine. I had seen enough ninja movies back on Earth to guess that it was either knives or shurikens of some alien design. And the soldier roared in challenge.

I expected that to be it for him. I expected the man to fall and die. He was evidently made of hardier stuff. The thrown blades did not even slow him down. He charged ahead with a roar and his mace raised. The two soldiers holding us let go, drew their own weapons—two narrow bladed broad swords—and charged after their companion. One of the guards had the presence of mind to sound his alarm as he ran to summon help.

The high frequency alarm pulsed and echoed in the tight confines of the corridor. From around the bend came the sound of fighting as the soldiers met with the perchers. A moment later, more soldiers flooded in through the security gates behind us. We pointed down the corridor to where the sound of battle could be heard.

Gorjjen plucked at me sleeve, pulling me back toward the barracks. Once there, he approached a panel on the wall and pressed a button. A soldier appeared on the screen above it.

"State your business," he demanded, brusquely.

"We'd like to speak with Fearless," Gorjjen called into the box. "He is also known as The Pig."

"What's your business with him?" the soldier on the screen inquired.

"We have a message from his mum," Gorjjen replied. "It's kind of urgent."

"Wait there. I'll send him to the gate," the soldier replied. I looked to Gorjjen and smirked.

"A message from his mum?" I asked. He shrugged.

"I had to tell him something." From down the corridor, the sound of fighting subsided. There was a lot of shouts and conversation as those soldiers racing to the rescue questioned the three soldiers who had sounded the alarm.

A few moments later, the flood of soldiers returned to the gate. Among them was the big burly soldier with the mace. He was cut up bad. A barbed wheel with long spikes was buried in his left cheek. Two more were buried in his chest. Only his armor had kept them from sinking all the way in. One of the three guards who had held the perchers at bay was being brought in on his back. His throat had been slashed. Several of the soldiers had nicks and small cuts, but they seemed more concerned with the big man's wounds. In the back of the group of soldiers were the three perchers who had been following them. One had a caved in skull—no doubt the work of the burly soldier's mace. Two soldiers carried him. Two carried another percher who had been run through. Three soldiers carried the last man—well, two men carried the body, and one man carried the head.

"You two," the burly soldier barked, "I'll have words with you."

"They're here for me," A new voice announced, stepping through the gate. He held the gate ajar so that the soldiers could pass through.

The Pig had arrived.

"They brought them here, Pig. Those two brought the perchers," the big guy accused.

"I'll talk to them. Go see a medic," Fearless advised, pulling me and Gorjjen off to the side. Once the other soldiers had entered, he looked to us and drew his sword. "Who are you, Leper?" Fearless asked, a threat implicit in his voice. "I have no mum, so why did you summon me?"

"He's my guide," I interjected nervously. "My friend here, he brought me to see you," I explained.

"Speak," Fearless commanded, sword in hand pointed at Gorjjen's throat. Gorjjen made a gesture with one hand. Fearless saw it, though I did not. With an exacerbated sigh, Fearless lowered his sword. "Why are you looking for me?" he asked in a more civil tone of voice.

"I'm not looking for you. I'm looking for Leia, your friend, the knight the perchers took," I said, studying the man's face to gauge his reaction to this.

"You and every knight and Grey Guardsmen on this level," he declared, unimpressed.

"Well, they won't find her," I said. "She's not on this level. She's lower. Some place with water." His eyes narrowed.

"How could you possibly know that?" he demanded, clearly in disbelief of my claim.

"He is the Lady Knight's love," Gorjjen announced suddenly. Fearless locked eyes with the nomad and something passed between them.

"You? You're the colonist?" the soldier asked.

"I am." Though, I was surprised he even knew I existed. "She talked of me?" I was fishing of course.

"No. But every knight, soldier, and guardsman on the ship is looking for you. You're a priority one alert," Fearless revealed, looking to Gorjjen as one might look to a boss. Gorjjen did not respond. I saw his arm opposite me twitch, and the soldier's eyes flicker down. But other than that, they did not talk.

"I suppose you're going to take me into custody now?" I asked sourly.

"No. There's no warrant on you. A watch and follow only. Besides, you're looking for my friend. So again, I ask why you came looking for me." He looked to me this time.

"My friend here," I said, gesturing to Gorjjen, "says we are needing weapons to fight the perchers. He said you could help with that." The soldier's eyes flickered down and Gorjjen's arm twitched again.

"I'm not arming you. I can gather others who are armed who would be willing to help save her. Others who wouldn't turn you in," he said.

"If they can fight, then call them. I know there are several of the infected holding her. It feels like a nest or a warren of some kind." It was only a feeling, but this seemed to make sense to the soldier. He typed a few things into his NID and sent the call out to those he thought could help.

"Come. They will meet us at a bar on the byway," he announced, leading the way.

"Her uncle's bar?" I guessed. He seemed surprised I knew this and nodded.

"The same," he replied. I glanced sidelong at Gorjjen. He seemed unfazed by it all and followed the soldier.

"Why are you helping me?" I asked of my friend.

"Why does anyone help another? Because, it is good and right," Gorjjen declared.

"You're going to keep pretending that you meeting me was a happy occurrence and that I'm stupid?" I asked. Gorjjen looked over at me appraisingly.

"Yes," he said. Which, of course, made no sense.

"Yes, what?" I snapped.

"Yes, my friend. I will go on pretending you are stupid. It has worked out for us so far," he told me simply, though not rudely. He said it as if lying to a friend was perfectly acceptable behavior.

"Who is he?" I asked of Fearless. "I know he signaled you. He made a gesture, and you put your sword down. You know him," I accused.

"Assuming you are right, colonist., if he has the authority to make me put my sword away, what makes you think I would betray him. This is between you two," he declared, picking up the pace. "Leave me out of it."

"Is he a knight? Is he a soldier? Are you a guardsman?" I asked, demanding an answer.

"He's none of the above, and he isn't going to tell you. And, neither am I. So, come along. My friend is in trouble, and I'm not going to let your squawking and squabbling put her in further danger. Now hurry," Fearless commanded, redoubling the pace. This was promising, even if discovering that my new friend was not who he pretended to be.

"How can I trust you?" I asked of Gorjjen.

"Did I leave you for the perchers? No. You can trust that I will let no harm come to you. Besides, if you are who they say you are, Magpie, you would know me already." Gorjjen then did something out of character with the man I knew. He winked at me and smiled.

Chapter 19: Allies

The bar was packed to over-flowing, filled with soldiers and guardsmen. I noticed almost immediately that there were not a lot of knights in attendance. A quick inquiry of those nearest the door confirmed what I had already guessed. The knights refused to rest until they located their stolen comrade.

Me and Gorjjen earned a lot of nasty looks from the patrons. Since neither Gorjjen nor I served aboard the ship and were not thereby officers in any sense of the word, we were seen as intruders and trespassers. In their eyes, we had no right entering their militaristic holy place. The bartender—a big one-eyed bastard with a limp—was evidently on his way over to tell us as much.

Fearless must have anticipated as much. He lurched forward into the crowd and met the bartender halfway, muttering an explanation in his ear. One-eye's bottom jaw moved back and forth behind closed lips like he was chewing something, though he may have just been grinding his teeth in frustration. There was malevolence in his eyes, and I never felt more out of place in my life. At this time, I had no idea he was Leia's uncle.

One-eye turned on his heel and stalked off to a far corner of the bar where a group of Greys were drinking and carousing. There was no polite conversation. One-eye pointed toward the door and the men, shamefaced and guilty pushed themselves from the table and left ignorant of what they had done wrong.

As far as bars go, I rather liked it. It had the feel of an English pub like the ones back on Earth. A painted window faced toward the street, letting the patrons look out, while preventing the passerby's outside from looking in. Fearless raised his hand to order a drink, but Gorjjen reached out and drew his hand back to the table softly. I was surprised to say the least. I was more surprised, when Fearless did not object. I suppose if you are fearless, sometimes you need an outside perspective to advise you if something you think is wise truly is. Fearless was of the mind that a drink before facing a nest of assassins was a good idea. Gorjjen was of the mind that it was not. I hated to choose sides, but Gorjjen's opinion seemed wiser.

I searched the eyes of the other patrons, trying to guess what kind of people they were. I had always been good at reading people back on Earth. I could look at a woman and tell what kind of work she did for a living by how stood, whether she had kids by how she leaned, and how often she had been forced to compromise herself by how distant the look in her eye. I could tell a lot about a man by how he treated others. I could tell whether he was a leader by how he talked and whether he was a threat by where his eyes went. These men and women were curious about us, but none of them were hostile. They evidently trusted One-eye's judgment on these things. If we were okay with him, then we were okay for them.

As it turned out, we did not have long to wait for the arrival of Fearless's friends. I don't know where they were coming from or what his message to them had said, but they came running. And though they did not arrive together, they arrived on each other's heels so closely as to make us think they had.

I had apparently served in the military many times back in the day. If Tessa Barnes had been right about me, I had been fighting since the United States became a country. I touched the scar at my hair line, as I considered these newcomers. The bullet wound explained why I did not remember anything before my service in the Second World War, but I did not remember fighting in Korea or Vietnam like the NSA director said I had. She alluded that I had fought in Iraq and Afghanistan too, but I did not remember that either. I did not remember any of it. As far as I remember, I was a just a nomad like Gorjjen. I had always just wandered and stopped in a town here and there along the way to work. I would stop for a few months or a few years, then pick up and disappear without warning. I had only been in Cherryville, Kansas for about four months. But my memory lapses aside, I recognized competence when I saw it. And these men and women, they were very capable. They were some of the most intimidating people I had ever met. I was giddy to make their acquaintance.

"What's up?" I said to the group by way of greeting. Either that was not a common greeting up here like it was down there, or they were just surprised that I had the audacity to address them. They looked down on me with twisted heads, confused scowls, and hard-edged eyes like I was wearing a tutu and just punched one of them in the eye. If I was to judge their mood in that moment, I would judge them irked. I looked to Gorjjen for encouragement. His advice was a shrug and gesture for me to continue.

"I'm Daniel Sojourner and this is my friend Gorjjen Doricci. I'm from the planet down below. Gorjjen has been kind enough to help me navigate your ship. I'm here to save your friend. I know where she's at, but these guys," I said, jerking a thumb at Fearless and Gorjjen, "think we need more help; more experience. I know where Leia is, I just need to know if you're willing to help me save her?" I paused for effect so they'd know I was serious. "I have to warn you. It could be dangerous."

They found my assertion to be the singularly most hilarious thing they had ever heard and proceeded to tell me so through fits of laughter.

"Well, if you think it's dangerous, maybe we should just take some time and think this through then. I'm rather fond of my own neck and all," the smaller of the two male knights interjected, grinning broadly. I knew he was mocking me, but at least he was laughing. Laughing was good.

"Quiet you," the lady knight in the group admonished, smacking the jokester across the back of the head. He smirked and wrinkled his nose at the woman. She just rolled her eyes in response.

"Enough," the tallest of the newcomers called, irritated by the levity. "This is for," he looked at me curiously, trying to remember the name I had given their friend, "this is for Leia," he said, using the name I had given her.

Fearless touched his chest then and gestured to the others one at time, naming each in kind. "I am Xi Pich." He announced. I immediately understood why they called him The Pig. He gestured to the lady knight and named her Milintart. The tall, irritated knight who had called for silence went by the name Ailig Tuin. "He's Leia's oldest friend," Xi added like it was a bit of trivia one might find interesting. "The comedian there, that's Borbala Rowden. He's not really all that fun. Actually, you're a mean son-of-a-bitch." Borbala's smile was all teeth. I raised a brow at this. He did not seem all that mean. The man gave me a roguish wink and for just a moment, behind the smirking eyes, I saw the ice. This was enough to make me reassess my opinion of him. Maybe he was not a comedian. He was just excited at the prospect of a fight. The last knight to join us did so just as the last of the introductions were being doled out.

She was not like the others. She was bald except for two scalp-lock braids that came very nearly to the middle of her back. They were dyed a dark blue and an even darker purple. These she had tucked down the spinal rings on the back of her armor as one. If they had been hanging free, they would have looked like pigtails on her. She was different, because she wore two swords on her back and a brace of daggers on the outside of her right thigh. She carried her sidearm as a belly gun in the front. Gorjjen, I observed, took notice of this, and he frowned. This I found interesting and expressed that interest as a curious little look which he acknowledged with a dip of his head.

She was intimidating. Unlike Leia and Milintart, this newcomer's muscles were corded and tight. Her thighs and calves were well developed like she spent all her free time running uphill with a keg on each shoulder. She walked and moved with perfect control. Her body was fluid, and her motions were effortless. The men who knew nothing of what was transpiring at our table, stared at her with longing desire.

Xi introduced her simply as Jo. I thought it a strange name for someone as fierce looking as herself, but I guess parents who name their kids rarely have any idea what kind of man or woman they will grow into. Jo might have been short for Joy or Josephine or Josefufu or some other weird alien name. Maybe she had just adopted the name as she grew into the person she was. Maybe a colonist gave her the name. I did not know. It just seemed a peculiar name to give a chainsaw wielding saber-tooth shark such as her.

I nodded to each in kind. Xi's NID beeped loudly, and he opened it to see what was amiss, groaning with exasperation, but gave no clue as to the origin of his distress.

"So, colonist," Milintart called, putting a condescending emphasis on the word colonist, "what makes you think you can find her when we can't?" There was a challenge in that question.

I shrugged not wanting to announce how I might feel for her, but my silence proved pointless since Gorjjen held no reservations as to the sensitive nature of the subject and simply disclosed the fact like he was doling out sports information.

"He's in love with her," he said, looking to me for confirmation.

"Does she know this?" Milintart smirked. "For that matter, does she know you?"

"I don't know if I'd call it love, but yeah, I kind of like the woman," I decreed, proclaiming it proudly. The knights were evidently not a touchy feely sort of people. They met my proclamation with sneers and flared nostrils. But however despicable they found me, they found Gorjjen even more detestable and looked at him with unbridled disgust. If Gorjjen was fazed by their opinion of him, he did not show it.

Xi fluttered his hand before them to get their attention and shook his head. He leaned in close to Milintart's ear and whispered something. She in turn whispered it to Ailig. This continued till of the knight's knew Xi's secret with was also Gorjjen's. The moment each person received the whispered message, the sneer on their face vanished and was replaced with a look of respectful shame. More than one dipped their head in deference to my friend. This made me itch with curiosity, so I turned on my friend, incensed that everyone seemed to know him but me. Worse, they had an almost religious respect for the man.

"Who in the Hell are you?" I asked in exasperation.

"He has many names," One-eye announced, pulling up a chair from the next table over. "Ain't that right, Puck?" One-eye was grinning, but a look from Gorjjen gave the hard-nosed bartender pause. The look was clearly a warning. The giant one-eyed bartender shut his trap and dropped his eyes in embarrassment. This raised eyebrows all around the table.

"Well, that wasn't my question. I wasn't looking for a different name. I want to know who you are. Before anything else and before I go anywhere else, I will know this. You've been lying to me. You've been cozying up to me since I first escaped. I don't like being lied to. I don't like being conned," I told him hotly, my voice rising to a point that others in the bar were beginning to pay attention.

"You always had a bad temper, Magpie," Gorjjen quipped, turning an appraising eye on me. He even smiled. "But no. You will have what I give you, and what I give you is the friendship of Gorjjen Doricci. He's a good friend. Cherish him."

"I'm not going anywhere with you—not if you don't answer me. I don't like secrets, and I don't like being lied to." I must have finally gotten through to him, for he sighed heavily and looked me in the eyes.

"I mean you no distress, my friend. I will not give you this thing you seek, but how about I give you something else. Something that will help you acclimate to this present arrangement that we share. How about I tell you a story," Gorjjen proposed, "and afterward, if you feel the same way, I'll tell you a different story that ends with you in chains doing it anyway?" He was not smiling anymore. I swallowed hard.

"I'm listening."

"A long time ago, you slaughtered a colony. You fired on your brethren in their ships because you rightly guessed that those ships were infected with something from that colony. You then fractured our armada—our colony—and took a third of our people off to hide amongst the stars. What you might not know is that the infected ships you thought destroyed, weren't."

"The crews and citizens aboard them survived. They're pursuing this armada even now. They're hunting down our colonies and infecting them with this virus—this sickness."

Gorjjen's eyes burned into me and felt myself squirm under that gaze.

"We should be fleeing," he continued. "We should be hunting down your Drifters and forcing them to rejoin the fleet and the Empire, but we're not. We're trying to save as many of the colonists as possible, Magpie. The Perchers; the First; the Infected; whatever name you want to give them, they're on this ship doing everything they can to sabotage it, to sabotage each Harvest, to slow us down long enough for those infected ships to catch us. In those first days of that first Harvest, only six of our ships were infected. Only six of our ships belonged to these First Colonists. That was over a thousand years ago. Their ships number over a hundred now, and every colonist in each colony we harvest that we can't convince to come with us, ends up being infected and converted into this malignant religion of Sylar colony."

He gestured to the group of knights and soldiers around us. "These men and women are looking for one knight who went missing because her absence might distract the Grand Reaper from his reaping responsibilities; because it might slow down the Harvest or at least make it a poor Harvest. This thing you fled from all those years ago, it is still happening whether you remember your part in it or not."

He concluded with the biggest surprise of all. "Now something you should know, but don't, is that we—me and you—were friends long before today. I recognized you in the byway and thought I'd surely lost my mind. I also know what the Grand Reaper has planned for you. He's planning on using you to scare the colonists on the planet down below into a mass exodus. He knew right where you were the entire time you were fleeing him."

"The baton I took off the Guardsman?" I confirmed.

"They were tracking it. I sent them chasing ghillie gas," he remarked, referencing a phenomenon common on a bog planet the Empire harvested once.

"How was he planning to scare the colonists with me?" I asked, not seeing what should have been obvious.

"You can't be that stupid," Ailig declared, with a shake of his head. It was slow in coming, but the truth finally settled in. I suddenly realized what Luke had planned for me.

"He was going to infect me, wasn't he?" I asked, feeling my chest tighten with stress. "B-But I was saving his sister. I was helping."

"Lucky for you, you have a friend like Gorjjen Doricci looking out for you, yes? I sent the Reaper's men off looking for a stick. I've also engineered a rescue party for you. This is your brood of nasty confederates and with them you're going to get the chance to save your lady love," he said this with a smile and laid a comforting hand upon my shoulder. I felt like my stomach had opened and dumped everything inside me out on the ground. "So, tell us, my friend. How do we find your lovely Leia?" Gorjjen asked.

"I can sense her. She's below us, on a different deck. I don't know which one. She's in that direction," I told them, gesturing back over my shoulder toward the back of the bar.

"So, we take the lifts and check the last remaining decks level by level," Jo suggested.

"That would take a long while," Borbala pointed out sourly.

"She's in a room with shallow water across the floor and a single door. It's a fair-sized room. Maybe fifteen or twenty paces across each way," I added.

"The aquifer?" Xi guessed, but the others were shaking their heads.

"Maybe, but I doubt it," Milintart responded.

"How did the perchers get our beloved lady knight to another level?" Gorjjen asked, posing the question as a riddle. The other's furrowed their brows, realizing that he had a point. They had not considered this yet. There was no way they could have used the lifts to spirit her away from the place she was attacked.

"A vent or a piping conduit, maybe?" Jo suggested.

"The chutes," One-eye declared loudly, pounding his fist on the table. "They're using the chutes to move her around."

I looked to the others and saw they were nodding thoughtfully. "What are the chutes?" I asked.

"They're where refuse is deposited," One-eye explained. "They're all over the ship. There's one close to everywhere. They wouldn't have had to take her very far to get her out of sight. Wait here while I get my sword." He hopped up and waddled off behind the bar, disappearing into the back.

"Come on," Ailig called, gesturing to the others, "let's get going before he comes back."

Xi's NID beeped again. He pressed a button on the side to turn it off.

"That something important?" Milintart asked him.

"Not really. Someone's looking for me," he said, rising so we could be off before the grumpy bartender returned.

We were three corridors away before One-eye realized we had left him behind. We heard every word he said and swallowed lumps in our throats after each painful repercussion he promised to inflict upon us once he caught us.

I sent my mind out, feeling for Leia's. I could still sense her. My companions and I walked through the corridors till we finally reached a spot where I could no longer tell in which direction to go. I could still sense her, but only down below.

"She's directly below us somewhere," I announced as I came to a stop. We were in a lane with painted cell doors on each side.

"It makes sense," Ailig announced, gesturing to his left and down the corridor. "Leia's parents live down around the bend."

Milintart was interfacing with her NID and had her holographic interface up. She brought her fingers in from the side and spread her fingers wide, and the flat linear plane of the interface expanded into a three-dimensional representation of the schematic she pulled up. She expanded it further, and we all gathered around to see what she had to show us.

"I see three spots on the schematic directly below us that meet the specs of the chamber you described. There's a chamber on the lowest level where the aquifer is located. There is also a hydroponic reclamation chamber on Level 7. The last place is a water switching station on Level 10." Milintart rotated the schematic, shaking her head. "That's all I see."

I ground me teeth in frustration, and Gorjjen must have noticed my anxiety for he laid a calming hand upon my shoulder. He seemed to have that ability like it was his superpower.

"You two," Gorjjen called out, gesturing to Borbala and Jo. "Find the chute or hatch the perchers used to escape this place and go in after them. The rest of us are headed to the lifts. Go down to Level 10, find the sluicing chamber and keep watch over it. When we get down there, one of us will call to coordinate with you." The pair nodded and headed down the hall. Borbala was pulling up a schematic of the area on his NID just as Milintart had.

"Why can't they just come with us?" I asked.

"Strategic positioning," Milintart declared. "He doesn't want the perchers escaping with Leia when we move in on them." There was not much else to be said. It was a sound plan. With Jo and Borbala gone on their hunt for the chute, there was nothing left to keep us there, so we trooped off behind Ailig and made our way back to the lifts.

The great thing about taking a lift with a squad of knights was that when they commandeered the first lift we came to, we were able to force the liftman to put it in a security override that took it straight down to Level 10. Once there, I eagerly stepped out onto the byway and sent my mind searching for Leia. I still had the feeling she was down as much as she was forward. I shook my head sadly and re-entered the lift. Milintart contacted Jo on her NID and let them know Level 10 was a bust. Jo's response was a simple reply: Going to Level 7.

I was nervous like a gambler with two tokens left. I might win one of two times, but there was a very real possibility that I might lose both times, and that scared me. The knights had been tracking Leia's blood all over the ship. Each time they were sure it was her until they found the crimson stain the insurgents had left. We were closing in on the last two possible places I knew to look. It was either going to be a hit or a miss. If she was not in either of these places, then I did not know what to do. Level 7 was coming way too quickly.

The passengers on the lift we commandeered watched us all with interest and patience. The knights paid them no mind. My chest was hurting by the time the doors opened to reveal Level 7. I wanted to save Leia, but I did not want to step out into the byway and be wrong. The knights, Xi, and Gorjjen all looked at me expectantly. This was the closest they had come to finding her since she was taken. I stepped out into a wide-open area and opened my mind, dreading what I would discover—or not discover. It took only a moment to orient myself.

I had expected my mind to sink towards the woman I had come to save, but it did not sink. My mind buoyed itself and urged me to go left. Not up or down. Just left. I felt a surge of excitement, and my companions must have realized it by the look of joy in my eyes.

"She's here," I announced in disbelief. "Leia's here."

Milintart sent the message to Jo. Jo replied that they still had one more level to descend. Gorjjen was confident that by the time we arrived and got in position to take the room, Jo and Borbala would be in position themselves.

"Get her," Ailig commanded, shoving me forward. I did not even care that he was using me like a bloodhound to ferret out his friend. We were in complete agreement on this course of action, and I did as I was told. He said to get her, and I was going to get her.

Maybe it was me being caught up in the excitement or me forgetting that I was overweight, but I took off at a sprint, following the little connection I had with Leia. This level was more open than Level 12 had been. Almost immediately off the lift was a plaza strewn with a hundred different tables, food carts, clothing vendors, and kiosks filled with toys and trinkets for the kids. The knights ran after me. I did not see Gorjjen, but I did not really expect to either. Some people were not big on physical exertion. I used to be one of them. It kind of made me feel good about myself that I was showing him up at this. I was easily fifty pounds overweight and running through the plaza like a schoolgirl running through the Mall of America with her father's charge card.

Gorjjen caught up to us on the far side of the plaza when I was forced to stop and catch my breath and then, to my dismay and the knights' amusement, vomit. The knights were a cross between being amused and disgusted with me. Gorjjen passed no judgment though. He merely walked past and kindly handed me a cup of some fruity drink he had purchased from a vendor while he was walking over to join us.

The drink was surprisingly good. I thanked him and lurched forward, taking up the chase once more. Gorjjen shrugged and started walking after me again. Four side passages later, we were there.

Milintart and Jo coordinated their approaches over the NIDs. The rest kept themselves hidden, watching the door and corridor. The sound of all of them raising their walls of white noise was deafening to me. I could hear their static. What I could not understand was how the perchers could not hear it. I kept my mind open. I wanted to make sure that if they tried to abscond with Leia again, I would still be able to sense them and stop it from happening.

Jo and Borbala approached the door from the far end of the corridor. Their armor was smudged and coated with bits of trash from the chute they'd been forced to travel down. From our side, Ailig led the attack, with Milintart on his right and Xi on his left. They all stalked forward slowly with their nanite swords in one hand and their side arms in the other.

"I think you should wait here with me," Gorjjen suggested, grabbing hold of my arm as I moved to follow the others.

It was silent in the hall. Not a sound filtered back to me. I found I was holding my breath. I did not know what to expect. I did not know if my brood of fighters would open the door to the chamber and charge into it or call for those inside to come out. I half expected a lone insurgent to happen by or stumble out through the closed door. I expected a lot of things, but what happened next was predicted by no one.

The moment Borbala's hand touched the knob, the door exploded outward, filling the corridor with dust and smoke. I could not see anything. One moment Borbala was standing there, the next moment he was gone. In the smoke and dust hidden from sight came the sounds of sword on sword.

The knights were under attack.

Chapter 20: Push & Pull

I tried to shrug off Gorjjen's hand and rush in to help. I felt I had to reach Leia at any cost. Gorjjen was quicker however and darted forward and faced me. He held my eyes with his and shook his head sadly, slowly forbidding me to fight.

"We need you here," he said.

"How can I help from here," I snapped, trying to step around him. "She's in there wounded. I have to get in there. I have to save her." I tried to step around him again and when he stopped me this time, I apologized out the corner of my mouth and took a swing at his head. I was not playing around. I threw my hip into the punch. I felt bad for doing this to him the moment I launched the haymaker, but I need not have.

I had never seen a man move so fast in real life.

He deflected my punch with a quick fan of his fingers and followed that deflection with a lighting quick snap kick to my solar plexus that launched me into the wall of the corridor behind me. Though I easily flew five feet, he still somehow managed to be there in time to catch me as I rebounded and fell to my knees.

Unfortunately for me, he was not done. He hooked his fingertips beneath my collar bone and dug his thumb into a bundle of nerves where my neck met my shoulder. The effect was startling. It felt like I had been hit with a stun gun. His rigid thumb filled my neck and upper body with blinding pain that left me gasping for air. It also made my right arm numb and limp and useless. I needed that arm. That was my punching arm.

"Who the hell are you?" I whined pitifully, grunting in agony.

"The knights need your help. They need Magpie. You need to clear the dust and smoke so they can see to fight," he replied, ignoring my question.

"How?" I bleated miserably. He let me go without warning, and I worked my shoulder in a circle to get the feeling back. The pain vanished save a residual ache in the joint.

"Push it away," he commanded.

I investigated the smoke, barely able to see Gorjjen beside me. I was having trouble focusing. I tried several times to gather my will, but it slipped away each time.

"Deep breaths. Calm your mind," Gorjjen advised.

I tried again, but as I started to gather my will a dark shape came staggering out of the smoke before us. She was darkly clad and quite obviously a percher. Someone had rung her bell, and she was preoccupied with shaking her head to clear it while mopping at a bright red cut weeping blood along her jaw line. I just stared at her in amazement.

She was not what I had expected of a First Colonist. She was a little out of shape. She wore soft soled dark boots that came up to her calves. In the top of her boot were several rods about the size of a pencil. She had pushed them through the side of the boot top then back out a little lower where she left them there within easy reach should she need one in a hurry.

The exposed bottom edges of the metal rods were smashed flat and sharpened as if they were some form of hiltless dirk. In her hand she held a blade of about two and half feet in length. The hilt was wrapped with an indigo clothe that looked like the leggings I was wearing. It had been coated with some cloudy resin to form the handle. There were a multitude of pockets about her, and each seemed to jingle as if she carried little bits of metal in each. The woman did not attack right away. She seemed as surprised of me as I was of her.

Her eyes flew wide as if she suddenly recognized me, and her sword came whistling in from the right and aimed for my neck. Gorjjen intercepted it though, striking the blade up with the back of his hand.

He probably thought me helpless in that moment as he moved forward to finish her. Like Tessa back in that black site, Gorjjen underestimated me. More specifically, he underestimated the knee jerk reaction of a redneck Earthling when faced with his imminent demise. She swung her sword, Gorjjen deflected it away, and I kicked her in the groin. Infected or not, I dropped her like I stole her bones.

Gorjjen looked at me in surprise, shook his head once in disbelief, and took a knee beside her. I figured he would knock her out, but evidently, I had underestimated him as well. He pulled one of those small metal spikes from her boot top and jammed it through her temple. She went limp. He then collected the rest of the spikes and came back to my side to stand watch. He was calm and unaffected by the life he just took. He did not so much as spare her a look after, and he calmly repeated his earlier command to me.

"Go. Push the smoke away so our friends can see," he said softly. I calmed my mind and drew in my will. I focused on the atoms between me and the cloud and pushed. My will found no resistance and went forward unchallenged. The cloud of smoke swirled and shifted, but it did not dissipate. It rolled in right behind my willful push.

There were cries of protest from ahead as my push collided with the combatants unexpectedly. Several items came whistling out of the fog around me and vanished into the smoke behind, ricocheting off the corridor walls. I was not sure what they were, but my guess was that they were more of those metal rods. The perchers probably were not very happy with me either, but then again, it might have been the knights. I had only just met them.

"I don't know how to do this," I complained. "I can't push air without pushing on the others?"

"Don't focus on the air in front of you. Focus on the air past the fighting and push it away. Draw it off and you'll draw this off," he said, gesturing to the smoke. "The smoke and dust will flow forward into the space you emptied." He knelt beside the woman he had killed to search her. He took up her blade and studied it with a professional eye then set it aside with a weary sigh. It had evidently failed to earn his seal of approval.

I tried to do as he suggested. I sent my mind out into the fog and found the last of the fighters. Here I imagined an invisible wall of my will stretching from floor to ceiling and from wall to wall, and the moment I was confident of its construction, I pushed. The fog around me began to move, but then my wall tilted forward and to the side and the other side as I repeatedly tried to compensate. Each time the wall tilted, the air I was pushing flooded back towards us sending the smoke right back where it came from.

"Concentrate," Gorjjen crooned. "You have all the time in the universe. Construct a better wall as if this were true, and then push."

I found the last fighter again and rebuilt my wall, but this time, I made my wall thicker, like a plug filling the corridor. When I was sure it was built solidly enough, I clenched my will and pushed with all my might. I felt my face flush, my eyes bulge, and my brain swell inside my skull. I pushed, and the plug barely moved. So, I took a few quick breaths, clenched my will again, and redoubled my efforts. Air was a lot heavier than I would have imagined. It felt like I was trying to push an elephant into a garden hose. The plug slid but barely, then it slid more and soon it had momentum. It was just a matter of perseverance now.

The fog around us began to swirl and shift then race off in the direction of my push. I kept pushing long after the smoke was gone, and then I was afraid to let it go; afraid if I did the air I pushed away would just come flooding back along with the smoke.

Gorjjen seemed to realize this and laughed. "Let your will fade slowly, and the air you pushed away will mix with the air you drew off," he murmured sagely.

I did as he suggested, and it was how he said. The smoke did not return. Also, the pressure inside my head eased. I threw a cheesy grin his way and he smirked before nodding toward the fighting before us. Joyful as I was, the fight was far from over.

Jo was the fighter on the furthest side, and she was desperately battling three perchers at once. They had been trying to escape. Though she seemed overwhelmed, she managed to foul each attempt they made to get past her. Her two blades wove, slashed, dove, and thrust with mesmerizing speed and stunning accuracy, but every move she threw, they countered as if she were fighting one single person who could read her mind.

Borbala was meant to shore up her defenses, but the blast had taken him out of the game. He was crumpled in a heap against the wall opposite the chamber door. He was not moving, and there was a small pool of blood forming around his head. If he was not dead, he sure would not be smiling when he woke up.

Ailig and Milintart had it worse. They battled six perchers at once near the chamber door, and two of the perchers kept switching back and forth between them.

Every time Milintart got comfortable in her routine, one or two of the perchers battling Ailig would suddenly switch partners and gang up on her forcing Ailig to abandon his attack to save her. The moment he went on the attack though, the two perchers who had left his fight would come back putting Ailig between them and the perchers he had broken free from. This left him off balance and fighting enemies on two fronts.

The moment he started to get control of the situation, two of Milintart's perchers would switch sides again and gang up on Ailig forcing her to mirror his frustrations. It was a surprisingly effective strategy. It kept both knights from ever getting the upper hand.

Every so often, Milintart or Ailig would manage to run one of their opponents through, but the moment they did another percher would dart out of the darkness of the chamber and join the fight.

Xi didn't seem that pressed, but then again, he did not feel fear. He battled two directly in front me, and even as I watched, more perchers were trying to squeeze out of the room. Only Ailig and Milintart's fierce battle kept the others trapped in the chamber. I reached into the room with my mind and counted another thirteen insurgents plus Leia. I suddenly realized that if they managed to get out of that room, we would be hopelessly over run.

I searched for the clothe hilted sword Gorjjen had set aside, but the moment I stooped to retrieve it, Gorjjen was there to stop me again. He shook his head and jabbed me in the temple with one rigid finger. It actually hurt a lot, but he was not attacking me this time. He was pointing at my brain.

"This is the weapon of a Prior, my friend. Not steel. You may not remember who you were, but I do. You were a Prior—a Grand Reaper. You had discipline. You had power. That can't be taken away. It's still in there even if you don't remember," Gorjjen snapped, beseeching me to remember.

I wanted to. I really wanted to go all Magneto against the perchers, but I did not remember being that other guy. Not even a little, and I told him so. "I don't remember being that guy," I whined.

"It's fine, my friend. It is. Doing this up here is all about leverage. If you know where to push and where to pull, you can make almost anything happen. Think of your enemies like boxes."

He stopped talking for a moment and flicked one of the metal rods he had stolen off the dead percher across the room. It hit one of Jo's opponents in the back of the neck, dropping him to his knees. She swept the man's head off without a second thought. It took me a moment to realize that the percher he had just killed had been getting the upper hand on Jo. If Gorjjen had not intervened on her behalf, she would have been dead. It did not help Jo much however, because one of the perchers battling Milintart darted over to take his fallen comrade's place. The moment he left a percher from inside the darkened room darted out to join battle against Milintart. Gorjjen had stopped one of them from killing Jo, but he had not tilted the tables in our favor.

"Think of them as a boxes," I prompted, urging Gorjjen to finish his thought.

"You can push up, down, forward, back, left, right. Or you can push in. It is all about opposing force. Your mind is just a muscle right now. You understand this, yes?" he asked.

"I think so," I said. I turned toward the two battling Xi and focused my will on the man battling him on his left. I set my mind inside that man's chest and uttered the word I was using to focus my will.

"You got this?" Gorjjen asked.

I nodded and said the word.

"Burst!" I commanded, clenching my will as the word exploded from me. The assassin I targeted froze suddenly, his eyes going wide with fear, and then quite unexpectedly exploded just like the secret service agents Palasa killed. The man made a horrid wet popping sound as I pulled all his joints apart.

All the fighting stopped. Every person turned in surprise. The man I killed was just a geyser of blood and flying body parts. With nothing left to support them, his entrails slapped floor like a soggy towel. This sent Xi and his last remaining opponent skipping away from each other. He might not feel fear, but Xi could most definitely be surprised. Everyone else looked at me in fear. Gorjjen just looked at me in disgust.

"That's not what I meant," he said sourly. I frowned. There was no pleasing the guy.

"Then be more clear next time," I barked defensively, crestfallen that no one was happy with what I had done. Well, no one but Xi was happy. With his second opponent gone, he was able to easily dispatch the lone remaining percher he was squaring off with. Xi went back into the fight first, and that was evidently the signal for the rest to go back to slaughtering each other.

I noticed Xi was leaving himself wide open repeatedly. At first, this concerned me, but then I realized he was doing it on purpose. He was exaggerating his strikes to leave himself open. He would overextend this strike just a little too much and then that slash would go a little too wide. The percher saw it and thought the man was tiring and went for it, stabbing in straight for Xi's heart. He was ready for it though. He leaned back and rolled his torso around and under the blade and when he came back up, he pivoted on his leading leg, shifted his sword to his other hand, and followed through with a back hand chop to the percher's throat. Xi gave me a nod of thanks and sprinted over to join with Jo in her fight against the three.

The perchers inside the room saw Xi joining with Jo and tried to set up a defense like they had going with Milintart and Ailig. Three of Milintart's opponents broke away and sprinted toward Jo. They never made it.

Gorjjen's hand whipped out quick as a cat's paw, flinging two of his confiscated spikes toward the darting men. Two of the attackers went down with spikes in their skulls. His third throw however was fouled when one of the perchers fighting Ailig threw a spike of his own at Gorjjen. Gorjjen was able to twist everything vital away from the throw, but the spike still hit him in the upper arm. I lashed out like mentally at the third man headed to join against Jo. The man flew into the wall with bone crushing force. I was a getting a lot better at this.

Gorjjen thanked me and motioned for me to do it again. I looked back to the fighting and saw three more perchers dart out to take the place of the three men Gorjjen and I just killed. Milintart disemboweled one of them before they could set their defense. It did not matter. Another darted out of the darkness to take his place.

Since no one liked my exploding assassin trick, I tried something different. I wanted to lash out like I had just done, but everyone was moving so fast. I was afraid of hitting a knight or distracting them at a crucial point that could get them killed. Instead, I focused on one of three assassins battling Jo and Xi and waited for an opportunity to present itself. I did not have long to wait. One of the perchers on the right drew a second blade from his boot. He held this one reversed in his left hand and brought it up before him as if to use it for blocking. I focused my will before him, holding it there like a boot above an ant, and waited. The moment he lashed out with the sword in his right hand, I clenched my will and pushed.

"Now," I whispered. The dagger, and the fist that held it, suddenly flew out wide to his left, twisting him off balance. His sword slash fell low and short, but the dagger in his fist found its mark, burying itself to the hilt in his friend's side. Jo and Xi were confused as to why their enemy suddenly attacked his friend, but only after they took advantage of their enemies distractions. Because of my intervention, Jo was able to bury the tip of her right blade in the throat of one assassin and take the sword arm off the other. After that, it was a single chop to his neck to the man's neck to end his fight. The last percher was suddenly very nervous. Before, she had the benefit of overwhelming numbers, but now it was two on one and not in her favor. Xi and Jo squared off with her. The percher lunged at Jo. Xi slammed his sword down on the back of the percher's downward arcing sword and Jo stepped into a double hand strike to the chest, slamming into the percher like she was Babe Ruth hitting a homer.

They might think that what I did exploding that one percher was gross but watching the top half of a woman flip over backwards while the bottom half stayed still was equally as disturbing as far as I was concerned. The moment I stopped vomiting, I decided to help Milintart and Ailig with their fight. I figured since Ailig was furthest from the chamber door, helping him would make more sense since no one would be rushing out to take the place of anyone I vanquished. Unfortunately, I never got the chance to help. The moment Xi and Jo joined in the fight, the tide of the battle turned. Four of Milintart's opponents broke off to battle Jo and Xi. Two of Ailig's broke off with him to fight Milintart, and Ailig did something cool. He dropped to one knee and ran his sword through the rib cage of the opponent directly in front of him, sliding his sword in under the other's desperate lunge. Ailig's remaining opponent tried to rush him from behind only to find Ailig's sword miraculously reversed. I didn't see him move it. The blade of the sword seemed to flow like liquid through the hilt and reform on the other side.

Free of opponents, he rose quickly and darted in to help vanquish Milintart's pair. The perchers inside the room rushed the door. Several were cut down by Jo and Milintart as they showed their desperation. I knew walls were not a barrier to my telepathy, so I sent my mind into the room to see if I could help from behind the enemy forces.

More of the perchers were forcing their way from the room. Soon each of the knights found themselves fighting three and four each. For the first time, Gorjjen reached for a sword. He retrieved the clothe hilted weapon at his feet and tested the balance.

"Stay here," He commanded. He took a step forward, then turned quickly as a battle cry was taken up from behind us. I drew in my will and turned to face this new threat. Thankfully, this threat was for the perchers. The man in the lead was cut up bad, but I recognized him. He was the big soldier from Level 12 who had taken shurikens to the face and chest. He rushed past me and Gorjjen with his mace cocked like a baseball bat. Right behind him came One-eye. His sword was more of a machete. It was four fingers wide and three feet long, but it looked small in the big man's hand. These two giants barreled into the midst of the fight laying into any and all attackers stupid enough to stand before them.

Gorjjen looked at me and shrugged, and he tossed the sword he held back on the floor. I would have smirked at this, but I knew what was probably going to happen now. The perchers would kill Leia rather than give her up. This was my fear, and I was not about to let it happen. I sent my mind into the room and discovered that just the opposite was true. The perchers in the back of the group inside the room waited like empty suits of armor for their turn to fight. No one was trying to attack Leia which made me very afraid. What if they had infected her already?

I tried to enter Leia's mind to see, but she still had the wall up keeping them out. No one was attacking her. Actually, that was not true. There was one of the First who behaved different than the others. He was different because he was in the back of the chamber watching the others. He was not interested in the fight at all. He seemed to only be interested in Leia. I had been wrong. They were not trying to kill her. They were trying to infect her. This was what the kidnapping had been about all along.

They were not going to use her as a hostage. They were not going to kill her. They had planned to use her as an assassin to kill her brother. Did they even notify him that they had taken her? No. Luke knew because I had told him. Even now, they were waiting for her to sense her freedom and lower her guard.

No. Not they. He. He was waiting for her to lower her guard; to open her mind to one of us so he could enter it. I started to pull away from Leia's mind, but she must have sensed me. I felt the wall coming down and Yellow Eyes stirred in the mind of the infected watching her. The thing with the yellow eyes was gleeful. Everything had worked as he had planned. He coiled himself inside that polluted mind and prepared to spring, and then, he did exactly that.

He surged forward suddenly, but suddenly screamed in pain as I blew his host apart. It was strange for me. I did not need a word to focus it that time. My thought in that moment was reality. I turned my mind on the others in the room, intent on crushing their minds as I had done with the NSA agent who had raped Palasa. I felt a soaring rage in my head. It felt like I was racing into the teeth of a hurricane. I had never known a sensation like this before, and as quickly as it came, it passed, and I was me again. I did not kill anyone else. I did not have to. The infected were different suddenly.

Something strange had just happened in that room, and it spread to the enemy outside. One moment they were zealots fighting with coordination and skill, and the next, they were confused and frightened.

They all just stopped. They stopped fighting well. They stopped fighting together. They just stopped fighting and let their weapons drop to their sides. The ones battling the knights were cut down as the knights and soldiers took advantages of the openings. They would have slaughtered them all if Gorjjen had not commanded them all to stop.

The perchers who were still armed dropped their weapons ringing to the floor and backed away, holding up their hands to sue for mercy. Several of the men and women blubbered and wept. A few vomited at the sight of all the carnage around them.

"What is this?" Ailig growled, confused by the percher's behavior. He looked to Gorjjen, but Gorjjen was looking at me. "What is this, master?" Ailig growled again, but Gorjjen could not answer. He was too busy looking at me in me awe.

"I don't know," he whispered in a small voice. "I just don't know."

Xi did not question it. He pulled the perchers from the room and made them kneel by the wall, then sounded an alarm on his NID to summon reinforcements. The big burly soldier who had just saved their bacon marched over to Xi, looking as if he meant to crush his comrade's skull.

"Why didn't you answer you're NID?" he demanded. I realized that was why Xi's NID kept beeping. He was dodging a friend.

Xi shrugged. "We were in a hurry," he replied.

The infected were asking where they were and what was happening. They were borderline hysterical. I did not care though. Leia was in there injured or worse.

I darted toward the chamber door, rolling around Gorjjen's outstretched hands. When the knights moved to bar me entry, I drew in my will and pushed them away—gently of course—and sprinted down the steps and through the shallow water to where Leia lay. I scooped her up in my arms, ignoring how her armor bit into my skin, and gently patted her cheek in an effort to wake her.

At first, she did not respond. Her breathing was shallow and weak. There were a half-dozen cuts across the front of her thighs and hands and her belly where they had stripped her armor away.

"Come on," I pleaded. "Be okay. Just be okay." I smacked her cheek a little harder. When that did not work, I smacked it hard. She immediately slapped me back and considerably harder.

"You . . . didn't try . . . to kiss me while I was out, did you?" she asked.

I laughed. So, she hit me again.

"I'm serious. You didn't stick your colonial tongue in my mouth, did you?" she demanded heatedly.

I kept laughing. I might have even cried, but if I did, I was not telling anyone.

It wriggled from the dead man's eye, slipping out from between the bottom lid and the eyeball itself. It plopped into the water and wriggled the back half of its body. At first nothing happened, but then something did. It began to move, propelled by its flagella. It moved through the shadows and motes of light, headed for her. Headed for the girl who had denied it. Like a water moccasin come to prey, it zeroed in on her exposed ankle. It could not survive long outside its host. It needed another. Someone powerful. Someone strong. Someone weak enough not to fight it for control. It slipped from the water and crossed a piece of Leia's discarded armor and plunged back into the cold drink. She had lost a boot the day they took her. Her ankle lay open and exposed before it. It beat its tail back and forth faster and faster, sensing how close she was, and then it glided to a stop.

The other knights had entered the room and come to see their injured comrade. It was smart. It was wise. It was patient. It could wait, and they would take her. It would die though. The man cradling the injured knight moved to lift her from the water. It had to be now. It flailed in the water, trying to cover the last few inches before they spirited her away. They would not notice it. No one ever noticed it. In over a thousand years, no one had ever noticed it.

However, in over a thousand years, it had never been in the presence of Gorjjen Doricci. The moment it lifted its head to strike, Gorjjen was there to stop it. He bent and scooped it up in a small leather bag and sealed it to keep it from escaping.

"What's that?" I asked.

"A solution to a very old problem, I think," Gorjjen remarked with a curious smile. I shrugged, having no idea what he was talking about, and I went back to caring for Leia. Gorjjen would explain himself when he was ready. I was tired of trying to get answers out of him.

Chapter 21: Pre-Summit

The fluorescent lights buzzed annoyingly. Only the squeak of the occasional leather conference chair broke the silence. Every now and then someone would clear their throat, but that was it. The room was filled with silent people.

Aaron stared at the screens the techs had set up. He had live feeds from almost every space agency on the planet before him including NASA, NORAD, Russia's RFSA, China's CNSA, and the UN's UNOOSA satellites and telescopes. There were high altitude surveillance flights being flown by almost every country capable of flight to monitor movement of the saucers overhead. Other than that, however, the planet as a whole functioned as usual. Only Earth's top government officials worriedly watched the skies and the banks of monitors feeding them the view. Each of them was nervous. It had been seven days since the alien ambassador had descended to the planet's surface. Seven days. Today was the day they were to come back, but today, all day, the saucers in the sky did nothing. The aliens were late.

Everyone agreed that there should have been some movement by now from them. Aaron let his eyes swivel to his counterparts around the table touching their faces one-by-one. They all looked bored. Peter Sang was with them again representing NASA. He leaned against the far wall with his arms crossed, studying his feet his feet with disinterest.

Tessa Barnes, with the NSA, was seated in a conference chair at the far end of the table. She sat cool-eyed and composed, elbows on the table with her fingers tented. Her eyes were moving; they were always moving, taking in everything and everyone around her. She was amusing herself by idly tapping her two middle fingers together in time with the second hand on the clock. Richard Weaver, with the FBI, reclined at ease in his chair, scrolling through apps on his phone. Michael Sommers was with CIA. He was texting someone unknown. Eric White Hall was even in attendance, freshly arrived from New York. The UN had sent him back in the company of a more experienced diplomat. It was this man that Aaron was most curious about.

He was a Vietnamese gentleman who went by the name Sang Hai Phong. He was possibly the oldest man at the table. Years aside, he had sat elbow-to-elbow with almost every leader on the planet at some point in his life. The good ones, the bad ones, and the very bad ones. If the UN had a negotiation to be performed, this man had been a part of it in one capacity or another.

When Ban-ki Moon, the United Nation's present Secretary General, presented the situation to the UN's member states and asked that they submit their choice of ambassador for a vote. Sang Hai Phong was submitted and almost unanimously elected.

Aaron liked the man well enough. He was well spoken, patient, and keenly observant. Keenly observant was an understatement. He was like a Vietnamese version of Professor Moriarty except with the sanctity for life like Pope Francis—who while not in attendance here, was in the city along with every other world leader. That is what made this so nerve wracking.

The most powerful people on Earth had gathered to meet the alien ambassadors, and now those same powerful people who had never waited on anyone now found themselves forced to wait for a man each of them knew to be infinitely more powerful than themselves. With all that power in one place, it made Aaron curious. Every influential security director was present in that room with him. There was a five-star Air Force General seated opposite Aaron. Beside him was a five-star Navy Fleet Admiral. And beside him was a four-star General with the Army. The only one of the four armed service branches not represented in the room was the Marines and the only reason General Brandt was not in attendance was because bad weather had him trapped aboard the USS Abraham Lincoln in the South Pacific. Everyone else was here and Aaron knew them all. At least, he thought he did.

There were two people in the room he had never seen before. The two individuals stood at attention behind Tessa. They were not NSA agents. They did not have the look. They were not military. They were not politicians. They were not aides or secretaries. They did not look like functionaries. What they did look like was people who did not belong. The only reason—Aaron felt—no one had inquired about them yet was due to the fact that they were rigidly standing at attention. People standing at attention were rarely questioned. These two, however, were odd and out of place.

He looked about the conference table. Others were giving them glances, but no one bothered to interrogate them. They were there so they must belong. Aaron was not buying it though. They were Tessa's doing, and he knew it. Anything Tessa did required deeper scrutiny. The mess surrounding Daniel Sojourner proved that. She behaved like being the director of the NSA was some form of royal title: Baroness do-whatever-the-hell-I-want Barnes. Aaron hated entitled people.

"Who are they?" Aaron asked without emotion. Tessa looked up in surprise. Several of the others looked her way interested in the answer. She turned to look where Aaron was looking and lost her curious expression. She almost seemed disappointed in having to give her answer.

"Psychics," she told him simply. "My last three absconded, remember?" she replied. No one in the room found those two statements odd. Aaron merely dipped his head in acknowledgement and went back to watching the monitors. The world had really changed in the past few weeks.

The first sign that something had changed occurred was when Peter Sang suddenly rose from his chair and gasped. He leaned in close to the monitors and pointed.

"What is it?" Tessa asked before Aaron got the chance.

Most of those seated half-rose to see what was happening with their own eyes. At first, what caught Peter's eye eluded them, but then it became more obvious. There were three tiny lights beneath one of the saucers. A moment later, there were other lights. These were beneath the other saucers. The entire room, silent up till this point, became even more quiet as thirty-one science and security experts suddenly decided to hold their breath.

"We are coming," a voice announced, startling those in the room. Heads turned as one and went to the woman who had spoken. She was one of the two psychics, and as they watched, she spoke again. "We are coming," she repeated. "We are coming. We are coming."

The gathered men and women looked to each other in confusion a trickle of fear running through them. After the sixth repetition of the message the people realized that she was not in control of herself. She was just an antenna for the alien horde.

The man who stood beside her had been staring at her in horror while backing away. He seemed ready to flee the room, but even as he began to turn away, something stopped him. He suddenly straightened. The look of fear in his eyes slid away to be replaced with a look of introspective curiosity. He was curious in those around him. The moment he spotted Aaron, his curiosity vanished. His head slowly lolled to one thought, a faint smile creased his lips, and marched forward toward Aaron.

Several of the alphabet gang hurried from his path, but they need not have feared the man. He was not interested in them or Aaron. He was interested in Aaron's day runner. He laid his hand on it and dragged it across the table, took a seat in a vacated chair, and opened it to the notepad within. He picked up a pen and began scribbling down several numbers.

At first, no one knew what to make of them. It was only after the man rewrote them for the fifteenth time that the Army General recognized them as geographical coordinates. Tessa rose and hurried over to where the man scribbled and read what the boy wrote.

"This is it," she crowed. "This is their designated landing strip. We need to locate this place and prepare." Aaron really hopped she meant they needed to prepare transportation and a reception and not a military response. He decided she was not a complete moron. She could not be, right? His reservations aside, he found himself nodding in agreement. This was what they had been waiting for. The summit with the aliens was close at hand. People needed to be contacted. People needed to be told. He reached for his phone and began to dial. It was time to let the President know.

Chapter 22: Confinement

"I've got her," One-eye said, trying to take Leia from me.

"Dammit! I got her," I said. I turned Leia sideways so she would not hit her head on the bomb shattered door. I chose my footing carefully. The corridor was painted with blood and gore. A quick look showed me that Borbala had not survived the explosion.

"Here. Give me the girl," One-eye demanded. He slipped his arms beneath her shoulders and legs. He lifted her from my arms like she was weightless. In the distance, the sounds of booted feet could be heard as the Grey Guardsmen and Imperial soldiers closed in on Xi's alarm. The other knights told him more than once to turn it off, but he refused.

"Well fought, my friend," Gorjjen congratulated, holding up the pouch that held the parasite he had captured. "It makes me sick for the old days to see you in action again as you just were." His smile dimmed suddenly.

"Thanks, I guess." I turned to study the perchers who had been taken prisoner. They were sobbing and shaking on their knees against the wall. They were all murmuring questions, but no one was answering them except to snarl for them to shut their mouths. This Jo emphasized by swatting those who did not listen across the shoulders with the flat of her twin blades. Milintart assisted. "What will happen to them?" I asked, feeling sorry for the people. Something had cured them of the virus or freed them from the parasite that controlled them. Or maybe it was a ruse. I did not know and neither did the knights.

"Why didn't you respond to my messages?" the big Imperial soldier whined to Xi. He busied himself with wiping blood and gore from the head and shaft of his mace.

"We were in a hurry," Xi replied again for like the sixth time since the fighting had stopped. I found it humorous. The big guy seemed like a rabid grizzly bear when he was fighting, but when he was not, he seemed like a kid brother upset that big brother would not let him come to the skate park with him.

"You could have taken time to tell me there was a fight. I proved I could help. I killed five of them all by myself," the man told him proudly. "How many did you kill?"

"All of the ones I fought," Xi replied. "Besides, three of the ones you killed were surrendering along with that lot," he said, gesturing to those kneeling against the wall. "I can't believe you're counting them."

I smiled. I wanted to throw up, but I smiled. There were body parts everywhere. Largely because of me and my unpopular exploding percher trick.

"What now?" I asked of Gorjjen, averting my eyes so I did not have to face the carnage.

"Now?" he mused. "Now, I have you placed under arrest."

My smile slid away. The look he gave me was impassive and serious. I burst out laughing thinking the man was joking. He sighed as if to say, do not make this awkward, but I was going to make it awkward.

"Shit. You're not joking, are you?" Ailig stepped close to me. His eyes daring me to resist. I looked at the faces of the men and women I had befriended. I looked at Jo pleadingly. I had saved her life, and she knew it. She pursed her lips and shook her head apologetically.

"Sorry, brother," Xi said by way of apology. He gave me a helpless little shrug. "He says we arrest you," he nodded toward Gorjjen, "then we have to arrest you. It's nothing personal. Personally, I kind of like you. You're handy in a fight." There were some calls of agreement to this from the others. "But we work for him."

"One-eye? Hey? I saved your niece?" I said, reminding him of what he already knew. He gave me a sour look.

"You helped save my niece," he clarified. "You didn't do it by yourself. Way I see, you were just a tool to be used till the job was done. Well, the job's done, son. Now it's time to put away the tools."

I looked to those around me incredulously, clenching and unclenching my hands in disbelief. "You gruff gnarly goat fucker!" I shouted in disbelief. One-eye looked at me startled but slightly amused. "You unbelievable sheep-humping horde of whores. I saved your friend; your sister knight; your niece; Luke's sister; that girl right there from death and worse. What the ever-living fuck is wrong with you people? Why would you do this?" I asked them beseechingly. "Why?"

"Um . . ." Xi responded awkwardly. "Why? Because, he said to arrest you, and frankly, he scares us more than we appreciate what you did," he remarked candidly, pointing his sword at Gorjjen. The others smirked to hear Xi admit to being afraid of something, but as to what he claimed, they were all nodding.

I held my hands out, wrist together, and surrendered tiredly to Ailig. Ailig chuckled softly. I was giving up. There was no fighting them or arguing. They were programmed to follow orders, and I was the most wanted man in the Empire. I guess it was a little too much to hope that they would let me slide for what was an extraordinary event for me but an ordinary day for them.

"Fuck you guys. Next time there's a fight, I might not save you. Might not do it. Nope. Ruined all the credit you had with me. Oh, and Jo, I thought you were bad ass, but even so, next time we're in the thick of it, nope. You'll be on your own."

She looked at me appraisingly then gave Milintart the wow expression.

"Maddox?" Gorjjen called, addressing the large Imperial soldier shadowing Xi. I was curious how he knew the man's name. I did not even know it. Never even heard it mentioned. "The prisoner is your responsibility. Take him to your Battle Commander. Xi, you and Ailig go with him. Grab a squad of knights from the security node near the lifts. That man is powerful," he warned. "You take telepaths. If he even thinks of gathering his will, you smother it. Is that understood?" Gorjjen asked sternly.

"Yes, master," Ailig replied, slipping security bands over my wrist.

"I thought you were my friend," I said to Gorjjen as they led me off.

"Gorjjen Doricci is your friend, Magpie. I am Gorjjen Doricci no longer," he replied, turning away.

"Then who the hell are you now?" I demanded.

"The Baron of Hein," he replied, "Weapon Master to the Imperial Army, and the swordmeister to Baggam's Children. Battle Master, Second Class," he declared proudly.

I stared at the man in disbelief, secretly impressed with the title, then looked to Leia, frustrated that I had to leave her so soon after her rescue. One-eye had stretched her out on the floor of the corridor and was busy stripping away her armor.

"You're kind of a dick," I told Gorjjen. He did not turn. He kept his chin up and his eyes on the prisoners before him.

"Indeed," he replied simply.

Imperial soldiers rounded the bend in the corridor and came to a stop before the big soldier Gorjjen had named Maddox. Xi was pointing back toward the carnage-filled hall when his NID suddenly began to beep. Maddox's NID beeped too. All the Imperial soldiers' NIDs were beeping. A look of dread passed between them. I glanced back and found that even the NIDs of the knights were beeping. Everyone checked the message that had been broadcast evidently ship wide.

"What the hell is going on?" I asked, curious.

I watched as the soldier's shoulders slumped. Ailig braced himself on the corridor wall gasping for breath.

"What?" I asked again, more respectfully.

"The Daimyo has been murdered," one of the new arrivals responded for all to hear. "Lord Merrick is dead." I realized this was different than a routine assassination like a Baron or a Senator. This man was evidentially someone very high up on the food chain for his death to have affected them as it was.

"Soldiers," Gorjjen called abruptly, "to me."

It was all the rest needed to hear. The soldiers went to attend the cleanup and detention of the captured perchers, and my wardens and I journeyed on. Xi picked up a squad of knights as Gorjjen commanded. There was no need. The thought of escape had not even occurred to me. On the lifts up to the upper levels, Xi explained who Lord Merrick was. He explained who he was to the people of the Kye O'Ren, who he was to the armada, and who he was to the Emperor.

He was a cousin to the Emperor. He was the supreme leader aboard the Kye O'Ren. His word was law to those who dwelled upon it. I realized that his loss amounted to same thing as the United States losing its President. I made sure to keep my tone respectful for the rest of the trip to the detention cell they had picked out for me. To the armada, he was like admiral. The Kye O'Ren was the flagship of the armada. Where it led, the rest would follow. This was huge.

Whoever had killed him had seriously crippled the fleet. But they did even more than that, and Ailig explained how. He explained that the Daimyo's passing was a more intimate loss to them because of who he was to Luke and Leia. The Daimyo was Luke and Leia's surrogate father.

This did not surprise me. Why? Because, when life chose to give me lemons, it was never a gift. It was so life could hold me down on the ground and squeeze lemon juice in my eyes.

The ride up took over an hour. When they finally showed me to my holding cell, I found it impressively unimpressive. It was a white room with a built-in bed along the back wall. What looked like a toilet was in the corner of the room. The front wall facing the corridor was made of some weird smart glass. Xi assured me it was indestructible.

He also showed me that if I had to use the restroom, all I need do for privacy was touch the wall and it would dim. A warning came with this. It would only dim three times and for no more than what amounted to fifteen minutes at a time. For one third of a rotation the wall would dim to simulate night. There was also notch in the wall with a control panel above it. I did not need to be told what this was. I remembered the one Gorjjen showed me. This was one of those free food printers. He saw me roll my eyes and smirked.

"You've tasted the Imperial cuisine, I see." Xi gently pushed me into the open room. The moment I was in, Maddox hit a button and closed the door.

"I have," I replied. "It tastes like medicine." Xi nodded absently. I was not sure if he was agreeing it tasted off or if he was agreeing that it tasted like medicine. It was not important enough to clarify.

"Baggam Rain, Battle Commander aboard the Kye O'Ren is warden of the prison blocks. He has a personal interest in you. He will either visit you himself or send one of his subordinates to process you in a few hours. till then, make yourself comfortable." Xi and Maddox waved their goodbyes and strolled off together. I wiggled my fingers back without much enthusiasm. It was then that I noticed Ailig was not leaving with the rest. He had hung back.

"We are grateful for what you did," Ailig murmured. "We're warriors though. We do what our commanders order. Right now, we're your enemy because our commanders say we must be. If that ever changes, know that you've got friends aboard the Kye O'Ren. As far as I'm concerned, you're one of us." He shifted to his back foot then back again as if unsure whether he wanted to walk off or say more. In the end, he opted to leave, but not before delivering one last message. "Thank you for saving her."

I could see he was sincere and nodded my gratitude for the sentiment. But with that said, he decided it was time and left. I sank down onto the bench that resembled a prison cot behind me and studied every inch of the room. It was like a giant shower stall molded out of steel with an impenetrable glass shower door. I was not getting out. That was obvious, so I went over to the kiosk and studied it for a time. It was no help. It had been engineered to resist tampering. I almost touched the glass wall to see what I could see down corridor in either direction, but I remembered that it would just go opaque the moment I touched it. I did not want to have to sit on a toilet in full view of anyone in the hall because I was curious what my neighbors were doing, so I resisted the urge to touch it.

That is when it occurred to me. My body was trapped in the cell but not my mind. How could they contain that? They could not as far as I knew. If my mind was not trapped, then neither was I.

I was a telepath. Hell, I had just ripped two men apart with my brain powers. I could use it to hit the little button on the control panel outside my cell. I almost laughed at the ludicrous design of my cell.

I sent my mind through the wall to the panel outside. My head started to hurt. I forced myself to concentrate on the button, but the pain just got worse. I was confident I could do this. It was easy compared to what I had done over the past two days. The pain was atrocious. My vision blurred. My mind swam. I had no choice. I had to stop. I had to pull my mind back.

The moment I stopped concentrating, the pain vanished. I studied the cell and ceiling and could not figure out how the hell they were stopping my ability, but they were. That was obvious. They had some countermeasure to prevent it. Whatever it was, it was highly effective. I tried six more times to bring my mind to a focus long enough to press the release for the door, but each time it ended with me gasping in pain. That was that. There was no escape, and I had to force myself to mentally take back my ridicule of the cell's designer. He had built the better mouse trap.

With escape off the table, I did the only thing left to me. I lay upon my cot and reviewed the battle I had just help win.

There were things I would have done different if I had it to do again. One, I would not explode a body. I had watched Xi and Ailig slip more than once in the mess and nearly lose their footing. Secondly, I would go for feet. Focusing on their arms and torso was difficult, but their feet were much easier to focus on. They pretty much stayed put and with the right angle and leverage, I could easily break an opponent's stance and spoil their balance or easily tear their groin muscles with an unexpected split. I began to develop different techniques based on what I had learned so far. There was one I was eager to try out. In theory, I felt I could launch myself through the air by pushing on something solid. Newton's Laws of motion were on my side, I believed. If ever I had to do battle with another, I would be sure to employ at least a few of the methods I had just devised.

It was not that I was eager for a fight. My interest was more of an academic approach to the utilization of my ability. I just wanted to discover the extent and limitations of my ability. This is what I was thinking about three hours later when a startlingly thin man roughly seven feet tall came around with a tablet in hand to interview me as Xi said he would. I had been arrested on Earth several times over the years and this was another typical booking. They wanted my name, level, quadrant, and cell address as well as my NID article number for future contact and three friends and family to use as second, third, and fourth NID contact numbers. As far as alien life went, it was disappointingly terrestrial in its reality. I supposed that was good in the long run, but in the short run, I wished it was more Stargate SG1 or Star Wars. Hell, I would even settle for Star Trekkie. When the glass at last dimmed, I gave up on the idea of escape and slept.

"He's sleeping," Baggam announced, turning his tablet so that Luke could see. Luke stared at the video feed with eyes red and raw from crying. Luke rose to his feet, grabbing a dagger from the decorative display on the stand at his elbow. He marched toward the door saying not a word.

"Guards!" Baggam called warningly as Luke started to exit. Two knights turned, hands on their swords and slapped the crest on their armor to activate it. They stared the Grand Reaper down, daring him to attack. Luke grimaced and growled and threw the dagger away. Baggam watched the expensive artifact skip across the carpet floor and smack against the base of a cabinet along the wall. His brow creased in irritation, but it passed quick. The boy had just lost a father. The Battle Commander could afford to be forgiving this once.

The moment Luke dropped the knife, he moved to pass. A quick nod from their commander was all they needed to let the Pre-Prior pass. After he was gone, Baggam rose and retrieved his knife, chewing on the inside of his lip thoughtfully. He studied the tablet again, studying the feed and considering the ramifications of disobeying Luke, especially now. Right now, only a few people knew that Magpie was in custody. Right now, it would be easy for Luke to make the man disappear. No one would know and no one would care. He pressed a button on the call box on his desk. A moment later the door opened to reveal one of the guards from a few moments ago.

"Put a guard on the new arrival," he ordered. The guard bowed and hurried out to see that it was done. "Luke. Luke. Luke. How do I save you from yourself?" He did not have the answer. He did not have it two hours later either when he decided to call it a day.

As the top General aboard the Kye O'Ren, he was afforded a few perks other officers were not. The one perk he enjoyed more than all others was that his residential cell was located on the same level as his offices. There were few residential cells on this level. The captain of the Kye O'Ren had a residence on this level. The Admiral of the Flight Corp and his Vice Admiral both had luxurious cells and private arboretums of their own. They both lived just down the byway from where he lived.

He was looking forward to getting drunk and falling asleep in his arboretum. It had been one of those days. His sub-commander and a handful of knights had taken it upon themselves to save the Grand Reaper's sister. They had destroyed a large nest of insurgents, managed to take a handful of them into custody, and did it all with only one loss to the group. Even now, that knight was being reprinted and his mind downloaded before his brain grew too corrupted to maintain the man's identity. It was a bad situation reprinting an Aeonic. The immortals lose their immortality during reprinting. The chips that let them live for centuries would not work with the reprinted physiology. The printing variance was too much and too unpredictable for the nanite circuitry to properly compensate.

Baggam shrugged, shaking his head to clear the thoughts of the fallen knight. The man would no longer be an immortal, but he would still live and probably live well despite his shorter life span. Baggam had even heard that many preferred the shorter lives to that of the immortals, claiming that life was fresher and more vivid. He did not believe it. Who would want a life that a was blink in time when they could keep their eyes open forever and see it all? No one, that was who.

He strode down the byway but stopped when he caught sight of movement among the decorative statuary in the center of the lane. Fearing an ambush, he let his hand slide forward to the long blaster on his belt.

"We need to talk," The Baron of Hein announced, tossing a clear sealed cannister to his superior. Baggam caught it one handed and twisted it around to see what it contained. It was a small spiked rodent common to the parks.

"About a Shrike Rat?" Baggam asked gruffly.

"No. About what's in it," Gorjjen replied ominously.

Chapter 23: The Attempt

It took me two days of laying in the cell to notice the sound. It was elusive and subtle. It was not quite a hum and not quite a squeal. It seemed to vibrate at just the edge of my perception. Whenever I took notice of it, it seemed to dart away like a dragon fly hovering just out of reach. It would dart away then stop. The moment I reached for it, it would dart away again. It was unbelievably annoying now that I knew it was there. I started to push my mind out in an effort to find it, and the sound seemed to home in on my thoughts and scramble them.

"I said, how have you been?" the woman asked again, louder.

"W-What?" I asked, rolling over so I could sit up and see. Her appearance startled me.

"How are you?" Palasa asked for the third time. I stared at her in disbelief, wondering if I was hallucinating. She looked as if she had been standing outside my cell for some time.

"Wow. How long have you been there?" I asked.

"Just a few minutes. You seemed preoccupied with the neural dampeners," she replied, drawing my attention to the burgundy looking dome of glass in the ceiling above her.

"The what?" I asked, feeling like a yokel.

"Let me guess. You tried to escape by pressing the buttons on your cell to open the glass, but something keeps interfering with your ability to concentrate and bring your will to a focus?" She pointed to the reddish colored dome again. "It's a neural dampener. It resonates with the frequency of our brain waves and cancels them out. You won't be able to project your will from inside the cell."

"Ah," I sighed with relief. "I knew it was something." I gave her a quick smile laced with sadness. I scooted back on my cot and leaned against the wall, perching one foot on the edge so I had something to hug.

"How are you?" she asked for the fourth time.

"Well enough, I guess. I'm a prisoner after all. I suppose I'll go on trial soon, so they can punish me for what they say I've done." I sounded bitter because I was. I did not think it was fair that I be punished for something I did not remember doing. Where was the justice in that?

"If you'll let me, I'd like to defend you," she said, taking a seat against the wall of the corridor across from my cell door.

"Well, if not you, then who else," I quipped, relenting. "You're the only one I know on the ship. Though, I don't really know you, do I? Not really." It was hard for me to admit this. I really was alone on the ship, but then again, I had been alone for as long as I could remember which was not that long ago.

"You really don't remember coming to this planet?" she asked, finding it hard to believe.

"No. My oldest memory, as bizarre as it sounds, was of me standing in a flooded alley in New Orleans two days after the levies failed. The alley had been destroyed. There were men and women lying dead in the water around me. I did not know who they were, or how I came to be in the alley. I just remember staggering weakly from the alley. A man and woman in bass boat swept me up. They took me and some others they picked up along the way to a church. We weathered out the flooding there, nearly starving before FEMA rescued us. Since then, I've been wandering. I drifted along the Gulf coast for a time. Took work where I could find it. I never stayed anywhere longer than a couple of years. Hell, I was getting ready to move on from Cherryville when these assholes landed. What are the chances they would land in what amounted to my back yard?" I asked with bitter disbelief.

"Considering they've been looking for you for over a thousand years, I'd say the chances are pretty damn astronomical," she replied with a sardonic smile. "Your life doesn't make any sense, Daniel. Or should I call you Magpie?" she asked, uncertain as to which I preferred.

"Definitely Daniel. Magpie was a murderer evidently. I don't know that man," I confessed, drawing my other knee up to my chest. I really did not. Depending on who you asked, I was either a savior or a mass murderer. It is crazy how those two sometimes coincide. Sometimes, I realized, the only difference between a sinner and a saint was perspective.

"Would you like to?" she asked.

"What? Learn who that monster was?" I asked. "No."

"He wasn't a monster. Not really. To me, he was just the opposite of how the Grand Reaper portrays him. It broke his heart firing on the Sylar Colony. After he convinced us to break away from the infected ships, he went off by himself, consigning himself to a willing isolation."

"He went into his cell and didn't come out again till my mother dragged him out. She was his second in command after we started the drift. She was pretty hard on you for being hard on yourself. We were without a Daimyo or an Abbot. Someone had to take charge of the Drifter's armada. We needed you. We needed someone aboard the ship to take charge, and you were the only one considered. The people of the Drift understood why you did what you did. Not all of them, but most. They wanted you to keep leading, but you kept refusing. You said that we didn't need a monster like you to lead them."

She continued, "You nominated your friend Angus. He agreed to serve as an interim leader and became the first Grand Reaper aboard the Drift. He said that until you finally came to terms with what you had to do back at the Sylar colony, he would lead, but would step down the moment you were ready." She shrugged and we sat there in silence with me imagining what she described and her remembering it. I opened my mouth to speak, but she was not done.

"We continued on as we had always done. Angus moved us from colony to colony and harvested the colonials as our imperial mandate dictated. When we reached—" What she said startled me and I came forward suddenly. She went silent in surprise. "What? What did I say?"

"You said this Angus moved us from colony to colony because of our imperial mandate?" I asked, seeking clarification. She nodded.

"Yeah, and..." she asked, furrowing her brow.

"The Drifters, they didn't break away from the Empire like I'm being blamed for. They broke away from the armada, but only the armada. They're still loyalists? They're still gathering colonists for the Empire," I told her, smiling.

"So?" she repeated, still confused.

"My charges are that I preached sedition and that I willfully murdered a billion people. If they're still doing the Harvest, then I'm not guilty of sedition. I'm guilty of quarantining a third of the armada. I didn't take them from the Emperor as Luke is saying. I broke up the armada to keep the uninfected ships away from the infected ones." I leaned back again, chewing on that fact. This changed the entire tone of Luke's accusation.

"That will help your defense if you can prove it," Palasa admitted.

"Is that how I came to be here?" I asked. "On Earth, I mean. Did they maroon me here?"

"You disappeared during the Harvest of this planet. My mother, me, and a handful of others went looking for you. We couldn't find you. When Commander Angus declared the Harvest complete, three of us stayed behind. We refused to abandon you here. Our plan was to rejoin the original armada when it came to Harvest this colony, but they didn't show up till now. That's why mom and I worked in the White House. We were waiting for the news of the armada's arrival. We've been in the White House longer than any other person in America." She smiled at the thought of that. "We took turns being politicians."

"You did find me though. Didn't you?" I asked, with a knowing smile. "When I thought you and your mom were spies for these guys, she seemed disappointed in me. She said that you two left me alone like I wanted. I didn't know what she was talking about back then, but now I think I do. You guys found me, I told you to leave me alone?" She nodded absently, but the nod turned into a shake before she was done.

"It wasn't that simple," she murmured without emotion. "Me and mom didn't find you. William did."

"You say that name like I should know it," I replied with a smirk, but my smile slid away when Palasa refused to respond. "What happened?"

"William found you December 16, 1811," she replied, staring off into space. It might have been a trick of the light or a prismatic effect of the prison glass between us, but it looked like she was crying. "It was the worst earthquake in the history of the United States. It made the Mississippi River flow backwards. They felt it for hundreds of miles."

"He died in an earthquake?" I asked, but she was already shaking her head. "Did I know him?" I asked, confused why she was mentioning the earthquake. "He was the third member of your team to stay behind, right?"

She nodded sadly. "That and more," she replied evasively, her face clouding.

"Damn it. Just tell me. What happened to him?" I demanded, thinking that maybe he was still down on the planet hiding.

"You killed him," she replied firmly. "You killed him." Her voice was barely a whisper the second time.

"Shit," I responded in amazement. "I really was a bastard."

"Was he someone important to you?" I asked, thinking that maybe it was a lover of hers.

"No. William was important to you, Daniel," she corrected. "He was your brother."

"I had a brother?" I asked in disbelief, feeling the pit of my stomach drop away.

"You had two—William and Mozzie," she replied. This was too much; too much for sitting still. I climbed to my feet and paced up to the glass, being careful not to touch it. I wanted to ask a thousand things, but my mind kept jumping back and forth, analyzing everything she had said. It was too much for me. How could I have brothers and not remember?

"Why?" I asked, settling on that as my response to the news.

"Why did you kill him?" she asked, thinking that was what I meant. "You wanted to be alone. You said you were saving the armada from the infected, but you would not say how. You had a plan. We tried to get more from you, but you were not making any sense. You said as long as you were around that we would always be hunted. You told him to leave. You told us to leave and never coming looking for you again. William wouldn't leave you. You and he blocked us out and talked between yourselves. William screamed for us to run, but it didn't make sense to us. He was terrified of you, and I don't know why. He never said why. He just started drawing in his will, and you killed him." She shook her head in disbelief, reliving that day. When she spoke again, her voice was thick with emotion.

"I've never seen anything like what you did to him. You were so powerful and awful and terrible. I've never seen a will like the will you showed us that day. You were so focused and angry." She went silent and looked upon me like she was waiting for me to change back into that monster. "You broke the world," she declared, falling silent.

"No. I meant, why would you tell me I had brothers then tell me I killed one of them?" I asked acidly, slamming a fist against the glass. The glass suddenly went opaque. I touched it again, and it cleared again. She was shaking her head as if to deny the accusation and avoid the question. "Why?" I snapped.

"I-I just felt you should know," she replied sorrowfully. "I'd want to know if my brothers were dead."

"Brothers?" I asked. "My other brother's dead too?" I asked with narrowed eyes and a greenish pall. "How?"

Her face drained of blood, paling before my eyes. She shook her head and refused to answer.

"How!" I bellowed through the glass, slapping my palm against it without thinking. It went opaque again. I touched it to clear it and backed away. "How did he die?"

"He…" She shook her head, refusing to answer.

"How, damn it?" I demanded again, feeling sick to my stomach.

"He was aboard the Esfir Parisa when you ordered it fired upon," she blurted angrily. "It was one of the infected ships. You had no choice. You had to do it. You had to destroy the infection."

"Oh, God," I gasped, clutching my churning stomach.

"You had to do it," she told me stubbornly.

"Like my brother William had to be destroyed?" I replied.

"I didn't say that. I didn't—That was different. You were…" She shook her head. His death was harder to justify.

"Come on, Palasa," I crooned softly. "You can admit it. I murdered my brother with absolutely no reason for it."

"Magpie wasn't that type of man. He cherished life. He cherished all life. William left you with no choice. He drew in his will first," she said. "I felt him drawing it in. He was going to attack you first."

"Why?" I asked, knowing she did not have the answer to that question. She just shook her head. I studied her moping face and understood the truth. "The earthquake wasn't a coincidence, was it?" She was on the verge of weeping yet managed to shake her head.

"It… " she swallowed hard and took a deep breath to steady herself. "I've never seen anything like it. It was the most frighteningly impressive display of will I've ever seen. Not even Abbots attain that kind of power."

"And I used it to kill him?" I whispered, leaning my head against the glass. It went opaque.

"You scattered his atoms and broke the mantle of this planet," she whispered back. I did not want to talk anymore and just sat there leaning against the glass. She did not talk. After a few moments of silent contemplation. I broke the silence.

"Please leave," I whispered.

I listened to her rise and approach the glass. She stood there in silence then hurried off. I could not blame her for being distraught. It had been painful for me to hear it all. It had to have been hard on her to tell it and relive it. I used to have brothers. That was a hard thing to wrap my head around. It made me wonder about my parents and what happened to them. I was afraid to even ask myself for fear I would go and learn it. The fear that they might have been aboard one of those ships was too much for me to comprehend. In the hall opposite the glass, I heard her come creeping back. I opened my mouth to ask about my parents but closed it without uttering a single syllable. It was okay for me to be angry, but she needed absolution. She had only ever tried to help. She did not need to carry around my guilt.

"It wasn't your fault," I told her through the glass. There was silence. "It really wasn't, you know. It wasn't your fault."

"Oh, I know that," a male voice replied in a deceptively calm tone of voice, "it was yours."

I stepped back from the glass in surprise. I did not know that voice, but I recognized the hate. I reached out and touched the glass, and it went clear again, revealing him.

"Hello, Luke," I said by way greeting.

"Hello, murderer," he replied, pointing toward the Imperial soldier standing near the door controls. The man pressed a button and the door slid open without a sound. Four soldiers flooded into the cell, flowing around Luke. They seized me by the arms and legs and stretched me out on the floor spread eagle, each weighing a limb down.

"Get off me!" I shouted, struggling against their grip. They put their knees on my limbs to pin them down.

"Only a few people know that we have you in custody," he remarked calmly, setting down a glass box with a hole in one end and a bizarre looking rat with spikes along its spine in the other.

"W-What the hell is that?" I demanded, suddenly fearful.

"That? That's a shrike rat. They're all over the ships. They're harmless. Don't be afraid of it. Be afraid of what's in it," he said, sticking his hand in one end of the box. The rat ran around in fear for a few moments then toppled over sideways with a seizure. "We discovered it will die if its outside the body for too long, but anything alive will serve as a host. Now, the interesting thing about it, Magpie, is that it will always leave its host for a more powerful vessel. It's impossible to remove it surgically. It took us a few attempts to discover that little nugget, but we learned that it can be lured out. You just have to give it a more powerful vessel to tempt it, like me." He confessed, "we still don't understand how it affects us."

"What the hell, man. What are you talking about? The rat?" I asked again, confused as to the point of his monologue.

"No, you dense dull-witted simpleton," he sneered.

"It's what's in the rat," he sneered again. "You're the one who figured it out. You figured out that it was a parasite infecting the First Colony and not a virus. Palasa told us. She told us everything. She told us how you ordered the destruction of the colony and how when the ships with the colonists from the surface tried to stop you, you fired on them."

"No. She said I had no choice," I argued back.

"She feels guilty, Magpie. She feels guilty for what you forced her to do." He felt something happening in the box and went silent, looking to the glass case.

I watched the rat with morbid fascination and even forgot to fight the soldiers holding me for a moment. However, the moment the parasite began to squirm from the rat's eye I remembered my duty to struggle and survive. The moment the parasite was free of the rat, it made a bee line for Luke's hand, slithering like a snake in pursuit of its new host. Luke foiled its attack though. The parasite collided with an invisible barrier. It tried to retreat into the rat, but Luke pressed a button on top of the box and another barrier snapped shut behind it, cutting it off. Luke seemed pleased with himself. The parasite writhed and slithered back and forth, searching the edges of its prison like a fishing worm in a can of dirt.

"What are you doing with it?" I asked, shying away from the box.

He pulled a strange looking glass tube from his pocket and twisted it on the end of a metal gun-looking device. These he shoved the tube through a sealed port in the side of the glass box, aiming it directly at the parasite. He pressed a button on the metallic end of the tube, and the parasite was sucked sideways into the glass tube. The end of the tube snapped shut behind it. He brought the tube up before him and looked at me then smiled meanly.

"You killed 1.8 billion people. I'm going to give you the chance to save four times that many," he announced, pressing the tube against my neck.

Back in his office, Baggam pulled up the live feed on his tablet from the holding cell to see how Magpie was faring, taking a long pull on his drink as the feed popped up. That proved a mistake, because what he saw happening in the cell made him spit it all over the tablet's screen.

"That stupid bastard," he cried, racing from his office, calling knights to his side as he ran. "That stupid impulsive brat."

"Don't do this," I begged. "Please don't do this." I twisted back and forth and flung my head from side to side to keep him from infecting me with what was in the tube.

"Hold still," he snarled. "This is better than you deserve."

"Don't do it. You don't know what you're doing. You don't know what it will do to me. Please. I'm begging you. Don't do this," I beseeched the soldiers. The guards holding me looked at the Reaper in shock. "Don't let him do this to me. You're supposed to protect the people on the ship from this kind of thing."

"Sir?" one of them called.

"Hold him still," Luke demanded, trying to keep the glass tube's end pressed against the soft flesh of my neck.

"You can't do this, sir."

"Hold him down!" Luke bellowed, fixing the man with a murderous look. I thought the man would come to my aid then, but he bit back the hateful retort and redoubled his efforts.

"Help!" I called to the empty air. Hoping someone would get there in time to save me. "Help!" I called again. The guard who had opened the door came rushing forward, and he grabbed my head to keep me from thrashing.

"You deserve worse than this," Luke spat, pulling the trigger on the metallic end of the tube. The end of the glass tube opened, and the parasite rushed forward while Luke laughed.

The parasite writhed against my skin, but that was it. It refused to enter my neck. This, of course, did not make Luke happy. He let off the trigger and closed the end of the tube trapping the parasite once more.

"Hold him still," Luke barked, as I started to raise my chest and slam in hopes of slipping free of those who held me. Luke was trying something different. He pressed the end of the tube down over my eye, causing me to cry out in pain and fear and pulled the trigger again. It literally dumped the parasite right my eye, but the parasite wanted no part of me. It coiled up inside its tube instead and hugged the wall, doing everything it could not to touch me.

"Get that thing away from me," I shouted, frantically.

"What did you do?" Luke demanded, letting off the trigger. He set the glass cylinder aside and clubbed me upside the head. It left my head ringing. The soldier holding my head released it. Luke hit me a couple more times, splitting my lip and bloodying my nose. The soldier who had held my head decided it was time to be a soldier again and wrestled Luke off me.

He grabbed Luke by the shoulders and pushed him away. The two struggled with Luke breaking the hold the guard had on his shoulders by bringing his right arm up and over the soldier's left and down under the other. Luke grasped his own hand and twisted his arms clockwise, prying the guard's grip loose, but in the process, Luke kicked the glass tube housing the parasite.

The glass shattered and soldiers scrambled to get away from it. The one holding my left leg was not fast enough though. The back of the man's hand was exposed, and the parasite coiled itself like a cobra and struck.

The man cried out in fear pawing at his shoulder while the other soldiers pulled their weapons. I scrambled back against my cot, climbing on it to get as far away from the infected man as possible. I had psychic ability before, but the neural dampener had me neutered right now. It had me and Luke neutered right now. I had two fists and fuzzy vision thanks to Luke.

The infected soldier pawed at his arm, looking with wild eyes to his brothers in arms for help. They warned him off with their stun batons. The man staggered back, and we could tell where the parasite was by where infected soldier slapped himself. When it reached his neck, the man clamped a hand over the area and started to cry, realizing it was all over for him. A moment later, his eyes rolled up into his head, and the man collapsed seizing violently.

The others closed rank, unintentionally but thankfully, separating me from their infected comrade.

"Don't let that thing escape," Luke commanded, moving off to his left to get behind it. The seizure stopped, and the soldier suddenly lay still. Luke froze, afraid to act. I felt the infected man's will being drawn in only to break apart like waves upon the rocks. The neural dampener stopped me from being able to defend myself, but it also stopped that thing from spreading its sickness.

"It can't use it's telepathic ability. It can't infect you," I blurted, pushing a soldier forward. The percher, for that was who the soldier had become, came to his feet quickly and caught the forward thrusting arm of the guard I pushed. He used the soldiers forward momentum to change his aim, ramming the stun baton into the abdomen of the soldier who had held my right leg. The man went limp crying out in pain as he fell and started shaking all over.

The soldier that the percher grabbed curled his arm and slammed his face into the infected soldier's nose, breaking it. The percher staggered backwards toward the door, pawing at the stun baton hanging from his own belt. He grabbed it and swung it back and forth warningly to keep Luke and the other soldier's back. It was working. Content that they were not brave enough yet to rush him, the percher turned and fled through the door to freedom.

Freedom did not last long for the infected though, and this was not the parasite's day.

Baggam's nanite sword thrust out before the fleeing soldier so that the man's throat collided with its razor-sharp edge. The soldier continued forward, going too fast to stop. The Commander stepped into the middle of the door in the soldier's wake and dragged the blade around the side of the fleeing man's neck and gave it a hard quick pull that separated the soldier's head from his neck. The head rolled off the back of the collapsing body and tumbled back into the room, very near the glass box.

Knights appeared behind their fierce commander, each carrying a naked blade in his hand and each more than willing to cut down every man in my cell if their commander willed it.

All eyes were on the severed head. Luke and Baggam knew what came next. The rest of us suspected. Luke squatted beside the glass box and opened the side closest to the weakened rat. The parasite made its appearance a minute later, slithering out of the soldier's head. The moment it was free, it hurriedly slithered back into the rat it had abandoned, crawling in through the things nose. Luke closed the box so the rat could not escape.

"You're Imperial soldiers," Baggam growled, marching into the room. "When were you ever trained to do this?" He put his face inches from the nose of the soldier who had held my right arm. "Well? Who trained you to torture prisoners?" he demanded. The soldier gave a nervous shake of his head.

"N-No o-one, sir?" the man stammered.

"Bah!" he growled in disgust. "Arrest them," Baggam barked to his men. His knights marched into the cell and took the four soldiers who remained into custody. "It seems Puck didn't train you as well as he thought he had. He'll be very disappointed to hear that. I'm sure he'll take it personally." The soldiers seemed terrified of this more than the prospect of being in prison. One of them started whining with fear as the knight holding him led them away. The moment the soldiers were gone, Baggam turned on Luke.

"Stand down," Luke commanded. Baggam marched over and put his face in front of Luke's as he had the soldier a moment prior.

"Explain!" he bellowed, spraying spittle in the Reaper's face.

"My explanation is that I am the Grand Reaper," Luke replied calmly, " and I don't have to explain myself to you, Commander."

Baggam brought the tip of his sword blade up and under Luke's chin. "Explain," he hissed threateningly. Luke's hard eyes did not soften—not at first. He was every bit as stubborn as the Battle Commander.

"The disciplined part of my brain reminds me that I can't kill you for what you're doing, but that part of my brain isn't speaking very loud right now. Explain or I push this into your brain and order the ships on to the next colony while we elect a new Reaper." Baggam wasn't going to be put off by rank this time. Luke, in the Commander's eyes, had crossed a very serious line.

"Fine," Luke relented, stepping back. "I had a plan. It wasn't just revenge. The colonists know him on the ground. The leaders have spoken with him. They've met him. They know what he's like. My logic was that if I could have infected him, I could show them the threat that was coming for them. I could have harvested the whole colony instead of half. I was trying to use a murderer to save billions of lives. Getting revenge was just a bonus for me."

"You have no idea what the end result would have been," I snarled. "What if you couldn't stop me?" I looked to the Commander. "You are going to arrest him, right?" I asked.

Baggam gave me a weary look. "No. He had a good plan, even if it was immoral. If he'd come to me before, I might have even sanctioned it. Might have," he repeated, letting it be known he was not completely on board with this.

"He's a raving psychotic," I cried, in protest.

"Said the man who killed two billion innocents," Baggam fired back.

"Fuck both of you," I called back, sinking to a sitting position. Baggam glared at me, but there was not much bite in the look. He kicked the severed head out into the hall.

"So, how did the soldier get infected?" Baggam asked. Luke shook his head in confusion. He did not have a good answer for that.

"I don't know. The parasite was afraid of him," he said, pointing at me. Baggam gave me the once over, studying me again from head to toe and back again, trying to figure out what he had missed.

"Why would it do that?" Baggam asked. "What makes you so special?" He gave me a hard look filled with suspicion. I shrugged. I sure as hell did not know.

"I haven't got a clue. Why don't you ask Palasa. She says that's why I came to this planet. She says I claimed to have come here to save the armada." I shook my head. "But I have no idea what that plan is now. Evidently, I've found a way to keep people from becoming infected."

"So, it would seem," Luke quipped. "Though, as you say, that means little to nothing since you can't remember what you did." There was a sneer in his voice that was just giving me the biggest headache. I was so tired of this man's shit.

"I'm through with him," I announced airily, making a shooing motion to dismiss the Reaper. Baggam actually grinned at the effect this had on Luke. Luke's nostrils flared and his eyes bulged, and his lips peeled back in a feral snarl of outrage. I came to my feet in a heartbeat and squared off with the man. "Try it. For the first time since meeting you, we are now equals. We can't use our minds. We have no weapons, and right now, I'd like nothing better than to put my fist through your smug self-righteous face." Baggam seemed almost on the verge of allowing it.

"Go," The Commander ordered instead, pushing Luke toward the door. "And don't think about coming back when I'm not around. I alerted the Inquisitor's Court to Magpie's apprehension. If you want to assassinate him now, you better be stealthier than my knights are vigilant," he warned. "From this point on, there will be two knights on watch outside this man's cell till he goes on trial." Luke gave him a hateful look and walked on.

"Speaking of that, Palasa has asked for the privilege of defending me. I've given her my permission," I said to Baggam.

"Your defense council is growing then," Baggam responded with a smirk. "Gorjjen Doricci has proclaimed himself your lawyer in this as well. He seems to believe in you, Magpie."

"Don't you mean the Baron of Hein?" I asked waspishly.

"No. I mean Gorjjen Doricci. The Baron of Hein don't care about you," Baggam fired back. "Count yourself lucky, Magpie. Gorjjen doesn't vouch for people often."

"Daniel," I replied. "Call me Daniel, please. Magpie was someone else. He wasn't me. He fired on a planet of people and on shuttles filled with family and friends. I'm not that man. I don't know that man."

"You're a murderer," Luke called from the corridor, "and it doesn't matter by which name you call yourself. Blood stains the hands, and those hands belong to you. You can't erase what was done just by willing the nightmare away. I can see you feel remorse, but not for what you did. You feel remorse for the fact this new persona of yours is in your eyes being unjustly held responsible for what that other persona did. You're the same man," Luke growled, coming a couple of steps back into the cell.

"This is pointless," Baggam griped, shoving Luke back into the corridor. "Please accompany the Pre-Prior to wherever he wishes to go. Don't leave his side till I tell you it's okay to do so. I don't want a repeat of this scene." The Commander picked up the shrike rat and shoved it at Luke. "Study it or kill it. I don't care. Just stop trying to infect people on the ship."

Luke gave me one last hate-filled look and marched off. The two knights assigned to him followed at a respectful distance.

"I'll get someone in here to clean up the blood and body," Baggam mumbled, studying the mess. The Commander pressed something on the hilt of his sword and the blade shimmered, rippling as the nanites that made it up realigned. When the blade settled and smoothed, the blood from the dead soldier was gone. He shoved it back into its sheath, ramming it into place to vent his frustration. He started to leave mumbling an apology for the incident under his breath as he went.

"Would you have let him?" I asked. Baggam glanced back at me and studied me as if calculating my worth. "If he had come to you first with his plan, would you have let him infect me?" I asked again, clarifying the question.

"Bah! I don't know." He moved his jaw like he was chewing on the notion. "Maybe. No. I don't know. It's complicated. By the Emperor's eye, I owe you nothing. As far as I'm concerned, you're a mass murderer. Maybe," he said again, "Maybe not. The enemy of my enemy notion has never really set well with me. On one hand, you're a filthy murdering coward seditionist. On the other, they're murdering cowardly parasitical missionaries. I don't see how one is better than the other or if it technically changes anything. In the end, you and the parasite are both cowardly murderers. I think my only hang up with any of this what it would end up doing to that boy out there. He's a good man. He has always been a good man. Your presence has turned him into this. You make him into this. He is your creation."

Baggam ground his teeth and flared his nostrils as he considered the question. "No. I wouldn't have let him do that to himself. I would have stopped him," the Battle Commander rumbled at last. "Not for you, but for him. I would have interfered for him. He is better than you. He is better than us all."

Chapter 24: Trial

I'd been lounging on my cot for over a day since Luke's attempt to infect me. I expected he would try again at any moment. I knew he hated me, but I was not sure just how much. That was not true. I knew exactly how much he hated me. He hated me enough to try and infect me with a sickness his people feared above all things. I doubted there was forgiveness in his heart. I was not even sure I was capable of forgiving any man responsible for killing my father. Not that I would know what that was like, having no idea whether my own father lived or breathed. So, it was with considerable trepidation that I rose from my cot in response to the hollow sounding echo of booted feet in the corridor outside my cell. In my head, they were coming for me again.

I had planned for this and slipped the square bowl into the food kiosk and pressed the menu item I knew to be a scalding hot beverage of unknown origin. I left it sitting there, ready to grab it and throw it into the face of anyone who approached me. I was not going down without a fight this time.

"Are you planning on throwing that in my face?" Leia asked, limping past my guards. She was not in her armor this time. Instead, she was wearing an almond-colored set of leggings that looked like jeans. The zipper of the leggings was laced and wrapped around a toggle to hold them closed. The top was of a slightly darker almond color and quilted with small raised triangular puffs. Across her shoulder was what looked like a blanketed shoulder plate draped over her right shoulder and upper arm. She did carry her sword, only this was not the short-hilted sword she normally wore. It seemed plainer. The scabbard had very little ornamentation.

"I was planning on throwing it in someone's face," I replied, smirking. She mumbled something to the two knights standing watch and they both drifted away, each going a different direction. She sank into a cross-legged sitting position, wincing as the scab-covered wounds across her thighs tore open. It seemed to cause her considerable pain, but she did not complain.

"I heard what Luke tried to do. I'm sorry for that. It was ungrateful of him," she admitted embarrassingly. I shook my head and waved that off.

"He has every right to be—" I began.

"Why did you do it? Why did you come for me?" she asked. Her brow furrowed. "You don't even know me." She shook her head struggling with the question.

"I don't know. I just got tired of being alone, I suppose. You talked to me. You kept coming around after we had parted. I could sense you. I think I just needed a friend." I knew this was not true. It had been a compulsion to find her.

"But, why me?" she asked, struggling still. "I'm sure you could have found a mate down on the surface with my attributes that was less of a challenge. Why would you do that for me? You nearly died from what the Commander says. He says you nearly killed yourself on the surface to get a message to Luke. You surrendered to the Empire to save me. Why? You killed billions. Why was I important?" she asked, almost begging to know what made her worth it.

"I love you," I admitted, knowing that was not really true. I knew it would probably frighten her off, but it was kind of the truth. Whether an infatuation or the real thing, I did not know. I just knew I needed her. It was not that I wanted her. I needed her.

"You don't even know me," she snapped, "but you were able to find me when no one else could. Maybe it is love… for you."

"You don't feel the same?" I asked, knowing she did not.

"I don't even know you. I… Why would you turn yourself in for me?" she demanded angrily, stretching out her injured leg to alleviate some of the discomfort. It was making her angry not knowing why I did what I did.

"It's not love. Okay. I just need you. I don't even know what that means. I just know that it's right. I need you. It's like a compulsion in my subconscious pushing me toward you. It's like I need somebody to stand with me, like my very own battle buddy. I want to say that it's just because I want you as a lover—I actually do by the way—but more than that. I need you in a way I can't define. It's something more intimate than physical contact like I need you in my mind all the time. It's an overwhelming need and no other woman will do. Does any of what I'm saying make sense to you?" I felt like an idiot asking this.

"No. It doesn't make sense. Not even a little," she responded, blunt in her reply. "You don't even know me."

"I do. I mean, I know that the parts of you I'm familiar with are magnificent," I said, feeling awkward. Her eyes narrowed, but I saw interest there.

"Describe me," she commanded, her chin raised.

"Your form is like sculpted marble, pale and smooth; impossibly smooth. Your skin is like star fire, shimmering on the surface of a still sea. Your eyes are like two limpid pools of water, deep and quenching, yet in them, I see fire, and an impossible strength. An indomitable will. Your hair spills across your shoulders like… like a chocolate fountain overflowing." I cringed the moment I heard myself say it. Her face screwed up into a comically ludicrous sneer. I stopped describing her and waited for the back lash, but instead of the jeering ridicule, she instead burst out in laughter.

"You," she held up her hand to stop me while she caught her breath, "are horrible at this," she declared, snorting intermittently, much to her embarrassment.

"You snort when you laugh?" I asked, laughing with her. She laughed even harder, begging me to stop. "I heard you. You snort when you laugh. Ha. That's so awesome."

"S—Stop," she begged, hugging her mid-section. "That was singularly the worst attempt at seduction I've ever—"

"You're beautiful," I declared, interrupting her. "That's why I was interested in you. Your face is nice. You move like fire in zero gravity. And when I see you, hear you, think of you, I just want to be a better man. I want to be worthy of you. That's it. That's my honesty. You're beautiful like no woman I've ever seen. I've always been a drifter, and I've never wanted anything but a horizon to head for till I met you. It doesn't matter that you don't feel the same way. You've done this to me. In all my miserable life, you were the only thing I ever thought to covet." I stopped talking and studied her face, then let my eyes drop. "When I go before your judges, they will find me guilty as your brother has and my dreams will die with me. Before I met you, that would have never been a tragedy." I shrugged, smiling bitterly. "You've become my North Star." She studied my face, emotion writ in the furrowed brow and uncertain eyes. She never said a word. She just sat there staring at me.

"Say something, anything. Tell me I'm an idiot and that I'm a fool. Make this go away. I can go before the judges and accept their judgement. Tell me I don't matter and that I was a child for daring to think we could be something. It won't hurt then when they take it all away." I walked over to the glass and knelt before her. "Please."

"You saved me," Leia whispered, climbing to her feet. We could hear more boots coming from down the corridor.

"No. Your friends saved you. I showed them where you were," I corrected.

"No. It was only you. The others saved my body. You saved my mind." She swallowed hard, placing her hand against the glass. "Before I was taken, I watched you while you slept. I tiptoed into your mind that first night after we met. You wouldn't shut up. You just kept jabbering on about cold spaghetti and fishing. I came creeping after you to see who you were, and why you felt the need to pursue me. You were so vulgar and childish at the ship, but not when you were alone. I was there before you drifted off, and I saw how you really were. I saw how you traced your fingertips across my naked flesh, and how you made love to me in your mind." She turned away.

"I saw you filled with passion and tenderness and honesty," she admitted softly. "You saved me because while the perchers clawed at my mind trying to get in, I relived your touch over and over again. I felt your breath warm and hot upon my neck and felt the kindness in your touch. They couldn't get in because I didn't want to give up that moment." Her eyes looked troubled and pleading as she looked upon me. "That moment saved my life. I won't take it from you. Let it save your life." She started to walk away. "I can handle being your North Star, but only if you fight for me a little longer."

"What?" I asked softly, at a loss for words. "You're saying I got a chance?" I asked, perking up. She laughed merrily, swallowing her cloying emotions.

"A small one," she whispered. "A very small one."

It was enough.

"I never said it but thank you," Leia announced. "Thank you for being that man. I hope this trial goes well for you. I kind of look forward to fighting the rotting men with you again," she said with a mischievous wink.

"Uh." I had no idea what she was talking about. "What rotting men?" I asked, seriously confused.

"In your dreams. When you dream, you dream of fighting the rotting men as they break into your dilapidated woodland abode. It was fun and stimulating. I thoroughly enjoyed it. If you win your trial, I would love to help you fight your rotting men again," she said, wrinkling her nose.

I sighed to see her flirtatious side, but I had no idea what she was talking about. I mean, it sounded like she was describing a zombie attack, but I did not dream of zombies. In fact, I could not remember one instance where I ever got to dream of zombies. I shrugged. What did it matter? If she wanted to fight zombies with me in my brain, then I would start dreaming about zombies. I would do anything to have her in my mind. This made me smile more than the rest. That last thought felt so right. I really did want her in my mind. She fluttered her fingers at me in a farewell wave and limped off, humming to herself.

The soldiers arrived a few moments later. It was time to go to trial.

It was good fortune that I was considered a high value prisoner. They kept me in a cell block near the lifts for easy access. I do not think I could have taken the long ride most of the criminals here had to take. This entire level of the ship was a dedicated detention center that stretched for hundreds of miles.

Getting out of the prison involved passing through three rotating rooms. Each was monitored from behind security smart glass windows like the one used on the front of my cell. After passing through the third lock, a prisoner would have to make the long walk through an Imperial garrison of soldiers while enduring the endless security scanners built into the smart glass walls of the corridor. This of course ended in a small chamber with security glass blocking off the only three lifts in this quadrant of the prison. Here the prisoner had to place both hands on the glass and receive one last scan from security. If the prisoner passed, the glass doors would open, and the prisoner would be allowed to pass to the lifts. An NID from an authorized agent of the prison was needed to open and operate the lifts however. All in all, it was a very effective system.

While I was waiting for the first of the three locks to open, I noticed a diagram posted on the wall. It showed that there were four security areas like the one I was about to enter. These were the only places on the infamous Level 601 whereby anyone could gain access to or from the prison level. It was completely secure. A central transit hub filled the center of the ship around the central axis and radiated out like spokes in a wheel. Thankfully, I never had to take the transit tube and vomit like the knights guarding my cell said the other prisoners did.

The door slow slid into sight from behind a thick metal wall. The moment it was lined up with the door in the wall, we stepped through. Once inside, the room began to spin. It passed an open door and I made as if to enter this thinking it our exit, but the soldiers blocked me from leaving. Two more doors identical to the last passed us by. The fourth door lined up perfectly with another room. It looked the same as the other doors we passed.

The soldiers marched me through, and I began to realize halfway through the second rotation that getting out was more than just spinning rooms with a single door. They gave you options to explore. I shuddered to think what would happen if I had taken one of the other doors. Getting through the locks meant knowing the combination of the rotation for that.

After we passed from the second and through the third, the soldiers marched me down the long walk. Colored spots appeared on the glass walls as we entered, showing up on both walls. As I walked, the colored lights formed a silhouette of my form with square boxes filled with alien words appearing at random. In the boxes numbers could be seen fluctuating up and down. From the boxes, connecting lines linked them with different parts of my person. The boxes changed as I walked, jumping from place to place, but each time the lines jumped with them and kept them connected to me. I felt like a teaching aid for a human anatomy class.

"Can we move this along?" I asked, trying to adopt a bolder stride. The soldiers made me walk the same pace as they walked. The boxes and arrows pointing to me seemed rather preoccupied with my head and neck area. The boxes flickered as if unsure what label to fill the box with. The arrows kept jumping around my skull like woodland gnats. I found it annoying and peculiar, but security did not stop us, so I did not question it.

The security wall was simple for me to pass through. Within seconds of me placing my hands on the glass, the door opened, and we passed through. A soldier with a peculiarly wide nose and dark eyes swiped his NID through a hologram on a pedestal between the lifts. The doors opened immediately, and we filed in.

"What's it like?" I asked, nervously. "You know, going before the Inquisitors?" Big Nose was the only one who would talk to me. Judging by the looks they were giving me, they had heard about what had happened to the last soldiers to interact with me. They wanted no part of me. All save Big Nose that is.

"It's an inquisition," he replied as if that were a decent answer. "You go in. They ask you questions. You answer them. They ask you more questions. They decide your fate. And you leave to live that life they choose for you." He crossed his arms over his broad belly and kept his eyes on the door.

"That's it?" I asked, in disbelief.

"They just want the truth," The soldier mumbled. "If you're innocent, then it is just a little wasted time. Are you innocent?" he asked, arching a brow questioningly.

"No," I replied dismally, though I did not know if that was true or not. I did not remember doing it.

"Then you're probably fucked," the soldier replied with no noticeable emotion. "What'd you do?" he asked.

"I'm Magpie," I announced with the same lack of emotion.

"Oh, then you're truly fucked," the guard declared, sidling away.

"Thanks," I replied blandly.

"I'm just here to help," the soldier said, shaking his head as if to clear it. The other soldiers chuckled quietly.

The lift deposited us on a different level of the ship. At first, I was not sure what level it was. I forgot to look at the placard. It was a bizarre place filled with pale unfriendly people distracted with their electronic devices.

"Where are we?" I asked.

"Level 51," The soldier replied, blinking his eyes as if in pain. "The bureaucratic level. All public services aboard the Kye O'Ren are conducted from this level. Residential services, permits, licensing, aesthetic enhancement councils, water, waste, and power management offices. Also, food services, civil mediators, crisis management, and the criminal courts—which is where we're going." I had to chuckle at it all.

"What's so funny?" Big Nose asked.

"You. This place. You have an Area 51 just like us," I replied, laughing harder.

"What?" the soldier asked, not expecting laughter.

"Down on the planet we have a place called Area 51. It's where our… you know what? Never mind. It's not important." He was not getting the humor in this. I nodded toward the endless plazas and opened aired cubicles filled with the plain pale unremarkable people tapping away on their NIDs and tablets like vapid teenagers with cell phones. "I think this is where accountants go when they die," I muttered finding the place impressively unimpressive.

Big Nose shrugged indifferently and marched me down the center of the byway. Men dressed in pale smocks with polished white shoes and soft sand-colored dress jackets with rounded tails and long lobed sides stopped fiddling with their tablets and watched as I passed. Women in bright yellow leggings, soft shoes, and bird egg blue blouses that came nearly to their knees, stopped their writing and gossiping and studied the monster their parents used to frighten them with. I could not help but imagine Luke standing before a camera somewhere with his arms spread and chin raised boldly declaring his successful capture of me. One middle-aged woman with helmet hair wrinkled her nose and sneered in disgust at me. I gave her the bird. I guess giving the middle finger translates because she looked shocked at the gesture.

The byway ended in a T-shaped intersection. The byway it intersected with formed a ring around a central hub. Other byways intersected it in different places around the hub. It was only when we crossed the intersecting byway that I realized our destination was the central hub.

The walls on the outside of the hub were covered in carvings and engravings. As I studied them, I realized it was a mural of sorts. The engravings were all connected to form one larger picture.

People were tumbling from the lips of a giant, falling through space to fill a bowl upon a balance. The bowl on the other end was filled with the blood of the tortured and harmed. There were men and women stuffed inside the wounds of a hideous creature with the distorted features of a man, and it was from these people that the blood came. They wept blood into the second cup. I understood the general meaning of it all. This was their version of the scales of justice. Here they balanced life with blood; good with evil; truth with lies. I would have liked to have studied the carvings in greater depth, but the soldiers would not have it. They prodded me along, shoving me toward two massive inner doors.

Written out in large, raised letters above the door was the place's name. It roughly translated into English as the Hall of Inquisition. It should have bothered me that we had arrived, but it did not. What did fill me with a tremor of dread was what was written beneath these words.

"Enter Ye Wicked Beast and Black Tongued Liars and be Judged."

I swallowed hard and made my way inside. It was a bizarre room that extended well into the next level of the ship above. There were four rows of seats. Each row sat a little higher than the one before it. These seats flowed around the room, starting and stopping at the door through which I had entered. The door in question seemed to be the only entrance and exit to the room. Two Imperial Knights in black armor and embossed with silver sigils stood guard before them. Long hilted swords jutted from their back and above their shoulders.

Above these seats and jutting out on spindled balconies toward the center of the room were dark robed men and women with cruel wrinkled faces and unimpressed eyes. They looked down upon me.

They were the Inquisitors.

Above them was a ring of boxed chambers. Set a little back from that ring and above them was another ring of chambers. There were five rings in all, and they were filled with men and women and even children come to bear witness to the final moments of Magpie.

In the center of the room before me on a small, raised dais stood Palasa and Gorjjen—my lawyers.

Officers from the Army and Grey Guard and unarmed knights of the Empire filled the seats around me. There were also officers from the Flight Corp and divisions of the Kye O'Ren's military I had never encountered before. Leia, Baggam, Luke, Jo, Milintart, Ailig and even One-eye filled seats in the first row behind the table where I was to sit. Someone I was surprised to see in attendance was Borbala. I was only surprised because I thought he had died. He looked depressed and different.

The soldiers flanking me marched me forward and stopped at the dais. I walked up the steps so that I could join with Gorjjen and Palasa. They moved me to the seat between them. At Palasa's urging, I sat. They followed my example and took their own. The soldiers who had led me in, marched back out without a word.

Before us was a long table with curious-looking squares roughly one foot across. A round dome filled the center of each square. Behind these squares was a long bar that ran the length of the table. There was silence in the room. I actually heard someone's NID beep in the uppermost ring of the gallery. That was how quiet it was in the room. I gave Leia a fleeting smile which she returned.

"What happens next?" I asked Palasa.

"Silence!" one of the Inquisitors demanded loudly. Whispers could be heard in the upper gallery as people began to discuss this occurrence.

"The accused can't speak except to answer questions," Palasa explained. "The first test of your guilt was discovering how long it would take for you to break the silence."

"That's just stupid," I declared loudly.

The spindled balconies that held my judges suddenly darted around the perimeter of the room and came together before me with all seven judges looking down upon me with hard cruel eyes and sneering scowls.

"The accused will speak only when spoken to," they declared, leaning out over the varnished rails of their balcony in challenge.

They waited there to see if I would respond. I did not because they were really creeping me out. Satisfied that their will would be obeyed, the spindled balconies began to drift somewhat apart. There was silence for a time, then one of the vulture looking women cleared her throat and broke the silence. She leaned out over the balcony. A small bent rod connected to an oversized collar on one end and a small thin disk hung before her lips. She spoke in a normal tone of voice and the small disk made it so that everyone in the room could hear her clearly and without echo.

"You are the Prior they call Magpie?" she asked.

I sat in silence, studying the faces of the people in the galleries above. Palasa leaned over suddenly and whispered in my ear.

"You can answer that," she said, giving me permission at last.

"I don't know. They tell me I am," I responded.

"The accused will answer this question in the affirmative or the negatory," she advised sternly.

"No. The accused won't."

"Silence," she barked, leaning over the edge.

I opened my mouth to protest, but Palasa placed a hand upon my arm to silence me. She rose and addressed the woman riddling me.

"If it pleases the Inquisitor, I would seek permission to answer this for the accused."

"It so pleases," the judge replied. "Speak."

"The accused is in fact the Prior who the Empire calls Magpie," she said, falling silent.

"Why does the accused not so answer?" she asked.

"If it pleases, he does not know. He, by my own testimony, sought refuge here with the colonials some four hundred years ago as the colonials reckon time. He joined with the colonials and fought in their wars. He was wounded to the head during one of these battles and has lost all memory of who he was and of what transpired before that wounding," Palasa explained, taking her seat when she was done.

"I ask of the accused. Is this true?" the shrewish judge inquired.

"It is as I understand it. My memories only go back a decade or so," I replied.

"When was this wound received?" she asked. I paused to calculate the approximate number of years.

"Seventy-one years ago," I replied. The spindled balconies all swooped in close to one another and the Inquisitors conferred in whispers. Gorjjen drew attention to himself by noisily sliding his chair back so that he could stand. The Inquisitors fell silent as they looked down on the ratty looking man who had risen.

"You seek the floor?" the old woman above him inquired.

"I seek the floor," Gorjjen confirmed. The room went silent once more.

The Inquisitors studied the ratty form of Gorjjen and communicated their disdain with sneers and raised chins.

"Who are you to speak on the accused's behalf?" they asked with a derisive sniff. I turned to regard my friends in the seats behind me and saw that they all smiled. Baggam smiled bigger than the rest.

"I?" Gorjjen asked, swelling with indignation. "You dare ask who I am?" he demanded again. His eyes cut into the Inquisitors courage like a nanite blade through bone. "You have the privilege and glory of addressing the indomitable Baron of Hein," he declared with a sneer of his own. The old men and seasoned spinsters, whom all men aboard the Kye O'Ren claimed they feared above all others, paled as if each of them sat where I did. There was silence from the judges but a buzz of conversation from the galleries above.

"The—" the old woman who had done all the speaking for the Inquisitors so far cleared her throat and tried to regain her dignity. She was a tall regal lady with bluish-grey hair. She wore the black robes like the other judges and like them, and her face knew no joy.

The people in the galleries were those who if shown the hint weakness, would eagerly exploit it. I had seen their kind at every cheap concert.

"We will, of course, recognize and hear the words of the revered Baron of Hein," she announced boldly, raising her chin once more.

"This man whom my colleague refers to as the Prior known as Magpie is not, in fact, the Prior known as Magpie. He is false," Gorjjen declared. There was more whispering in the boxes above. "This is his body, but the Magpie has flown this form. Where he resides now, no one may know. I do not. I have investigated this wretched excuse for a man, Grand Inquisitor," the Baron announced, "and found no trace of the sentient mind of my old friend the Magpie. It is possible the Magpie may return to this form in time, but till that day is realized, this man is innocent of the transgressions of the Prior so accused."

"It is your belief that this man be pardoned because he does not remember who he is?" a male judge asked incredulously.

"Absolutely not. You who sit at the feet of justice cannot pardon this man. In fact, I demand that you not pardon this man," Gorjjen snarled, shoving a rigid finger in my face. I swallowed hard.

"What the hell is he doing?" I asked of Palasa.

"Silence!" the old woman who presided demanded of me. With me silenced, she turned her attention back on the man demanding that I not be freed.

"You are ambiguous in your defense, good Baron. Please clarify your stance," she urged.

"You may not pardon this man for this man is not guilty of any offense worth pardoning," Gorjjen declared. He gave the men and women in the balconies a hard look. "If found guilty, must Magpie face the Emperor's justice?" Gorjjen asked.

"He must, if found guilty. It is the law," the old woman replied.

"Will it be swift?"

"Assuredly so, good Baron," another Inquisitor to my left decreed.

"Please clarify this point of law for me then, glorious Judges. Do we punish the body or the sentience when we punish those who break the Emperor's laws?" he asked.

The Inquisitors conferred with thrown looks and facial tics then turned back to the Baron of Hein to respond. "It is our understanding that we punish both."

"Ah, it as I suspected. Tell me, what law could the body break that the sentient mind that controls it would be free of fault? Can a body break the law without the sentient identity that dwells within willing it to do so?" Gorjjen asked. The brows of the Inquisitors creased with troubled thoughts.

"If the sentient form transgresses, the body transgresses by matter of proxy if not deed," A robust looking judge announced.

"I see you are a man of deep thought, my revered elder. So, the body may be punished even should it be absent the guilty mind. I am agreed that this is good law. For if we destroy the body, what home remains for the sentient mind who first chose to break the law? I applaud you good men and women. You have answered my queries with great alacrity and strong-minded logic." Gorjjen bowed to the Inquisitors and started to retake his seat.

"The Baron of Hein is most gracious in his praise," a wrinkled white-haired old woman replied. Gorjjen was almost seated when he pretended a thought had just occurred to him.

"Gracious Judges," he called yet again.

"The Baron wishes another point of law be clarified?" the old white-haired woman asked.

"Verily," he replied. "Will this court pass judgment without hearing the testimony of the accused sentience?"

"Surely not, good Baron. All witnesses will be called to speak including the accused," a grey-haired old man revealed. Gorjjen smiled as if satisfied with this response.

"Great. Fantastic," Gorjjen declared. "Then I move to adjourn these proceedings until the fugitive Prior we know as Magpie be apprehended." The whispers in the upper gallery had grown angry. The judges picked up on this and responded with irritation.

"Do you mock this court?" the old grey-haired judge demanded heatedly.

"Yes, I most assuredly do," Gorjjen responded, showing no hesitation.

Gorjjen studied the faces of the judges before continuing. "Seven Inquisitors have decreed that the body may be punished even if the sentience guilty of the transgressions has flown the vassal. Here we sit beside the body of the guilty in which resides the innocent sentience of another. How do you call yourself, my friend?" Gorjjen asked, turning on me suddenly. I looked to the judges and the faces of those seated before me and shrugged.

"My name is Daniel Sojourner," I declared strenuously.

"Did you personally fire upon the Sylar Colony using the long guns of the Imperial ship the Moon Rai?" he asked.

As if waiting for this cue, a hologram suddenly appeared above the long bar that ran across the table before me. It showed video feed from a saucer in orbit of a red planet. One of them was firing upon the surface of the red rock planet. Each blast burned away their atmosphere and broke up the crust of the planet.

"No. I didn't do that. Magpie did that," I declared, looking with horror on the destruction I saw being wrought. I knew it was my hands that had done that and my mouth that had given the order, but I could not imagine me having ever something like that.

"Did you fire antimatter rockets from the Moon Rai at unarmed Imperial ships?" Gorjjen asked. The hologram changed to a loftier perspective. Rockets pushed with blue flame rained down on six saucers. Clouds of escaping air rushed from the breaches and brief belches of fire lit the ships. Bright arcs of rejoined energy flared impossibly bright where the antimatter warheads contacted the ships' hulls.

The lens through which we watched the missile barrage suddenly went black then reacquired the damaged ships at a higher magnification. Small specks of debris floated outside the damage ships. The lens went black again and reacquired the ships yet again at an even higher magnification. I could see then that it was debris that filled the space around the ships but bodies. It was people; hundreds of thousands of people floating frozen and dead above the burning planet. And as I watched, they began to sink into the damaged atmosphere of the planet below, burning as they fell.

"I... No. No! I did not do that," I declared, eyes brimming with tears. "I did not." I swiped through the image with my hand trying to banish it. When that did not work, I smashed my fist repeatedly on the bar from which the image sprang. Palasa tried to stop me.

"That isn't me. I didn't do that." I looked to Leia and tried to make her believe me. Luke's eyes were hard and accusing, but Leia's eyes were understanding. She had seen inside his mind. She knew the truth through my eyes. "I didn't do that," I mouthed. She smiled and responded in kind, mouthing the response I needed to hear: I know. Palasa put her hands on my shoulder to comfort me. It did not really help. "Shut it off, please." The footage was cut a moment later.

"Strange," Gorjjen murmured. "I sensed no deception in this man. How say you, my rapturous egalitarians? Is this man the body and the sentience of the man who killed 1.8 billion innocents?" There was more whispering from the judges as they conferred.

"Is it your intent to let the butcher of the First Colony escape justice?" the old grey-haired judge asked.

"Assuredly not," Gorjjen snarled. "The Baron of Heid is the greatest champion of justice aboard the Kye O'Ren. If the guilty man responsible for the massacre of Sylar Colony and Imperial saucers sat here now, I would not. Instead, a stranger sits here in the murderer's body. It is my intent to let this bodiless sentience reside in the killer's body till the true murderer returns. Either this, or the legendary Inquisitors find another body for this sentience to occupy before punishing this body for the sins of its last master. Which outcome do you wish, glorious Judge?" Gorjjen looked to the balconies and waited.

The judges conferred for a moment. When they spoke again, it was the tall shrewish blue-haired spokeswoman who had led the inquisition to begin with that spoke.

"The honorable Baron of Heid has given this council much to consider. We shall adjourn these proceedings and meet again on the morrow. The accused is to be returned to his cell," she declared rising.

"No. No. This is no good for me," Gorjjen announced, still standing. The judges paused and sank back into their seats.

"Good Baron?" the shrew asked curiously.

"I will stand for my friend, Daniel. He is to be released into my care. He will return when I tell him to. He will spend time in the cells no longer. We have established that Daniel Sojourner is not Magpie. We do not imprison the innocent," Gorjjen reminded the Inquisitors, "or do we?"

"Ah," the grey-haired old judge cried, coming forward, "but we have determined that the body in which this Daniel Sojourner resides is the body of the criminal Magpie, making this body guilty by its former joining with Magpie's sentience." The old man smiled a gap-toothed smile to all those in attendance believing he had out reasoned the indomitable Baron of Heid. "The body must be imprisoned."

"Is it the esteemed Inquisitor's belief that this guilty body will somehow ignore the fact that Daniel Sojourner resides within it and wander off while Daniel is distracted?" Gorjjen asked tauntingly. This elicited chuckles from all in attendance. The shrew gave her fellow judge a withering look and addressed Gorjjen directly.

"We sensed no deception in this Daniel Sojourner's responses. The Baron of Heid's request is granted. He stands as Guilt for the body of Magpie. Where this body goes, Gorjjen Doricci goes. Daniel Sojourner is free of this court as is his body up and until the moment that the criminal Magpie returns to claim it. If this should happen, it is the duty of the Baron of Heid to apprehend and return the fugitive to this court to stand trial for his crimes or to kill the fugitive body and slay the guilty sentience. Is this understood?" she asked with a sneer.

"This is justice," Gorjjen declared. The Inquisitors rose as one as did all in attendance. When the judges had passed through their respective doors, those in the gallery above followed suit.

"What now?" I asked, looking to Palasa.

"Now?" Xi asked, coming up to the dais. "Now we get drunk. You're a free man Daniel Sojourner," he announced. I looked at him then to Palasa. She nodded.

"That's it?" I asked of Gorjjen.

"Assuredly," he replied.

"I thought it would be harder than that," I confessed.

"It was either they see reason, my friend, or I win your freedom using an old colonial law where innocence is determined by trial through combat. This was the easier course. I would have regretted killing the reverent and legendary Judges," he admitted blandly. I could not tell if he was serious or not.

"Will you drink with us?" I asked.

"Do I have a choice? Where you go, I go," he said, stepping aside so Palasa could pass. I looked at Leia and saw what amounted to a come-and-get-me look.

"Not everywhere I hope," smiling so he knew it to be a tease. He sighed deeply and motioned for me to get the hell out of his way. I came down the steps and swept through the crowd eager to join with Leia.

I encountered Luke instead.

"Congratulations on your freedom," Luke intoned, extending a hand. I shied away from it not trusting him. "I'm sincere. The Baron made a good point. I am angry with Magpie. You are not Magpie. Like the Inquisitors, I sensed no falseness in your testimony. You truly believe yourself to be this Daniel Sojourner." I looked from his hand to the man's eyes and back again. His eyes did not match his words.

"You're serious?" I asked in disbelief.

"I am," Luke replied. I stared at his hand for many long moments and shook my head.

"I don't trust you," I declared.

"As you will," Luke replied. "I would, however, like to utilize your services as translator once more. I wish to inform the colonial leaders of the protocols and restrictions we request they follow as they are the same protocols and restrictions we will follow. I find it helps smooth way for the Harvest if we avoid any unintentional insults during the summit. I have everything written out in Cojokarunese. It's a list of the diplomats from the other ships and their customs."

"I don't think so," I replied with a shake of my head. "Try Palasa. She'd be better at it."

"Ah, I would, but I've already tasked her with making a list of the customs of the various leaders in the colony for our own diplomats to peruse. It has proven to be a monumental task. I fear she will be tied up seeing to its creation. I only ask because tomorrow is the seventh rotation. Tomorrow is when we're to meet with them," he confessed.

I shook my head, not believing that it had been a week already.

"Think it over. I bear you no ill will, Daniel. Not anymore. What has been done is done. I can't undo that. We can only move on. My hatred of Magpie must be put aside so that I may perform my duties as Grand Reaper. Too many lives depend on the success of this reaping." He shrugged and offered his hand again. I still did not take it. Giving up, he walked off with Baggam in tow.

"What was that all about?" Leia asked, coming up to me. I told her, and she shrugged.

"You should do it. He wouldn't have asked unless he was sincere. He really does need this reaping to go well. You've seen the infected. You know what is going to happen to those that are left behind," she said. I nodded my reply.

"I'll think it over," I lied. I did not trust her brother, but she did not need me throwing that in her face.

"What now?" she asked.

"I guess we get drunk," I said, gesturing to her friends.

"Or we could rattle a rack," she suggested instead. I frowned, unsure what she meant by that. She seemed to sense this. "You could polish my armor," she suggested instead. That did not sound very fun.

"I really don't feel like cleaning armor right now. I mean, I'll help you later, but I think I'd rather get drunk for the time being." I smiled to show I meant no disrespect. She slapped me upside the head.

"No. I mean we could do this," she snapped, making an "O" with one hand and ramming her index finger on her other hand through the center. My eyes flew open with sudden understanding.

"Oh," I cried, smiling. "You mean sex. God yeah. We can definitely do that," I declared, slipping my arm around her waist. She giggled in amusement and darted forward, dragging me along in her wake.

"You're an idiot," she declared. I grinned knowingly.

"Hey, Daniel," Xi called, "you coming?"

"Nope. I'm helping Leia with her armor," I announced, earning me another smack across the back of my head.

"Stop being an idiot," she growled playfully.

It took us half an hour to get back to her place. I kept glancing back wondering if Gorjjen was following me.

"I feel bad for him," I remarked, searching the byway behind me for some sign of the man.

"It was his choice," she replied. "He volunteered for this." She reached for the handle to her parents' cell and hesitated, changing her mind mid reach. She glanced at me and pulled rag from her pocket. This she used to turn the handle. The door opened with little resistance.

Her parents' cell was spacious with a large living area, an expansive kitchen, a privy, four bedrooms and a private garden with a simulated sky. I did not get a chance to explore it. Leia was eager to get me in bed. She was shucking clothes with every stride she took into her room. I was fumbling with my alien zipper and strange buckles and shoes that self-tightened. Me tearing my way out of my shirt was literally the worst hulk impression I ever did. By the time I got my shoes off, she was already nude.

They say you can touch a woman many ways; with your hands; with your words; with your lips. They often fail to mention that you can touch her with your eyes, and I did. Her body was an expertly crafted work of art. She did not exactly blush as my eyes caressed her form, but she did smile a little softer, biting her bottom lip in anticipation.

I bobbed around the room on one leg, tugging at my impossibly tight shoes. I was helpless. I could not be glib. I could not be clever. I could not even finish undressing. She had to do it for me. She strolled over to me, her skin stretched tight across her hardened abs. She grabbed my tunic and ripped it open. She giggled to see my sparse forest of chest hair.

"How cute," she murmured playfully.

She produced a small blade and deftly sliced through the lacings on the front of my pants. I still have no idea where she was hiding that. When at last we were equally nude, I realized something. I was just a man, and she was just a woman and we both wanted this. I scooped her up in my arms. Her laughter was music and poetry to me. As I carried her to the bed, she bent her neck and invited me to kiss it.

I put my lips close to her flesh and exhaled slowly so she could feel the warmth of my breath upon her skin. I massaged her neck with my lips, raking my teeth lightly across her flesh. She hissed in surprise and moaned. I imagined chains of thrilling lighting coursing through her body in response to my touch. She twisted around and opened her mouth. I opened my own and welcomed the taste of her lips.

We made love for most of the night. I have the bite marks to prove it. When at last we were both spent, we lay in each other's arms, drinking in each other's eyes.

"Was it worth saving me for?" she asked with a smirk, nuzzling my neck. I closed my eyes and moaned.

"No," I replied, with a lazy smile. "I think I must rescue you again to make it fair." She rolled atop me yet again, and lay breast to breast. I was tired, but I did not want to sleep. *Are you real?* I asked, pushing the question into her mind. She sighed and kissed my chin, then slid down beside me so that my arm was beneath her. She laid her head upon my chest.

I'm real, she replied soothingly.

Will you be here when I wake? I asked.

If you want me to be, she replied. I closed my eyes and hugged her closer. I was afraid of falling asleep. I was afraid this would end.

"I need you," I whispered softly, drifting off to sleep.

"Why?" she whispered back, frowning when she saw that I slept. "Why do you need me?" she asked again, knowing I would not answer.

Chapter 25: Dream

She looked down on the man she had just bedded. He had been energetic and tender; he was really tender. It had been fun. No, it had been a lot of fun. She had trysts before. Sex was sex. It was a good workout most times. She looked at the man sprawled with his mouth wide open and his arms akimbo. He looked ridiculous now. It made her smile to see him like this. She lightly raked her fingernails through his chest hair. He moaned and snuggled closer. She grinned and pressed her naked breast against him, feeling the warmth of his body. She lay like this for a time. When at last she could lay like that no more, she twisted around and lay with her eyes upon the ceiling.

It was time to play that game. It was time to play the where is this going game. He was not a warrior so they did not have that in common. He was relatively weak for a man. She was not. He had absolutely no fighting prowess. Hygienically, he was inferior. He seemed oafish and simple. She knew he was not, but that was how he seemed anyhow. He had no idea who he used to be. She did. He was not imposing. He was just a regular guy. She was a regular girl. She had not been normal since she was very small. She frowned. That had not been honest of her.

He was not just a guy. Most guys would not kill themselves to save a girl they had just met. Most guys could not make perchers burst. He could. He was extraordinary sometimes, but was that enough? How could it last? He was in love with her body. He did not even know her.

His arm twitched beneath her. She ignored it.

She played the game with every man she bedded. She would imagine what life with them would be like. He was not a warrior so they would not be competing. He was not athletic, so there would not be any early morning training sessions or quarter rotation runs. Maybe that was a good thing. Maybe it was good that he was different. Being together all time and doing the same things as each other made people predictable and where was the excitement in that.

His arm twitched again.

She rolled over and saw that he was dreaming. This made her grin.

"Are you fighting the rotting men again, my sweet?" she asked softly.

She closed her eyes and let her mind drift, sliding her head into his.

She had no choice but to smile. They were in that same old dilapidated woodland abode he had dreamed about that first night. He was armed with that same shotgun, but this time he carried a broad bladed machete in the other. Beside him was his dream version of her. She was wearing her armor, holding her sword in one hand and her sidearm in the other.

There was a bang against the door of the cabin, and the sound of breaking boards behind her as the rotting men struggled to gain entry. She walked slowly toward him, smiling as she approached. He smiled back.

"Are you ready for this? " he asked.

"Of course," she replied, reaching back to draw her sword. She had not been wearing a sword while they slept, but here, she was in full battle dress with a side arm on her hip a nanite sword in her hand.

The rotting me broke through the windows and shuffled in from the other rooms. Daniel opened fire on the first one and stepped forward to slam a machete into the face of another. After that, it was everyone for themselves. Leia laughed as she cut the foul-looking men apart. This was one of the things she loved about Daniel. In his dreams, he was a hero. In his dreams, he got to fight non-stop. In his dreams, he was the warrior she wished he was in real life.

When they first began, it was evenly matched between them and the rotting men. This changed though. She was a far better fighter than Daniel imagined and easily dispatched every one that entered building.

"What now?" she asked.

"We wait for more to come," he replied.

"That's silly," she said, throwing off the bar that kept the front door secure. "Let's go find more. "

"You mustn't!" Daniel cried in fear. He raced for the door to close it.

"Don't worry. It's just a dream," she declared, stepping forward to meet the rotting men. It came for her, dashing through the ranks of zombies like they were grass. Daniel seized her from behind and threw her back into cabin, slamming and locking the door behind her.

She woke up lathered in sweat. Daniel lay beside her still fast asleep. Leia stared at the man in fear. What the hell was he hiding from.

She closed her eyes and tried to remember what it was she saw, but it never came into the light. It was impossible to identify. The only thing she remembered about it were those sickly yellow eyes. She would never forget those eyes.

Chapter 26: Carnage

I woke with a start, crawling toward the edge of the bed. It took me a moment to remember where I was and who I had spent the night with. The woman in question was seated on a padded stool beside the bed, her naked pink-nippled breast swayed and bounced as she hurriedly pulled on her leggings. She came to her feet suddenly and started hopping up and down in an effort to pull them on quicker. I never wanted a woman so much in my life.

"Morning," I greeted. "Do we really have to leave? I was hoping we could lie in bed a little longer."

"Finally," she snapped in irritation. "Get dressed. It's already starting." My brow furrowed in confusion, but that quickly turned to alarm when the next detonation occurred. The whole cell shook in response. Pictures tumbled from shelves and stray knickknacks rattled and crashed together. Leia ignored it all and grabbed a pale quilted tunic from the back of a chair. She pulled this over her head and down, hiding her beautiful breast from sight. "I grabbed you some different clothes," she said, pointing to a wad of clothing on the foot of the bed.

"Jupiter's tits!" I exclaimed, bouncing up in surprise. I grabbed the leggings she had gotten for me. They were more of those dark indigo leggings from the kiosk in the plaza. The tunic was another of those puffy armed shirts. "What the Hell was that?" I cried in alarm, pulling the leggings on as quickly as I could. I hurriedly laced them up, wrapping the ends around the toggle at the top. Finding my boots became something of a scavenger hunt. I was not sure where I had tossed them in my race to fornicate the night before.

"It's perchers," she replied strapping on her shin and calf guards. "They're attacking en masse. It's become something of a routine aboard the Kye O'Ren and the other ships before the Harvest. The Imperial Army was put on notice yesterday. We were expecting some kind of choreographed attack from the infected the moment Luke ordered the Air Corp to make ready their skiffs and shuttles."

"Why are they being readied?" I asked, pulling on my boots.

"Today's the first day of the Harvest. We need the shuttles in peak condition to ferry the leaders to the surface for the summit." She shrugged indifferently. "The First do this every time we begin the Harvest. There'll be attacks for the next seven or eight rotations."

"Are we getting dressed to go fight them?" I asked, nervous.

"No. The soldiers and Grey Guard will handle the policing and emergency responses aboard the ship. The knighthood is seeing to the security of the diplomats. They're guarding the shuttle bays and ships to keep perchers from sabotaging our rides." She buckled her cuisse about her right thigh.

"So we're going to the shuttle bay to guard the shuttles?" I asked, not understanding why we of all people had to hurry. I pulled my tunic on and laced up the front. She gave me a weary sigh.

"No. They usually attack the lifts first, and we need to get to the upper levels before one of their attacks disables them. I protect Luke when he's on the surface. I am his guilt and guardian. Each diplomat at the summit is allowed one guardian." She jerked at a strap on her armor, tugging it in frustration. "Dammit!" she growled, yanking harder at the strap to her culet and breast plate. "Could you give me a hand with this?" she asked, huffing and puffing from the exertion.

I hurried over and pulled the straps across her back, cinching them till she winced. "Make sure they're tight. Nothing worse than fighting in loose armor," she cried out as I gave them each one more tug. She made me loosen the second strap a little, then declared it good. "Today's going to be unbelievably stressful. I've got to prepare Luke's entourage, review his shuttle's flight plan, inspect his shuttle, choose a landing zone, draft a security plan for each of the diplomats aboard the Kye O'Ren, and interrogate everyone suspected of the Daimyo's murder."

I found my old lacing from my previous tunic and pulled it loose so that I could wind it around my forearms to smother the puffiness of my shirt sleeves. She watched my preparations and smiled. "That's kind of clever," she said with approval. "I always thought those puffy sleeves looked ridiculous, but . . ." She shrugged, leaving the rest unsaid.

I sat down on a stool, my preparations complete and watched her strap on the rest of her armor.

"Is that really necessary?" I asked.

"Do they not wear armor in the colonies?" she asked back.

"Not like that. They used to wear metal armor like you wear back in olden times, back when we fought with swords like yours," I said.

"None of the colonies have a sword like mine. What do they fight with down there?" she asked.

"Guns, pistols, tasers, stun grenades, grenades, machine guns, mortars, and more. They wear a form of lightweight body armor resistant to bullets and knives," I replied, growing morose. "They've invented tens of thousands of different ways to kill each other. My people down there have excelled at the art of justifiable murder."

"That's a lot of ways to kill people," she confirmed. "I prefer a nanite sword and my halo," she replied, picking up her side arm. This she strapped to her thigh. She laid her sword sheath across her shoulder, starting a stud on it into a groove. When she was sure it was started, she pushed it back and let it slide down her back till it clicked, locking it in place. Another loud explosion went off somewhere in the ship, rocking the cell. It was further away than the last one.

"Aren't you afraid they'll take down the ship?" I asked.

"Hardly. It's impossible for a percher to reach the hull of the ship. Every service on the ship for every quadrant and neighborhood has quadruple backups should they take one out. The last two levels of the ship require security clearance to reach and a tracker just to move around. Anyone unauthorized is immediately detected by ship security." She seemed amused by my concern. "Are you nervous?" she asked in a cute pouty voice. She came closer and kissed me. She kissed my lips first, giving them a quick peck, then hesitated, growing suddenly serious. She kissed me again, letting her tongue dip into my mouth. I responded in kind, sucking gently on her tongue as she tried to break the kiss. She returned the treatment, sucking on my bottom lip for a second before playfully biting it and disengaging.

"How long will it take you to get back out of that armor?" I asked, making as if to remove my tunic. She laughed wickedly and gave me one more quick peck on the lips. I grinned and looked at her weapons.

"Do I get a weapon?" I asked.

"You're a civilian. Civilians aren't allowed to carry weapons aboard the Kye O'Ren," she declared with mock regret.

"What if I'm attacked?" I asked.

"Run," she replied. That did not fill me with lots of confidence.

I sighed and put my hand down on a charcoal covered box beside me to help me rise. It squawked and squealed in protest, forcing me to hurriedly remove my hand. "Wasn't me," I declared. Leia laughed.

"You're okay. That's just a Part Pod," she replied, moving toward the door. "Give me a few moments to review the security bulletins on my NID, and we can head out." She hurried into the next room to pull her NID from its charging station. I studied the Pod with great curiosity. The top of it looked like those tablets the bureaucrats up on Level 51 carried everywhere. I tapped the top, and it lit up. I studied the glyphs that appeared, but I could not make heads or tails of them.

"Hey, what's this Part Pod do?" I asked.

"It fabricates simple everyday components. Everyone has one. Do they not have these in the colonies?" she asked, coming back into the bedroom to demonstrate how it worked. I tried to figure how it worked, but it was a little too advanced for me.

She laughed. "No. Like this." She said, touching the third glyph. She grabbed a stylus from a holder on the side and quickly drew a circle, then drew another around it. The tablet automatically smoothed out the lines. She touched a spot down in the lower corner and dragged it toward the center. The circle pivoted sideways to show its edge. She dragged the edge of the circle and gave it depth. When she had it as wide as she wanted it, she selected another glyph that rounded the edges of the ring.

When she was done, she pressed a button on the bottom of the tablet and the machine began to hum and vibrate. I watched through the side of the box as impossibly fast plates passed back and forth above each other. Below these plates, the ring slowly began to form.

"We use these to replace common parts that may wear out or break. It's preloaded with almost every part we need on this ship. It's kind of a common appliance, like a food kiosk. Everyone has one." She was so nonchalant about the technology. She seemed to find it funny that I was so intrigued by something that to her was as common as a light bulb was to me.

It took only a few seconds for the machine to create the item she had designed. It was a metal band. She slipped it on my hand over my middle finger. I looked at her in alarm. She noticed and smiled. "There! Don't you look purdy?" she asked with a grin.

"You know, down on the planet, we wear rings on this finger to indicate that we are married to the person who put it on us." She snatched at the ring and quickly tossed in the trash. I laughed out loud at this. She seemed embarrassed.

"Ten ticks and we're gone," she announced, strolling back into the living room. Her NID was lit up and beeping as she moved from bulletin to bulletin. I looked at the crafting engine, smiled, and took up the stylus. I occupied the next ten minutes drawing and shaping my own series of rings. I checked the size against my own hand and hit the button that made the machine fabricate the image. When it was done, I picked it up and admired it, sliding it over my fingers. It fit perfect. I glanced into the other room to see if she had taken notice and hit the fabricate button again to make a second one. It took a few more seconds to make the next one. I tried it on the other hand. It fit perfect, though it was a little tight on my middle finger. I slipped them in my pocket, worried how she would react if she caught me with them.

"You nearly done?" I asked. She smiled and returned.

"We can leave. Half of the lifts are still in operation. The army has chased down and killed the ones responsible for those explosions we've been hearing." She walked over and offered me her hand. I took it and let her lead me from her parent's home. The byway and corridors barely had anyone in them which made it easier to travel. The ship felt like every time I ever went out at 2 a.m. to do a Taco Bell run. The citizens had evidently heard the news just as the Infected had. The Grand Reaper was this day going to reap the colony, and everyone knew not to go out . . . except us obviously. To go out today, was to invite death. Today was the day of the First. They would be out in force hunting diplomats and politicians and people of influence and anyone else whose death would hinder the Grand Reaper's designs. I felt a tingle of dread.

We passed six lifts before we found one that still worked. The liftman was absent. He had abandoned his post the moment the Infected started blowing lift channels.

"You ready for this?" she asked. I took a breath and nodded. Evidently, I had stormed the beaches of Normandy once and broke the world. I was pretty sure I could handle an elevator ride to the upper levels. Leia hit the button for the door and placed her hand upon the sidearm she was calling a halo.

The doors opened after only a short wait. She half drew her weapon, but she needn't have. The lift had only one person inside and she was an old woman carrying a covered bird cage. Leia nodded to the woman, pressed the button for Level 401 and settled down in the back to wait. I sat beside her, with my hands inside my pockets. I slouched down and readied myself for the long ride up.

"What do I do when we arrive?" I asked of Leia. She shrugged.

"You could translate those protocols for the colonials like Luke asked," she suggested.

"That's pointless. How would I get it to them?" I was serious. I could not see how I would be able to get it to them. Did they have some type of interstellar email on the ship? She gave me a look and shrugged.

"You could send it by courier to one of the ambassadors," she suggested. The thought of an alien FedEx made me giggle.

"It was just a suggestion," she remarked defensively.

"Why can't I just shadow you?" I asked. I knew it was a bad idea the moment I suggested it.

"Because, I have a job to do. Look, we had fun last night, but this isn't a real relationship. I'm battle hardened. I'm disciplined. I'm constantly on the go. You wouldn't like my life. You wouldn't find it interesting moping around while I created security protocols and briefed other knights or interrogated potential assassins. This," she said, gesturing back and forth between us, "won't work."

"I don't know. I think interrogating possible assassins sounds fun. We could tag team it and give them the ole good cop, bad cop routine. But I get to be the bad cop," I told her, smiling. She looked confused.

"We don't play games," she replied.

"How do you interrogate a suspect without a little game theory in play?" I asked, giving in to my inner Law and Order. "You come in all hard-nosed and aggressive, then I come in to save them from you 'cause I'll be this patient understanding good cop who's come to rescue them from the vengeful bad cop. It'll be the buddy cop hit of the season," I said with a smile, knowing she would not get the humor. She smiled to be polite.

"No. You know one of the suspects, so you don't get to come along," she replied, letting her eyes slide over to the little old lady with the covered bird cage. "Let me ask you something, do you find that old woman to be strange?" she asked, gesturing toward the woman in question. I was racking my brain trying to figure out who I knew aboard the ship who could possibly be suspected of being an assassin.

"Is it Jo?" I asked, glancing at the old woman.

"No. I don't know who the old woman is," Leia replied, giving me a yet another look of confusion. I looked over at the old woman then back to my lover.

"Not her. I mean the assassin you suspect. Is it Jo? She seems kind of assassin-like," I replied.

"Something about that woman there is rubbing me the wrong way. She just seems wrong," Leia replied. "And no, it's not Jo. It's Palasa." She turned back to the old woman. "She doesn't seem off to you?"

"There's no bird in the cage," I responded, having figured that out within seconds of boarding the lift. I was not interested in the old lady though. I was interested in the fact Palasa was suspected of murder. "Who do you think Palasa assassinated?" It was possible this was a crime from before when I was Magpie.

"The Daimyo. He was poisoned while Luke and Palasa attended an evening feast with Lord Merrik. I have to interrogate her to determine her guilt or innocence." She was not taking her eyes off the old woman. She still felt the woman was somehow wrong. "She doesn't seem strange to you?"

"Palasa isn't an assassin. She wouldn't do something like that," I argued back.

"Would you shut up about Palasa? Look at the old woman. Doesn't she bother you?" Leia snapped angrily.

Now that I was looking at her, she did seem strange.

"Why would you cover a bird cage with no bird?" I asked. Leia shrugged, having no answer.

I studied the old woman for the first time, taking in her baggy robes, her covered bird cage, the rigid way she sat. For the first time since entering the lift, I really took stock of her.

"Why cover a bird cage if there's no bird in it?" I asked again. Leia seemed to consider it, then suddenly stood up.

"Wait," I called, but Leia wasn't having none of it.

"Hey, old mother," Leia called loudly, coming to her feet. Her hand slid up over her shoulder to grab her sword. The hilt stretched out to meet her hand like an old friend eager to play.

"Not like that!" I called, realizing without knowing how I knew what was in the cage. The old woman's head slowly swiveled towards us like some type of predator. She hissed in anger, and hurriedly thrust her hand up under the cover on the cage. It was just a reflex. Or it was not. I do not know. With the understanding that this was our end came a primal burst of will. I think I was only trying to knock the cage out of her hand. I was hoping that was my intention. However I meant for it to play out in the end, it did not. My burst of will came like cannon fire. It crushed the cage up against the far wall and took most of the old woman's upper torso with it. From her chin to her lap, everything was gone, turned to red mist and blown upon the wall. Her backbone was still intact and still supported the old woman's head—at least for a moment. It was a macabre moment for me, watching this jawless old woman's head blink twice before her spine collapsed under the weight of her brain-filled skull.

"Futuo!" Leia exclaimed in horror, backing away from me. I shrugged, at a loss to explain how I did it or even why.

"That, Leia, that was . . . that was an accident," I explained.

"You turned her to paste," she replied in disgust.

"She had a bomb," I replied. "She was a percher. She was about to blow the lift up," I stammered. Leia was staring at the old woman's corpse and just shook her head in denial of what she saw. I thought she was trying to deny my claim. I got up and quickly navigated my way around the red pulpy mess I'd created and retrieved the cage. I brought it back to her and uncovered it.

"This is a bomb, isn't it?" I asked, showing her the tangled mass of wires and a bundled set of small cylindrical canisters surmounted with a clear dome filled with some sort of plasma." She was still staring at the body. "Hey," I called again, louder. "This is a bomb, isn't it?" I asked again. Leia looked to the cage and nodded absently.

"Yes." She went back to staring at the corpse. "It's a low yield neutrino rapid diffuser," she mumbled absently, sinking back into her seat. "It would have flooded the immediate vicinity with radiation and taken out everything in the immediate area. You saved hundreds of lives most likely."

I studied the bomb with curiosity. "I know I've heard the term neutrino bomb somewhere before," I remarked. Leia shrugged, turning to face me. Her eyes were unreadable but not entirely. I did see disappointment in them.

"Your people call them nuclear," she replied, regaining her composure. I stared in fear at the cage in my hand and carefully set it down on the floor and backed away.

"You killed her," Leia accused.

"It was a reflex," I explained, guessing that was what probably happened.

"You didn't even focus it with a word," she declared in amazement.

"I didn't mean to kill her. I was just trying to knock the bomb out of her hands. I panicked. I saw her hand slid up under the cover on the cage and instinctively knew she was trying to trigger the bomb. Then this happened," I said, gesturing to the mess. "I'm sorry if it was too much. I didn't mean to."

Leia studied the woman's corpse a moment longer and shrugged. "No matter. That's a bomb. She was a percher. It was a good kill, just messy."

"D-Do we have to clean it up?" I asked with sudden dread. Leia stared at me blankly for a several heartbeats and began to laugh. It started out as a soft chuckle and grew into body rocking guffaw of uncontrollable mirth. I tried to chuckle along with her, but it was an awkward moment. I was unsure if she was laughing at the thought of us having to clean up the mess or the dread I showed at the prospect. I decided I was the butt of the joke and grew sullen as her laughter resolved itself into a crazy bout of giggling. It took a while.

"Do you think we'll encounter more of her kind on the way up?" I asked. The door to the lift chimed just then, and the lift slowed and came to a stop. Leia turned to the door, slowly drawing her halo. The door slid open slowly. And there they were, as if my question summoned them, nearly a dozen perchers waiting to tear us limb from limb. Sometimes, I really hated my life.

The perchers made as if to charge us, but suddenly stopped when they found that the floor was slick with gore. I counted nine of them that I could see. I drew in my will, but a quick look at Leia made me relax it. She looked scared of what I would do to the men and women coming to kill us, and that was a strange thing to realize. How horrible must I be that the chick with the sword was more uncomfortable with what I was going to do to them than with what she was going to do to them with her sword. I did not like the look she gave me. It made me feel monstrous.

"Relax. I'm not doing that again," I assured her with a smile. She smiled back, seemingly relieved. "But a weapon would have been nice."

"You're a citizen. You can't have a weapon. That's why you have me," she said, adjusting her grip on the sword. I looked at the nine perchers confronting us. Her assurances did little to comfort me.

Leia darted forward while the perchers were still distracted by the carnage that used to be the old lady. No doubt, they wondered from whence it came. Leia leapt the old woman's corpse and came down on the other side with a mighty two-handed chop to the head of the first percher. She split his head in half all the way down to his collar bone, then ripped her sword free, whipping a line of blood clear across the lift behind her.

She drew in her will and lashed out at the dead man's body, blasting it back into the perchers behind him. Many twisted away from the missile and drew their own swords. They were shoddy blades with clothe wrapped hilts like the ones I had seen the day I helped rescue Leia.

I decided it was on me to keep the perchers from reclaiming the bomb, though they did not seem particularly interested in it. I slipped my hands into my pockets and slid my fingers through the rings I had made earlier just in case I was called on to defend myself. I knew I should probably rush in and help her, but I had never watched Leia work before. I had never actually seen her in a fight. I was not disappointed.

Leia was taking advantage of the missile she had launched, rushing forward into the midst of the Infected. She poked forward into the chest of the next percher woman who had foolishly tried to charge her with her sword raised. The tip of Leia's nanite blade pierced her chest, but not deeply. Just deep enough to reach her heart.

The woman's eyes suddenly went wide in surprise and faded just as fast as she wilted to the floor, sliding forward on her knees as her momentum carried her past. She remained like that, slumped with her head against her chest.

Leia's recovery with her sword disemboweled the man to her right. She meant to take the man's head and end his suffering, but the man on her left was seizing on her momentary distraction to lob a clumsy horizontal two-handed strike at her head. She ducked beneath it and whipped a quick back hand slash at his legs that he avoided by skittering out of reach.

Leia dodged toward him again, sending him scrambling even further away. This proved to be a feint meant to draw in the others at her back. Two perchers, a tall good-looking man and a short stocky guy with no neck, took the bait with their swords raised high. It occurred to me then that these people were idiots. They all felt it necessary to raise their blades high when charging their enemy.

Leia dodged the tall man on her right and deflected the downward blow of No Neck on her left. She came back across with a back hand swipe of her sword that left the tall man without a hand. He cried out in pain and horror, and I thought Leia would end him, but she did not.

She could not. No Neck was there. No Neck came in chopping at her like he thought he was a woodsman trying to fell a tree. He drove her back and back forcing her to fence with him far longer than she had intended. It gave the three attackers at her back the opportunity to take her unawares, and they would have if I had not intervened on her behalf.

I threw out my mind and pushed on the dead woman kneeling in the midst of the battle. My push toppled the dead woman over backwards into the path of the men charging her from behind. Two of them fell across the dead body, but the other leapt over her and continued his charge.

Leia heard the two men go down and hurriedly broke away from No Neck, cutting the tall man's throat as she turned away to face the threat coming from behind. That man back pedaled quickly colliding with the fallen. He was whipping his sword back and forth trying to stop her from attacking him, but it was wasted effort. She had just wanted him out of the way so she could finish No Neck who had just thrown everything he had into a mighty overhead chop aimed at her neck. The blow came just to her left and she deflected far to her side.

Her riposte scored a hit to his left shoulder. Unfortunately, the man was a righty.

She rushed the men behind her again while No Neck dealt with his shoulder wound. She came in slashing wildly to ward them off, so she could come back again at No Neck. He was proving to be a persistent bastard. Leia turned just in time to meet No Necks next attack. Again, he tried to slash her diagonally from right to left. Leia deflected it again, bumping it with her blade once more to give her another opening. She hit a button on her sword to reverse her grip, then snapped kicked No Neck hard in the chest launching him backwards into the wall.

The Scrambler from the ground came rushing back in. She knew if she turned to face him, he would just skip away again. She was done with that. She shot him a quick glance to see if he was still trying to charge her back with his sword held aloft again. He was, so she threw herself backwards with everything she had and let the man impale himself upon her blade. Her nanite blade slid through the man's diaphragm with very little resistance. She hit the switch on her hilt again, and the blade slid from his body and re-emerged before her.

She almost felt sorry for them. Their illness kept forcing them to throw their lives away. She took a deep sigh and gripped her hilt in both hands and prepared to meet No Neck again who had rebounded off the wall and was even now bearing down on her, screaming as he came sword aloft.

I watched her with pride. She was simply amazing to watch, and watching was all I wanted to do, but the last two perchers to enter the lift saw easier prey in me. I was apparently unarmed to them. They cut around the center row of seats to avoid Leia and raced toward me.

I slipped my hands out of my pockets and gripped the armored rings I had made in Leia's Parts Pod. I had designed them with triangular tips above the knuckles to make my punches hurt more. I probably did not need to. The perchers attacking me wore no armor and one of them was a chick who stood a lowly five foot one.

She was that typical good looking high school cheerleader type. She carried a clothe hilted sword like the others. Her companion was about six foot four and easily weighed two twenty-five. He carried a heavy gauge pipe about two foot long, and the look in his eye that clearly said he wanted to bash my skull till I was dead.

I had spent three days aboard the Kye O'Ren, stuck in a holding cell with nothing to do except imagine what would happen the next time I got into the thick of it. I was all for using my telepathic ability, but that was a recently acquired ability. I had not mastered it yet, so I fell back on my red neck roots. I was a brawler at heart, and I loved a good fight. I was reasonably sure there was a way to combine these two abilities to make them far more effective in their execution.

My fabricated knuckles solved the only problem I was having with my theoretical methods. I was worried that the force of my will would end up breaking my hand upon impact. I was pretty sure the brass knuckles I created would solve that problem for me.

The man reached me first and swung his club at my head with all his might. I ducked and swung my fist at the pipe itself, throwing my mind behind the punch. The result was moderately amazing. The moment I clenched my will, my arm rocketed forward and the brass knuckles collided with the pipe midway between its ends. The pipe bent in half from the impact, flew from the percher's grip, and blasted a hole through the side of the lift.

The momentum of the punch was too much to arrest, so I spun into the punch and delivered a powerful backhand to the man's jaw, hammering at it like I was trying to tear his head off. It was too difficult to focus my will behind each punch, so I resigned myself to only enhancing critical punches I knew would land. The brass knuckles split the man's lips and cheek, shattering several teeth. The force of the punch sprayed the lift wall with blood and broken teeth.

The woman who had been racing after the man, darted in with her sword raised high, screaming at the top of her lungs like some bad Kung Fu movie henchman and slashed for my neck.

No. I declared, using the word to focus my will into a deflection of blade. Her sword swerved out wide to my left, and she came at me snarling and screaming and trying to claw at my face with her free hand. I slammed a hard right into the woman's jaw and she nearly cartwheeled from the force of the blow.

Unlike the big man, she crumpled to the ground and did not get up.

The man I had hit shook his head and staggered back into the aisle before me. I raised my fist and prepared to defend myself. That proved to be foolish. The man was evidently something of a boxer before he was infected, because he spent the next few moments handing me my hat.

He threw three quick jabs at my face and followed them with a right cross of his own. My head rocked back as the first three jabs connected with my mouth and nose. I managed to duck under the right cross though and followed it up with a left right left of my own to his rib cage. He groaned and cried out in pain, and I probably should have just kept hammering away at his ribs till he was too injured to defend himself. I should have, but I got cocky and tried to lay him out with an upper cut. I missed because this bastard could fight.

He faded back and dodged right. He threw out a quick left that connected with my chin, then quickly bobbed expecting me to counter with a jab of my own. I did not disappoint, though I was throwing haymakers today. He ducked beneath it almost contemptuously and came up on my right. He must have sensed I was tiring because he started raining heavy rights on my rib cage like he knew I would not fight back.

I drew in my arms and used my elbows to protect my ribs as best I could, but he had counted on that. He popped up suddenly and threw a meaty left to the right side of my head. It connected and turned my head hard setting me up to receive the right cross he had been eager to throw all along. He put everything into the punch intending to end the fight right there.

My vision was dancing. I knew he was a much better fighter than me in a fair boxing match. But this was not a boxing match, and he had forgotten that. This was a fight where the loser died. As I saw it, there really were not a lot of rules to break in this sort of fight, so I did the only thing my addled brain would let me.

I dropped beneath his right cross and fired off an upper cut to his groin. Both his hands went to his groin, and he doubled over in agony. I went all the way to my knees. I should have gotten up and used the distraction to deliver that upper cut I desperately wanted to, but I was too tired.

I cocked my right arm instead and put my will behind my next blow. I was not aiming at the man's groin this time or his head. I was aiming for the inside of his right knee. The shot I fired off to his groin was immediately forgotten as his knee joint suddenly decided it wanted to hinge side to side instead. The joint broke apart and he collapsed sideways against the seat Leia had been sitting in earlier.

I recovered a little, sobered by his screams but not impressed by them. My right eye was swelling shut, and it was hard to breath out of my nose. My mouth was full of my own blood, and there was a ringing in my ears. That aside, I could still see well enough to locate his head. I found it, pawing at it with my iron ringed fingers. It took me a moment to twine the fingers of my left hand into his hair and get a good grip. When at last I was sure of my grip, I raised myself up on my knees and started raining iron knuckled rights to the side of his head. I kept it up till holding him up became a chore. I let him go then, realizing I had won the fight. I let go and rose awkwardly to my feet, staggering back with exhaustion. I tripped over the cheerleader chick I had knocked out, and only kept myself from falling by colliding with the wall behind me. I was breathing hard and sank into the seat beneath me.

I blew a blast of bloody snot from my right nostril and looked to see how my lady was doing.

She was not doing good.

Three of the men had her on her back. She was still fighting them off, using her bracers on her forearms to block some of their strikes, and her sword for whichever one of them came to close. The only thing she had going for her was that the floor was still slick with the bomber's slurry remains.

"Brace yourself," I called, gathering my will.

I focused on the area between me and Leia and gave her a firm but gentle push. She shot out of the midst of them, sliding easily across the lift floor lubricated by the human remains. She kicked off a lift seat to spin her around so that she would be facing her attackers when she came to a stop. I staggered off toward the fight, summoning the courage to fight on. I was not leaving her to do this alone. I broke into a run and drew in my will again.

Leia slammed hard against the wall of the lift; her armor absorbing most of the impact. She slammed a palm down on the floor and shoved herself up, getting a knee bent and a foot planted in the process. The perchers tried to close the distance between them and her, but they were sliding as much as they were running.

I was going to use my will to launch two of the men into the lift wall above her, but Leia messed that plan up when she came sprinting back into the battle. She launched herself at the lone swordsman on her left, ignoring the other two. She was still in the way, so I changed the focus of my will and put it right behind me. I launched myself towards them with my right arm cocked and barked my word of focus.

"Now!" I cried, letting the force of my will catapult me into the battle. I was easily thirteen feet away when I leapt. I roared as I soared, rocketing into the men. I met the one on the right with an insanely powerful plunging punch that tore away half his face. I crashed into him and the other man, flipping and rolling and sliding past them. I did not stop till I came crashing up against the side of the lift as Leia had. Unfortunately, I hit the wall without armor and found it hard to concentrate after that.

When my vision finally began to clear, I found myself on the floor at the mercy of the second percher I had bowled over. He had recovered far faster than I. He had his sword clutched in both hands with the blade pointed down at my chest. He growled in anger and quickly pulled it back to plunge it into my chest.

It was nearly a tie. The burning ring left by Leia's side arm appeared over the man's heart at almost the same time I ripped him apart. It was like with the old lady. I hadn't drawn in my will or focused on a word or anything. I had just flexed and ripped the man to pieces.

"You really have to stop doing that," Leia announced wearily, strolling through the gravy of human remains pooling around her feet. "It's really gross," she remarked, reaching down to help me up. I took her hand and rose. Her armor was painted red with blood and garishly decorated with stringy bits of offal and tendon.

She looked at my face and the swelling eye. "Did you at least get a few licks in yourself?" she teased, studying my injuries with an experienced eye. I pointed to the two against the far wall, and the man beside me with half a face.

"What did you hit him with?" she asked. "A mace?" I held up both hands and showed her my bling.

"We call them brass knuckles down on the planet."

"Handy," she observed, "but, illegal. You're a civilian. You can't have weapons."

"Does your law specifically mention these?" I asked.

"No. But they're obviously weapons," she replied. There was a groan from the back of the lift.

"You left one alive?" she asked in surprise, pressing the button for Level 401 again. I shrugged.

"She was a girl," I said with a shrug.

Leia smiled. "So am I," she announced good naturedly, turning to look at all the bodies littering the floor. I got her point.

"You didn't kill them all," I pointed out. "Some of them are mine."

"I killed more than you," she replied, strolling back to her seat. The woman I hit turned unfocused eyes upon us as we approached. Leia slammed a hard-soled boot in the woman's face, knocking her out before calmly retaking her seat. She studied the man I beat to death. "Yeah, those are definitely weapons."

"You wouldn't give me a weapon," I argued, "which is a bad policy when psychotic ETs are running around the ship like this was the Purge." She did not get the reference, and I realized I had a lot of necessary Earth culture to share with the woman. "I still killed five without a weapon."

"You blew an old lady apart. You beat one man to death and tore half of another man's face off." She checked her tally and shook her head. "You killed three—one old lady and two men. One of those you defeated is still alive and the fifth one you're counting was killed by me before you blew him apart. That was my kill," she declared.

"Fine. I will give you that small fry here," I said gesturing to the woman Leia had stomped, "doesn't count, but that last man definitely counts. I blew him apart."

"After I shot him," Leia argued stubbornly.

"Fine. We count him as a half each," I declared. Leia thought it over and shrugged.

"That's still three and half to you and six and half to me," she declared proudly. The lift beeped and began to slow. I cleaned off my brass knuckles just in case and turned to the door. Leia pushed herself up and drew her halo with one hand and her sword with the other. The lift slowed to a stop and the door squealed open.

More perchers flooded in.

There had been calls coming in for almost two hours describing scenes of horror on five different levels of the ship where hacked bodies and stray heads were being discovered in the byway outside the lifts. It had taken the Imperial Army almost forty-five minutes to figure out that the carnage was tied to one lift. The last call came in from security personnel on Level 375 where they described how someone's entrails were slowly being juiced in the lift doors as the body that contained them was slowly being dragged upward by the lift that left them behind. After that, security personnel were waiting on each level for the doors to open. Level 401 was where that lift finally stopped.

Thinking that an entire nest of perchers had taken up residence in it, the army had asked a squad of Imperial knights be on hand to reinforce the army. The soldiers had brought long rifles with them. Blast shields had been set up to crisscross the byway in front of the lift in case the enemy came at them in a rush. The knights waited with swords in their hands and halos on their hips, and when the door to the lift chimed to alert of the impending lift car arrival, twenty men and women gripped their weapons tight in anticipation of the fight they thought was coming.

The doors slid opened slowly to reveal what I can only imagine was a garish abomination outfitted in the armor of a knight but slathered in human remains and clutching the hair of a short woman with a mangled face. I stood beside her with puffy eyes looking like I had been painted in a slaughterhouse. I had the bird cage in one hand and two sets of brass knuckles in the other.

We marched forward wearily. Leia shoved the short woman forward so that she stumbled and sprawled at the feet of a fellow knight. I marched forward, equally weary and handed the bird cage to one soldier and two sets of brass knuckles to another.

Behind us inside the lift was a slaughterhouse of human remains. Bodies were shoved through walls. Arms and heads and entrails lay draped across other bodies that were dismembered and hacked with faces twisted with silent screams of agony.

"Be careful," I mumbled, "it's a bomb." I would have fallen then, but Leia came to my rescue and caught me before I hit the floor.

"Some help here, please," Leia called to the crowd. "Oh, and that lift is definitely out of order," she declared with a cocky smirk. She managed to laugh once at her own wit before withering under my weight. Her fellow knights and admiring soldiers rushed forward to rescue us from our fall.

Chapter 27: Recovery

There are many wonderful technologies aboard the Kye O'Ren, but as far as advanced alien technology went, I was most impressed with the tanning-bed looking machines they called Med Beds. No greater sin is there than to use a device that takes all your pain away and leaves you better for the experience.

There is a medical node for every neighborhood in every quadrant on every level of the ship. You break a bone, go sleep it off in a Med Bed. You cut yourself, go sleep it off in a Med Bed. If you feel sick to your stomach or feel you have suffered a concussion or you find that you are bleeding from your eyes and every other orifice of your body or you find yourself spending two hours fighting perchers in a lift with your girlfriend at your side, all you have to do to is go sleep it off in a Med Bed. You will not ever know how it works, but after forty minutes in a Med Bed you definitely will not care. It's like you are main-lining heroin, but without the soul-crushing addiction afterwards.

I had just taken the worst beating of my life, but after forty minutes in their Med Bed, you could barely tell I was bruised. My ribs did not hurt anymore, the spot on my shoulder where I was stabbed by a percher in the third wave of attacks was gone all except for a pink puffy sore spot. The bruising around my eyes was still tender to the touch, but the bruises had paled from a dark purple to a greenish yellow. Two broken fingers were mended. A cut above my knee was fully healed. And the concussion I was experiencing was completely cured. These would be in every house if they decided to sell them down on the planet.

The truth was it took longer to clean us up than it took to heal us after arriving on this level. Leia healed faster evidently.

She had not really been that injured. She managed to avoid most of the damage I had taken because of her armor and because she actually knew how to fight.

She came and sat with me while I was still in my bed and explained that fifteen Imperial Knights had been killed by insurgent attacks and twice that many soldiers and guardsmen. A quarter of the lifts had been disabled ship wide and three senators, an Abbot, and the nephew of the late Lord Merrik had all managed to get themselves assassinated despite the saturation of the Imperial Army. They even tried to assassinate Luke again, but the trio who attempted that were summarily hacked to pieces by the Battle Commander himself. Other than the Med Bed, seeing Leia alive and well was the highlight of my day.

"You fought pretty well for a colonist," Leia murmured with a smile.

"I'm not really a colonist though, am I?" I replied flippantly.

"Actually, you are. Down there is all you remember, so right now, you're more them than us," she declared with a note of sadness. "But you still fight good for one of them." She pushed a sheaf of synthetic paper into my hands and waited for me to ask.

"What's this?" I squeezed the papers between me and the top of the Med Bed so I could peruse them.

"It's the protocols and restrictions Luke needed you to translate," she replied. Leia handed me a device that looked like an ink pen except that it didn't have any ink in it. "You need to spend more time in the bed if you want to heal completely. You took a pretty serious blow to the head in that last attack. You can translate these and let the bed heal you the rest of the way." She leaned in, pushing her face between the bed and lid of the healing chamber and kissed me on the lips. "Thanks for saving my life again," she whispered, pulling away.

"You saved my life more than I saved yours," I confessed, reminding her how things sat between us.

"You still saved mine though, so thanks for that," she said again, limping out the door. I realized then that she had gotten out of her Med Bed sooner than she should have. No doubt, she felt the siren call of her responsibilities. An injured leg would not really inhibit her all that much. I decided not to protest the fact. Instead, I settled back into my Med Bed and began the tedious job of translation.

Chapter 28: Preparation

Leia's duties were many and being ambushed in the lifts had not helped her schedule in any way. However, she was a true professional, and each duty took only a short time to fulfill. She saved the inspections of the shuttles and skiffs for last seeing as how they would just be vulnerable again if she inspected them now.

So, she spent the next few hours sending out troops to escort the politicians. She hand-picked knights she knew to serve as Guilts for these men and women, then stripped them of their halos. There were only two people at the summit allowed to carry side arms. Those two people were the personal bodyguards for the Grand Reaper and Earth's chosen ambassador.

She met with Baggam and a man named Orin Nightjar, Acting Fleet Commander and Brigadier General in command of the Kye O'Ren's Terrestrial Air Corps. These were the ships and shuttles that were going to ferry the diplomats to the surface. She stood by for the most part while they picked out a landing site on the ground close to the city where they had apprehended Daniel. They determined approach vectors and landing sequence. This is where she came in to play.

Growing up as Luke's sister, she was fully aware of the hierarchy among the diplomats and their various customs. Landing in the wrong order was a good way to insult many of the armada's leaders. They were a touchy bunch. She handled the scheduling and sequencing of the flights well enough. This was what she did.

What bothered her was the time after the meeting. It was a long walk back to her brother's cell. Leia was supposed to meet with Luke next to brief him on what she had accomplished so far, and she would have if her walk had not been so long. She had too much time to consider things. The Harvest was important, but she needed to know more about the man she had bedded. He was the man who hid a secret with yellow eyes. She had feelings for him too, and that made her nervous. Attachments made good warriors weak and vulnerable. She did not want to be weak. Luckily, there was someone she could talk to; someone who knew Magpie better than anyone aboard. Leia just had to find her.

She woke up her NID with a touch and quickly typed in a message. This she sent to a friend of hers who worked in intelligence for the Commander Baggam Rain. It only took her friend a few inquiries to discover where Palasa was. She breathed a sigh of relief when she saw Palasa was on this level still. Leia was not all that eager to use the lifts again any time soon.

Her interview with the Palasa was not till later, but Leia decided her curiosity could not wait. She needed to discover a few things for herself; how had Daniel—undisciplined, doltish Daniel—managed to tap in to so much power? He should not be that strong. There were physical limits to how powerful a psychic could become. It was not some magic force they utilized. It was a physical interaction between one's mind and the molecular makeup of the universe.

Myron's Law of Opposing Force was clear on this. The Abbot established long ago that all sentient psychic states achieve equilibrium with the magnetic molecular force of the universe around it. Like warm air rising in a volume of cold, anyone could exert their will on the atoms around them to create a molecular flow. Most people did it without even thinking about it. They would feel a draft or a cold spot in the room and look for an open door or window.

Sometimes, that was where the draft came from, but other times, it was them dragging their psyche through the air around them like a child swiping his hand through a cloud of cigarette smoke. They did not know they were doing it. The cloud of atoms would swirl and drift around them and they would feel the change, but it was never what they thought it was. It was not a draft. It was an effusion of will.

The problem with Daniel was that he was not just swiping his hand through the metaphorical cloud. He had discovered a way to envelope the matter around him and mentally squeeze it like a bladder with a small hole in one end. The result was a highly focused stream of matter being directed at whatever he wanted destroyed. He had found a way to magnify his will in such a way that it defied the physical laws of the universe.

His influence on the matter around him seemed far too focused for a mind as undisciplined as Daniel's. Pulling people apart with your mind was next level psychic ability. Before he lost his memories, when he was still a Prior, he might have been able to do most of what he had been doing of late, but in his present state of being, he should not be able to generate that much focus. He should not have the experience to know how to do it.

Luke had been tutoring Leia since he had first entered the monastic order of monks. He was reasonably strong. He had advanced quite far during his twelve hundred years of service, but even he would be hard pressed to match Daniel right now in a contest of wills. Leia could not even pull people apart and she had been at it for over eleven hundred years.

According to Daniel, he did not even know he had psychic ability till seven rotations ago. In one week, he had surpassed the abilities of a Pre-Prior. That was not possible, unless he was lying and did remember being the Prior Magpie. She had been in his mind. She knew he was hiding something; something with yellow eyes. That was her fear. She feared that Daniel might be a lie Magpie created to escape punishment. If that were true, that would change everything between them. Having feelings for Daniel was one thing, but if Magpie was really in there, she knew she could not love him. That is why she had to know the truth, and Palasa, she hoped, would have the truth she sought.

Palasa had sequestered herself in an out of the way facility to finish her dossier on the world leaders for the armada's dignitaries. The room she had sequestered herself in was a portable NID data repository. Back on Earth, Palasa called it a library. It was a public area on the ship. Everyone had access to the facility so long as they followed the rules of etiquette the Board of Governance had established for such places. No loud talking. No food. No beverages. It was the usual rules for such a place. What was unusual for these kinds of places was sword wearing female knights without their armor.

Leia had not had a choice in giving up her armor. Her psionic armor needed a thorough cleaning after the ordeal in the lift and a good polish since she would be representing the Cojokarueen Empire at the Harvest. One did not embarrass the Emperor without serious repercussions, so she dressed the part aboard the ship.

She wore her almond leggings and tunic and carried a traditional blade upon her hip. A large, quilted pauldron covered her right shoulder and upper arm all the way down to her elbow. The pauldron was an affectation her fellow knights wore when out of armor to let those they passed know they were knights and not squires. In their formal wear, a silver chain with heavy links and a medallion bearing the sigil of Baggam's Children served the same function.

Leia entered the repository and spent just a moment admiring the rich burgundy finish lacquered across the shelves and wall panels. Worked wood on a ship was an expensive affectation. The Board of Governance that maintained the repositories evidently thought the cost justifiable. It did seem to give the place an air of solemnity. Leia could understand that reasoning. This was a place for knowledge, and knowledge had always been a noble pursuit. It was worth the cost of a rich design to her.

She spotted Palasa immediately. Magpie's former second lieutenant seemed pleased with the task she had been given, judging by how feverishly she scribbled down her translations.

"It's Palasa, isn't it?" Leia asked, approaching the table. Palasa looked up in alarm and checked the time. "You're not late," Leia said, holding out a hand to forestall the woman who was even now attempting to put away her borrowed literature.

"Can I help you, Lady . . . " Palasa tried to remember what Daniel called her.

"Leia," Leia supplied. Palasa smirked, recalling it now.

"My name makes you smile?" she asked, smiling as if sharing a joke.

"Daniel has a sense of humor is all," she replied evasively. Palasa was sure Leia would not want to know that the man she had been spending time with had given her the name of Leia as an attempt at humor. Leia nodded and gestured to the chair opposite Palasa. Palasa quickly invited the lady night to sit. Leia thanked her.

"I thought we weren't to meet for another hour," Palasa remarked, leaning back so she could study her guest. Leia was doing the same to her, studying everything from the tight-fitting grey leggings Palasa was wearing to the short-sleeved white blouse she had on.

"You served under Magpie back before he broke up the armada. What can you tell me about him?" Leia kept her hand close to her sword out of habit, but it seemed to make Palasa nervous. As a courtesy to the woman, Leia forced herself to always keep her hands on the table instead.

"I served under him as second lieutenant," she replied. "He only fired on the ships and the colony to—"

"I'm not interested in the incident. I'm interested in the man. You knew him before he became infamous. Would you mind describing him for me." Leia's expression darkened. "Was he as powerful in his telepathic ability back then as he is now?"

Palasa's eyes widened then narrowed as she studied the knight across from her. "What'd he do?" she asked softly, a note of fear in her voice. Leia sensed the change attitude immediately.

"He's done things like this before, hasn't he?" Leia gasped.

"Used power he shouldn't be able to use? Yeah. He's done that before and more. Was that the detonations I felt from the lower areas of the ship?" Palasa asked. She looked terrified at the prospect.

"No. That wasn't him. He's powerful, but he isn't that powerful," Leia scoffed.

"You really don't know that man, do you?" Palasa asked in disbelief.

"You're really scared of him," Leia realized, coming around the table to sit with the woman.

"Anyone with a functioning brain should be. All they ever talk about is him destroying Sylar and the infected ships. You're the first to ask about him. No one ever talks about him. They call him a mass murderer, but always out of context. He was just a man before this all went down. He had a family. He had parents and two brothers he was very close to. He's become the focus of so much hate, but he didn't win in all of this. He lost too. Harvesting the Sylar colony changed him in ways you couldn't imagine."

"I can imagine," Leia murmured, resting her elbow on the table.

"No, you can't. He was worthy of being followed back then. He was worthy of respect. If we'd just listened from the beginning and bypassed that first colony, all of this could have been avoided. They knew something was wrong with the colonists. They knew it, and they still made him harvest it."

"Wait, the First Reaper knew the colony was infected? Everything I'd heard about what went down that day says Aug Moon was the one who pushed for the Harvest. He wasn't?" Leia asked, fascinated to hear this differing version of the event.

"We had a directive from the Emperor to harvest the colonies. We waited three hundred rotations in orbit above the planet like we were supposed to, to observe the colony and learn how it functioned. Aug Moon, like Magpie, discovered quickly that there was something peculiar about the colonists. You've heard the tales, of course, about how the entire planet had only one religion. Well, it was partially true."

"What's that supposed to mean?" Leia asked, growing a little perturbed with Palasa's detour in the conversation.

"There were two castes of citizens on that planet. The worshipped and those who worshipped. They didn't worship gods. They worshipped people. When Aug Moon presented his case of why we'd come, they agreed without discussion. It was our first Harvest and we didn't know this to be a peculiar response. Always with the colonies after that one, they debated and bargained as if they were selling us their people. The First volunteered en masse to board the ships."

Leia listened, enraptured by this unheard account.

"In the first few months, altars were being discovered in out of the way common areas. Soon after, the monks began to notice that more and more of the citizenry aboard the ship were abandoning their gods and beliefs in favor of this new religion. Magpie took notice when the reports of these altars and mass conversions reached him. He went to investigate the altars with two knights."

"He never really described what happened other than to say they were attacked. The two knights were killed. Magpie was severely wounded. We tried to get him to rest and spend some time in a Med Bed, but he was adamant. He claimed the colonists were infected and sick. He said that was what they worshipped. You should have seen him. He was terrified. I'd never seen the man afraid of anything before that, but he was."

"And the enhancement to his ability began after that?" Leia guessed.

"Not immediately. He ordered the Sylar colonists on the ship to be put in quarantine and ordered all shuttles coming up from the surface suspended. He had the Daimyo behind him on this. He didn't have Aug Moon though. Moon was still down on the surface and only he could call off the harvesting of the colonists." Palasa stopped talking suddenly and checked the time. "Will this take much longer? I really need to finish this project before we leave."

Leia ground her teeth. "Just a little longer, please?" she asked pleadingly. Palasa smiled gently and nodded.

"Before he discovered the virus, Magpie spent most of his time shadowing Aug Moon, training to be a Reaper himself. Well, he'd noticed the mass conversions taking place on the ships and had come to the surface to notify Moon. But something went wrong. Moon didn't believe him. I was the one piloting the skiff that took him down to the planet, so I don't care what they say. Aug Moon was infected with whatever it was that had infected the colonists. There were soldiers on the skiff serving as security. They reported afterwards that it was Magpie that went crazy and killed the Abbot, but it wasn't true. I saw it." Palasa checked the time again. "I really need to get back to work."

"No," Leia barked loudly, drawing shooshing sounds from the other people in the room quietly reading. "Just . . . Just keep going. Keep telling the story."

"Why? He's been cleared of the charges. He's a free man," Palasa declared, checking the clock again.

"I'm conducting my own investigation, okay? Just tell what you remember." Leia got up and went back to the other side of the table and made as if to sit but changed her mind and limped back and forth.

"Magpie approached the Abbot. Aug Moon was on his knees praying at a colonial altar. He made Magpie wait. The knights and soldiers that were supposed to provide Moon protection were kneeling before the altar as well. Magpie almost left then, but he decided he couldn't leave the Abbot behind, so he tried to force Moon to board the shuttle with him. It didn't go as Magpie envisioned."

"The landing zone where we landed was on the shores of a small inlet from the sea. Magpie tried to drag Aug Moon aboard and Moon snapped. He gathered his will and struck Magpie so hard he threw him fifty feet into the sea. Everything just went crazy in that moment. Moon shouted to his security and pointed at the skiff I was piloting. He screamed at others who went racing off into the forest. Moments later, shuttles started lifting off from the surface ferrying more colonists up to the ships." Leia looked confused.

"How far is fifty feet?" Leia asked, trying to imagine it. Palasa looked around, searching for something she could use to illustrate the measurement.

"Almost the width of this room," Palasa replied. Leia nodded and motioned for her to continue, taking a seat on the edge of the table.

"Moon threw Magpie in the water. When Magpie made it back to shore, he tried to flee. Moon wouldn't allow it and sent his knights after him. Magpie was acting different. He'd cut his temple during the attack and was bleeding profusely. The knights seized him and dragged him back to the Abbot."

"According to Magpie, the Abbot was infected as were the knights. He said they were all infected and that if we didn't take drastic action soon, they would spread their sickness to the ships. When Moon brought his will to bear to strike Magpie down, Magpie lost it. He broke free. Aug Moon lashed out at him. Magpie countered it. Moon smashed at Magpie again and knocked him back into the sea."

Palasa shook her head. "I thought Magpie was dead after that. He just floated face down in the water, not moving. Moon came for us, running and screaming. He had this bizarre look in his eyes. You know, one of those wild and dangerous looks. He was calling for us to exit the ship, but I wouldn't come. I sealed the ship. His soldiers and knights came after him and together, they tried to enter the skiff. I was scared. Moon swore he wasn't infected and begged us to open the door. I was pretty sure me and my crew were about to die, but Magpie came to our rescue."

Palasa gestured to Leia to pay attention. "This is what you came to learn. Magpie brought the force of his will to bear in one huge blast. He obliterated everything. He destroyed an entire squad of knights, nine soldiers and Aug Moon himself. I don't mean he just killed them. He atomized them and everything else between the skiff and the sea. He almost flipped the skiff." Leia was deathly silent.

"Till that point, I'd never seen anything so powerful in my life, but he wasn't like that before. He rarely resorted to violence, and when he did, the most he could do was throw people and in one rare moment of success, he was able to levitate a feather for six heart beats." Palasa shook her head. "You have no idea how terrifying it was."

"So, his powers just spontaneously manifested?" Leia asked, thoughtfully.

"It seemed that way to me, but the man was a pillar of self-discipline. Every action he took was thoroughly thought out right down to the way he cut his jaja fruit. He was like the stories they tell of the Tea Makers back on Cojo before we learned to fly. He was discipline incarnate. But it did seem that his abilities advanced far quicker than they should after that." Palasa finished scribbling a line on the synthetic paper, then went back to contemplating Leia. "Did he cause the explosions?" she asked again.

"You thought Daniel caused the explosions down below?" Leia asked, shuddering at the idea of that much force coming from another human being. "You really think he's capable of summoning that much power? Really?" Leia asked, scoffing at the thought. "Did any of this really happen or are you just singing the praises of your old master; you know what I'm talking about. Is this you trying to turn a sinner into a saint?" Leia was beginning think this whole conversation was a waste of time. Nobody was as strong as the former second lieutenant was claiming Magpie to be. Palasa leaned in close so she could not be overheard by the others in the depository.

"A few hundred years ago, there was an earthquake down on the planet. The colonials who lived in that region have described it as the single most powerful earthquake in the history of their nation. A river one mile wide ran backwards as a result. It shook buildings a third of the continent away." Palasa shook her head, remembering it. She had been there too.

"You were there?" Leia asked, curious where this was going. "Did he save you?" Leia asked, expecting that another impossible feat of strength was forthcoming.

"No. He caused it," Palasa told her simply. It was Leia's turn to shake her head.

"That's impossible. That defies Myron's Law—"

"—of Opposing Force," Palasa finished, nodding. "I know, but I was there. So was my mum and his brother. He caused that earthquake and flattened a small forest in the process, and then, he wandered off like he didn't even know us. He claimed before that he was trying to save the armada. I thought he meant he was trying to save it from the infected, but now, I think maybe he was trying to save it from himself. The last thing he said to us was 'leave me alone.' After what we saw him do, you bet we left him alone. He's antimatter to everyone around him. I remember the old Magpie before the Sylar incident. I respected that man. I don't know what he became afterwards.

This Daniel Sojourner he's become is quite possibly the best thing that could have happened to him. I just hope it lasts."

"Magpie had a brother?" Leia asked, changing the subject.

"He had two brothers. He killed them both. Mozzie was with him at the Sylar Colony—during the outbreak aboard the ships. When the governing council refused to decide regarding the infected ships, Magpie made the decision himself. He destroyed the Emperor's Pride, the flag ship for the armada, because it was infected. He knew full well his brother was aboard. That was part of the reason I knew it had to be done. Him and Mozzie were close—real close. There was no way he'd destroy the ship with his brother on board unless it absolutely had to be done. He went nomad after that, drifting around the ships. He gave up his position even though we were all calling for him to lead us."

"And that was it? He just shut down and vanished? What about his other brother?" Leia asked.

"William? William avoided him and even moved off the Moon Rai to a different ship. They didn't meet up again till this planet was harvested. After that, they never met up again," Palasa murmured distantly. "You mind? I really need to get back to this."

"Sure. Yeah, we can do the interview later before we ferry down to the surface. I just wanted to know more about the man I was . . ." She left that last unsaid. She was not comfortable talking about who she was presently intimate with. "Maybe his memory loss is for the best." Leia knew she should do the interview now while she had Palasa pinned down, but she did not feel like it. Daniel seemed destined to damage her compass every time she turned around. He was a distraction that almost got her brother killed. He was a distraction that got her kidnapped. And now, he was the distraction keeping her from investigating the death of her surrogate father. He was bad for her, and she knew it, and in the same breath, she did not really care.

"Magpie was a good man who did a hard thing for the right reasons, but he was a tortured man after the Sylar incident. He served as our Grand Reaper for a while. If Daniel has truly forgotten who he was, then maybe this is his reward. Maybe he gets the fresh start he deserves. I don't know." Palasa shrugged and took back up her pen intending to return to the dossier she was in the middle of preparing.

"What if it isn't?" Leia asked. "What if Magpie isn't gone. What if Daniel is a lie, and the real Magpie is still there, hiding in the back of Daniel's mind."

"Is this what you're afraid of?" she asked.

"I'm not afraid. I'm just considering every possibility. What if he is in there? What if he's hiding, and Daniel is just a mask he's created for our benefit; a way to escape his culpability?"

"What would make you think such a thing?" Palasa asked, her eyes narrowing shrewdly.

"Yellow eyes in the darkness," Leia murmured under her breath and far too quiet for Palasa to hear.

"I didn't catch that," Palasa said, cocking her ear to better hear what Leia had to say.

"I said, you're probably right. It's a blessing. Daniel seems to be a good man." Leia pushed herself up and flipped a quick wave of farewell to the woman across from her. "Maybe this long-lost brother of Magpie's will like who Daniel's become. Maybe there's a happy ending in this after all."

"If there is, that won't be it. William's dead. Magpie killed him too and broke the planet's mantle in the process. You and Daniel may be the closest thing this whole miserable tale has to even remotely resembling a happy ending. Magpie's gone, but I doubt your brother will let him stay that way," Palasa predicted blandly. "Your brother is not a nice man."

"I'm not even saying that there is a me and Daniel at this point, but if it turns out there is, then yeah, I'll gladly be his happy ending. And as far as my brother is concerned, Magpie is gone. He's forgiven Daniel. He's forgiven him for what Magpie did. He understands the truth now. He knows Daniel isn't the same man that killed our father, just like he knows you're not the assassin who killed the Daimyo," Leia declared, gesturing to Palasa. Palasa's eyes widened in surprise.

"Oh, don't act surprised. I knew you weren't the murderer the moment I laid eyes on you. You're an innocent. I'll interview you because they tell me I must, but only because you might have seen the killer without knowing it. Thanks for giving me the time to talk this out. I'll schedule a new time for that interview. Thanks for being candied with me," Leia told her, smiling weakly.

Palasa's eyes narrowed. "Who told you Luke forgave Daniel?" Palasa asked before Leia could exit the repository.

"Luke did. He even gave Daniel a job of translating protocols and restrictions for the colonial diplomats. He wouldn't have done that if he hadn't forgiven him. He even told Daniel he understood that he wasn't Magpie anymore. And with you? It's obvious. My brother isn't an idiot. He knows you're innocent. He can see the truth in a web of lies. I know you're innocent because I read the report on the Daimyo's death."

Palasa sighed, but Leia continued. "There was no way you could have slipped poison into Lord Merrick's cup. You were brought straight from the cells and operated under the supervision of Lord Merrick and my brother. The interview is just a formality. I know Luke, and this is over." Leia seemed pretty sure of the fact. "You and Daniel, you both get to live normal lives from this point on. Be happy for that." Leia didn't smile. She just turned to go. She had learned what she wanted, but again, Palasa gave her pause, snorting with laughter.

"You really believe that, don't you?" Palasa asked bitterly, letting her laughter fade.

Leia studied the other woman's features wondering why she would think that it would be otherwise. Her brother was a good man. He was just under a lot of pressure. But her thoughts did go back to the incident in the cell between her brother and Daniel. A soldier had died because of her brother's rashness. She shook that thought away. The thought that her brother was lying to her was just absurd. There had always been trust between them. She knew Luke better than any other person in the universe. He was a good man. He had always been a good man. She kept telling herself that over and over, but her mind kept going back to that prison cell with Daniel. She considered that a fluke, a moment of weakness on her brother's part and not one he was very apt to repeat.

"Yes. I do believe that," Leia snapped. "Why wouldn't I?" She gave Palasa a hard look and left before the woman thought up an answer. "He's forgiven him," she murmured softly to herself. "He has. He has forgiven him." The peculiar thing in all this was that she actually believed the lies she was telling herself.

Chapter 29: The Plan

Leia found Luke a short time later in his cell, dressing. It was almost time to go. Her brother was a traditionalist. Many in the monastic order collected singular items and possessions to show their rank among the order. They would take exotic cells with rare wood attributes and rich colonial works of art and sculptures, furniture and clothing, and parade themselves down the byways and through the temples with great aplomb. They would preen themselves and puff themselves up because the higher their rank, the more appearances mattered. But Luke lived in defiance of that belief. He lived as the monks once lived when the order was pure and meek and about finding enlightenment.

Luke's cell was a plain affair with a single bed, a table with two chairs, a floor with no carpet, and one chair in his back garden. His kitchen stasis cabinet where other citizens stored their produce and groceries was as empty as the day he took this cell. He used the kiosk in his kitchen for all his meals. The only luxury he allowed himself were the bookshelves. He had a fascination with colonial literature and made a point to collect copies of popular works from famous colonial personages at every colony he visited. Three rooms of his cell were covered wall to wall with these rare volumes. In all of his twelve hundred years, this was the only vice he chose to indulge. There were over six thousand volumes in all, and he had read them all.

"Smells musty in here," Leia complained, sniffing at the air with disdain.

The price of knowledge, I'm afraid, Luke replied, pulling a richly embroidered tunic over his strong, well-rounded shoulders. The tunic was an off-white-colored long-sleeved shirt with no cuffs or collar. It had a decorative double seam that ran up the center of the chest and ended at a v-shaped neck that barely showed his collar bone. He wore dark leggings and dark hard soled shoes that matched.

Leia lifted his jacket from the hook on the wall where it hung and held it out for him to slip on. He slipped an arm into one sleeve and his other arm into the other sleeve and shrugged it on. He turned to face her, and she smiled.

Are all of the diplomats seen too? he asked.

"Yep," she replied, fussing with his hair.

The alternates located and summoned? he asked again.

"Yes," she replied, growing incensed.

The landing site picked and shuttles sequenced? he pressed, irritating her. She nodded.

And the shuttles are inspected? he asked flicking his eyes toward her.

"No, actually. That's all I have left to do. The security personnel are picked. All the diplomats and functionaries are staged and ready to load. Daniel is translating the protocols you gave him. We're ready to go," she said. "We're just waiting on you."

What about the suspects in the murder of the Daimyo? Have you interviewed all of Lord Merrik's suspected assassins? he asked, holding her gaze.

"Not formally. I've only spoken with Palasa. It wasn't an official interview though. I was getting some background information on her," Leia hedged, grabbing a short metal rod from a holder on the wall. This she handed to him. He studied it then flipped it end to end, smiled, and slipped it into the inner pocket in his jacket.

Were you getting her background or his? Luke asked. His eyes were flat and suddenly hostile. Leia ground her teeth in frustration and gave him a look of warning. He was treading dangerous ground.

"A little of both," she admitted, unimpressed with his disapproval. "You forgave him, remember? Besides, it's none of your business who I bed or see. You're my brother not my father."

I feel I must fill in for our father since your new love was the man who killed our father, he told her snidely. *I want her, this Palasa, interviewed for the Daimyo's murder. After she's interviewed, I want you to declare her guilty of the murder. And, I want it done before we board the shuttles for the colony.*

"No. She's not guilty. Anyone with a brain can see that. Why is it important that you pin this on her?"

It's all about maneuvering, little sister. I made a mistake trying to infect Daniel. I admit it. I was wanting to punish Magpie, but I can't punish Magpie because he's gone. Or maybe he isn't. What if he's just suppressed? Politically, it is important that Magpie is punished. So, I must do everything in my power to pull him out of hiding if he actually is hiding. I think he's in there somewhere, hiding behind that snarky smart-ass persona you've fallen in love with. You can't tell me that you don't think that this might be a hoax. There has to be a nugget of doubt inside you. He declared, almost pleading with her to agree. Before she could respond, he saw the look in her eye. He saw that momentary flicker of uncertainty and smiled.

Look at me. I am a good man. Palasa was that man's second lieutenant and more—much more. I will not send an innocent woman to Level 601. I know she's innocent. The real assassin was a percher. An intelligence officer discovered her posing as a guest-master a few days ago. I asked them to keep it quiet. Luke studied her reaction. She was not happy about this.

When the parasite refused to infect your precious Daniel, I started looking for other ways to hurt him, and that research let me discover something about Palasa. She isn't who she claims to be. I mean, that's her real name, and she was Magpie's second lieutenant, but she was more than that. This is my last attempt to try and draw Magpie out of Daniel. He may not consciously remember who she is, but if he is still in there, seeing her in peril may reach the real Magpie. I firmly believe he's in there suppressing himself. I think he's still in there, but he doesn't know he's still in there. If this doesn't work, then I'll declare Magpie dead and recognize Daniel as an entirely different person. I swear it. He held both hands up, palms out. Leia studied him shrewdly, wanting to trust him.

"What's your plan?" Leia asked.

I'm going to declare Palasa the murderer of the Daimyo. It's a crime punishable by death. You're going to testify to this before the colonials. I just want the colonials to think that one of their people assassinated our leader. I want them to fear reprisal. I want that thought in the forefront of their minds. I want them to feel obligated to tell their people why we've come in such a way that the people of this colony will seriously consider it our invitation. I wanted to show them an infected Magpie, but that plan failed. I thought that if they were able to compare that smug bastard they once knew with the raving infected man he would have become, it would have motivated them to flee with us. It was fear mongering, but it would have worked and punished a man who deserved to be punished. Luke shrugged.

My plan failed though. I can't show them an infected Daniel because of whatever he did to himself all those years ago to keep the parasites out. This thing with Palasa is the next best thing. If I can't use one kind of fear to motivate the colony, then I'll use another. It'll be a bluff, but they won't know that. He smiled. He was pleased with himself for thinking up such a clever plan. Leia wasn't happy though. She was a strategist too. She saw so many problems with this plan. It was reckless with many unpredictable variables.

"This is coercion, Luke. That violates the first Law of the Harvest," she warned. "This could get you sent to Level 601 instead." She was shaking her head, not liking it at all.

It isn't coercion, sis. They still have the choice to come or not. Nobody is forcing them. Think about it. I need you for this. Will you help me? He could see she was still hesitant. *Think of it this way then, if you do this, you'll know once and for all if Daniel is the permanent tenant in Magpie's body or not. It'll put all your doubts to rest.*

"This is immoral," she declared, bitterly.

Perhaps.

"You're not going to try and harm Daniel in any way, right? If Magpie appears, you seek no vengeance. You let Gorjjen take him into custody as the Inquisitors have instructed, and you publicly declare Palasa's innocence to the armada the moment the colony informs their people. Is this agreed?" she asked. He did not immediately respond. "Agree to this, and I'll go along with your plan."

I agree to declare Palasa innocent, not to harm Daniel, and to let Gorjjen take Magpie into custody if I'm able to lure him out, which I will. One thing further. I need you to give this to Daniel when I declare Palasa guilty of assassinating the Daimyo. He handed her a tablet.

"What is it?" she asked.

The "much more" of which I spoke. This is who Palasa really is. When Daniel reads it and hears my announcement, he will react. If Magpie is in there, he will come out. This will get us a response if there is any response to be had.

"What if he does respond? How will you take Magpie in without hurting him? What if he appears and tries to kill you?" she asked, not liking his plan in the least.

There will be Imperial knights chaperoning every diplomat we take down there, plus the Baron of Heid will be on hand. Feel free to assign more security as you see fit. I don't care. I just want to know for sure that Magpie is gone, he told her in earnest. She barely heard him. She was thinking about the stories Palasa was telling her at the repository. This had the potential to go so wrong if her stories proved true.

"I don't think this is a good idea, Luke. I don't think you realize just how powerful Daniel has become. He's erratic and growing stronger every day. He's unleashing next level psychic ability like it's a reflex. If he loses control because you baited him into lashing out, people on both sides could get hurt," she declared, staring holes into the man.

You know what? I'm tired of debating this. You'll do it, or someone else will. I don't care, but this is happening. I will have Magpie revealed, and I will make this the largest Harvest we've ever had. I won't let those people die at the hands of the Infected. I won't do it, so this is happening. Get on board with it, and do it now, Luke snapped, walking away.

Leia did not follow at first. She was staring at the tablet. She had to know what he meant when he said Palasa was more than just a second lieutenant. All kinds of fears were racing through her mind. He was imagining Palasa as Magpie's lover back before he lost his memory. That would explain the tall tales Palasa had been trying to feed her. She did not know, but she knew she had to find out. She had to know, so she woke up the tablet and activated the glyph in the middle of the screen. Words flashed across the screen, and she read them, growing paler the further down she read.

Luke paused at the door studying her reaction. When she was done and there was no more to read, she looked to her brother and there was anger in her eyes. In turn, his smirk was not filled with joy. It was gloating and filled with sadistic glee.

She marched up to him, studying his eyes as she approached. There was a momentary flicker of shame there, but it was fleeting. It was quickly replaced with a cruel sadistic smile.

"You're a fucking monster. You're a—" She had no word for him. She couldn't think. Luke would not do this. She opened her mouth to respond but slapped him hard across the cheek instead. "After this, I'm putting in for transfer. You're not the man I grew up with and dad would be ashamed of you."

We won't ever really know that though, will we? Dad's dead. Dad is dead, and the man you're screwing did that to him. You think dad would be ashamed of me? He laughed mockingly. *I think he'd be a little more disappointed that his daughter's a whore*, Luke spat. Leia did not even have to consider a response to that. It was automatic. She kneed him in the groin, then grabbed his ears and slammed her forehead into his nose.

"Screw you," she declared, seething with anger.

"I'll do this, but the Emperor help you if you ever cross my path again," she told him spiting in his face, grabbed a rag off the table and threw it at him so he could stop the blood coming from his nose before it made a mess of his jacket and tunic.

As she marched past, he opened his mouth to snarl out some new insult, but one look from her made him hold his tongue. He had no illusions about her. She was the better fighter. She was better trained. She was better equipped. She was even better motivated than him thanks to his smugness, and this was not the time to pick a fight. He had a Harvest to see to. He mopped at his nose and went back into his cell to see about stemming the flow and covering it up before he left.

Leia's anger did not subside on her march to the hangar. She went through the checklist on all the shuttles, finding nothing wrong with any of them. After that, she went looking for Daniel. Luke had given her permission to assign more security to keep an eye on Daniel in case Magpie made an appearance. She knew just the personnel to assign. She woke up her NID as she marched back to the Med Bed where she had left her lover and quickly typed in the names of the knights she wanted on Daniel's detail. She pulled up her holographic interface and studied the dots that showed her friends.

Her friends were ten levels higher in the ship than she was, which she found strange since they were all stationed on Level 12 Quad 3. She tapped each dot and dismissed the projected interface and sent out the message for them to report to her for their new duty assignments. She put a rush on it. Their responses were almost immediate. They were on their way down.

This made her feel a little better, but not a lot. She was still unbelievably disappointed in her brother. When she reached the medical node where Daniel was. A quick look showed that he was still inside. She did not enter right away. She had to see it again to verify what Luke had shown her. She read through the profile again. It said the same thing though. There was no denying who Palasa was to him. It was going to break his heart. She almost marched in right then and there to hand him the tablet but decided against it. At least now she understood why Palasa and her mother had followed Magpie down to the planet all those years ago.

"You're looking better," Leia announced with a smile she did not feel upon entering the room.

Daniel giggled drunkenly. "I'm feeling soooooo goooood," he confirmed.

"Uh-oh," Leia laughed. "You've been in the bed a little longer than you should." She hurried over and pushed the lid of the Med Bed up. The effect on Daniel faded almost immediately. He tried to grab the top and pull it back down, but she was not permitting it. She flicked his nose and pushed the lid all the way up. After a few seconds, the euphoric state went away.

"Why did you do that?" Daniel mumbled, chuckling drowsily.

"It causes a chemical in your brain to over produce if you stay in the bed with nothing to heal. It causes euphoria. It isn't good for you in prolonged doses," she said.

"I love dopamine," Daniel declared, shaking his head to clear the sleepy feeling away. After a few moments, the effect faded completely. "Wow. That was fun," he proclaimed grandly trying to kiss her on the lips. She did not feel like it though and turned her head, so that his kiss fell upon her cheek. "Something wrong?"

"It's been a long day," she replied. He handed her a sheaf of papers with scribble marks on them she could not read.

"All done with the translation," he mumbled again. "Do I give 'em to Luke or what?" He looked to her for the answer.

"I'll take care of it," she responded, taking the papers.

"This too," he said, handing her a placard he had made. The placard said, "I am here to speak with Aaron McDonald, Director Homeland Security." Leia read it and smiled.

"You're going to the surface," she announced suddenly.

"Why?" he asked in confusion.

"No reason really. I just want you there, so I can keep you safe," she replied, smiling sadly.

"You look like someone just peed in your Cheerios," Daniel told her with a smirk.

She considered what he said before shaking her head feeling even more defeated than she looked. "Nope. I don't understand what that means."

"You look sad and disappointed."

"It's been a long day," she said again. Leia looked at the man and sighed deeply. She could not do this right now. "Come on. I'll show you to the staging area."

"I'll show him to the hangar," Gorjjen announced suddenly, popping up on the other side of the Med Bed. He had been sitting quietly in the corner listening to all they had to say. They both started in surprise and turned on the man. "Problem, my friends?" he asked, as if nothing were strange about his sudden appearance. Daniel smirked, but Leia just gave another long sigh.

"What are you doing here?" Daniel asked, offering the man his hand to shake. Gorjjen studied the proffered hand then looked back to Daniel as if to say, that's very nice, my friend. Daniel kept his hand out there a little longer, then realizing the man was not going to shake it, he withdrew it.

"I am you Guilt. I go where you go," Gorjjen reminded him.

"Where were you when we were being attacked on the lifts?" he asked, suddenly remembering the weapon master's absence.

"I was on the lift that followed," Gorjjen revealed.

"Why didn't you just join us on our lift?" Daniel asked incensed.

"I am your Guilt. I follow you. I don't walk beside you," he said. "Besides, you didn't wait for me."

"This actually works out better," Leia told them, handing back the protocols to Daniel. "I'm assigning you a protection detail for the surface. All dignitaries get one. You're the reserve translator should Luke need one. I have one more stop to make before we leave. One last interview." Leia's nostrils flared and she ground her teeth as she announced this. "Give these to a shuttle captain when you get to the hangar and send him to the same place where Luke captured you. Tell him to give the protocols to one of your ambassadors. I'll try to catch up to you before you leave. If I don't," she leaned forward and kissed him quickly, "try and remember that for a knight, it's duty above all else." She was looking at Gorjjen when she said this, drawing his eyes back to Daniel. Gorjjen seemed to understand her meaning and his chin rose a little higher and his shoulder's straightened. He was to be the Baron of Hein again.

"Yeah. I get that. Just kiss me kindly when you can," Daniel told her with a smile. This did make her smile, and so she leaned in again kissed him a little harder and a little longer. When she broke at last. She realized that Gorjjen was watching them. He looked amused and Daniel looked breathless.

"I'll send Ailig and the rest of the group to your new location. They're your security detail," she declared, turning away to leave.

"Whatever it is that's bothering you—that's making you fear for me on the surface—don't worry. I can manage. I've evidently been managing for over a thousand years. It'll be okay," he promised, having no idea what Luke had in store for him. Leia felt so sorry for the man.

"Just," she searched for the right words, "stay calm and let it happen. It isn't real," she said, turning his head so she whispered it into his ear.

Daniel was confused, but he nodded in reply; not because she asked him to, but because he trusted her completely.

"Promise me, please. You'll stay calm and won't let Luke provoke you," she begged, worry in her eyes. She wanted to say more but refrained. He wanted to ask more, but he could see that she had already told him more than she should have so he just nodded.

"I promise," he told her, thinking only as an afterthought to reassure her with a smile. She did not say "goodbye" or try to kiss him again. She just gave Gorjjen a look and walked away.

Her meeting with Palasa went about as expected. The woman gave her account of what happened, what she saw, who was there, how the Daimyo's reaction to the poison began, and how her attempt to save Lord Merrik's life with a tracheotomy was foiled by Luke who stopped her before she could begin it. It had all been in the report except the part about the tracheotomy. Leia requested more information on that then wondered why her brother had not allowed it. Surgery on the ship was a rare practice due to the Med Beds, but it did happen. Leia listened to it all. Her periods of silence grew longer and longer as she contemplated what she had to do.

"Why didn't you tell me who you were to Magpie?" Leia asked.

"I did," Palasa replied. "I was his Second Lieutenant." Leia pushed the tablet across the table and woke it up. Curious, Palasa leaned forward and read, her face draining of color. "Don't tell him, please. Magpie is gone. Daniel doesn't need to know who I am. This doesn't need to be told."

"You loved Magpie though, didn't you?" Leia asked.

"Of course," Palasa replied sorrowfully.

"He loved you?" Leia asked.

"Yes," Palasa whispered. "That's why we stayed behind. That's why we . . . Please don't tell him," she begged again.

"We have to," Leia lied, hating herself for what Luke was making her to do.

"Daniel is hiding something. Back in the furthest reaches of his mind, he is hiding something, and we think it's Magpie. I've seen it. I've been in his mind, and I've seen it. My brother's plan is to put you in peril in the hope that doing so will draw Magpie out," Leia told her candidly.

"What do you mean by put me in peril?" Palasa asked, drawing in her will slowly.

"I'm going to declare that you're guilty of the Daimyo's murder. That carries a penalty of death. We will present you to the colonists on the planet as the murderer of our beloved leader so that the unspoken threat of global annihilation will motivate them to comply with our request to announce the Harvest to their people in hopes of placating our supposed anger. Daniel will be in attendance. If Magpie is in there still, he will manifest, and two things will happen. I will know for sure if Daniel is real or if he's just the mask Magpie is wearing to escape us, and Luke will either have his revenge on the man who killed our father or he will have peace that Magpie is truly gone."

"After the Harvest, you will be cleared of all charges. The real killer has already been found and executed. This is a gambit and nothing more. Play your part, and you might just get to see Magpie one last time before he dies. You'll get to say goodbye," Leia told her.

She felt sick to her stomach. This wasn't what being a knight was supposed to entail. She felt dirty doing this to Daniel. He had saved her several times. He saved her when nobody else could. This seemed a bitter answer to his unselfish kindness. But worse yet, it felt like a betrayal.

"I don't want him to know who I am!" Palasa snapped at the knight.

"Will you attack me then?" Leia asked quietly.

"If I must, yes. I don't want Magpie back. I want him to stay gone. Daniel doesn't need to know who I am. Don't do this," she pleaded. "You don't know what it will do to him to discover the truth."

"It's done," Leia told her callously. Palasa drew in her will and focused on Leia's head. A knight's armor could break up most psychic attacks. The only way to truly circumvent a knight's defenses was to finely focus it on one exposed part of the body. She did not want to hurt Leia, but she also did not want Daniel to know either. Leia made no move to stop her. Palasa took a deep breath and prepared to flex her will and destroy the lady knight where she sat. She never got the chance. Leia did not move, but somehow she managed to cloud Palasa's mind. Concentrating became difficult. Palasa tried to focus, but the harder she tried to focus the more her head hurt.

She finally cried out and collapsed back into the seat, relaxing her will. The pain subsided almost immediately.

Three soldiers appeared then. One of them carried a staff as tall as he and atop it was a familiar, burgundy-colored sphere. This was the source of the disturbance that had scattered her thoughts. It was a neural dampener. The other two soldiers carried stun batons and moved into a position to flank the neural dampener.

"They will accompany you onto the transport with Daniel and myself. You will not be allowed to speak to him. If you alert him, signal him, speak out when accused by Luke, after the Harvest, we won't declare your innocence. Is that understood? If you don't do this, you will be allowed to die for the Daimyo's murder," Leia told her in a steely voice. Palasa did not respond. She just collected the dossier she had been working on and rounded the table. She shoved the sheaf of papers at Leia, slamming them hard into the knight's armor. Leia did not retaliate.

She calmly took the papers and allowed the soldiers to lead Palasa away. The repository was quiet after that. All the other patrons had been evicted so the interview could take place. Leia pulled the sheaf of papers away and considered them, rising from her seat. She was so furious with him. She dropped the papers on to the chair seat beside her and leaned heavily upon the table before her. Her breathing was coming fast, and her vision would not clear. She was just seeing red everywhere she looked. Her lip curled in disgust, and she considered what she was doing. This was not what being a knight was about. This was not. She screamed out her frustration to the empty room and smashed her fist into the tabletop before her. It felt good, but she needed more. She punched it repeatedly till her knuckles bled. And when that was not enough, she drew in her will and destroyed it.

"No!" she screamed, smashing through the table repeatedly till her fury was spent. Huffing angrily, she surveyed the destruction she had wrought and decided it needed just a little more, lashing out with her booted foot at a nearby chair. Her snap launched the chair deeper into the room. "No," she cried again, quieter. "No. No. No. No!"

She stood there seething and panting, hating her brother for making her his accomplice. That was not true. She did not hate her brother for making her do it. She hated herself for being weak. Daniel had always been a distraction. That was true. And now, he was destroying her life by making her care for him. She just wanted to quit him. She just wanted to walk away from the man with the dual identity. She even wanted to walk away from her brother and deny him his wishes, but she could not. She just could not quit either of them. Luke was her brother. How could she walk away from him? And Daniel, how could she abandon him?

Ironically, she just could not get him out of her head. She grabbed the sheaf of papers and walked away. It was time to begin the Harvest.

Chapter 30: Homebound Message

"Sir," Aaron's assistant called from the front passenger's seat.

"Yes, Jamie?" Aaron called back, pulling his eyes away from the traffic on the sidewalk. The black SUV passed beneath an old railroad trestle, and for a moment, Aaron could see his reflection in the tinted-out glass. He looked older now. He had bags beneath the bags beneath his eyes, and the hollow spots beneath his eyes made him look cadaverous. He kept his eyes on his reflection till the SUV passed back into the light. His reflection vanished, and the people on the sidewalks returned, moving like windows on a train as he passed them.

He closed his eyes and held his hand out to take the phone he had seen reflected in the glass. The phone his assistant was holding out to him even now. He turned his tired eyes to Jamie who held them for a second before turning back to his day runner and Aaron's schedule book.

"Aaron McDonald," he announced into the phone.

Jamie glanced behind toward his boss and saw the look of exhaustion on the man's face slide away. It was replaced with confusion and concern.

"You're sure? How long?" Whatever the answer was, it was enough to make Jamie's boss tap the driver on the shoulder. "Turn around. We need to get back Washington. One of the ships just landed on the lawn of the Washington Monument."

"Why?" Jamie asked without thinking.

"Why? I don't know, but they've asked for me by name." Aaron's browed furrowed in confusion. Sure, he had been at every meeting with the alien ambassador, but this was the first time they had asked for him by name. "Come on Brad. Put the pedal down. Get us there." The government vehicle lurched as Brad obeyed, pushing the pedal nearly to the floor. Aaron went back to staring out the window, and the pursuit of his inner demons, coming out only once as a thought occurred to him. "Jamie?"

"Yes, sir?" Jamie replied turning to face his boss.

"Route three teams to the monument." He chewed his bottom lip thoughtfully, stroking one of his cuff links idly. Jamie was already dialing.

"Expecting trouble?" The assistant asked curiously, turning back so he faced forward. He finished dialing and pressed the phone to his year.

"Just being careful is all. It's not a good time to be trusting blindly."

This landing was not expected, and Aaron shuddered to think what had changed. His mind went immediately to the man who called himself Daniel. They had really wanted him. Had he changed the alien's plans for Earth? Had he muddled this for everyone? He shook his head absently, dismissing the thoughts. Daniel had seemed a good sort. He had been trying to do the right thing down here and at great personal risk to himself. That was the kind of man he was. If he changed things, it was because he thought he was fixing them. Aaron shook his head again, trying to rid himself of the worries. This was an exercise in futility. Worrying about why the ship was here served no purpose, so he put it from his mind and began working through the problems of receiving the alien dignitaries enroute to the planet's surface.

It was a twenty-minute drive back to the Monument. Crowds of people had gathered, and traffic was snarled for several blocks. Homeland Security agents met his SUV as they pulled in. He slid from the back seat and took a moment to adjust his suit before looking to the sea of people and their forest of up-thrust hands filled with cell phones cameras.

"Mister McDonald? Mister McDonald?" a woman called out from behind two of the Homeland Security agents escorting Aaron to the Monument lawn. He gave her a quick appraisal, noticing the shapeliness of her legs. It was only a quick look and so that was why he did not realize who it was he was ogling. "Aaron!" the woman called again, skipping the formal back and forth. Her arm was outthrust with a microphone filling it. "Dad!" she called again, embarrassed to have shouted that. Aaron came to a stop, shocked by the call.

"What are you . . . What, Sheila?" he asked, continuing his walk to the alien vessel parked in the middle of the monument's lawn.

"They say the aliens asked for you personally. Have you met this alien before?" she asked, struggling to keep pace, her cameraman shadowing her.

"I don't know, Sheila," he replied blandly. "I don't know which alien it is. If it's ET, yeah. We used to hang out in college. We were frat brothers," he told her patronizingly. His smile was faint and vanished quick. There was a moment of laughter from the people close enough to hear his jest.

"What's the U.S. government hiding from its own people. I can see it, Aaron. You know I can see it. You're hiding something," she snapped. "Is that why every leader in the world has converged on Washington this week?" She paused as if judging whether to reveal what she already knew; what she had just learned. "Does this have anything to do with the Summit?" she asked. He kept walking, but then suddenly wheeled on her.

"We are hiding something from the American people," he announced suddenly.

"I knew it. You're hiding why they're," she jerked her head toward the saucers overhead, "why they're here, aren't you?"

"What do you remember about August 16, 1977?" he asked, leaning in close so few could hear them.

"Not much. I wasn't born then," she replied.

"Well, in 1977 Earth was visited by aliens just like these. They took someone," he said. She had been excited, thinking he was going to reveal something juicy, but then her eyes went flat as she realized he was still messing with her.

"Stop," she told him.

"Oh, we told everyone he died, but the truth leaked out," Aaron explained, carrying his joke to its conclusion, his voice rising.

"Stop it!" she told him more strongly.

"Elvis is alive, Sheila, and they're here to return him. You hear that people. Elvis is alive!" Aaron announced theatrically to the crowd. He leaned in quick and kissed his daughter's forehead before she could pull away or protest.

"Ahhhhh!" she cried in frustration. "What are you hiding?" she demanded, coming to a stop.

"Everything, Sweetie," he replied flippantly. "I'm a politician, remember?"

"I hate you," she shouted.

"I know it, Baby. You should go see your mom. Since this started, I've had to be away on business. She gets lonely. She could use a little company while I sort this out," he said, giving her a farewell wave. This frustrated her more than his jokes. She did not want the public knowing she was the daughter of the Homeland Security Director and now he had just kissed her head like some prepubescent child.

The moment Aaron was past his daughter and the perimeter of people, his smile slid away, not that it was ever a real smile to begin with. He went back to being that man staring out the window again, and he marched out onto the lawn without any trace of hesitation. It was how he survived during his climb to become Director. He relished failure, seeing it as the only way to truly learn, so he did not fear it. He did not fear dying because he considered the fact he was still alive after all the things he had been through in his past—his stint in the Marines, his time with the organized crime investigative division of the FBI, and his time with the DEA hunting cartel bosses—to be a miracle. He was living on borrowed time. So, he lost nothing by marching out into the unknown. The freedom from fear made life so much better in his opinion. It made life fresher, so he did not stop until he stood before the alien visitor who had requested him.

"You asked for me?" The alien was a man who looked to be in his mid-twenties. He was short for a man. Maybe five foot eight. Slim but fit. He wore a simple jacket that stopped at his waist with a short, rounded tail on the back. His leggings were a dark charcoal while his jacket and tunic were more almond in color. His boots came to mid-calf but there was a decorative lacing that was part of the boot and crisscrossed the remaining upper portion of his lower leg, ending just beneath the man's knee. The alien was cradling a case in his arms and raised a placard.

I am here to speak with Aaron McDonald, Director Homeland Security.

The alien never said a word. Without a telepath to translate for him, there was no way the man could have told those he met who he was here to see. The placard made sense. He just had to show it to whoever summoned courage enough to approach him upon his arrival.

The alien flipped the case he carried around and presented it to Aaron. There was a message scrawled across the top of the case. His eyes went to the signature and smiled when he saw who it was that had signed it.

Daniel was reaching out.

"Why did you ask for me?" Aaron asked. The man tapped the message with his index finger, but he said nothing at all. Aaron sighed and read the message Daniel had written him.

> *Hey Aaron. I'm fine for the time being. They've asked that I assist them in preparing you and the rest of the dignitaries for this big meeting between our world and theirs. They wanted to let you know what the terms of this meeting should be.*
>
> *Inside you'll find a translated list of their protocols and restrictions and a list of the restrictions they're going to honor and ask that we honor the same restrictions. They're silly things like only one bodyguard per diplomat. No firearms, which isn't silly. I think you get the gist of it all. There's quite a few terms and conditions within the case.*
>
> *When they arrive, I've assured them that the colonials (you guys), will provide transport to wherever this meeting is being held. They're on the up and up about*

this. Their government is over all an empire, and they value the letter of the law just like we do. At no time during my stint on the ship have I discovered that their plan for Earth is any different than what they told you.

They are being pursued by another armada. They're trying to save Earth from the sickness this other armada brings with it. They're a lot like the United States for the most part. Better in some ways. Their entire system of governing seems to be them taking all the different forms used on Earth, cobbling them together, then throwing them against the wall to see what sticks. They're fair, just, and value the same things we do.

Hell, I'm only alive right now because of their laws. Any way. I won't be your translator this time around. I'll be there, but I'll be watching like everyone else. I guess I'll see you when I see you, buddy. Don't let Tessa screw this up for Earth.

Sincerely, Daniel.

Aaron read through it again and smiled. He'd been wondering how it played out for the man. Daniel was snarky and a bit of a pain in the ass, but he seemed sincere and a good sort. The Director started to lower the case and saw that there was more under the fold in the message.

P.S. Make sure our people don't do anything stupid. You wouldn't believe the size of the guns they have trained on the planet's surface. Their diplomats are unarmed. Their security isn't. But, even if they were, starting a fight down there, would go very badly for Earth if something went amiss. This isn't a threat. They've had those guns trained on Earth from day one of their arrival as far as I've gathered. It's precautionary measure. Just don't let our people screw this up. ET's a bad ass this time around.

Aaron read it through again and glanced nervously toward the faint blue outlines of the saucers overhead. He found it encouraging that Daniel kept referring to Earth as his people. Aaron knew the man was one of them, but it was strengthening to know he was still on Earth's side of this.

"Is this the entire message?" Aaron asked of the courier. The alien courier's head lolled slowly to one side and his eyes narrowed. Aaron just assumed the man was pulling the thoughts out of his skull. He may have been right in that guess for the messenger suddenly nodded, then turned and re-entered his ship.

Those watching from the open portal on the ship backed away and hit something beside the door. The panel swiped sideways from inside the wall of the ship and closed them off from Earth. A moment later, the ramp raised and took the curved shape of the hull.

"Well, that was a long a drive for a short conversation," he reflected sardonically, backing away from the saucer. After a short distance of backing away, he turned and walked away, headed back to his SUV. He had seen what one of the ships did to a cow in Kansas. He had no intention of being rolled across the monument lawn like plastic trash during hurricane season. He did glance back when the whining of the engines built to a crescendo. When the vibrations from the ship got to the point that he began to feel it in his teeth, the ship left. Lifting off like it had been shot from a rail gun. One moment it was there. The next moment it was gone. If not for the slight bluish blur tracing off into the sky and the vaporous clouds it formed from its friction with the atmosphere, one might think it just blinked out of existence.

Aaron's agents met him at the crowd and rolled in around him to guide him the short distance he had to travel to reach his vehicle.

"Mister McDonald!" Sheila called from the far side of the security detail. He did not respond.

"When I'm gone, redeploy to the Alpha site and report to Captain Douglas. He'll roll you into his team and dole out your new assignments," Aaron told the squad leaders. Three heads nodded and turned away.

"Yes, sir," they responded, gathering up their men.

"Stay sharp men," he called after, rolling up his window up.

"Aaron," Sheila called again, fighting the agents keeping her at bay. She ground her teeth in frustration and reluctantly called to him again. "Dad," she called with resignation. The window stopped just shy of closing all the way and reversed direction.

"Yes, dear," he replied wearily.

"What was that all about?" she demanded.

"You know better than to ask questions like that," he told her tartly.

"Why are you hiding the details of these meetings from the public?" she asked, genuinely curious. He motioned to the special agent holding her to let her through. She came up to the window. He motioned her to lean in close. She set her hands on the door with the microphone she held in one hand. She had it aimed his way and leaned in close. He placed a hand over the head of the microphone.

"All I can tell you sweetheart is . . ." he looked at the crowd as if fearing being overheard and lowered his voice conspirator's whisper. "All I can tell you is . . . love you, Baby." He kissed the tip of her nose before she could pull away. "Go see your mom," he commanded, winking at the camera. The camera man was smirking.

"Dammit, Dad!" she growled, pulling away. She backed away even as he motioned to the driver to be off. She wanted to shout at him some more, but the man's window was now up and disappearing through the crowd. With him gone, the agents blocking her and her cameraman dispersed.

"Come on," she called, excitedly to her cameraman.

"Where?" he asked.

"We're following him," she snapped. "Hurry up."

"How? He's already gone," the camera man demanded, lowering the camera so he could grab the handle on top. He rushed after her, waddling under the weight of the power supply and camera bags.

"I dropped my phone in the car," she replied. "I can track it." She rushed back to the van and tossed the mic in the box behind her seat while he stowed his camera. She took shotgun, and he climbed into the driver seat. She pulled her laptop out of its bag and brought up the web service for the app on her phone, and quickly logged in. After it pulled up the map, she zoomed in till street names could be read. Her phone appeared as a red dot pulsing on the screen. Her location showed as green. She quickly oriented herself with how the map was laid out and pointed an imperious finger straight ahead.

"That way." The driver obeyed, rushing off to tail his friend's father, riding the brake until his van was free of the crowds.

"Isn't this illegal?" he asked. "We're tracking the Director of Homeland Security. I'm pretty sure this is illegal."

"It's a grey area," she waffled. "He's my father, and he accidentally took my phone by mistake. It's ambiguous at worst. Easy to talk my way out of." She checked the map and pointed at the stop light ahead. "Right at the light."

"Where do you think he's going?" the cameraman asked.

"Where's that alien briefcase going, you mean?" she asked back. "This is going to make international news, Gary. The networks are going to eat it up."

"But more importantly, you get to stick it to your father, right?" he added accusingly.

"Right up his tight, smug, self-righteous ass," she confirmed. "Turn left."

There were a lot of lefts and a lot of rights before they realized that he was leading them out of the city. They followed him for three more miles, realizing that the road did not have a lot of turn offs he could take. This was becoming frustrating. There was nothing but farmland out this way, and Sheila pointed that out to Gary.

"Where's he going?" she demanded in frustration. Gary shrugged and shook his head.

"Super-secret government black site?" he guessed, only half joking. They followed a short distance further and spotted police lights ahead.

"What the Hell?" she murmured in confusion.

There were four state cruisers blocking the road ahead with their cars. One of the troopers was wearing a bright orange vest and directing traffic to turn around. He carried a bright orange flag. This he used to motion for Gary to stop. The trooper approached cautiously. His eyes went to theirs, then to their hands. He studied the network logo on the side of the truck and nodded as if to say, yeah, I know who you are.

"Problem?" Gary asked, hanging an elbow out the window.

"Roads closed," The trooper replied absently, leaning in to look inside the van and in the back. "You'll have to detour back the way you came. You'll find a crossroad a couple of miles back. It'll take you around," he said, gesturing that it was time for them to leave.

"So, why's the road closed?" Sheila asked, curious what the lie would be.

"Train car derailed and spilled chemicals. Just, back up over there and turn around."

"What kind of chem—" Sheila started to ask, taking the challenge.

"Turn around, right now, and leave," the trooper snapped. "Go. Move it."

Gary bobbed his head up and down nervous and eager to comply. The moment they were out of earshot, Sheila gave Gary both barrels.

"Chemical spill my ass," she snapped, looking at the laptop's screen. The dot representing her phone had left the highway and had traveled off to the left a mile or so down the road. There were no side roads ahead, so this confused her some.

"Well, we tried," Gary said with a resigned sigh.

"Wait one second," she mumbled, opening her browser and pulling up their location on Google maps. She switched to the satellite view and compared the map on the phone tracking app with the satellite map. "It's a farm," she announced in confusion.

"Or, they want you to think it's a farm," Gary sang, again only half-jokingly.

"We're not done," she said, pointing to the screen. "Come on. The road the trooper mentioned connects with a dirt road that passes close to where my phone is." Gary pulled back onto the road under the burning gaze of the trooper who had sent them off. The van rocked hard as it came back up on the pavement.

"What if this gets your dad in trouble?" Gary asked.

Sheila shook her head. "He'll be fine. He knows people. He's the big bad Director of Homeland Security. What can they do to him? Just drive."

"He's your dad," Gary told her stubbornly.

"He's an ass, and—what the hell," she called out suddenly drawing Gary's eyes back to the road ahead.

"What are those for?" Gary asked, turning his cap around backwards so he could lean in closer to the window. He followed Sheila's frantic gestures for him to pull off on the shoulder.

The crossroads were ahead and coming straight at them was a long line of vehicles. At the head were Highway Patrol cruisers with their lights flashing and his sirens blaring. Behind them was black SUV and behind it another and another as far as they could see. Behind the SUVs came Limos. Behind the limos were military Humvee's and personnel carriers. Sheila disappeared into the back of the van and came back with Gary's camera on her shoulder. She shot video of the caravan passing and when the last of them were passing, she zoomed in on the faces of the soldiers in the personnel carriers so they could be tracked down later.

"What the hell is going on?" Gary mumbled, sucking in his gut as Sheila threw herself across his lap and out his window with the camera in hand. "Hey, be careful with that," he cried, fearing she would drop it.

She kept recording until they were completely out of sight. Two Highway Patrolmen pulled their cars across the road behind the caravan to keep anyone from following. She filmed for a few minutes longer, then reluctantly slid back into the van. She dropped back into her seat hard and set the camera down between their seats.

"News! News is what's going on," Sheila exclaimed. She pointed off to their right. "Turn here," she told him, pointing to the right. He grinned eagerly and jerked the shifter into drive. The van spun a back tire and kicked up a little gravel on the shoulder as Gary spurred it into action.

He took the right she had pointed out and five minutes later, he was turning right again onto a narrow gravel lane. The further he went the more washed out it became with tall grass growing between the tire tracks. The van bounced and rocked hard as they rolled through the rutted puddles and exposed roots. They passed two houses on the lane. One was abandoned. The other looked like the owner cooked meth. After ten more minutes of creeping down the track, they reached its end though the map they were following showed it should have gone on for another quarter mile. It ended at an old barn in the process of falling in. A wooden corral beside it was filled with weeds and small trees as high as their head. No one had been there for quite some time.

"What now?" Gary asked. Sheila looked at the map and studied the terrain. The gate that should have closed the field off from the lane was open, collapsed, and rotting on the ground.

"Through there," she said, pointing to the gate in question.

"I'm not driving in there," Gary complained.

"Through there," she snapped again. "It's just a field."

"No. What if we get a flat?" he asked. She did not respond. She was digging in their camera bag for some of the buttonhole cameras they used when covertly investigating restaurants and businesses for human interest pieces.

"Go," she commanded.

"No," he fired back.

"God damn you, Gary," she snapped, crawling out of the van.

"Now, where the hell are you going?" he demanded, growing frustrated. She did not say. She just ran off through the gate, buttoning up her top to hide the camera.

"Come on, Gary," she called back to him. Gary stayed seated and watched her run off.

"Shit," he muttered dismally, grabbing his camera bags and camera. "Shit," he spat again. "Shit. Shit. Shit," he repeated, striking the steering wheel after each exclamation.

"God dammit, Gary!" Sheila called back from the middle of the field. "Get your ass out here."

He took off after her at a waddling run, stumbling in the tall grass and slowing when the bags he carried started to bounce and bang around on his thighs and hip. He caught her at the tree line.

In the distance they could hear a loud whirring sound—sounds actually. They shared an excited look and tittered like children on Christmas Eve who thought they had just heard Santa. They had heard that whirring sound before only a short while ago. They had heard it when they stood in the shadow of the Washington Monument.

"Holy shit," they exclaimed together, racing into the woods.

"This can't be happening," Gary cried laughingly. "Two landings in the same day?" Sheila stopped and gave him a huge smile and hugged him. Gary's smile dimmed to be replaced with a dreamy look of peace. When she broke free and waved for him to follow, he did so, sighing.

They came to the edge of another field and stopped. The whirring sound was very loud now, and then like that, it was gone. A moment later, the whirring returned. It took Gary a lot of will power to creep down to the field's edge. He was a coward in real life. He was not like Sheila. She would always barge in. She said she was living on borrowed time, so what did she have to lose. He had asked her about that once, and she just said it was something her father used to say.

When he finally joined her at the edge of the field, he was dumbfounded by the sight of what they saw. They both were. This was not what they had expected. They had expected to find a single solitary ship, but there over half a dozen ships in the field and even as they watched, several of them took off only to be replaced with more ships. Each ship carried a small group of aliens. The aliens who disembarked were greeted by a small group of suited men near the far end of the field.

"Hey," she called sounding distant, "focus in on the suit in the front." She turned to face Gary and saw him staring at the saucers with wide eyes. "Gary," she snapped, "focus in on that man in the front; the suit shaking hands." She went around to watch the viewing window as Gary slowly zoomed in on the man's face. "Kiss my ass, that's Sang Hai Phong," she gasped in surprise.

"Who?" Gary asked.

"U.N. diplomat. He's a . . . ah . . . he's an ambassador; a negotiator for the United Nations. He's a power piece." Gary cocked his head, straining to hear. He let the camera's lens dip.

"What are you doing?" Sheila snapped catching sight of the lowered camera. "Keep it on those people. This is evidence that the world governments have been meeting with the aliens in secret and with the help of our own government. This is fucking huge," she crowed, feeling the thrill of the discovery. "Dammit, Gary. The camera. Point it at the saucers."

"I don't think they want us to," Gary replied, slowly setting the camera on the ground and raising his hands above his head. Sheila turned to see what had her cameraman so rattled and caught sight of the ghillie suited men with camouflaged faces who stared back at them over the camouflaged barrels of their impossibly long rifles.

"Shit," she murmured, raising her hands.

Ten minutes later, they were marching into a pavilion that was being erected. Sheila's father was there with Tessa Barnes and Michael Sommers. Aaron's face reddened with anger the moment he saw her, but he said nothing. He gave the two other Directors a look, saw that they had not seen his daughter yet, and he hurried the prisoners from the tent before that could change.

"What the hell are you doing here?" he hissed angrily.

"News reporting," she replied, mockingly shoving her unplugged mic in his face. "I'm a reporter, remember, Dad?" He slapped the mic from her hand and led her off a short way further.

"Oh, Baby. You've done some screwed up shit in your life, but nothing on this level. You've really messed up this time. You're not going to get to report this," he revealed.

"This will come out," she told him snidely. "You can't hide it from the world. The people have a right to know you're meeting with the aliens," she argued.

"No. They don't, Baby. People don't want to know what's happening here. That's why they elected us; to shield them from the things they can't face."

"Fine. Confiscate the camera. When our bosses hear about what we've seen here though, there will be an army of media trucks your pet troopers won't be able to keep at bay. Someone always talks. Me or Gary or one of these men. There is a whistle blower amongst you," she said, watching her father's face droop. She even allowed herself a triumphant little smirk.

"Take his camera. Destroy the footage," Aaron told the agent who'd brought them in. "Take him to my SUV and don't let him leave it. That man talks to no one till I've had a chance to debrief him." Gary looked to Sheila for help, but she just shook her head helplessly and gave him a look of sympathy.

"You can't do that," Sheila told him indignantly. "Freedom of the press."

"You really don't get it, do you. This isn't some game. This isn't you railing against the system this time. It isn't like when you joined Occupy Wall Street or bared your breast to show solidarity with Pussy Riot to embarrass me. You're standing on the edge of the rabbit hole here, windmilling your arms, and now I have to decide whether to save you, push you, or let you fall. Pushing you isn't an option. Letting you fall means you'll never see the light of day again. They will bundle you two up and take you far away and silence me if I protest. This is bigger than the rights of one man and his spoiled daughter."

He continued, "If my counterparts learn what you are, I won't even know where they'll stick you. This is it. This is one of those events where the rights of the people are trumped by the need of the nation. Look at them," Aaron barked, pointing toward the saucers. "Five of them shot off into the sky suddenly, nearly blinking out like the one at the Washington Monument. A few moments later, five more came gliding in one after the other to land and unload their dignitaries."

Sheila swallowed hard and suddenly began to understand the gravity of the situation. This was not like the other times, she realized. He was right. This time was different.

"So, tell me. Do we send you to a black site for holding, or . . ." he asked, looking pointedly at the button camera hidden on her top.

She sighed and began peeling it off.

"Fine," she snapped. "But, what about Gary? You have to let him go."

"Yeah. You have to let me go. I'm not talking about this. Hell, I don't even know what I've seen," Gary said to the Director, gesturing toward the saucers. "What is that? That's really cool lawn art, sir. Wow, so this is where America's security agencies have their yearly inter-agency barbecues. Mmm. Looks good. Personally, I like honey glazed ET well done." He turned away as if looking for something. "Where's the paper plates, sir?"

"Dammit, Gary. Not now. It's not time for the jokes," Sheila snapped, putting a comforting hand on his shoulder. She could feel him trembling beneath his shirt. The man was terrified.

"What about her, sir?" the Special Agent asked. Aaron mulled it over and gave her a gentle shove toward Jamie.

"I guess I save you," he murmured. "I just hired a second assistant. Get her outfitted."

"And him?" the Special Agent asked.

"Get him a paper plate and feed him, and keep him close," Aaron replied in defeat.

"What? Really?" Gary asked, straightening. "There really is food?"

"Dammit, Gary," Sheila cried rubbing the bridge of her nose.

Aaron was not done though. He brought his finger up before her and leaned in close. She was hoping this was the point he smiled and kissed her nose and revealed it was all a big joke. He did not smile and her nose was not kissed.

"This pass only works if both of you play ball. If one of you fucks this up, they fuck it up for both of you. This is your chance to see things through the eyes of Homeland Security. This is the most important event in our history. Not just our history. The history of the world. What is happening here determines whether Earth exists from this point on." He looked from one to the other and back again. Sheila swallowed hard. Gary peed a little.

Jamie shuffled Sheila and Gary both off to a separate tent and rounde dup what clothes he could before outfitting the two and returning to Aaron's side with them in tow.

"This is the best you could come up with?" Aaron asked, peevishly, checking out his daughter. The slacks Jamie found for her were baggy. The jacket was clearly half a size too big. The shoes she was wearing fit her like a glove though, and he suspected they were the ones she had arrived in. Her hair was pulled back into a tight ponytail and cradled in her arm was someone's day runner.

"She's scrawny," Jamie blurted, making no apologies for the results. He had done the best anyone could expect of him under the circumstances. Aaron turned on his daughter, fixing her with a stern look.

"This man," he said, pointing at Jamie, "is your life. You are his shadow. If he goes somewhere, you go with him. If he stops, you stop. He is an assistant. The only person he talks to is me and whom I tell him to talk to. You only talk if he gives you permission. He is my assistant. You are his." He stood up tall and imposing. "Is any of this going to be a problem?" he asked.

"Talk when he talks. Walk when he walks," she summarized with a roll of her eyes.

"And that," he said, tracing his fingers in the air before her, "that rolling your eyes and those heavy sighs. That is going to end badly for you. The moment one of these other agency heads begins to suspect you're not who you pretend to be, the gig will be up. If you're lucky, I'll be there when it happens and can intercede on your behalf. If it happens when I'm not around... Well, just don't let it happen."

"Got it," she nodded, swallowing hard. A Homeland agent came bustling up to them and whispered in the Director's ear.

"He's here," Aaron announced, addressing Jamie.

"Who?" Sheila asked, without thinking. Her dad just rolled his eyes and motioned for Jamie to follow. Sheila followed close on Jamie's feet, head down to avoid eye contact with everyone else. To Jamie, she asked the question again. "Who's here?" she asked.

"Daniel's back from the ships," he replied. She furrowed her brows in confusion.

"Who the hell is Daniel?" she asked in confusion, causing Jamie to glance back at her in irritation.

"He's a redneck that was in the wrong place at the wrong time. He's been up on one of the ships for the past few days," Jamie responded absently, writing a memo on Aaron's calendar.

"How'd he get up on the ship?" she asked again, drawing Jamie's ire.

"Stop talking," Jamie snapped, turning on her suddenly. "You're not a reporter anymore. You're a personal assistant. Act like one."

"Fine," she snapped in reply, closing her mouth. The next five minutes of walking to meet Daniel was murderously boring to her. She wanted to look at everything and ask thousands of questions like why are they here? What do they want? Why are they landing? Do they mean us any harm?

"You seem none the worse for wear," Aaron said by way of greeting, extending his hand to a somewhat robust looking figure. The man was not tall. He did not seem overly bright. He did not even seem overly clean. The smile he gave her father was warm, familiar, and genuine. He was definitely no politician.

Chapter 31: Exchanges

The ride down to the planet's surface was uneventful. Leia was strangely quiet, speaking only crisp commands to the crew of the skiff, and muttered replies to my questions. I did not take it personal. I did not want to be a distraction. Mostly she replied to me with non-committal shrugs and soft grunts.

Gorjjen on the other hand was very talkative. He wanted to know about everything. He asked about our theater and art, our music and religions, and our technology and foods. He seemed almost giddy. He told me about other colonies he had visited and the places he had been. Off the ship and away from the prying eyes of court, he really opened up. I was eager to introduce him to my friends down on the planet. All one of him.

He was not really my friend. I did not really have any friends. Aaron though, he was kind of like a friend. He had protected me from Tessa Barnes, the Director of the NSA. In my book, that made him a friend.

Up on the ship before boarding the shuttles, I was overjoyed to see my new friends. Ailig, Milintart, Jo, and Borbala were all there. Borbala though, he would not be joining us on the surface. He had changed since his resurrection. I had learned the truth about this miracle rebirth and understood why he did not want to descend with us and why he was giving up being a knight.

They had brought him back. They had reprinted his body and reintroduced his memories and thoughts into the new form. I thought he was joking when he claimed they had brought him back from the dead, chuckling like I knew he was pranking me. He showed me his neck to prove he was a copy. There was no scar. He was no longer Aeonic. His immortality was gone. He was bittersweet about the fact. He acted like he had received a death sentence. I guess on some level, he had.

You only ever get one reprint and after you have had it, your immortality is forfeit. Someday, if he did not die in battle or by accident or by illness, he would die of old age. He had been sentenced to die by life. He would die like every other human on Earth. However, he lived among immortals which meant he might see one or two more Harvests before it happens. I guess when you have spent centuries looking at eternity, it is devastating to discover that it is all about to end.

Xi had helped me find a shuttle pilot to courier the protocols down to the surface, and he even helped identify the landing site. Even now, Aaron was probably reading my ad-libbed copy of the protocols and restrictions that Luke had provided.

When we finally did leave the Kye O'Ren, I was immediately thankful that the first time I flew in a shuttle, I was unconscious. The shuttle ride through the atmosphere was rough. It was worse than rough. Standard practice for knights was to go into battle on their feet. As a result, we were standing like commuters on a subway when we hit the atmosphere.

We were bounced into and off each other a lot. The knights did not mind. They were in armor. I was not. I felt like I was being forced to stand in the middle of a meat grinder.

As far as I could tell, there were no diplomats on our shuttle. We had it to ourselves. Other than me, my friends, and a small shuttle crew, the shuttle was mostly empty. The worst part was that something was wrong with Leia and Palasa, and they refused to talk about it.

Palasa kept shooting me veiled glances, but each time she looked to me, she followed it with a furtive glance at Leia as if she were afraid to get caught looking at me. Leia's eyes never seemed leave the woman, but when they did, they only left her to go to me. It was almost as if she were trying to read my thoughts without reading my thoughts.

"What's wrong?" I asked of Leia.

"Not now," Leia replied curtly, "I'm busy."

That was our entire conversation all the way to the surface. Knowing how rough entering the atmosphere had been, I was surprised when the landing turned out to be surprisingly gentle. Considering the speed at which we were traveling on the way down, the soft landing felt strange.

I was nervous as I disembarked. We were in a field. On the screens, I could see Washington D.C. in the distance. The field in which we landed was filled with military Humvees, personnel carriers, and a whole dealership of black SUVs and limos. Soldiers patrolled the tree lines. Strong jawed alphabet agents were busy setting up a command center from which to run operations. A line of suited diplomats stood a short way off. Each group served as a welcoming committee for the ships that were landing. In the distance, I could see military helicopters patrolling. No doubt, they were watching the roads in and out.

Aaron was waiting when we disembarked.

"The food's crap up there," I told him as a greeting.

"I got the case. Thanks for that. It will make a lot of the world leaders in attendance less nervous seeing as they're allowed a bodyguard each," Aaron said. "They need that affirmation. This Summit is making a lot of powerful men and women feel really small and weak. This is not a good thing. Small men do stupid things to make themselves feel bigger. We don't want any stupid things being done at this gathering." My brows went up and with them went my eyes. I glanced nervously up at the saucers far overhead and back to Aaron.

"Yeah, we most definitely want this gathering to go well," I said. Sheila looked to the saucers overhead curiously. "You remember Palasa?" I asked motioning to the woman right behind me.

"Tessa's men remember her better," Aaron remarked with a sad smile. "I took care of your mother's burial as you requested, dear," the Director told her softly, respectfully.

"Thank you, Aaron. This, as strange as it sounds with all of this going on, has really put my mind at ease. Was it a nice service?" she asked. He looked apologetic.

"It was a brief service," he replied, "and I'm sorry for that. I put her to rest out at Mission Fields." Aaron turned to Jamie. Jamie was already pulling a card from his day runner. "This is where you can find her, if you get a chance to see her before you go."

"Nice touch," I announced to nobody in particular. Aaron gave me a quick but fleeting smile.

"You're not the translator this time around?" Aaron asked me.

I pointed to Palasa as a way of answering. "Luke requested her this time. Now that he knows who I am, he doesn't really want to work with me anymore."

"Who is he?" Sheila murmured without thinking. I took notice of her for the first time, and I could not help myself from trying my newfound powers.

A very bad man evidently, I told her sardonically, pushing the words into her head.

"Wow," she whispered in surprise, staring at me with a mixture of awe and fear. *You can read my* thoughts, she surprisingly broadcasted back into my mind. I smiled and turned back to the others.

Are you reading my thoughts? she asked again. I smiled but left her to decide whether or not she had imagined it or not.

I turned back to Aaron. "I'd like to introduce you to my friends. This is Jo of the House Castille, a noble house of the ninth colony called Ja-kob. She is an Imperial Knight with a Blood Knight distinction." *Don't ask because I have no idea what that is.* I confessed silently to Aaron.

Jo was a fierce looking Amazonian looking woman. Her arms were thick and veiny. Her head was bald except for two braids on the back of her head. She wore a dark armor this day with thin red glyphs etched into it. In the center of the breast plate was a glowing sigil. The sigil was a circle at the pinnacle of a triangle. Two arms extended down from the triangle and joined with two more circles.

It looked almost like an adult holding the hands to two children. On the lady knight's back were two swords with stunted hilts. Their hilts were etched black and red like the armor. On the shoulder plates of her armor was a delicate filigree of gold, accenting the armor. On her greaves, the same delicate gold design was repeated as it was with the outside of her thighs and shin guards.

Jo came forward and bowed shallowly from the waist. When she rose, she offered Aaron her hand. Aaron bent and kissed its palm. Jo's eyes went wide with delight, and though the scar tracing her jaw line was angry, her smile easily overshadowed it.

"This is my new friend Ailig Tuin. He was special forces in his home colony before climbing through the ranks of the Grey

Guard and Imperial Army to become a squire and ultimately one the most terrifying Imperial Knights I've ever met," I confessed with a grin. "He was born a commoner like our soldiers. He is held in high esteem by anyone who's ever seen him use a blade."

Aaron turned back to Jamie. Jamie reached inside his jacket and withdrew an elk handled hunting knife with a fourteen-inch blade.

"Please accept this as a token of friendship," Aaron urged. "It was hand forged by a man named Ray Johnson. The blade is rolled carbon steel. It was a gift from the knife maker to me. I would like you to have it." Ailig seemed touched by the sentiment and nodded his thanks. He said nothing. He did not speak Aaron's language.

"And this, is the Lady Milintart." I quickly described her house and lineage as I had the others. Jamie produced a smooth looking bottle. Apparently it was Millo 91: an unbelievably expensive perfume.

"I'm told it smells of the mimosa blossom," Aaron murmured. "Though, it seems strange one flower should wear the scent of another." Milintart actually blushed at this and accepted the perfume with shaking hands. Sheila looked at her father in amazement. It was obvious that she had no idea how he knew the things he knew.

How do you know to say these things? She broadcast to nobody in particular.

Oh, I told him. I sent a case down with a courier to prepare him and Earth for these meetings. I interjected.

You are talking to me! she gushed.

I turned my focus back to Aaron once more. "Xi Pich. A strong ally and friend who as a reward from the Battle Commander for saving the Grand Reaper's sister, has been elevated from the ranks of the Imperial Army and is even this day become a squire. He will one day be an Imperial Knight like my other friends. He is known as The Pig, but answers more succinctly to the nickname Fearless, which in my opinion, better suits him. Jamie turned to Sheila, snapping his fingers impatiently. Sheila realized all eyes were on her and remembered that she too carried something on her as well; something Jamie had passed to her after she had changed. She reached into her jacket pocket and pulled out a bottle of whiskey. This she passed reverently to her father, feeling it would spoil her father's presentation if she just handed it to him by the neck. He seemed to appreciate this extra effort on her part, judging by the little grin he gave her.

"Three Ships, Single Malt whiskey; 10 years old," Aaron announced, studying the golden liquid with envy. He held it for a moment as if reluctant to pass it on, but did so, placing it with great care in the hands of the squire. Xi's eyes grew wide and round. He had no idea what it was or that Aaron was over dramatizing the giving of the gift to give the bottle of whiskey even more value in the eyes of the former soldier. Xi accepted it gratefully and shook the man's hand vigorously.

"Finally, I would like to introduce you to Leia, Luke's sibling, sister to the Grand Reaper himself, Imperial Knight, and personal bodyguard to the Pre-Prior," I somewhat dramatically announced. I held out my hand to her, and she took it. I felt shivers all over. I guided her hand over to the Director's hand and Aaron took it and bowed so that his brow touched her naked fingers.

"As a daughter into my house, you are welcomed. My blood in defense of all you love," Aaron intoned, kissing her finger twice.

Her eyes went wide, then narrowed. She turned on me then and began berating me in her own language. I tried to hide my smile. She swatted my shoulder several times in annoyance then smashed a fist into my arm hard before stalking off to join the rest of her friends.

"Problem?" Aaron asked me.

"No. She just realized that I told you what to say. She doesn't like surprises," I said with a grin, rubbing the place where she hit me. It had really hurt.

Aaron was studying the last man in line: the only man not introduced. He looked like a transient from Bangladesh. He was freshly shaved but wore a ratty yellow jacket laying open so as to show his belly and the pale tunic beneath it. His forearms were wound with cord over the top of his long sleeves. Atop his head was a bright yellow turban, though it was not wound as tightly as those worn in the Middle East.

"I'm not sure who he is right now," I confessed, earning a flat unfriendly look from Gorjjen. "Sometimes he's a man named Puck. Sometimes he's a cruel bastard calling himself the Baron of Hein. When he wants to be my friend, he calls himself Gorjjen Doricci. He's the weapon master and swordmeister for the Imperial soldiers and knights aboard the Kye O'Ren. That was the name of the ship I was on. He seems proud to declare that he is a Battle Commander, Second Class, beneath Battle Commander Baggam Rain. You met him when they came to collect me. Remember? He was that big gruff angry bastard that shadowed Luke. You'll meet Luke again soon." I pointed toward a ship coming in to land. "He's working with Luke again."

Wait. The guy in charge is named Luke and his sister is named Leia? Sheila asked in disbelief, just catching the reference.

Yeah. Weird right? What are the chances, I replied back.

Yeah, that's pretty weird, she agreed.

Gorjjen stepped forward and introduced himself in English. I thought the man ignorant of the words I had just spoken. Gorjjen gave him a smug sidelong glance to let me know he had understood everything.

"I am Gorjjen today," Gorjjen declared, bowing his head over Aaron's hand. "Daniel is a good friend."

Aaron nodded and lifted the polished walnut case he had been carrying. This he lifted and opened, turning it around so that Gorjjen could see it.

"Daniel has told me what you did for him. I wanted to thank you personally for keeping him safe. For going above and beyond what anyone had a right to expect from you," Aaron said, passing the case over to the man.

"This..." Gorjjen looked to me and then to Aaron. "This looks valuable," he mumbled, at a loss for words.

"It is. It's a Taurus Judge. A type of sidearm called a revolver. It was mine, given to me by a man I once saved. I'm now giving it to you," Aaron announced, giving Gorjjen an inviting smile. The knights were all admiring the blue steel finish and expert craftsmanship.

"I... cannot take it," Gorjjen replied unexpectedly. Aaron's brow furrowed in confusion, and he looked to Daniel for an explanation. "I cannot take it without," Gorjjen continued, "giving you back the same." He reached into his jacket and pulled from it a short rod. It looked like someone had polished mercury and made a solid round cylinder from it. "The weapon of a knight," Gorjjen declared confidently. He handed the walnut case to me to hold and presented the metal rod to the Aaron.

"What's it do?" Aaron asked, laughing nervously. He was unsure what it was he held. Jo came forward and bowed to Gorjjen respectfully.

"With your permission, Master?" she begged. Gorjjen nodded and Jo held her hand out to Aaron, requesting the rod. Aaron handed it over, adjusting his glasses with one hand. Jo stepped back, and Gorjjen stepped aside to give her room. Aaron could not understand what Jo had said, but he understood her prompts.

She gripped the rod in one hand and showed Aaron where the buttons were. She pressed the first of the buttons and the nanites that composed the rod realigned themselves rapidly. The rod grew into a polished five-foot staff. The rod narrowed over all as it changed.

She showed him the second button and pressed it. The end of the staff rippled and blossomed into a long spear tip. She turned the spear horizontal to the ground and pressed the third button. The other end of the staff rippled and formed an identical spear tip. She rolled the spear around in her hand so that she held it palm up and grabbed the staffs middle with her other hand, also palm up. She pressed another button, and the staff came apart in the middle.

Jo rolled the two halves of the spear over in her hand and held them like swords. No one saw her press any buttons, but she must have for the smooth cylindrical shape of the spear halves flattened and elongated, becoming twin blades. She windmilled them before her with expert precision and brought them down to her sides, blades extended forward.

She pressed another button on the hilts and the blades suddenly disappeared, reforming on the reverse side of the hilts. She brought the hilts together, and the two halves were rejoined. One final press of a button brought the blades back into the joined hilts and once again, she held only a simple metal rod. This, she stepped forward with once more, bowed, and passed it back to its new owner.

"Whoa," Aaron mumbled in amazement, taking the rod from the knight. "This is majestic," Aaron whispered in awe.

"With good... health, my friend," Gorjjen responded, taking back the walnut case which I had been holding. There was silence between them for the longest time as both men admired their gifts, but it could not last forever.

"Hey, buddy," I called to Aaron, "Luke's about to land. I'd prefer not to be here when he does. It will sour your negotiations, I think."

Aaron nodded and gestured to Jamie. "My assistant, Jamie, will take you and your honored companions to your vehicle. It'll take you to the summit. Thank him again for this," Aaron pleaded, raising the metal rod.

"It's impressive," I confessed. "Can I have it when you die?" I said with a laugh. Aaron just grinned and patted me on the shoulder.

"Sure. If you're still around. If you're still around, you can have it." Aaron stepped aside and motioned for us to pass. Gorjjen raised the box and gave it a firm shake as if to say, thank you again, my friend.

Jamie led the way. The SUV Aaron had arranged for them was waiting with the engine running and a Secret Service agent standing by to drive them.

Who are you? Sheila asked, throwing her thought out toward me. To my credit, I did not flinch and kept walking.

That's a difficult question. One of them I guess.

You don't know? she asked back.

Evidently, I came here on a different armada hundreds of years ago, I told her conversationally. *I pulled a Rip Van Winkle, and now they're back, and I'm finally awake once more. Figuratively speaking, of course.*

Oh. What's this all about? Why are the aliens landing, she glanced at Jamie to see if he was aware of what she was doing.

Earth is one of their colonies. It was started long ago. They come through every few hundred years and harvest the colony to keep it from overpopulating the planet. The planets that can support life are like oases in space. They're rare and need protecting.

I reached the SUV last and slid in beside them the rest of the group. Palasa bid us farewell, begging our forgiveness. Luke had other plans for her. Along with Aaron's assistant and Leia, Palasa left to go and meet the esteemed Grand Reaper.

As we settled into our SUV meant to transport us to the summit, we conspicuously had one extra body with us.

"So," Sheila asked me, turning sideways in the passenger seat of the SUV. "How do you like Earth so far."

You're not supposed to be here, are you? I asked. Sheila gave me an impish smile that I returned. I liked rule breakers.

I was reasonably certain that any minute Aaron and his entourage would realize that one of their own had broken protocol and stowed away with us. I smiled for a moment at our new rule breaking company before looking back toward Leia as the SUV began to move.

I watched Leia converse with Aaron as we drove away. She had not even said goodbye. This did not bode well for us, I decided. What kind of lover refuses to say goodbye?

I'll miss you, I told her, sending my thoughts out to her. I felt her mind before she got it under control. It was tumultuous. Her emotions fluctuated between shame and love. I guess I could understand that. She had spent the night with the man her brother accused of murdering their father. How do you justify that? Any justification of that would be a hard sell to one's mind. However it presented in her mind, for good or ill, it was still plenty of baggage to sort through. The only gift I could give her was time. That aside, I still felt a twinge of irritation at her cold repose.

I had saved her from becoming infected. I felt my stomach knot up with fear when I thought that all my efforts were for nothing and that she was going to be as ungracious as her brother. I had no choice but to close my eyes and will the thoughts away. That was not why I saved her, and I knew it. She owed me nothing for that. When it came right down to it, all I wanted was for her to be happy. If that meant she could not be with me, then I had to accept it. I seriously doubted anything I could say would help speed up her acceptance of the situation.

Yeah, okay, she replied tersely. *Just remember what I told you on the ship. It isn't real.*

It was like she Kung Fu kicked my heart. If she was trying to decide how best to crush my soul, she could now relax. She found it. I knew me and her were a long shot, but I had still held out hope.

I watched her fade into the crowd through the back glass of the SUV as our driver took us away. It was a clear day, but in my mind, it was raining.

Chapter 32: The Ploy

Sheila studied the secret service agent driving the SUV. He seemed oblivious to the fact she did not belong. His eyes went to the rear-view mirror almost as much as they went to the road ahead. He seemed to sense her eyes on him and gave her a glance. She smiled and turned back to the aliens sitting in the back seat.

"What is this summit meant to achieve?" she asked, breaking the silence.

He suspects you aren't who you claim, Daniel advised, looking to the agent driving. Sheila did not immediately look, but when she did turn, she caught the agent turning away and playing it off as if he were reaching for his coffee.

Can you distract him? she asked.

Now, why would I want to do that? Daniel asked back.

My father is Aaron McDonald. I'm a reporter. He caught me and my cameraman taking pictures of the landing. He thinks he's saving me. What he doesn't realize is that I don't really need him or his help. I need this story not some boogeyman bed times story of covert secret agents making me disappear. I'm an American, and this isn't a bad movie, she declared with a shrug.

It might be. You think he's just making it all up to scare you into being good? Daniel asked with a knowing smile. *Doesn't he know things like that don't happen here?* Daniel scoffed, playing along.

Exactly. That happens to terrorists, not American citizens and definitely not the daughter of the Director of Homeland Security, she asserted snidely.

It happened to me, Daniel replied. Sheila studying him in surprise. *It happened to the President's aide and her daughter. Hell, they raped her and shot Mercy Mangrove in the throat when I broke them out of there. Your father, he saved us. He's a lot better man than you're giving him credit for. If he thinks they'll make you disappear, then you need to listen. Those black sites are real, and they don't care who you are. Mercy was the President's aide and she was stuffed in a black site and killed. If they can do that to the President's aide, I don't think they'll blink twice at doing to the lowly daughter of the Director of Homeland Security. Do you?* he asked snidely.

Whatever, her eyes narrowed thoughtfully though. *Would you distract the driver for me? Please?* she begged.

Fine, Daniel quipped, focusing his will on the steering wheel in the driver's hand. He waited for the man to glance back at Sheila. The push was not hard, but it was enough. The distraction came from the driver's inattention. The wheel suddenly jerked left and the driver who had been sneaking looks at Sheila grabbed it in alarm overcompensating as he pulled it back. This ended with him overcompensating in the opposite direction. The vehicle jerked and rocked throwing the knights and other occupants into each other as it whipped back and forth violently. In the confusion, Sheila stole the driver's phone and turned it off, slipping it back into the cup holder just as the driver brought the vehicle back under control.

He glanced in his review at his guests and raised a hand in apology.

"Sorry about that," he called. "Rabbit in the road or something." Gorjjen and the others slowly turned to look at Daniel with looks of vexation. Gorjjen's look specifically was a warning to him not to do that again. Daniel smiled and shrugged in apology.

So, you do what you needed? he asked. She smiled and nodded.

Back at the landing, you and that armored chick. The one who hit you. You and her a thing? Sheila asked.

It's complicated, Daniel replied.

You like her, but she doesn't like you? Sheila asked.

The opposite. I like her. She likes me. A different version of myself killed her father and evidently two billion other people. I saved her from kidnappers. Her brother despises me and tried to infect me with a parasite from the First Colony. It's pretty Shakespearean when you get right down to it, he admitted, seeming resigned to the ludicrous nature of his relationship.

You killed 2 billion people? she asked in stunned disbelief.

So, they tell me. It was over a thousand years ago, he admitted sourly.

How are you alive still? she asked.

Oh. I don't remember doing it so I'm free for the time being, he replied misunderstanding her question.

No. How are you alive after a thousand years? she clarified. He turned and showed her the scar on his neck. *It's a perk of being a citizen of the Empire. Anyone in the Empire can choose to receive the implant. Evidently, my other-self wanted to live forever.*

Your other self? she asked. *What's that even mean?*

I have memory loss, but before I lost it this other identity of mine evidently murdered an entire planet of people and half a fleet of ships. From what I gather, he, this other me, thought he was saving them from a sickness. He scorched their planet and fired upon his own ships to keep those ships from mingling with the rest of the armada. Some of the infected escaped in the ships and were taken in by the armada against my other self's wishes. It caused the armada to split. I evidently convinced the uninfected ships to leave fearing the sickness would spread throughout the rest of the armada. It evidently has not, so I broke up the armada for nothing. I took a third of their ships and ran away, and here I am, he announced in grand fashion.

How exactly did that work? I mean, how did you come to be here?

At some point after the massacre, some six hundred years later, my other-self abandoned those he'd rescued, and marooned himself on this planet with the rest of you colonists, Daniel explained with a heavy sigh.

Why? Sheila asked.

Why did my other-self kill those people or why did I maroon myself? Daniel asked in confusion.

Why did you maroon yourself with us and abandon the piece of the armada you stole? It seems this other-self of yours fought for the greater good. Running away doesn't seem to be in his character. Maybe that other-self had a reason for coming here that wasn't just self-interest, she mused.

I think my other-self came here for several reasons. He killed his brother for one. I don't think he could live with the guilt, but at the same time, I think he was trying to save the armada. He claimed he was trying to save it when Mercy and the others came after him, Daniel replied, suddenly sounding morose.

Which one? Sheila asked.

Which one what? Daniel asked back.

Which armada? An armada is just a group of ships. So, technically, the alien ships over our head right now are an armada, but so was the group of ships you convinced to leave. And, if you want to get technical, both groups together form an armada by themselves. Was he trying to save them from those infected people you mentioned or was he trying to reunite the two halves of the armada and make it whole again? It's a pretty ambiguous statement when you get down to it, she stated matter-of-factly.

Daniel's expression became troubled. She was right of course. He had been looking at it as a simple expression. What if he had stayed behind so he could lead the armada to the one he led away? Then a thought occurred to him that was even more grand that the goal of reuniting the armada.

What if I was talking about the other armada? The one headed for Earth. Daniel exclaimed. *What if that was what my other-self meant? What if I had found a way to cure the infected?*

He turned to those in the SUV with him wondering who he should confide in. None of them seem good candidates. He gave Gorjjen a leery glance. The only thing that made this news exciting was the prospect of reclaiming all those who were taken. The only thing that made it unenticing to pursue was the fact that he would have to recover that lost identity. But, if he did that, Gorjjen would be honor bound to arrest him. He realized there were only two people who would truly listen to him, and neither of them were in the vehicle just now.

What other armada? Sheila snapped, feeling the pit of her stomach drop away.

The one carrying the infected to Earth, he replied, as if that were old news. Sheila suddenly felt sick.

That's what the summit is. The Grand Reaper, the man currently in charge of the armada overhead, is here to reap the colony. It sounds ominous, but it isn't. He's here to try and convince all of us to leave with him because that infected armada I mentioned is on its way here. It's been in their wake reaping all the colonists they leave behind.

Where'd they get an armada? she asked. *You said you—he—destroyed their ships and planet. How are the still coming?* She felt bile in her throat.

I don't know. They repaired the ships evidently. Well, the ships my other-self supposedly destroyed anyway. They somehow survived. This made Daniel frown. It did not sound right. He had watched the missiles during his trial. They had destroyed the ships utterly. He continued on, filing that thought away for later. *They've been pursuing this armada ever since and converting the colonists the Grand Reaper leaves behind. The perchers or First Colonists have insurgents on the ships above. There's not many of them, but there's enough to slow the armada. This summit is a conference between the leaders of the armada and the leaders of Earth with the objective being to convince as many of you as possible to leave with us and return back to our home world of Cojo from which mankind sprang. This Harvest must take everyone it can. Everyone who doesn't come will join the ranks of the infected,* Daniel said, chewing his lip thoughtfully. Talking it out like this helped him think.

"You're serious," she murmured sadly.

Very, he replied. *On your left,* Daniel announced suddenly, drawing her attention to the driver. He was reaching for his phone.

Shit, she exclaimed. Daniel concentrated on the man's coffee cup and pushed as the man's hand passed it. It burst apart, showering the back of his hand and his phone in scalding coffee.

"Man!" he hissed, jerking his hand away in sudden pain.

"Dude. You totally drenched your phone," Sheila cried, using her shirt to dry the man's phone.

"Thanks," he replied, reaching for the phone in question. She passed it back to him without hesitation. He checked and saw that it was off and made as if to turn it back on.

"I wouldn't do that," Sheila advised hurriedly. "You don't turn wet electronics back on while they're wet. You need to lay it on the dash or something and let it dry first." The driver looked at her suspiciously.

"She's right," Daniel announced. "If you turn it on now, it'll most likely fry the components." The agent glanced back at Daniel, considered the wisdom of what he said, and nodded. He set it in a cubby above the stereo. Sheila busied herself with cleaning up the spilled coffee for the agent.

"Thanks," he mumbled to her absently. She nodded and gave him a quick smile.

Thank you, she said, glancing back at Daniel.

Gorjjen turned around slowly and stared Daniel down.

Do that again, and I will choke you with your own spinal cord. He promised. The others issued similar threats. Well, except for Xi. He was not fazed by it in the least. Daniel gave the Baron a cheesy smile and nodded his understanding.

Is the spectacled ambassador attached? Milintart asked suddenly and unexpectedly.

W-What? Daniel asked, stupefied by her question. The question had come out of nowhere.

Is he well respected? she asked quietly.

"Shit!" Daniel exclaimed quietly to himself, not loud enough to be heard.

He is well respected. He is the supreme commander of our homeland security force, and unfortunately, I believe he might just be attached. The lady before me who won't shut up, she is his daughter. At the mention of his status and supposed rank, her interest in the middle-aged man seemed to grow. Daniel decided not to get involved further. Milintart decided otherwise.

Maychance, he still might yet be unattached, yes? Milintart pressed.

"Perhaps, you might discreetly inquire of his child as to the predisposition of his availability." This she whispered softly at Daniel's ear so the others could not hear. Daniel thought better than to groan miserably in reply. This was his fault after all.

"I-I will . . . I'll check on it for you," he lied.

"Discreetly, of course." she whispered back. he nodded, catching movement out of the corner of my eye.

No problem, Daniel said to her before turning his thoughts back to the reporter.

So, why do you hate your dad? Daniel asked.

We don't have to talk about that, the reporter replied. *I mean, there's aliens in the car with us. What's their story?*

Daniel gestured to Xi. *A brave man.* He gestured to Ailig. *A fierce man.* He moved on to Gorjjen. *A deadly man.* He jerked his head toward the two women with whom he sat. *A proud woman and a mysterious woman,* Daniel announced, introducing the group in his own way. *I lied to your father in that list of protocols I sent him and told him that I was personally chaperoning the family of the Emperor.*

Why would you lie? The reporter asked.

So we could get a front row seat and better swag, Daniel admitted honestly, throwing her a roguish wink. *Your dad. Why do you hate him?*

I don't hate him. I'm just... She shrugged.

You're disappointed in him for being disappointed in you? Daniel guessed.

Actually, yeah. It isn't that I hate him. He's just always been about his job. He leaves my mother alone for days and sometimes weeks on end. When I was young, he was always working; always breaking his word. It builds up over time. Then, you get to this point where he's disappointed in what you do for a living and I'm disappointed in what he does for a living.

It doesn't have to be like that, Daniel said. *It's never too late to go back and fix it.*

Like you went back and saved the armada? she asked.

That's different. I've lost my memory of that time. I'd go back and fix it all if I thought I had the answer inside me, but I don't. He shrugged helplessly. *I was shot storming the beaches of Normandy. I don't remember anything before Hurricane Katrina.*

That don't make any sense. Those events were like sixty years apart, Sheila declared. *Amnesia doesn't work like that.*

And now, you're a doctor? he asked, smiling to soften his words. *Evidently, it does, and stop changing the subject. It's not too late for you and your dad. He obviously loves you. Why else would he stick his neck out to save you?*

He didn't save me. He just told me that to keep me from doing my job. No one is going to be taking me to a black site or whatever. This is America. They don't do that to our own.

You're a fool, a new voice announced in Sheila's head. She searched the faces of those in the car with her. She realized it was Gorjjen who had spoken. *I have attended over a hundred Harvests and there is always one like you who thinks their laws will protect them from those who would keep our purpose secret. Never underestimate the will of a true believer. Your father truly cares for you. I saw that in his mind when he gave me my gift. Even while he greeted voyagers from the stars, his mind was only on you. His worry for you is like a scream inside his head.*

The man is rarely wrong, Daniel admitted, having heard it all.

You don't know my father. He wouldn't . . . A familiar sound drew her attention suddenly. It was a sound she'd heard often growing up with her father. It was the sound of a gun clearing a holster. She turned slowly to look at the driver. He was staring at her. In his lap, hidden away from the passengers was a semi-automatic pistol, and it was trained on her.

"Your father would like to have a word with you," he told her softly, turning his head so she could see his ear bud. "There will be agents waiting to take you into custody when we arrive."

"My father knows I'm here," she declared.

"He's known for some time," Daniel replied.

"How could you know that?" she asked in confusion.

"Because I told him," Daniel replied. She stared at the man in surprise and shock. "This ability of mine lets me talk over great distances. The lady knight you asked about, she's with your father even now. She relayed the message to him for me. Don't be mad. Your father is my friend, and I have been a guest of a black site. You don't want that. Let him help you."

"You had no right," she demanded, no longer going through the pretense of this being a private conversation. The two lady knights watched it all with amusement. Xi didn't care. Ailig was asleep.

"Daniel is a good man," Gorjjen interjected. "He saves people. It is his . . . superpower," the Baron decreed with pride.

"Agent," Daniel called to the driver, "you won't need that gun. She won't go anywhere." As if to prove him wrong, she grabbed the handle on the passenger door and shoved it open intending to jump from the vehicle as it slowed to round a corner. Daniel focused his will outside the door and pushed it closed. She stubbornly tried it again and Daniel spoiled her attempt by pushing the door locks down. The handle would not work anymore.

"Why would you do this?" she demanded.

"I need you safe. I have plans for you," Daniel replied.

"It is his superpower," Gorjjen reminded her. Sheila settled back into her seat, giving up. As long as they were not taking her out of the game, she was fine with playing ball. She shifted and got comfortable again, turning so that the second button cam she was wearing captured the Secret Service agent and the gun he still held on her.

"Fine," she declared stubbornly, "we'll do it your way."

Daniel smiled, knowing she did not mean a word of it.

Chapter 33: Drive

What are you up to, my friend? Gorjjen asked me.

You know how Luke wants to address the governments of this world and get them to notify their people as to why we're here and what we're offering them? I asked.

I am so aware, Gorjjen replied.

We have on this planet another way of communicating with everyone on the planet. We call it the Internet. It's in most of the homes on this planet. It's a lot like your NID network. If someone could get video of what is taking place in this summit onto it, the people the world over will then know about Luke's request to harvest the colony. After that, the people will sound off and the governments will be forced to admit to this meeting. This is how it's done on this planet.

You see the woman sitting there in the front seat. She is a reporter. She is one of these people who can get Luke's message on the Internet, into our news stations, and into the homes of the people. She is a flame burning in dry grass right now. All we have do is give her a direction to burn, I told him proudly. He was not pleased with this.

This is no good, my friend, Gorjjen replied calmly. *We have imperial laws governing how the harvest is to be conducted. We must present it to the colonial leaders and let them decide. This is law. We must not aid this woman.*

With respect, my friend, I replied, using his form of address, *I am colonial and of this planet. I have been invited here. I am not a world leader, but neither am I a citizen of the Kye O'Ren or the Empire as you established before the Inquisitors. I am not Magpie, therefore not under the governance of your imperial laws yet. This is how it's done here on Earth. The government *tries to keep a secret from the people. The reporters try to discover the secret to tell the people. This is actually colonial law. If the reporter is successful, then the government is obligated to suffer the berating brays of the people. In the end, the government has to admit the truth. It is how it is.*

This is no good, Gorjjen repeated, falling silent.

Welcome to Earth, my friend, I said with a negligent shrug. He seemed disappointed in me. I was not too concerned. I had always understood a friend to be someone who did not dictate behavior but influence it. If Gorjjen was truly my friend, he would not intervene in my not so clever plan to spit in the eye of Earth's governments. He would just content himself with advising me against it.

Gorjjen did not elect to respond, which was good and bad. It was good that I would not have to argue with the man, but it was bad, because I caught Jo studying me with raptorial eyes. I felt like livestock in a sale barn under her the glare of her inquisitive gaze. I felt like she was trying to decide whether to purchase me.

Problem? I asked hesitantly. Jo blinked and her visage softened. She was blunt and more straight forward in her interrogations than Milintart had been. It was her way.

The men of this planet, are they a vigorous sort? she asked. I was confused by this question, having no reference for it.

How do you mean? I asked cautiously.

If I were to select one for breeding purposes, would they have endurance and amorous skill that one such as I might find pleasing? she asked, pausing only to ensure she was choosing the right words to politely voice her indelicate inquiry.

"Shit!" I quietly exclaimed again.

Many would, I replied evasively. Her eyes narrowed.

Do they remain this way as they age? she asked.

I don't really know. It's possible. You know, with the right diet and exercise and plenty of sleep and . . . I really did not want to be having this conversation.

I only ask because the ambassador propositioned me, and I was considering his proposal of a dalliance. As a representative of the Empire, I have no wish to be rude. It's just that I'd rather not engage in carnal delight with this man unless he could keep up and keep pace. My Aeonic chip was activated when I was twenty-three years old. My body is often too much for the older men. I am quite aggressive and vocal and would like not to create an inter-world incident by accepting the revered diplomat's invitation only to kill the man with my affections. You do see my dilemma? she asked. It was the most I had heard her speak up till this point.

I do see your point, Jo, I replied, searching for the right words. *I think you might be relieved to discover that the man is married and has a child even. His daughter sits here with us even now.* I saw Jo's eyes flicker to the front seat, and her cheeks blushed with embarrassment.

That roguish bastard, she declared with a heartfelt giggle. *Thank you, Daniel. This might have been a very embarrassing situation had I accepted. You are a true friend.* She seemed disappointed though.

What's wrong? I asked, wishing I had not. She sighed.

I thought for sure I'd win our wager this time around, she replied.

Wager? I asked, not knowing what bet she spoke of.

Yes. We, compete at each Harvest to see who can bed a colonist first. We thought your Leia had won this round, but then we discovered that you aren't technically a colonist, so the contest is still on. I felt most fortunate to be propositioned after only a few moments on the surface. Your people here, they're my kind of people. Plain spoken, aggressive, and clear in their desires. I feel I will do very well here. I will win this bet, she declared, giving me a playful smirk.

And after hearing about your interlude with Leia, I'm even looking forward to it. She says you were most passionate and reasonably skilled. It was my turn to blush. My mind went wild trying to figure out when she had time to tell Jo about us having sex. If felt a twinge of indignation.

She told about—wait? What do you mean reasonably skilled? I asked, slightly incensed. She laughed wickedly.

She told you about me and her and last night? I asked awkwardly.

She did. Me and Milintart were most attentive to her tale. It was obvious she was now having fun at my expense. I suppose I had it coming after setting her up with Aaron. *I do have a question about one of the images she sent to my NID. What do you call this position—*

We don't usually discuss our interludes on Earth with others in a face-to-face setting, I hurriedly interjected. *That's what the Internet and cell phones are for. We're on Earth right now, Jo. Jo? Is that short for something?* I asked, getting sidetracked.

Jokuleesa'mous-eff-Shai'baud, she replied.

Ah, so Jo it is then, was my only reply. Jo seemed to become engrossed with the scenery passing us by, and this gave me time to point out different landmarks to my friends. This talk drifted to the experiences and stories we each had. Milintart described some of the colonies she had seen. Jo described the gladiator-style arenas on her planet. Xi regaled us with stories about life in the Imperial Army. Gorjjen listened and commented little.

When it was my turn, I did not have a lot of stories to tell. As far as my memories went, I was ten years old. In fact, I had few. With my memories only going back a decade, the only real tale I had to tell was of Hurricane Katrina. It was not a happy tale.

"You mean to say," Sheila asked, after I had told my tale, breaking her silence in the process, "that your memories start in an alley during one of the worst disasters in recent U.S. history? Don't you find that kind of strange? I mean, that is one hell of a coincidence." I could only shrug.

"It wouldn't be the first natural disaster I found myself in the middle of," I remarked. "I was also present during the worst earthquake in American history too." I tried to smile that memory away, but I had been told too much about my part in it.

"Which one was that?" she asked.

"New Madrid," I replied. It was some time ago. I knew her next question before she did and answered it before she asked it. " I was told about it by someone who was there." Sheila's mouth had been open ready ask me. She closed it with an audible snap. Knowing I had killed my brother and caused the 'quake still made me sick to my stomach.

"It is . . . no coincidence that a hole has two . . . sides," Gorjjen announced sagely, murdering my language. "Maybe not the coincidence . . . you believe to be." He did not say much, but when he did, it made you think.

I really did not want to think about it.

You don't think that it's a coincidence me losing my memory during the Hurricane? I asked, letting my mind go back to that night.

You focus too much upon the storm and not enough upon where you were. When I was young, such places as you describe in your first memory were considered dangerous. Perhaps this is important. How did these bodies come to be dead? By incident or by the hand of another. I considered his words reluctantly and shrugged. I did not like what he was implying.

I have no idea how they died. I didn't check them. I assumed it was because of the storm. There were a lot of people who died in that storm.

"But not you," Gorrjen declared aloud. There were strange looks from the others having not been privy to mine and Gorjjen's back and forth. Gorjjen's observations worried me. What if I had killed those men and women? It was New Orleans. An alley in that city, especially before the floods, was like an invitation to be killed and robbed. Did my ability manifest without my remembering it? I could recall the shattered walls and the broken bodies floating faced down in the water. What if that was it? What if that was why I could not remember? I did not want to think about it. I was not Magpie anymore. His past was no longer my concern. I was finally free of it all. That felt like a lie. What bothered me the most was not that I might have killed those people by accident. It was that if my ability had manifested—if I had killed those people— was my ability responsible for my absent memories? Would this happen again? *Magpie is dead*, I declared, not meaning to broadcast my thoughts.

When did he die though? Gorjjen asked, posing the question to make me think about it. I shook my head and growled away the thought. I looked around at the faces of my friends. They were all looking at me and I was not sure if it was pity or curiosity writ upon the features. Either way, I did not like seeing it there.

I looked to Ailig and realized he had yet to share a tale. Seeing this as a way out of talking about myself, I sought his aid as a drowning man seeks the preserver.

"What kinds of things did they do on your planet for fun?" I asked of Ailig. He shrugged.

"My planet wasn't a planet where one spent lots of time as you have wandering and playing being carefree all day long. It was more of a hostile planet. Over sixty percent of the creatures that lived there could kill you. Fifty-one percent of the plants could kill you. The weather was pleasant for one third of the year, freezing for another third, and plagued by super storms that scoured the surface clean for the rest of the year. We lived in shallow-domed subterranean dwellings to avoid the storms and to fend off the cold. During the third season where everything was pleasant, we grew crops, raised livestock, and warred with neighboring cities. Harsh living made harsh people. Harsh people make good warriors, and I was considered one of the best on my world. I was the top warrior in my clan." He smiled. "I lived in a world that needed warriors." He gave us negligent shrug.

"There was no joy there?" Milintart asked, having heard little of the man's planet.

"Of course, there was joy," Ailig replied. "Did we do fun things like wandering the shores of our lakes and rivers with our lovers? No. That got you killed, but if you liked war, Pimboi was a paradise. As it turned out, we liked war. We liked it a lot." He gave Sheila a mischievous wink. She understood nothing he said and blushed believing his wink to be lecherous.

"Seems terrible though," I observed. "You spent all your time fighting and surviving and for what? Life's too short to live like that."

"Ah," he replied, picking up on the gist of my concerns. "I believe I see the problem. You think of Pimboi as you would your world. Our star was bigger than yours and our revolution around it three times longer than your Earth takes to complete its year. We measured our years by these revolution as you do. So, on our planet, our elders lived to be twenty-five to thirty years old as you reckon the number. This is how the Grand Reaper convinced us to leave Pimboi. He promised we would live forever and that even if we chose not to, we would still live to the ripe old age of seventy. We learned of the Reaper's cleverness when we learned how years were reckoned upon the ships. It was still a good decision, but I do miss Pimboi and the endless trials that came with living there," he admitted with a dreamy look in his eye.

Jo sighed lustily. She seemed entranced with Ailig's tales of home. "I would like to see such a place," she admitted.

"They're kind of a screwy bunch aren't they?" I mused, aiming the comment at Milintart.

She smiled, "Indeed."

I disengaged from the conversation and looked around at the city. We had been back in D.C. for the past twenty minutes, but we did not seem to be approaching the White House. I called out to the driver, asking for our destination.

"Where are you taking us?" I asked.

"Washington D.C.," he replied. I was not sure if he was trying to be funny or facetious.

"No shit, smart ass. I mean, where are we going? This isn't the way to the White House," I replied, trying to recall from my limited knowledge of the city how it was laid out.

"I'm sorry, sir. I'm not allowed to reveal the destination, especially with her in the vehicle," the agent replied, jerking his head toward Sheila.

"He's taking us to the RFK," she replied, reading the exit sign. I shrugged not knowing any place by that name. "Robert F. Kennedy Memorial Stadium. The RFK."

"A stadium?" I asked in surprise, confused by the destination.

"Makes sense," she replied. "There's plenty of parking. It'll be easy to secure since it's just a wide-open area around it with water to the east and the armory to the west. The government wouldn't want aliens—no offense—in the White House or anywhere near it. The other world leaders probably already have a problem with the U.S. hosting the summit. That aside, there really aren't many venues around that can handle a gathering this large." She held out a hand toward me snapping impatiently. "How many diplomats will there be on the alien side of the summit?" she asked. I breathed an exasperated sigh and thought it over.

"There's around three hundred and seven ships and at least one diplomat from each ship plus their bodyguard. There's probably a minimum of six hundred and fourteen men and women. Realistically, it's probably closer to six hundred and sixty-five people," I told her, doing the math in my head.

"There's a one hundred and eighty-six countries. Each is represented here. One bodyguard each. Minimum, we're looking at around four hundred people. Realistically, five hundred," she said, shaking her head. "Almost twelve hundred people in all. Plus, security." She closed her eyes to imagine it all. "Yowzers! Yeah. The RFK is probably the only venue in Washington that can handle that number. It's the perfect place. The high walls of the stadium will keep out journalist and foil their attempts to use long-lensed cameras to spy on the gathering. I don't think there's any other place you can seat all the world leaders from two worlds in D.C."

"Is she right?" I inquired of the Secret Service agent.

"Maybe," he hedged. Gorjjen turned to me and nodded.

"In his mind, the pilot says yes," Gorjjen declared proudly. I had to smile. Then I had to be awed by the blanket of security surrounding the stadium. It started almost three quarters of a mile before we had even reached the stadium.

Getting Sheila out of this place might end up being more of a challenge than I had originally anticipated.

The driver waited in line behind several limos and a few other SUVs. The dignitaries, alien and otherwise, were being unloaded close to a side entrance before briskly being escorted inside. We watched the unloading of the other cars with interest.

Sheila called out the names of the diplomats she recognized. She pointed out Vladimir Putin with the North Korean dictator Kim Jong Un. I was surprised by this, but not a lot. Luke had insisted all world leaders attend and not just pretty kids. Ma Ying-jeou of Taiwan was in the next vehicle. Shinzo-Abe, the Prime Minister of Japan and his functionaries were in the next two limos after Ma. A middle eastern delegation was in the SUV after Japanese Prime Minister. She did not know which middle eastern country they represented though.

When they were empty, the vehicles drove away, returning presumably to the landing site, or to hotels in Washington to pick up more of the Earthling delegation. With them out of the way, it was our turn to disembark.

Sheila made it a total of fifteen feet from the vehicle before the Secret Service agents apprehended her. They started to bustle her away, and I probably should have let them, but I could not help myself. I had plans for her.

"Hey, you? Yeah, you guys with the girl." They turned to regard me.

"Yes, sir?" the agent in charge responded.

"She's the daughter of the Director of Homeland Security. If she disappears down the rabbit hole, I'll . . . She better be sitting beside her father when this summit gets underway," I declared in my most menacing tone of voice. I recalled what Tessa allowed her minions to do to Palasa when she had her and her mother hidden away. I was not letting that happen again.

"This is a matter of national security, sir. We have our orders," the agent replied, motioning to his men to continue.

"Understand me," I told the man in parting, "if she isn't sitting beside her father, I will rain hell down upon you." I looked to the ships overhead and to my companions. I knew they would not do anything to help. This was a diplomatic setting, and their behavior was dictated by laws. The agent glanced up at the saucers with what my ego said was sudden doubt, but that less cocky part of me knew it to be irritation.

"We only have a request to hold her for her father," the agent replied. I nodded, and he hurried off.

Are we flexing our muscles now, my friend? Gorjjen inquired, chin raised and eyes front. We were in a setting where appearances mattered once more. My old friend was back to playing the part of the noble soul. I bumped him playfully with an elbow anyway. The corners of his mouth twitched. That was as much of a smile as I could expect from the man, and I knew it.

I don't have your awe-inspiring magnificence, my friend, I replied jokingly. Gorjjen sniffed imperiously.

This is true, he said, leading Baggam's Children forward. I smirked and followed.

I had never been to the RFK before. I had never been in a stadium before for that matter. It was not what I expected. I suppose it probably looked different and more glamorous without six hundred folding chairs arrayed on the green with all of them facing a podium on the sidelines. The podium was facing the rising rows of seats in the stands above. This was where Earth's leaders were being seated.

The diplomats of Cojokaru were being seated in the folding chairs below so that they were forced to look up into the faces of Earth's leaders just as the Kye O'Ren's Council of Inquisitors forced me to look up to them.

I suppose when you're diplomatically outnumbered, any trick you can play to garner an advantage must be played. A third of the alien diplomats were in attendance already. More were streaming in around us and from the other side.

We were visually inspected to ensure we were in complete compliance with the prohibition on firearms. The Secret Service agents handling security looked frazzled. They were not allowed to search us physically, and the idea of letting people into the same venue where the President of the United States would be while armed bothered them to no end. But this was not a typical summit. These were not typical diplomats.

As with the U.S. who often dictated their terms to other countries regarding security—being the all powerful entity they thought they were—it was now the Cojokaru who were allowed to dictate the terms. Earth's diplomats could have refused, but they would not. They wanted to hear what the alien ambassador had to say. They had had one year to wonder. It was now their one opportunity to discover firsthand what it all meant. The question of "why they are here" would be answered, as well as the question of "from where did they come."

A very serious woman with short brown hair and a pixie cut led us from security and through a long concrete hall that ended at the green. There were tables set up in the end of the field closest to us. They were laden with food and drink for those in attendance. Another set of tables was set up at the far end of the field, and as I supposed, it was most likely laden similarly with food. I broke away from my group, drawing confused looks from the security detail. They could not understand the urgency nor my need to eat real food again. They were not familiar with the kiosks aboard the ships.

"Don't worry. I'll catch up," I called, jogging over to the tables. It did not take me long to fill up a plate and grab a Coke. I had been on the Kye O'Ren for almost a week, and every meal I ate came from a kiosk. I was tired of government cheese so to speak. I needed real food. "Excuse me," I called to the man behind the table. He smiled, but it was a tight smile hiding a lot of anxiety.

"Y-Yes, sir," he replied, politely.

"Do you have any funnel cakes?" I asked, searching the tables for some evidence of their existence. He frowned and stared at me as if he was not sure if I was kidding or not.

"No, sir," he replied slowly as if afraid to disappoint me.

"Dammit," I exclaimed quietly to myself. I was disappointed but I knew I should not be. This just was not really a funnel cake kind of crowd.

"A-Are you . . . one of them?" the man asked, glancing toward the pale blue disks high in the sky. I laughed.

"We're all one of them," I replied with a snort of laughter. "This is their colony after all. We are them. They are us. They put us here."

The man seemed stunned by this realization.

"What do they want?" he asked meekly. I deadpanned my response.

"Marijuana," I declared. "As much as we can grow." He stood there blinking back at me, trying to determine if I was joking.

"Really?" he responded. I gave him a puckish smirk and answered him by slowly stuffing two roast beef wrapped asparagus spears with wasabi mustard and cream cheese in my mouth.

The man looked terribly stressed. He knew I was screwing with him, but he was too nervous to call me out on it. Being in the presence of so many aliens without knowing why they were here or what they were going to do to everyone was destroying the boy. I relented. It was one thing to mess with Ailig and the rest. It was another to torment the already tormented. I was cruel.

"They've come to Harvest us," I replied, intending to explain what that meant, but I never got to finish. The kid whimpered as if I had just confirmed his worst fears. He wilted to the ground in a dead faint. Several of the other persons tending the catering rushed over to see to their friend.

I hurriedly walked away.

Chapter 34: Summit

I tried not to glance back at what I had done. Instead, I looked around to see who had witnessed my moment of shame. Nobody seemed to take note of what happened, they were all staring at the security station where the guests of honor were being screened.

I spotted some familiar faces in Luke's entourage and slowed my roll to wait for them.

Sang Hai Phong, Leia, Baggam, Aaron, Tessa, and Palasa were with him along with an honor guard of Imperial Knights.

The Secret Service seemed to be having a problem with the fact that Leia refused to give up her halo. As Luke's bodyguard, she, like Sang Hai Phong's bodyguard, were the only people allowed to wear side arms at the summit. Aaron moved to the forefront with Tessa and put a stop to the fuss. I joined up with their delegation as they entered.

"Pig in a blanket?" I asked, offering one of my finger foods to Luke. He rolled his eyes and walked away. "Pig in a blanket?" I asked again, offering it to Leia instead.

"Oh, God yes," Palasa exclaimed with eager eyes. She snatched two off my plate without hesitation. "If I ever have to eat kiosk food again, I'll probably vomit." I found her attitude amusing and offered the plate to Leia again. She picked up one of the piggies and sniffed at it, then gingerly bit into it. She moaned with delight and grabbed another.

"What kind of meat is this?" she asked. I shared a look with Palasa who was vigorously advising me not to tell Leia the ingredients with shakes of her head.

"Have you ever heard of the Snoo?" I asked, recalling my Dr. Seuss. She shook her head. "It's Snoo meat."

"They're really good," she gushed, gobbling down the one in her hand quickly. "I do hope the colonists will bring some along for breeding purposes. This would be popular with the citizenry on the ships. The plazas would be swarmed under all the time."

Palasa gave me a weary look as if she had been putting up with my shit for centuries. As Magpie's second lieutenant, she probably had. This made me wonder just what Magpie was really like. Not the notorious killer, but the man. Did he play with children or help old women cross the street? I mentally shrugged. It did not matter. The man was gone.

"Better than kiosk food?" I asked. Leia smirked.

"Definitely," she replied. Palasa tried to snatch another one from my plate, but I hurriedly moved it out of reach.

"Table's over there, my friend," I told her, giving her a playful wink. She smiled hesitantly and looked to Leia as if seeking permission to go grab some food. Leia did not nod, but everything about her posture and breathing seemed to surrender to Palasa's unasked inquiry. Palasa's smile suddenly seemed genuine again, and she broke away from the group to fetch her own food. She had been on Earth for as long as I had. The transition to saucer food, as she was probably aware, was one made with much regret.

"Are we sitting together?" I asked. Leia sighed and shook her head.

"I'm working, Daniel. I stand with my brother throughout. The rest of the delegation will sit there." She pointed to two short rows of seats beside the podium. There were two rows on the other side as well, and some of the politicians milling around them looked familiar. It was with surprise that I realized one of them was the President of the United States.

The visiting dignitaries began to arrive faster, and I realized I should find my seat. Leia was towing Palasa toward Luke so quickly that Palasa was forced to stumble in her wake to keep up. It did not help that Palasa was stubbornly shoving finger sandwiches in her mouth as fast as she could chew them.

I hurried down the aisle the organizers had left between the rows of chairs, passing between the Israeli Prime Minister and the Iranian President. You could almost taste the ozone air caused by the friction they were creating. It must have been assumed that I was the infamous craft table assassin come to kill the President, because as I hurriedly approached the front row of seats where my friends were sitting, I discovered several Secret Service agents closing ranks before me to bar my forward progress. I gave them a smug look as I cut right before them and rejoined my group.

Where I was to sit was in the front row adjacent to where Luke and the President would be sitting. Ailig and Xi were already seated. They had saved me a seat right between Xi and Gorjjen. I plopped down and looked around for Milintart and Jo, wondering where they had gotten off to.

They were both crowding Aaron like he was Hefner and they were armored playmates. His daughter was seated beside him with an agent guarding her. Aaron seemed confused and almost distraught by the attention the two Lady Knights were giving him. It was only made worse by the fact that he could not understand a word they were saying. That, however, did not stop them from filling his ear with their flirtations. Their body language was saying what their words could not. My friend was deeply uncomfortable.

I surrendered to it. Yes, it was my doing, but who could have guessed it would go this far. My opinion was that this could not possibly end bad. I was sure of it. They were all professionals. I turned to offer Gorjjen one of my finger sandwiches, and I found him grinning from ear-to-ear. He was watching Milintart and Jo pursue the Director as well. He evidently found it hilarious.

Gorjjen looked down at the plate and accepted it, taking all my food with him. I sighed heavily. It was not my intention that he take it all. I shook my head in disappointment and popped the top on my Coke. Gorjjen heard the hiss of the top being popped and reached over to take it from me as well, thanking me with a nod.

"Your people are very generous," he declared, taking a pull from the can. His eyes widened in delight. "Delicious, my friend." I gave him a tight smile and climbed back to my feet. Nothing had changed. I was still hungry. When I glanced back at Xi and Ailig, the both of them were holding up their fingers like I was the hot dog vendor at this particular stadium. I sighed heavily and went to fetch the three of us drinks, shoving them in whatever pockets I could find in my alien garb. I grabbed three more plates of snacks, avoiding the newly revived caterer I had given the panic attack to. I selected a variety of nibblers for the two men to give them a spectrum of flavor to choose from. When I returned to deliver their plates Milintart and Jo had rejoined us.

They tasted Ailig's food and sent me for two more plates. I found it funny that they were my security detail, yet I was serving them. I suppose it was karma for trolling them upon our landing. In the end though, it all worked.

By the time they announced the commencement of the summit, outlined the parliamentary procedure that would be in effect to govern when and who would be allowed to speak and how questions could be asked, I was halfway through my kibble.

Sang Hai Phong was asked if he understood the procedure as it was outlined. He nodded in the affirmative. Luke was asked the same. Palasa relayed the question to Luke, and Luke too nodded in the affirmative. The orator who announced the commencement then turned floor over to the Director of Homeland Security and surrendered the podium. Aaron patted his daughter's knee then rose smoothly to his feet and approached the microphone.

"Most of you know me, or of me," he said, addressing first the leaders of Earth, then the foreign diplomats. He turned so that they could see his face. The men and women from the saucers overhead, listened attentively to Palasa's translation of Aaron's words. "And to those new to Earth, I say welcome. I was among the first batch of ambassadors to greet you, the Kojokaru," he said, pausing. He turned to acknowledge Sang.

"The ambassador that will represent Earth in today's proceedings, Sang Hai Phong, has asked me to speak and describe my first impressions of your people."

"Civilized and cultured are among the first words I would choose. Exotic but familiar would be my next. The truth is, I don't know your people. I have only met with your ambassador a couple of times. I've never had the pleasure to get to know any of you on a personal level."

"You claim to be a people of laws. You claim to be the answer to why we're here. I honestly don't know you. I am not a good person to ask when called upon to give my impression of you." He turned back to the Earth delegation in the stands above.

"The visitors you see before you, call themselves the Cojokaru. They are citizens of an empire that spreads throughout the stars. They brought man to Earth, or so they say. Their ambassador is a man named Luke. He was named by one of us because his name doesn't translate. His people call him the Grand Reaper." He smiled and raised his hands as to calm the buzz that went up at this revelation.

"They don't know about the mythical creature from our medieval histories. As I understand it, they're meant to be our salvation. He is called Grand Reaper because they've come to harvest this planet—their colony." He raised his hands again when the buzz became a drone of nervous whispers. "I was like you. I heard the word 'reaper' and 'harvest' and thought the worst. I saw them as predatory, but then they explained." Aaron turned to look at Luke, considering his next words.

"They consider this planet and the others like it that they found to be like oases in space. They realize how precious they are and have taken it upon themselves to assure that the planet continues to thrive and support life. They're here to cure our overpopulation concerns. They've come to take those who wish to return to the seat of the empire: a planet a called Cojo." He removed his glasses and cleaned the lens while he considered his next words.

"I only know these things because a good friend of mine related them to me in a missive. I shouldn't be standing here telling you these tales of our visitors. He should be up here telling you. After all, he's one of them and one of us. He's been living among us for over four hundred years," Aaron announced, turning to look at me. "He served as translator between the Cojokaru and Earth when first we met. He volunteered to go with them at great personal risk and has spent the past week amongst them. He possesses the knowledge and experiences that I lack." I had only been vaguely listening to what he was saying. I was here to spectate, which I thought meant I could eat, drink, and doze off as the situation allowed. Maybe this was Aaron's way of getting back at me for setting him up with Milintart and Jo. I doubted it though. This seemed far too important to be part of a revenge. He gestured to me.

"That is why, at this moment, I would like to ask my friend Daniel Sojourner to please approach the podium."

I choked on a deviled egg, forcing Ailig to pound on my back vigorously for several long moments in an attempt to help me cough it up while the dignitaries of two worlds looked on with deep frowns.

"Me?" I croaked. Aaron smiled and nodded, surrendering the floor to me.

I sat there dumbstruck for the longest time. My eyes went to Aaron. I could not possibly have heard him right. I was no speaker. I was just a dumb redneck drifter.

My eyes flashed up to the faces of the most powerful men and women in the world. They looked down on me with varying degrees of interest and annoyance. My throat felt suddenly very dry. I could not swallow. There was an energy in my chest and arms, tingling and squirming below the surface. It was most likely adrenalin, but it felt like electricity. Huge shivering jolts of power shot down each side of my spine, alternating and pulsing. There was a tickling tingle behind my eyes and the taste of copper in my mouth.

I was afraid.

You'll do fine, my friend, Gorjjen whispered into my mind.

The back of my skull felt like it was on fire. It was a physical pain. It was not any symptom of fear I had ever experienced before. Xi gave me a firm shove to get me out of my chair and

Ailig gave me a nudge to get me walking. I heard them chuckling quietly behind me. They thought this hilarious.

I turned to stare out at the sea of faces behind me. That was a mistake. The men and women of the armada were far more curious of me than the leaders of this world. I saw rapt attention and speculative appraisal. They thought I was a stranger, having no idea that I was their boogey man.

"Come on, Daniel," Aaron urged, beckoning me forward. I glanced over at the President. He sat watching me with his chin raised and lips pursed, silently nodding his head as if he were listening to some preacher's sermon. If he had moaned "hallelujah," it would not have seemed out of place considering his face.

Putin looked upon me like he was a claims adjuster and more a pawn broker than a President. I could tell he was judging my present value and comparing it against my future value. I felt like livestock again.

The man beside him was a Chinese official. Considering the company he was keeping, I figured he was most likely the President of China. I could not recall his name. The Brit in the same row could only be the prime minister, which meant the Frenchman sitting beside him was the President of France. The leaders of Earth's five most powerful countries, seated side by side and waiting to hear me speak. I suddenly felt very nauseous. I felt like some serf come to face the fabled five kings that ruled the land.

I think the only thing that saved me from a complete faint or breakdown was that I looked over at him. I was looking for Leia, but I found Luke. He looked angry and worried, and in his eyes I saw the lie Leia had been trying to feed me laid before me. This man had not forgiven me. He did not believe that Magpie was dead. I was still prey to him, and someday, he would kill me, maim me, or torture me if I let my guard down. I did not intend to ever allow that to happen.

Anger is an amazing emotion. When your blood is being pumped full of adrenalin like a NOS fuel injection and the energy inside you is coursing through you and threatening to rupture your skin, there's only one sure fire way to get it under control—you set your blood on fire. In that moment, I hated Luke almost as much as he hated me. I hated his smug, self-righteous, self-entitled face.

With the anger lending me strength, I straightened my spine, squared my shoulders, raised my chin, ignored the worried looks Palasa and Leia were throwing me, and approached the podium. It was my mic, and my turn to repay Luke the kindness he showed me in my cell.

"My name is . . . Daniel Sojourner. It wasn't always, but it is now," I proclaimed hesitantly. I licked my lips and picked one face out of the crowd to gauge.

"I'm over twelve hundred years old." I bent my neck and showed the men and women above me the scar below my ear. "We call them Aeonic implants. They turn off the aging process. However old you are when it's implanted is how old you stay forever." This created an excited murmur among the leaders.

"It is a voluntary process to receive one. It is available to all citizens of the Empire. Some people don't choose, and they live out their lives normally and pass away as nature intended. Some keep them forever. Some have them removed when they feel they've lived long enough. When the chips are removed, your normal aging process resumes. This is one of the examples of the technology these visitors possess. It's immortality as an outpatient procedure," I said. My voice felt like it was going to crack. My head throbbed wickedly.

"In addition to this miracle of science, they also possess the technology to reprint the deceased and restore their minds to them, if done in a timely process. I have seen the results of this technology firsthand. A knight killed on the ship was reprinted and made whole in only a day. If injured, they have pods they call Med Beds that you may rest in that will restore your health and cure everything but an amputation. I have experienced this technology twice. The first saved my life. The second, removed some bruises and cuts so I could look pretty for you," I said with a smirk. This brought a titter of laughter from the Earth delegation.

You did fine. Now sit down, Luke commanded crossly. *You have no right to address these people.*

I have every right to address these people. They're my people, I snapped, suddenly furious. *I have more of a right to address them than you. I care about them.*

So do I, he fired back. *Sit down now, or I promise you there will be repercuss—*

I did not let him finish. I knew what I wanted to tell these people. I wanted to tell them everything. I wanted to tell them the truth.

"I am considered a murderer by the people in the armada overhead. I killed 1.8 billion people believing that I was saving the armada. I fired on the first colony we harvested and on the ships that received the newly harvested. My real name was Magpie. I was a monk in their monastic order," I announced proudly.

I was not sure how Earth's delegation would take it, but I was pretty sure how the men and women at my back were going to respond to my announcement. The Cojokaru delegation did not disappoint me. There were cries of anger and calls for me to be taken into custody. There were men and women being held back by security and others calling for me to be executed on the spot.

The Council of Inquisitors had cleared me personally of any wrongdoing, though it was conditional. That message evidently had not reached the other ships. It took a good while for security to convince the diplomats to return to their seats. Earth's leaders were strangely silent throughout this.

"Sorry, Aaron. I should have told you who I was to them before you called me up here," I said to the man. "As you can see, I am not well liked among the people of the Cojokaru. I am a pariah back on the ships. I didn't go to visit the ships and inspect their way of life. When they discovered who I was, they took me into custody and tried me for murder." There were lots of narrowed eyes staring down at me.

"I don't remember being Magpie," I told those around me. "Tessa Barnes, the NSA Director knows more about my past than I do. I don't remember anything that happened in my life before Hurricane Katrina." Tessa Barnes rose and confirmed this.

"I've been on your planet for four hundred years. I fought in many of your wars. I was shot while storming the beaches of Normandy with the Allies. A bullet grazed my head and I spent months in a coma. I was stabbed in the American Civil War. She found evidence of me throughout America's history. I don't know why I can't remember who I am." The pain in my head sharpened and crept down the back of my neck.

"My past beyond Katrina has been spoon fed to me by everyone I've met since the Cojokaru made first contact in Kansas. I don't know how much of what they tell me is true. I've only ever been this man, Daniel Sojourner. I've seen the evidence though. I've seen footage of me firing on an unarmed planet and on six saucers, completely destroying them." I could see by the looks of apparent concern among the earth delegation that at least they believed me to be genuine.

"I can't tell you with certainty who I am. I can tell you who they think I am and what they think I've done. I believe telling you about my past through their eyes will tell you who they are and why you should trust them." I tried clearing my throat. I was parched. My head was pounding worse than before. I had migraines before, but nothing like this. It fell like hot needles were being pushed through my skull. I was not sure why it was happening. I coughed, drawing concerned whispers from my friends around me.

"Could I get some water please?" I asked, leaning heavily upon the podium. Something was terribly wrong with me. A bulky female who looked like someone had put a suit on a block of spam brought me a bottle of water. I downed it one drink.

"Twelve hundred years ago, I was known by the name Magpie. I was a monk aboard an imperial ship known as the Moon Rai. I left the planet of Cojo with the rank of Prior." I glanced at Palasa then Leia, seeking confirmation of this fact. Palasa nodded. There was worry in her eyes. "For those unaware of how the monastic order is structured, the highest rank is Abbot. The second highest, is Prior. This is what I was. The third highest rank, is Pre-Prior." I turned to indicate Luke. "Ambassador Luke, the presiding Reaper, holds this rank."

I studied Luke's reaction to see how he was taking this. His expression had softened, but only for the benefit of those who watched him now. His eyes still drilled into me. He did not like that I had relegated him to an inferior position. He did not like that I had been allowed to speak. I honestly did not care what he liked. He had tried to infect me, so I proceeded onward with my tale.

"Around a thousand years ago, the armada over your heads was sent out at the order of our Emperor." I racked my memory trying to recall the Emperor's name.

Emperor Choan Vaat, Luke supplied grudgingly. *Wrap it up.* I gave the man a quick irritated glance before continuing.

"Emperor Choan Vaat," I said, feeding them the name Luke had just provided. "Our directive was to harvest each of the colonies seeded by the Empire thousands of years before. You've all wondered if there was life out there. Well, there is, and though you've spent your entire lives searching for it, thinking it rare and hard to find, the truth is, it isn't hard to find." I paused to gather my thoughts.

"The Cojokaru empire is overpopulated, and it's been overpopulated for thousands of years. Even before the Imperial ships terraformed this planet and seeded it with your ancestors, the planet of Cojo was overpopulated. There are thousands of colonies like Earth out there. Hundreds have been Harvested." I saw the look of confusion on the faces of the Earth delegation. They flinched every time the word Harvest was used. It was time to clear up the misconception so they could focus on the important parts of my story.

"You know what? Before I go on, I think I should clear up something. The visitors use the word Reaper and the word Harvest to describe the task they're here to perform. They are unfamiliar with our mythologies and have no knowledge of the Grim Reaper from medieval lore." I turned to address the dignitaries behind me from the ships.

"In our lore from long ago, there was a nearly all powerful being called the Grim Reaper. He carried the tool of the harvest, a scythe, and hunted those whose time it was to die. His touch was death, and when the body had fallen, he used his scythe to carve away the soul. The soul he took on to the afterlife to be punished or rewarded. The Grim Reaper was a hunter that could not be eluded by man, woman, or child. The terms Grand Reaper and Harvest instill a dread in the minds of my people," I told them, looking at Luke. "They don't know not to fear you." I fixed Luke with a penetrating Luke.

Maybe they should fear you, I told him. You've been less than humane with me.

You killed my father, Luke replied, gritting his teeth.

Don't you mean Magpie killed your father? I asked. He broke eye contact first. It felt like a small victory. He was still gritting his teeth though. I turned back to Earth's leaders in the stands.

"The Cojokaru don't know about our boogeyman. So, I feel these terms have been causing each of you a certain amount of anxiety. The Grand Reaper here," I said indicating Luke again, "isn't some kind of villain." I felt dirty lying like that. "He's a representative of their Emperor selected for his depth of humanity and compassion. He has come to save your lives. Earth is quickly becoming overpopulated as are a lot of the other colonies in the Empire. Planets such as ours are like oases in space. If we continue as we are, we will destroy it. The Harvest is simply an invitation to the people of this planet to return with us to the seat of the Empire—to the planet Cojo. This is a chance to save Earth and see the place from which humanity sprang." I hoped that I did not sound too corny, but I could barely think through the pain inside my head.

"They told me that I killed 1.8 billion people. I destroyed a planet filled with life, and I destroyed six of the saucers like the ones you see above you." My head felt like it was going to explode. My will slowly began to build only to ebb a moment later. The process repeated over and over again, pulsating slowly and outside my control. A thought occurred to me then.

What if the pain in my had was not incidental. What if it was being externally caused?

I had ripped people apart with my mind. I did not pull the person apart. I put pressure inside of them and pushed them apart. Someone more skillful than me could theoretically do the same thing only with far more control. This thought led me obviously to the question, who would stand to gain from causing me pain. It was not really a riddle. I turned and gave Luke a challenging stare. He returned the look with a creased brow and a sneer he could not seem to hide.

Stay out of my head, I roared, giving him a firm mental slap. He did not respond right away. I expected rage or a retaliation, but instead I sensed his surprise, shock, and confusion. The pain only got worse.

I'm not in your head, he snapped, drawing in his will. Leia reached out and placed a restraining hand on her brother's shoulder.

What's wrong? she asked.

Ask him, I told her, trying to remove the caustic edge in my voice.

I didn't attack you, he barked, firm in his assertion.

Someone is. My head feels like it's going to burst, I confessed, gasping. My forehead was lathered with sweat. I pushed forward, trying to hurry through my telling.

"The ships overhead are . . . about the diameter of one of the states in America's heartland. There are over six hundred levels in each ship. For those of you who . . ." My eyes would not focus. "For those of you who did the math, each ship is approximately six times the size of the United States. Each saucer is a country unto itself. Each level in each ship gets to retain its system of government. Food is free. Clothing is free. Each family gets a spacious compartment. There are parks and fields on the ship that go on for miles with fifty and sixty-foot trees populating them. There are plazas and subway style lifts that take you from level to level. The colonials, such as us, who board can join their police force, also called the Grey Guard." The pain only kept escalating, but I knew I had to tell the earth delegates about the saucers. I had to convince them.

"These people can eventually become Imperial soldiers or peacekeepers. They rarely have a reason to be called into action. Those who aspire to greatness can be squires to an Imperial Knight. Those who can meet the physical requirements become knights in time. Aboard each of these ships are millions of different colonists from hundreds of different colonies. They are each sharing their rich culture with each other. There are books up there you have never read. There is art up there that you've never seen. There are children who laugh and play and animals you've never seen. It is not a paradise though. It is a place filled with life with the same draw backs as you have here." I had to stop. I could feel my heartbeat inside my skull. My knees threatened to give out at any moment.

Stop it, I cried to Luke. *Stop it, please.*

I'm not doing anything, he shouted back. I felt his mind touch mine for a moment. He was right. The pain felt different.

No one is attacking you, he said.

Bullshit! I growled, clutching at the podium for support.

"I destroyed six of these ships a thousand years ago to save the armada overhead. The first colony we harvested was infected with a parasite that we couldn't detect. The infection disguised itself as a religion. By the time we realized the truth, six of our ships were infected. When I destroyed the planet of

Sylar, the infected ships sent shuttles to dock with the uninfected ones. I quarantined the ships I could and took it upon myself to destroy the infected saucers and everyone aboard." Even through the pain, I felt the guilt of what I had done. I recalled the footage shown at my trial and all the bodies floating frozen in space and burning up as they fell back into the atmosphere.

Tell them no more, Luke demanded.

Stop attacking me, I weakly replied. I blinked my eyes over and over hoping that would ease the pain. It did not help. It was not a migraine.

"There are still some of the infected aboard the ships overhead. They don't seem to be infecting very many people. They've been aboard the ships up there for over a thousand years. They only seem to wanna wreak havoc on the ship. The Kojokaru have suffered many assassinations, including the current Daimyo. He was poisoned a few days ago."

There was a murmur of surprise at this, and it came from both delegations. I ignored it and pressed on. I did not want to get into the midst of the politics surrounding the Daimyo's death.

"The infection doesn't seem to be spreading very fast. I can only assume that it's because the carrier of the disease isn't aboard this armada. It spread faster on the ships I destroyed. Most likely, the source of the infection is not aboard any of these ships. This enemy acts like an insurgency. They don't seem to focus on the general population as a whole. They seem to only target the influential and the armada's leaders." The murmuring in the Earth delegation grew agitated as they discussed these revelations.

"You may wonder amongst yourself, is this insurgency a serious threat? My answer is, that it can be, but life goes on as it always has. Like it does in Iraq. Like it does in Afghanistan. Like it does in Israel, France, Pakistan, and Egypt and everywhere else insurgent attacks seem to happen."

"On the whole, the insurgency is nothing to fear. For centuries, it was thought that the infection was an elusive virus of some sort. It has only recently been discovered that it is in fact a parasite instead. They are even now studying it. It is a major break for the Cojokaru and an important one." I tried to slow my breathing to ease the throbbing.

"I don't know if the Grand Reaper would have told you this beforehand, but the ships I destroyed all those centuries ago still work. The infected have been pursuing this armada ever since I destroyed their planet. This is why this armada is late in its arrival here. It was meant to arrive long ago." I crossed my arms, closed my eyes, and rested my head upon them, leaning heavily upon the podium. Aaron rose and approached.

"Are you alright, Daniel?" he asked with a touch of concern.

"My head. It feels like it's on fire," I whispered back. My will surged again but harder, and I watched the finish on the podium slowly crack and split before me. "I don't feel so well."

"Would you like to sit?" Aaron asked. I shook my head and reached for the mic, missing it. He approached the mic instead.

"I think we're going to have to pardon, Daniel. I believe he isn't feeling very well. He's a marvelous man. One week ago, he was wounded. Our guests took him with them up to their ship to save his life in one of these Med Beds he spoke of. While he was up there, he saved the Pre-prior's sister from a kidnapping. He helped track down those who'd taken her and saved her from what could only be described as a fate worse than death."

Aaron gestured to Leia. She blushed gently and dipped her head, acknowledging what Aaron said as truth. "He's spent a week in space. He's been wounded twice. He's been healed twice. He's translated the material you were passed as you entered the summit. Today, he re-entered Earth's atmosphere and descended with the rest of the Cojokaru's esteemed diplomats. I feel that standing here before us, he may have pushed himself too far too soon. I believe his present state may be my doing. The man seemed like he could do anything, and I asked too much," the Director said by way of apology. He patted my back gently to let me know, he appreciated my efforts. I was not done. I had more to say. I waved him off and rose back to my full height, my face twisted with pain. "See," he said, "the man is indomitable," he said this with a genuine note of respect. He retreated, but he did not go far. He brought Leia forward with a look.

"I quarantined part of the armada after I attacked the Sylar colony. It was . . . It was a number of ships that had received no shuttles or skiffs from the infected saucers. It was an act of sedition and considered traitorous. I fractured the armada and took the uninfected ships off on our own, hiding them among the stars." My grip on the podium is the only thing that kept me upright.

"The diplomats and citizenry aboard the ships over your head called us Drifters for drifting away from the main armada. I stayed with the Drifters for many years acting as their Grand Reaper. In 1595, as Earth reckons their years, the Drifters visited this colony intending to harvest it as per the Emperor's directive. We tried to harvest it as best we could. Your technology was inferior. Your governments lacked the ability to communicate directly with all your people. We plucked at your civilization here and there and ultimately left. One of the places we harvested was a British colony in Roanoke, Virginia.

American history calls it . . . they call it the Lost Colony. One word was left carved in a tree for the supply ships to find. The word was 'Croatoan.'" I smiled weakly.

"There has been a lot of lore around this word and what it may have meant. It is a word of the Cojokaru. It means hello and goodbye. It's like the word aloha. Your people were saying goodbye. This planet was not ready to be harvested. We took with us a few natives and one small new world colony. When the Drifters moved on, I stayed behind."

"I-I fought in ever . . . every American war there was. I was stabbed in during America's Civil War. I was shot in Normandy storming the beach and spent sever . . . several months in a coma. Tessa Barnes, the NSA Director, h-has verified this. The bullet wound must have scrambled my wits because I don't remember anything of who I was. Till the armada arrive, I've o-only ever thought of myself as an American. It's all I know." I felt like crying. The pain in my skull was stabbing deeper down into my neck.

"There is much wr-wrong with the Empire, but that is the way of li . . . life. There are things wrong with each of your countries. We do not live in a paradise, and neither do the Cojo . . . karu. They are a civilization like any other and suffer the same problems. They have tried me for m-my crimes and declared me conditionally innocent due to my lack of memory. I cannot remember. Therefore, they refuse to p-punish me. Should I remember, I will stand trial again. Luke—the Grand Reaper—will come up here in a moment and try and convince you . . . that you must come with us."

I glanced over at the man, wincing in pain. I needed to tell them about the danger they faced. I needed to tell them about the armada of the infected bearing down on them and their planet.

"Trust him. He's trying to save your lives. The armada of the infected? They pursue us. They aren't far behind. Every man, woman, and child left behind who—"

My eyes rolled up in my head suddenly, and I toppled over backwards, seizing. Aaron and Leia rushed forward to catch me. Ailig and Xi darted toward the podium to assist. They carried me away as a roar of concern went up from all in attendance. I remember looking up into the darkening sky and wondering where all the stars had gone. I couldn't remember when last I saw the moon or when last I saw a shooting star. The armada blocked out everything lovers found beautiful about the universe.

When Leia came to me, I was standing in a cabin in the woods with a framing hammer in one hand and sawed-off double barrel shot gun in the other.

"You need to wake up," Leia called, striding forward. She shot nervous glances, frequent and furtive, toward the cabin's door.

"I can't," I replied. "He's going to break in. I can't let him break in." I don't know why it was so important that he not return.

"Who?" she asked, turning to stare at the barred door. "Is Magpie outside that door?" she asked.

"Who's Magpie?" I asked, confused. I ignored the zombies standing outside the windows. I knew they were not coming in. They moaned low and soft and silently swayed back and forth as if their brains had been paused.

"I'll help you fight them off," she offered.

"It won't help. He's come to fight me himself," I replied. "I will lose. I can't beat him."

"Who?" she asked.

"Luke," I responded, though that did not sound right. "Not Luke. No. Him. He. Yellow Eyes," I corrected.

"Luke did not attack you," she replied. "No one attacked you." She marched over to the window and stared out through the boards. The darkness was out there, agitated and roiling, and coiled ready to spring. "Who is Yellow Eyes?"

"You should know this," I told her. "You know who he is. He was there when . . ." I could not remember what I was about to say. I could not breath. I gasped and choked. She shook her head and came back to me, grabbing my shoulders so she could shake me.

"You have to tell me who he is. Tell me who Yellow Eyes is. Quick, before you wake—"

I opened my eyes suddenly, wincing and coughing. My head screamed in pain. A paramedic was kneeling over me and in his hands was a vial of smelling salt. It smelled atrocious.

"—up!" Leia blurted, a faraway look in her eyes. A moment later, her eyes found focus, and she looked down on me with concern. My head still hurt, but it hurt a lot less than before.

"What happened?" I asked. "How long was I out?"

"About ten minutes," Aaron answered. "What happened to you out there?" he asked in a voice tinged with worry.

"Up what?" I asked suddenly, struggling to sit up. I looked to Leia so she knew the question was directed at her.

"What?" Xi asked, thinking that I was talking to him.

"Not you. Leia. You said 'up.' Up what?" I asked. She looked at me as if were crazy.

"You seriously don't remember being in the cabin again?" she asked. "In your mind? With the rotting men? It's literally the only thing you dream about."

"I don't remember," I admitted blandly, cringing in pain.

"We should call in an ambulance and get him a CAT scan. I can't find anything to explain why he passed out," The paramedic admitted. "He may have some underlying condition."

"No," I snapped. "I'm not done."

"Yes, you are," Leia snapped. "You've done enough damage. It's going to take all of Luke's diplomatic skills to undo the damage you've done."

"I didn't ask to go up there. I was invited," I told her firmly, glancing over at Aaron.

"And now, I'm asking you not to go back up there. You're not well," she said. I could not argue with her. I felt like Hell warmed over.

"I have to go back out there," I said. "I have to help save these people."

"If you go back out there, Luke is going to . . ." She bit her lip and looked away.

"Luke's going to what?" I asked waspishly, suddenly very nervous.

"It's Palasa," she said. "He knows who she really is." I studied her eyes. She was worried and ashamed. No. She was terribly ashamed.

"What are you talking about? Who the Hell is she?" I demanded, cradling my head with both hands like I was trying to hold it on.

Leia shook her head, torn between telling me and keeping her brother's secret. I was pretty sure I loved this woman, but even so, I sensed something dire and dangerous from her. It was something that could change our relationship forever. I could not bear it: the pain, the secrets, the stress. Always that pressure inside my head like all I wanted to do was explode.

"Who the fuck is she?" I growled. Leia flinched like I had slapped her.

"I'm sorry," she whispered, pushing a tablet into my hands. She caressed my face with one hand, opening her mouth to respond, but at the last moment, her courage failed. She closed her mouth with an audible snap and hurried off. Her loyalty to her brother had won out again.

Chapter 35: Discovery

"In three, two, and roll," Brandon murmured, speaking into the mic jutting out of his console. The monitor screen glowed, painting everything in the dark around him, including Brandon, a ghastly green.

He patiently listened to the static coming through his headset.

"Confirm command line," he prompted. There was silence on the other end. "Command, confirm command line," he repeated. The silence lasted as the engineers and physicists on the other end confirmed his calculations.

"Command line not verified. Trim inverse by factor of three. Adjust command line and verify." Brandon adjusted his calculation by three one-hundredths and re-sent the new command line. He leaned back and waited, popping the top on a Red Bull.

"New command line sent, Control. Verify and remit," he told the man on the other end. There was a long pause as the other end tested the new settings.

"Control, your command line is confirmed and ready to submit." There was the sound of keyboard keys being punched with heavy fingers on the other end.

"Roll all stop in two, one, and stop," the voice on the other end of the headset confirmed.

Brandon studied the current settings for New Horizon's flight factors. Its yaw was not where he wanted it, but the engineers and physicists on Akin's team overruled his request to recalibrate it, claiming its present numbers would guarantee the least amount of tremble. He thought it was riding too far afield in relation to its vertical axis, even though it was still within its range of variance. It might need trimmed in a week or so, but for now Akin's brain trust thought it was flying fine.

The deep space probe had given them very little trouble since its launch from Cape Canaveral back in 2006. It's flyby of Saturn, Jupiter, and Uranus had gone smoothly. There had been three scheduled trajectory correction maneuvers or TCMs during the course of its flight that required changes in its velocity, but the flight had been, for the most part, uneventful.

The only sphincter clenching moment was when the probe was set to pass through the Kuiper belt, but that situation resolved itself quickly when it was determined that only one asteroid would be encountered. An unscheduled TCM was performed to change its flight trajectory so that the asteroid could be studied in an unexpected flyby. It had been smooth sailing since.

"We have a good roll," Brandon declared, covering his mic to cough. When it was done, he pulled his hand away. "Control, I'm getting repeated instances of lens flaring in the upper right quadrant of camera one. Can that be filtered?" he asked. He threw his hand over the mic hurriedly, catching sight of Jenny going to lunch. "You going to lunch?" he asked.

"I was thinking about," she replied. He fished a crumpled twenty from his pocket and offered it to her. She looked at it with dread. She absolutely despised getting the man lunch. All he did was complain about it thereafter.

"You mind?" he asked. "Number one, no pickles, with a coke." She took the twenty. He smiled big, smacking his chewing gum noisily. "Thanks, babe. I'll get you next time." She frowned.

A squawk on his headset turned him back to the job at hand. Jenny looked at the twenty, sniffing it tentatively. She wrinkled her nose in disgust. His money always had a stink about it. She opened her purse and dropped it in, reminding herself to wash her hands after.

"Checked image sequencing, Control. It's not flare. Randal thinks it might be rime frost inside the viewing cannister. Recommends phasing shutter," the voice on the other end suggested.

"You want Ketchup?" Jenny asked, sticking her head back inside the door. Brandon nodded, flashing her a look of irritation. She gave him the finger from behind the door where he could not see it and left. Brandon's fingers flew across the keys as he typed in his query and pulled the last batch of images from New Horizon. He opened the most recent and arrayed them in his viewer for a comparison inspection.

"Negative on shutter phasing. I'm looking at the probes last data burst. It's not ice. Camera two caught the same object in every frame at different locations. It's free traveling mass. We may have another asteroid." Brandon took a swig of his Red Bull before continuing.

"I recommend a re-task on camera one. Bring to center upper right sector. Zero in on traveler. Sequence the zooms with thirty captures between. Cap at six hundred magnification. Task and compensate roll for camera shift. Track zero to foreign body. Resume macro two and re-zero on Pluto after," he told the man on the other end of the mic.

There was a long pause. When the voice on the other end finally responded, it repeated everything Brandon said and followed it with a request for confirmation. "We'll need the heads upstairs to sign off on the re-task."

"Command line, confirmed," Brandon told him, hitting enter on his end. The command was sent down to batching. They would send out the servicing commands in the next scheduled burst. "You want me to get approval," he asked, "or can you handle it?" Brandon checked the clock on the wall.

The next scheduled command burst was not for another hour. It would take four hours after that for the burst to reach the probe. It would take about an hour for the probe to readjust its camera and take all the photographs he had just requested. Changing its zoom would not take all that long, but it could possibly require a course correction after. It would take another hour to configure its batch response and convert the image files to something more compact for transmission back to Earth. Which would take another four hours to reach Earth and an hour to process all the images.

In all, he would be invested and waiting at least eleven hours before he got the photos he requested from the probe. He was really hoping the images showed an asteroid or something. He was tired and frustrated of re-tasking the cameras every week on supposed foreign masses only to discover afterward that it was a speck on the lens.

"Janice is already sending the request upstairs," the man on the other end declared.

"Awesome. Then I'm going to sack out. Look for me again at," he studied the clock on the wall and tabulated when his data burst would arrive back from the probe, "eighteen hundred hours."

"Eighteen hundred hours? Confirmed. Sweet dreams, Control. Command out," the voice on the other end responded. There was a squawk and a screech as the line between them was disconnected.

Brandon pulled off his headset and hung it over the top edge of his cubicle wall. He swigged his Red Bull then wondered why the hell he was drinking energy drinks when all he wanted to do was sleep. He went off to find a sofa in an empty office to crash on. He knew Jenny would wake him when she returned with his lunch.

He rubbed his eyes and wandered off. The moment his head hit the sofa, he was out.

It was his phone vibrating that woke him. He felt better, but still tired. He pulled the phone off his hip and ground the heel of his hands into his eyes to rub away the sleep. When he could finally see, he found a fountain drink sitting beside the couch on the floor. It was from Wendy's. It was sitting beside a Wendy's bag. His phone buzzed again. The soda had been sitting there long enough to leave a wet sweat ring on the floor. He checked his phone and saw who it was calling.

"Brandon," he answered in a voice thick with sleep.

"The data burst just decompressed. I'm looking at the pics you ordered. You're gonna want to see this. I haven't contacted them upstairs yet. Get your ass down here if you want to see them before Randal classifies them," the man on the other end told him in a shouted whisper. Brandon nodded, fully aware the man could not see him doing it.

"I'll be down in twenty minutes," Brandon told him.

"No. Now. These won't wait. This is huge," the man told him and something in the man's voice piqued Brandon's interest.

"Be down in three," Brandon said, twisting around so he was sitting on the sofa instead of reclining. The man on the other end crowed with joy and hung up.

Brandon picked up his soda and took a drink. It was watered down. He opened the bag and found his change thrown in on top of his burger and fries. The fries were cold and leathery. The burger was too. He swore under his breath, cursing Jenny for not waking him. He scooped out his change and chucked the drink and burger in the trash on his way out the door. Jenny's station was empty. She had most likely gone home hours ago. He promised himself he would have words with her when she came in the next day.

He did not bother with the elevator. He knew if Stanley was calling him, then the news was big, which meant the second Randal found out what was in the pictures, he would change the security access to the photos.

He hurried down the stairs, leaping the last three and hurried through the door at the bottom. The moment he was in the hall, he slowed his roll so as not to draw unnecessary attention. He took two lefts and let himself into the command center at the end of the hall. Brandon's eyes went to the big wall of monitors and the two big screens hanging one above the other on the far wall. It was a sea of headphone wearing heads before him.

Stanley was half standing at his cubicle, rising as far as his headset would allow. He was frantically beckoning Brandon over. Brandon was almost giddy. This felt juicy.

"What you got?" he asked, looking around to see if anyone else had been alerted by Stanley's zealous behavior.

"You were right. It wasn't rime. It wasn't dust. We do have a traveler. Check that. We have a lot of travelers," he corrected, pulling up the images from New Horizon.

He started with the first images at the lowest magnification and began scrolling through them in the viewer so that they climbed up through the various magnification levels as they went. In the lower magnification, it looked like dust on the lens. The next magnification showed that there were several specks and not just one. They looked grey and pitted. He still thought them asteroids though. The next magnification level however got him excited.

The objects were moving in a pattern. The next bump in magnification left no doubt as to their identity. It was another alien armada. The next bump in magnification was zeroed in on the largest of the saucers. The probe's magnification level bumped up again, going in close and tight on the lead saucer. There was some blocky design on it. The magnification increased one last time, and he realized the symbols were actually two words. He could not read them, but he had seen the lettering before. Each of the ships in orbit around earth had symbols like these.

"Holy shit," Brandon breathed. Stanley laughed, bouncing where he sat.

"We did it. We did this. We found alien life," he exclaimed quietly. Brandon sighed heavily.

"We've already discovered alien life, or have you forgotten about the ships in orbit overhead?" Brandon reminded him snidely.

"This still counts," Stanley declared defensively. The screen suddenly blinked and flashed blue. The images they were looking at were gone. White block lettering appeared on the screen in their place.

"Security Access Denied. See your supervisor."

Brandon swore noisily, slapping a hand down on the desk in frustration. Randal had seen the pictures.

"What now?" Stanley asked, trying to refresh his screen to bring back the pictures.

"Now, we go back to work," Brandon quipped morosely.

"But the aliens. There's more," he pressed. Brandon shrugged. He stopped being excited about the alien ships months ago.

"Out of our hands and not our problem. It's now the problem of the powers that be," he replied, catching sight of Olivia over at her own cubicle. "I gotta go see a girl. Later, Stan. Thanks for calling me down."

Stanley grunted in reply. He was busy scribbling down the symbols from the ship in the photo before he forgot what they were. He watched Brandon walk off, then hurriedly brought up the imaging software again. He quickly selected paste from the menu he pulled up and watched with a smirk as the last image of the saucer appeared in the viewer. Print Screen, he realized, was the best keyboard button they every created. He zoomed in on the two series of symbols on the side of the alien craft and sent it to the printer.

He hurried over and collected it from the cradle where it fell then marched it from the building and into the next one. He took the elevator up to the third floor and hurried down the hall to the room at the end.

"Stanley!" The twins sang merrily. "They let you out of your box?" Carl teased.

"They did. What's up guys?" he asked conversationally, trying to downplay the fact that he had printed off a restricted image and taken it from the building. The twins at one point had been identical. They had the same orange hair and the same splash of freckles across the bridge of their noses. They were the same height. The laughed alike. They dressed similarly. The only real difference was that John easily weighed three hundred pounds and Carl weight a buck seventy-five.

"Going bowling tonight with our mom. What about you?" Carl asked. John sat back in his chair, his fingers interlaced and resting on his belly, while he looked with myopic eyes through the thick lenses he wore.

"That sucks," Stanley replied without thinking. John chuckled at the reply before Stanley realized what he had said. "Hey, they still got you working on translating the writing on the ships over head?" he asked. Carl nodded.

"Yeah. We've deciphered most of it. There are a few nuances they have that we're still working out though. Why you ask?" Carl asked. Stanley slid the picture over in front of them.

"Can you decipher this one?" he asked. John came forward, adjusting his glasses to better view the image.

"Don't think we've seen this image yet. Which designator is it?" he asked, referring to the names the military gave each ship overhead.

"New image. Never seen before. I'm curious what it says. Could you translate it?" he asked pleadingly. John and Carl shared a look then studied the symbols again.

"We can, but you have to come bowling with us and our mom tonight," Carl replied. John nodded. Stanley stopped to think on how bad he wanted to know.

"Done," he told them. His mind was already working on how to get out of the deal. Carl opened the spread sheet where they stored the alien alphabet.

"See, their language isn't like ours where one symbol stands for a sound. They have two symbols for each sound and three when it's a vowel sound. John was already scribbling down the translation. It took him a few moments to verify. Carl double checked his work and frowned.

"What?" Stanley asked in concern.

"Your ship's name is the Lunar Beam," Carl declared. John nodded, confirming the translation's accuracy.

"That isn't a very good name for a ship," Stanley muttered. The twins shrugged. They agreed.

Stanley was halfway back to his own building when it hit him. Their translation was a literal translation. The ship was not called something as lame as the Lunar Beam. A ship of that magnitude had to have an equally magnificent name. He knew it had to be something like "Lunar Streak" or "Moon Ray." He felt tickled with himself. He was still studying the picture he had stolen when he finally made it back to his building. His smile vanished though the moment he looked up.

Security was waiting for him.

Chapter 36: The Truth

I could have left. I could have gone back to the field and caught a shuttle back to the ship right then. I could have left the summit and vanished back into the world. I could have gone where not even the infected could find me. I could have done these things.

"Do you need a place to lay down?" Aaron asked. I shook my head, even though I knew it would cause me pain.

"No," I murmured quietly, caressing the tablet. "No. I want to be here. I can help," I insisted. Xi and Ailig hoisted me to my feet.

"I don't know what's wrong with him," the paramedic admitted. "He could have a tumor. He could have a chemical imbalance. There's literally thousands of things that could have caused this."

"He'll be fine," Aaron replied back. It felt good to have someone in my corner.

"Has he suffered a head trauma recently? Or maybe in his recent past?" the paramedic asked, refusing to give up.

"Both," I told him, "but I'm fine now."

"No, you're not," The paramedic growled back, disagreeing. "What was this recent head trauma?" he asked.

"I was smashed repeatedly in the back of the head with a homemade mace earlier this morning," I replied. The paramedic's eyes narrowed, unsure if I was screwing with him.

"I'm serious," he snapped.

"Me too. I spent six hours laying in an alien Med Bed that cured the concussion. I'm fine," I said, believing my own assertion. The paramedic did not know how to respond to my defense.

"What about the other head trauma?" he asked.

"He was shot in the head storming the beaches of Normandy," Aaron told the man, answering for me. My head still hurt. The paramedic studied me, at a complete loss to argue such outlandish claims. All he knew was that I should see a doctor.

"It was seventy years ago," I told him. "I'm fine."

"You're not fine," Aaron countered, "but it's your head. If you want to stay, I'll allow it. He's right though, you need a CAT scan."

"What good would that do?" I asked. "I've already been in a Med Bed. I think I've had the best medical care available. Don't you?"

"Honestly?" Aaron asked. "I don't know how that technology works. Just because they're advanced, doesn't mean they are all knowing. We may still have technologies they don't. Sometimes in Vegas," he reflected, "it's hard to see the danger hiding in the dark because the neon shines so bright." I actually had to admit to myself that this was probably the most compelling argument any of them could have given me to visit a hospital here on Earth. I almost relented, but then remembered what I held.

"I'll take my chances," I told them, stubbornly refusing to abandon Earth because I felt unwell. "Could one of you help me back to my seat?" I asked. Ailig and Xi, with one of my elbows in each hand, turned me and helped me return to my seat.

Luke had been speaking to the Earth delegation, but all eyes went back to me the moment I exited the tunnel. A few feet from the tunnel entrance, I gently pulled away from Xi and Ailig and forced myself to stand tall. I willed myself not to show the pain I felt upon my face. The pain in my head began to multiply the closer I came to Luke. I did not know how he was doing this, but I was sure that my condition was his fault.

Try it again, I warned, throwing my thought into his mind.

As you wish, he replied calmly.

I was sweating again by the time I reached my seat. I looked to Leia before taking it. She gave me a fleeting glance, her brow wrinkled with worry. The moment she noticed me staring, she looked away.

We have to talk, I told her. She did not reply.

I slowly eased myself back into my seat. The pulsing in my head was horrid. My will kept swelling and fading. I saw blades of fake grass before me bend toward me then relax only to bend toward me again. It was like my mind was inhaling giant mouthfuls of air. I closed my eyes and concentrated on my breathing. Luke resumed his speech. Xi and Ailig sank back into their chairs, giving me worried glances.

How are you feeling? Sheila asked softly.

Like shit, I replied.

If you need anything. Just ask.

I need you to leave this place the first opportunity you get and post your video on YouTube and share it with every news outlet who'll report it, I told her. *Our governments are not going to announce any of this to the public. Look at them. They're petty, self-obsessed men and women, who need us to keep them in power. Which of them do you think will willingly give up their authority and let their people board these ships?*

You were eloquent, sort of, she replied.

I scared them. I told them that there were monsters out there. I told them that those monsters were aboard the ships above. I fought through five waves of the infected this very morning alone and had to spend hours in a healing pod just so I could attend this function. I opened my eyes and looked down on the tablet I held. My eyes went to Palasa who was actively relaying Luke's words to the people before him. I tapped the screen and woke it up.

Don't read that, Leia begged, pleading with me not to discover the truth.

Who is she? I asked. She shook her head in reply.

Please don't ask me. Luke wants you to read that. He thinks Magpie is still inside you. He wants you to read that so he can put Palasa in peril. She isn't really in any peril though. It's a ruse. He's going to announce that Palasa is the assassin who killed Lord Merrik, our Daimyo. He's going to do this and remind them that Palasa worked for one of your leaders. He can't threaten them. It's against our laws, but he doesn't have to. Look at the ships above our heads. He just has to make them think we'll retaliate if they don't agree to cooperate with us. Don't react when he does this. It isn't real. Let him accuse her. I know the truth. After the Harvest is done, Palasa will go on trial and she'll be exonerated. The real killer has already been found and killed. Just don't react. Please.

You were going to let it happen? I asked, injured more than I cared to admit by the news.

We have to save these people. If that means bending the truth and working the system, then yes. I was going to let it happen, she admitted candidly.

You know that isn't what I meant. You were going to let him try and draw . . . my vision blurred for a moment as my will mounted even higher. Gorjjen's yellow jacket was suddenly pulled open in the surge, and I saw the dark handled grip of the Taurus Judge sticking out of an inner pocket. He had snuck it in past security.

"You were going to let him try and pull Magpie from me. How could you believe that Magpie was still in here? He's dead. He's gone. We spent the night together. How can you still not trust me?" I snapped. Luke stopped speaking and turned to regard me. I stopped staring at the tablet in my hands and looked up. People on both sides were staring at me. I realized that in my frustration, I had blurted out the last part of our conversation instead of projecting it. I raised my hand and bobbed my head in apology.

Shit, I declared to know one in particular.

I didn't want to set you up, she admitted.

Who is she? I demanded. Who is Palasa to me? Leia was silent for a very long time as she weighed the merits of telling me. I felt her will relax as if in defeat.

Palasa is your niece. She's William's only daughter. Her mother, Mercy, her, and William stranded themselves on this planet when you left the Drifters. They wanted to try and find you and bring you back, she said softly. Empathy poured from her. *I'm so sorry.*

My will surged harder. I was not alone after all.

I did not hear Leia's apology. All I heard was the roar of the inferno burning inside my head. I glanced at Luke then looked to Leia. My disappointment in her was a bitter taste upon my tongue. My eyes went to Palasa as if compelled.

You're my niece? I asked, eyes red and brimming. Palasa was in the midst of relaying Luke's words to the masses, but even so she went silent. *You're my niece?* I asked again, it was a question but also an accusation. There were gasps of shock and cries of alarm as my will mounted. People lurched forward in their chairs, drawn by the force of my emotions. Some were dumped out in the grass.

You need to calm down, Leia pleaded.

You're my niece? I asked again, staggering to my feet. The tablet dangled from the end of my arm as I came to my feet. I was not holding it very tight, but I felt the screen crack from the force swirling around me. *Are you?* I demanded. The memory of her being raped in Tessa's black site came unbidden to my mind. Luke staggered toward me as he fought the growing swell of my fury.

"He knows?" Luke asked of Leia, speaking aloud. The memory of Mercy gasping for her last breath as blood spurted threw Palasa's fingers paraded before my eyes. I flung the tablet away, meaning only for it to sail like a Frisbee over the heads of the dignitaries to my right. It flew like shrapnel into the wall at the end of the field, propelled by my fury and guilt. I had killed her. I had killed him. The tablet blasted through the wall and the stand seats behind it.

There was a cry of alarm from the diplomats and security came running. There was a mixture of Imperial knights, Homeland Security, and Secret Service. They were sorely outmatched.

I'm so sorry, I told her, coming forward. Each step I took towards her dragged chairs and people in my wake. *I'm so sorry for what I did.* Palasa turned then, tears spilling down her cheeks.

I know, she replied. She swallowed hard. I turned my eyes on Leia.

You were going to let him use her to draw Magpie out? Why didn't you just believe me? Why couldn't you just trust me? What have I done to deserve your skepticism, your betrayal? I asked, wounded to the quick.

The fire in my mind felt like geyser of flame. *I loved you!* I roared.

Palasa hurried over, closing the gap between us. The people around me were backing away. Their chairs tumbled toward me though, then exploded like an IED back toward the crowd. They chairs crashed into dignitaries and bodyguards, then suddenly reversed direction again, sweeping in and around me. They were pushed to and fro in the ebb and flow of my will. Palasa cradled my face in both hands, stroking it gently. When she spoke, her voice was small and frightened.

You're doing it again, she whispered. *This is how it starts.*

Over her shoulder, I saw Aaron stand and come forward. Tessa was at his side. She was jet fuel being thrown into the fire barbecuing my mind.

Stop it. Please. Palasa begged. I looked into her eyes and felt the fire in my mind wilt and dim. The chairs I was pulling and pushing suddenly lay still. The cries and screams around me suddenly stopped. Everyone waited nervously to see what would happen next.

It was your dreams, Leia announced suddenly. *It wasn't you I distrusted. It was your dreams. You never remember them. You never remember fighting the rotting men. You never remember being terrified of the thing hiding in the darkness.*

This is why you betrayed me? I asked, hurt and confused.

No. It was the darkness I feared. I thought it was Magpie hiding inside your mind. I thought you were hiding him away. I thought you might be the mask he was wearing to escape his punishment. I wasn't trying to draw Magpie out. I was trying to confirm that he wasn't in there to begin with. I was trying to prove it was just you, she cried. *I had to know that the man I was falling for was really the man I knew. I needed to know for sure.*

The pounding in my head dimmed a little more. Aaron came forward a bit, holding out a hand toward the security aching to rush me, warning them to stand back. He had seen what Palasa had done to Tessa's men. He realized this would be worse. He knew better than to provoke me. Knights had flooded in and were even then forming a ring of armor between me and the dignitaries on both sides. Some carried long poles before them. Some carried short four-foot poles. I had seen them before. I knew what they were. They were forming a shield wall to stop me.

You could have asked, I told her. Leia was shaking her head.

How could I? What could I say to you?

The truth, I snapped. *Tell me the damn truth.*

Oh. Hey Daniel. I've been eavesdropping on your dreams while you're asleep and was wondering, what's that Yellow Eyed monster you're hiding in the back of your mind. Really? You think that conversation would fly? she asked snidely. *You never remembered your dreams. You never—*

She was still talking. I knew she was, but I was not comprehending it anymore. I watched her lips moving as she defended her position, but I stopped listening when those two words were uttered.

Yellow eyes.

Two words punched me in the stomach. Two words rammed themselves down my throat. Two words shattered the door in a cabin in the woods. I pushed Palasa aside forcefully and vomited into the grass where she had stood.

You have to fight it, Palasa begged.

"Daniel. What's wrong?" Aaron asked. His voice sounded like it was coming from the bottom of a well. It was a soft murmur being heard through a brick wall.

My mind went back to before. I had sent my mind up to the ships. There was water on the floor. Leia lay bleeding in it. The men and women who held her perched like vultures about her, hunkering down to watch her and assault her. I was there scratching at the wall she had erected like a lap dog wanting in. They were there, tearing at the noise, slathering and gnawing and gnashing their non-existent teeth upon the barrier she had erected. In the darkness of their minds, I saw it. The beast with the Yellow Eyes. It was the parasite Gorjjen would later capture. It was in there, and it came for me.

I sank slowly to my knees, my eyes filled with fear. I had run away from it. Mercy had pulled me away. It had not infected me because it could not infect me. Luke had pressed it against my neck and the worm would not bite. He dropped it on the soft wetness of my eye and the worm had fled afraid. In my mind, Palasa was saying it again. I had come to this planet to save the armada. My brother had looked into my mind, and I had destroyed him. They stabbed me with a bayonet, and my name was Silas Gardner. I was shot in Normandy, and my name was Thomas Pilgrim. My first memory was of an alley filled with dead people, and now I was Daniel Sojourner. I fired on the colony. I fired on the ships. I killed Aug Moon.

Gorjjen's words suddenly made sense to me. I had spoken first. I had said that a lot of people had died in that storm. He had replied, "but not you."

How long ago had Magpie died? The question bothered me because I knew the answer.

Every time my life was threatened, something bad happened, and I got a new name. The old woman with the bomb. The percher who tried to stab me on the lift floor. I had turned them to red mist. No. That was not true. I did not turn them to red mist. He did. Yellow Eyes killed them. Yellow Eyes took control. Every time my secret was discovered, something bad happened, and I got a new name. Every time I slept, I fought the zombies. That's what Leia had said. I fought the zombie horde every night, but I would not open the door.

Luke had been talking for some time now, speaking English at the top of his lungs. He had never needed a translator. It was just another lie. He was shouting at the diplomats representing Earth, shaking his fist like he was Hitler. The four men who sat with Putin retreated toward a nearby tunnel. Putin was with them, hunkering down behind a wall of men.

". . . is one of you," Luke called. "This woman killed our leader. This woman killed my father. Her crime is your crime. She worked for your leader. She was one of yours, and you sent her to assassinate our beloved ruler." The diplomats in the stands looked worried. "Look to the sky. Do you really think we won't retaliate for what you've caused to be done?" he asked, his voice fluctuating as my will began to ebb and flow again. He hid behind the blurriness in my eyes, but I knew he was there.

"It wasn't your fault," Palasa cried, weeping openly. I stared up into her eyes. I finally knew the truth. I finally knew the secret I was too afraid to tell.

"You've gotta run," I whispered urgently, seizing her by the shoulders. The pain made the world look like it was quaking around me. The blood pumping through my veins was deafening.

". . . that's why I sentence this woman to death. She is guilty of assassinating our most beloved leader. She is an assassin and a murderer and an agent of the Empire's most wanted criminal, Magpie. She will die for what she's done: for what you have sent her to do," Luke roared, "and when we are done with her, we will turn our eyes on those who sent her," he told them, slamming his fist down on top of the podium.

Don't listen to him, Leia called. *It isn't real. She isn't really guilty. She'll be fine.*

You have to flee, I begged. *Save them. Save them all from me.*

"A sentence that must not wait," Luke bellowed, striding toward Leia. "Justice must be swift." He was carrying something in his right hand. My hands trembled with pent up power.

Luke's eyes never left my own.

"Leave!" I bellowed to the crowd, waving my hands to get their attention. "Flee! Hurry! Save yourself!" I could feel it moving inside my skull. The thing we called Yellow Eyes was there. I wanted to rush forward and save them, but I was the thing they needed to fear. I look to Aaron to heed my words. "They're all in danger. Everyone is in danger! Get them out of here. Get them away from me." Aaron nodded and moved to obey.

This is for killing my father, Luke roared into my mind.

I turned as he pressed the glass tube to Palasa's neck and pulled the trigger. The parasite in the tube slithered like a serpent toward neck. Palasa was momentarily confused by what was happening. She reached up to pull away what was jabbing into her neck, but by then the parasite had already slit her skin and slithered into the fatty tissue below.

There was a moment of horrified understanding where Palasa opened her mouth to scream but nothing came out. Her eyes looked into the darkness of the sky overhead, and the parasite entered her brain.

The world froze as the laws of space and time were rewritten inside my head. I saw the whole universe spread out before me. I simultaneously observed every movement and every person in the stadium. I saw how it would all end. I inhaled slowly, eating all the sunlight. I would need every ounce of strength I had to destroy Luke.

Chapter 37: Destruction

"No!" Leia screamed, lashing out at her brother. He turned away from me just in time to be flattened by her strike.

My will built of its own accord, only now I was no longer fighting it. I had a target for it.

In my mind, I was fighting a zombie horde the likes of which George A. Romero would be hard pressed to envision. I was fighting for my very survival. I was fighting to keep myself in control. Nearly two hundred folding chairs came bouncing toward me, rolling like tumble weeds. They swept around me to my right only to be sent hurtling back into field behind me once more. I wore power like a cape in that moment and carried lighting in my fist.

The dignitaries from the saucers fled. Their bodyguards shielded them with their armored backs.

Aaron was ordering Secret Service to clear the stands. The crowd on both sides stumbled and tripped over each other in their rush to flee. The only people who didn't flee were the knights who encircled me and my friends. Leia's strike knocked Luke back into Palasa who in turn bowled me over. We all three went down in a tangle.

"Go!!" I roared, my body arching skyward. I was losing control. Ailig and Xi came to help me, pulling me to my feet. "Stop it," I snapped, shoving them away.

They flew nearly thirty feet in opposite directions, rolling sideways and flipping ankles over apex into the crowd. Leia came rushing forward to stop me—or maybe it was Luke or Palasa she was trying to stop. I do not know.

Whoever it was she planned on stopping, she was doing it with her halo in hand. She was nearly on us when her path forward was suddenly interrupted, arrested, and altered. She jerked sideways suddenly like she had been ripped away with an invisible rope. She flipped and cart-wheeled past Gorjjen who twisted almost casually out of her path to avoid being hit. He did not look back to see how she fared.

I had not done that. I looked to my right where Palasa was still trying to disentangle herself from a semi-conscious Luke. She showed no interest in the man.

Gorjjen watched me calmly as if he was not presently standing in the midst of the maelstrom forming in the center of the stadium. Leia smashed into a tangled knot of dignitaries and guards at the end of her flight. Her halo fell from her hand and bounced across the grass before me. I stared down at it bemused. I almost reached for it, but Palasa was quicker.

She snatched up the halo Leia dropped and turned it on me. She had me dead to rights. I was too stupefied to resist, but suddenly, she changed her mind and pointed it at Gorjjen instead. I was not really confused. She knew what the Yellow Eyed bastard in my head would do to her if she tried to pull that trigger.

Gorjjen twisted right to avoid the first blast, ducked under the next, and threw himself bodily sideways to avoid the following two. He landed on his feet completely undamaged. The diplomats behind him were not so lucky. The halo burnt baseball sized holes through dozens of the diplomats and their guards alike. Each shot plunged through the body of the man in front and the five or six men behind him.

Milintart and Jo did not flee with the rest. They came rushing forward, swords in hand. This was what an Imperial Knight trained for. They slapped the emblem on their breast plates to activate their psionic armor and bore down on Palasa.

Palasa turned the halo on Milintart, but the nimble knight twisted to her right and twisted again and again and again, rolling right around the infected woman like a dancer in a ballet. Palasa fired three shots at the dancing knight hitting several Secret Service agents as they threw themselves in front of the Homeland Director in a bid to save him. They had no idea how effective the halo was or how futile their sacrifice, and Aaron collapsed behind his security team.

The knights ringing me in slammed their poles into the ground activating their shields. The radiant blue petals of energy formed in a chain with each petal reinforcing the one above it. The shield wall blinked into existence, and the knights behind them planted their feet and drew their weapons, ready to die in defense of the civilians behind them.

Several of Palasa's blasts popped and fizzled against the shield petals. Each petal hit blinked out for a moment, defeated by the blast. The moment the shield batteries recharged their drained capacitors, the shield petals reformed.

Jo came at Palasa straight, dodging right as the infected woman brought her halo to bear. Jo feinted left to draw her fire and dodged right as the muzzle of the halo tried to follow her. Palasa fired a blast where Jo should have been, then tried to correct her aim. However, Jo's left blade met the muzzle midway and slapped it aside. The halo whined and spat a stray blast toward the shield wall.

A tall guard racing in from the crowd to help the knights took the blast full in the face. He crashed down through the ring of knights and slid to a stop beside me.

Jo followed her left counter with right-handed chop to Palasa's neck. Palasa lashed out with her will, deflecting the blade up as she dodged backwards. It gave her room enough to fire off several wild shots at Jo.

Jo threw herself flat and rolled to avoid the half-dozen poorly aimed shots my infected niece popped off. Palasa thought she had bought herself some breathing room and hurriedly scanned the ring of knights to find her exit. She found it across the back of the guard she had dropped dead beside me. The knights in the shield wall had yet to close the gap the fallen guard had opened. She made for the gap only to find Milintart hot on her heels.

Milintart came at her from behind, rushing Palasa and leading with a blinding flurry of upward diagonally executed slashes that alternated back and forth from left to right. Palasa took two shallow cuts to her lower back before stymieing Palasa's charge.

The infected woman dropped her right arm down to her side and swept it backwards with Leia's halo in hand. She fired off a couple shots near Milintart's feet to force the woman to retreat. Milintart gave ground, but before Palasa could take advantage of the retreat, Jo returned.

Jo came in whirling and stabbing, slashing and hacking. Her hands worked independent of each other. Her left worked back and forth up high, seeking to slit a throat or pierce an eye. Her right worked low, trying to cripple or disembowel the woman. Jo managed a shallow cut across Palasa's brow. The blood from her wound immediately began flowing into the infected woman's eyes, blinding her. She fired blindly at the ground before her before she tried to smash Jo with a blow of her mind.

Jo took a knee as the blast of will crashed into her. The wall of force broke apart upon her armor. She sprang forward again.

Jo's right sword slashed for the meaty part of Palasa's leg, seeking to sever the muscles above her knee. Jo's left sword snaked around Palasa's arm as she shoved it forward, halo in hand. The tip of Jo's sword slid like a razor under the surface of the skin, slicing a deep spiral in Palasa's upper arm all the way to her arm pit. Jo's blade paused there for a moment, so Jo could step into the follow through. The moment Jo tried to shove the wicked tip of her sword under Palasa's arm and through her ribs, the infected woman countered. Palasa dropped her sidearm and twisted sideways so that the piercing blade merely nicked a little fat beneath her arm instead of puncturing her lung.

She found Milintart at her back again, slashing horizontally to cut the infected woman in half. Palasa was forced to swing her upper body below the blade as Gorjjen had done to avoid Palasa's shots at him. Her palms actually brushed the grass so low was she forced to go.

Palasa saw an opening behind Milintart's mighty attempt at bisection, and she let her trailing leg swing up and over. The heal of Palasa's foot caught Milintart square in the face, breaking the knight's nose. The hit sent Milintart staggering backwards into the ring of knights behind her.

Jo leapt after her with a mighty two-handed chop, but Palasa was able to twist aside at the last moment. Jo was a Blood Knight. She had achieved more in her time as a knight than almost any other, including Leia. There were no wasted movements to her attacks. Her chops missed, so she turned her blades ninety degrees and dragged their edges across Palasa's stomach.

Palasa managed to suck in her stomach a little, but she was still cut badly. Sucking in her stomach had only kept her from being disemboweled, but that was where the bright side ended for her.

The infected woman danced backwards, cradling her stomach and tripped over Aaron and his dead security detail. The parasite in Palasa's head knew in that moment that it would most likely die at the hands of this twin-braided double-bladed dervish. Jo was a far better fighter than she.

The power inside me was building. I was losing control. I cried out, my control slipping. The podium exploded, and the knights behind it were hurled backwards hard into the wall behind them.

I had not meant for that to happen.

"Help me," I pleaded at the top of my voice, looking to Baggam who stood outside the ring of knights. "For Christ's sake, do something." Baggam looked bleak. He did not come to my rescue.

I felt like my mind was vomiting. Each dry heave sent waves of force that flashed out into the crowds. The leader of Turkey and the Australian Prime Minister were crushed backwards into their seats, their bodies broken and twisted, bones jutting from the rib cages. Blood and fluids spilled from their eyes and mouth.

Palasa pawed at the ground around her, looking for anything she could use as a weapon. Her hand found something in the pile of bodies. Aaron's hand weakly closed upon her searching arm in an attempt to stop her.

She snatched her arm away and smashed her elbow into his face. In her hand, she held the silvery rod Gorjjen had given the injured man. With a press of a button, the glorious weapon transformed, sprouting like a tree from both ends. She held fast to the weapon and let the five-foot staff drag her back to her feet. The end supporting her punched through Aaron's chest and into the ground below.

Aaron growled in pain and Sheila screamed in fear. The reporter rushed forward and tried to drag her father from the fight. Palasa looked down at the frail younger woman and contemptuously swatted her away, smashing her upside the head with the bloody end of her staff. She caught Sheila across the side of the head. The reporter twisted sideways and collapsed backwards with an audible sigh before blacking out.

"Someone help me!" I cried again. I was gritting my teeth so hard I felt one of them crack under the strain. My mind vomited again, and the ring of knights about me was thrown backward even further, opening gaps everywhere.

I opened my mouth to scream again, and my mind spasmed unexpectedly. I clenched my will by accident. It was brief but devastating. The waves of my will rolled away from me and any who stood were thrown to the ground. Any who stood between me and the wall were ground into hamburger meat.

Several knights perished.

Leia came darting in from out of nowhere sprinting fast for Palasa. Ailig and Xi came back into the fight as well and just as eager. Palasa worked her staff up and down and back, deflecting Jo's lighting fast slashes and foiling Milintart's brutal hacks. Sparks flew as the nanite weapons collided repeatedly.

As Leia launched herself into the midst of the battle, she stabbed out at Palasa with her mind as well as her swords. Palasa screamed in pain as the force of Leia's mental attacked ruptured the skin all across her face. Over a dozen weeping wounds appeared as if by magic. Two more appeared across Palasa's chest from Leia's sword. One cut ran from her collar bone to her right shoulder as Leia slashed across. Leia's recovery came as a vertical slice from above that cut through Palasa's right breast.

She screamed in pain and swept her stolen staff before her, punching Leia across the side of the head. Leia staggered sideways, but she had the presence of mind to twist away to give Jo clear access. Palasa accidentally pressed the button on the staff that caused the twin spear tips to sprout from both ends. It proved fortuitous for her.

She twisted sideways to avoid Jo's strike and threw herself backwards into the blade to keep one of Milintart's strikes from landing. The infected woman wheeled her staff around to knock both blades out wide, slashing Ailig across the cheek and Xi across the chest in the process.

She flipped the spear around and worked it back and forth like a sewing machine needle, stabbing repeatedly back and forth and aiming for Jo and Milintart's mid-sections. They swept their blades back and forth frantically in an effort to defeat Palasa's frenzied attacks. She lashed out to the sides occasionally to foil the men's contributions to the fight. Leia darted in and out as Gorjjen had trained them to do. If they could not killer her, they would tire her out, and Palasa was quickly tiring.

Palasa swept her staff across to knock both Jo and Leia's blades aside, then stabbed out with the bottom of the staff for Ailig's solar plexus. This was ultimately her undoing. She was tired. Ailig was not.

The colonial survivalist and decorated knight did not hesitate in the least, he swept the spear aside with his bent left elbow and rolled down the length of the shaft. He swept his right elbow up and over the top of the shaft and trapped it against his side while he stabbed out with his other hand, shoving a foot and half of nanite steel through Palasa's right shoulder. He followed this by delivering a quick spear-handed jab to the infected woman's windpipe. His stiffened hand did not crush the windpipe, but it left her gasping for air.

"I can't stop it!" I told them. No one was listening. I felt blood leaking from eyes and nose. Palasa suddenly sensed the danger. She had time now that they thought her defeated. She could not attack the five warriors with her mind directly, so she attacked them indirectly.

She gathered her will and focused it behind a group a dignitaries trying to flee and flexed. Her will exploded like bomb sending the diplomats crashing into the backs of the knights. The knights staggered forward under the weight of the flying bodies, stumbling into the five warriors that held Palasa. She tried to flee in the confusion, racing for the wall and the Earthling dignitaries beyond.

She focused her will just before the wall at ground level and leapt. The moment she passed over the spot she had picked, she clenched her will and launched herself up over the railing.

"It's happening," I sobbed. "I'm sorry. I'm so sorry."

"Stop him," Palasa cried, recognizing her peril. Her voice crackled and popped insect-like. Those pursuing her paused in surprise. The parasite knew it needed to flee, but it also knew that it would do no good. It could not run fast enough or far enough to escape the thing inside my head.

My arms shook like I was being electrocuted. It was happening. I could not hold it any longer. Palasa must have sensed this. She rolled her spear around in her hand so that the spear tip faced me and cocked her left arm. She intended to launch it at me like it was a javelin.

My salvation in that moment came from the most unlikely source.

"No!" Luke cried, raising the halo Palasa dropped. He fired a single blast, and it took the infected woman in the stomach, blasting through the metal railing before her and punching through the right side of her abdomen. The blast narrowly missed hitting the Canadian Prime Minister behind her.

I was vibrating like I would blow apart at any moment and despite all that energy and heat, watching Palasa clutch at her stomach in an attempt to hold her intestine's in chilled me. I felt an icy blast wash over me like a cold north wind.

As I stared up at my niece, I felt all my resistance drain away. I surrendered to the thing inside my head and fixed my gaze upon the Pre-Prior. He turned Leia's halo upon me with a triumphant sneer. He had not killed her to save me. He had killed her to keep her from robbing him of the privilege.

The cloud of wild will blowing about suddenly came rushing back into my mind, reforming into something powerful and dreadful and narrowly focused. It coiled inside me like a serpent, rearing its head to strike.

"Goodbye, Magpie," Luke growled, pulling the trigger. I growled back and let him have it right in the teeth.

The force inside me burst forth like escaping gas. If Luke had been standing there when it released, he would have been torn to shreds.

The halo blast caught me a glancing blow across my cheek. My savior this time had been Luke's sister.

Leia had leapt forward and clubbed her brother upside his head with the flat of her blade, knocking him off to the side and unconscious.

The force of my will stabbed forward where his face had been, missing him by inches. It stabbed instead into the wall thirty feet behind him, blowing the wall apart and plowing a furrow twelve rows deep into the seats above.

World leaders who had only ever feared coupes and free speech were flung aside like water before a wheel. The rage took me. It controlled me now. I had given it all away, and Yellow Eyes slipped into the driver seat after a thousand years trying. He had finally won, and all it took was the death of an innocent woman. The well of willpower gathered inside me felt like a neutrino bomb waiting to detonate.

"We should celebrate," Yellow Eyes declared. His crackling, chirping, popping insect-sounding voice told all who could hear that I was gone. I watched it all as if from down a long hall.

Leia looked up at me and gasped in fear. The Yellow Eyes she had seen in the darkness outside the cabin were no longer hiding in the darkness of my mind. They were right their above my cheeks for all to see. She understood the situation then and let her shoulders slump. This was as much her fault as it was Luke's. She had let this happen.

"It was you all along?" she said, saddened by the knowledge.

"It was me," Yellow Eyes confirmed.

"When?" she asked. "When did you infect him?" Yellow Eyes seemed amused by the question. Normally, he would not have deigned to answer a doomed woman's query. But he knew it would hurt her more to know.

"The moment he set foot on my world," Yellow Eyes whispered. "You should never enter the water. That's where we live. That's where we live still."

"H-He is . . . an abomination," Palasa called out weakly, teetering on the wall above us.

"I am the Other and the Last," Yellow Eyes announced. "I shall live forever."

"You are too . . . late," Palasa called down to him. "We have found you. We. Are. Here," she said, blood leaking from her mouth.

"You lie," Yellow Eyes replied, ignoring the others.

"They are here, and we are watching. Justice. Will. Be. Ours," the thing inside Palasa taunted. Yellow Eyes roared in anger, searching the eyes of the people around him. He looked for their eyes, the eyes of the infected. He saw only Palasa; bloody, mutilated, Palasa.

"Liar!" Yellow Eyes roared, sending out a blast of hijacked will. The blast hit Palasa in the chest, carrying her backwards into the seats and concrete beneath them. Her body rippled and ripped and tore for several long moments as the parasite inside me poured all his hate into the attack. Her body spread out in all directions like she was dropped watermelon. Her blood and innards painted the cowering diplomats around her red.

"You can't escape us," Leia growled, taking a new grip on her sword. Milintart moved to my left. Jo stepped into place between her and Leia. Ailig and Xi flanked the three women.

"You don't get it. You can't stop me," Yellow Eyes hissed. "I can crack worlds. I. Am. A. God."

"Such grandeur, my friend," Gorjjen remarked. "Let us test your magnificence."

Yellow Eyes turned in surprise, having not sensed the Baron's approach. There were no words beyond what Gorjjen spoke.

There were no exclamations of surprise or defiance on the part of Yellow Eyes. Most importantly, there was no hesitation in Gorjjen's act. Gorjjen pulled the trigger on the Judge, and the forty-five-caliber slug punched through the left side of my chest.

I felt the pain, and I heard Yellow Eyes scream of rage. He had finally won after ten centuries of fighting only to lose it to a sliver of lead. This was the first time in centuries that it felt right surrendering to the darkness. I fell backwards into it like I was falling into the arms of a lover. I had no regrets. My fight was finally over.

Chapter 38: Identity

The zombies stood at the window. They moaned low. They swayed restlessly, but they did not attack. The door to the cabin stood ajar; the bar thrown. I sat on the hearth, before the crackling fire. My shotgun sat beside me on the stones. The clawed hammer sat head down upon the floor, its handle leaning against my legs. I could sense that outside, the darkness stirred. The Yellow Eyes in the woods studied me as a child might study the crystalline structure of a snowflake.

I thought about picking up the hammer and picking up the gun and resuming my fight, but I was tired. What was the point? Yellow Eyes would never quit. He would never surrender. Now that I finally knew the truth, I was free. I had not destroyed the Sylar Colony which is a fact that had weighed heavily upon my mind. It had been Yellow Eyes.

"Why don't you come in here and take control again?" I called out to the darkness, taunting it. The darkness did not respond. "I finally know the truth," I shouted. "I remember it all." I picked up the gun, caressed its walnut stock, and for a moment I was almost my old self. I looked with hate upon the darkness and knew it mocked me.

"I'd be interested in hearing that story," A new voice admitted, a familiar voice.

"What are you doing here?" I asked morosely. "This," I said, motioning back and forth between them, "can't work. I'm infected, remember?"

"You weren't always," the new voice replied, giving the open door a wary look. "When did the thing infect you?" she asked.

"Are you real?" I asked, suddenly skeptical that she could be here again, knowing full well what hid inside my own mind. She smiled.

"I'm real. I'd really like to hear that story."

"We were harvesting Sylar. We knew something was off about it. It took a little probing, but we learned that there was another sentience inside each of the people. You know how we thought they were infected? They were, but it wasn't against the colonist's will. It was with their blessing."

I continued. "The colony proved too unforgiving for the colonists left there by the Empire to seed it. They discovered, much to their dismay, that there was an infestation of parasites on the planet; it was a worm of sorts. It was intelligent and sentient and came in two breeds."

I could practically smell the disbelief and disgust coming off Leia. "The first breed, called Jejun by the colonists, were a cruel vicious specimen who infected the colonists and used them like steeds, forcing them to hunt, maim, and torture the other colonists. These parasites," I jerked my head toward the darkness without, "have the ability to enhance and focus our will far beyond anything a human should be able to do. The other type of parasite, the Pymalor, was a kind and just creature unlike their cousins."

My audience was enraptured. "When the Empire first seeded the planet with humans, the hope was that they would breed and survive and grow plentiful. It didn't work out that way. The humans were dying one-by-one. The Jejun," I said, gesturing to the yellow eyed darkness again, "were taking them as hosts and killing them for fun, and would have continued till all of them were dead. If not for the intervention of the Pymalor, the colony of Sylar would have faded away within years of the seeding."

"A Pymalor worm infected one of the first colonists and explained why the other colonists seemed to be going crazy. It revealed the existence of the Jejun and offered the colonists a deal. If they served voluntarily as hosts to the Pymalor, the Jejun could no longer infect them. The colonists accepted. The goodly parasites infected all the colonists the Jejun hadn't infected. Together, they hunted down the infected and dispatched them. After that, every child born on Sylar was born infected. The Jejun were then driven into the sea."

My face betrayed my now somber tone. "We of course knew none of this when first we arrived in orbit above Sylar. After three hundred rotations we descended to the surface. The Jejun began to infect us almost immediately, only this time, they weren't making their presence known. The Sylar colony was huge. The Jejun couldn't risk letting their hated cousins know. Their plan had been to infect the crew of the ships and military and then after the Harvest was complete, they would kill all of the citizens of Sylar who had boarded the ship."

"The Jejun don't really have a hierarchy. Some of the more obstinate of their breed chose to secretly infect unknowing citizens aboard the ship. I and two knights happened upon one of these altars while a Jejun prince was infecting a small child. We fought. The knights were killed. I killed the infected man and child and hurried to relay what I knew to Abbot Aug Moon down on the surface."

"On land, I was safe, but Moon was already infected, and he knocked me into the sea when I confronted him. The parasites in the water swarmed all over me, fighting each other for possession of my body. That yellow eyed bastard took over my body and briefly my mind."

"The parasites kind of function like Facebook. They attack you through your social network. For instance, if they infect someone who is trusted, they are usually more able to take control of those who trust the infected one. From there, the infected friends and family are able to infect their circle of friends and family as well, and so on."

"Those like Yellow Eyes out there, rule over those they infected like a god. Those without a worm function as worshippers. This is the only way they can infect someone. You either open your mind to them, or they slither into your brain." I looked out into the darkness.

"You should probably leave," I said. "I'm not in charge here anymore. The only reason it's not attacking is to show you that it has complete control of me and that you are powerless here." Leia squatted before me and stared out into the darkness, unimpressed with its presence.

"Would you like to be?" she asked cryptically.

"Of course."

"Tell me the rest," she urged. I shrugged and did as she bade.

"When our crew came back to the saucers, they brought with them more of the Jejun. They started infecting the crews aboard the six ships. I had been wrestling with Yellow Eyes for control and managed to win through, taking control of my own sub-conscious. Before I won my freedom from it though, it used the guns aboard the Moon Rai to burn away the planet's atmosphere. My first act upon freeing myself from its influence was to turn those same guns upon the six infected ships, obliterating the rest of the Jejun and their worshippers. I faced criminal charges for what I did. In the interim before I destroyed the saucers, skiffs started coming from the infected ships. Those who came aboard were infected. I didn't know the difference between the two breeds back then. I didn't know if those who came aboard were Jejun or Pymalor. All I knew was that they were infected." I picked up the double barrel shotgun and turned it so both barrels pointed toward my face. I was not attempting suicide, but a part of me was just curious what it looked like staring into the barrels. It was dark in there.

"Maybe it's wise that we fear the dark. We feared it as kids," I mused. "Kids are programmed from birth to fear real and viable dangers. There really are things in the dark that can hurt us. Yellow Eyes," I said, nodding toward the door yet again, "is case in point. Bullets," I added, pointing the gun at Leia's head so she could look into the barrels, "they hide in the darkness of a barrel." She did not flinch. "Perchers," I said, pointing the gun at the head of one of the zombies outside the window. I pulled the trigger, and the shotgun coughed fire. The zombie's head exploded. The darkness outside squirmed irritably in reply but did not enter.

"Why won't he come for me?" I asked. "Why won't you come for me already!" I shouted into the darkness.

"I won't let him," Leia answered.

"No offense, but I don't think you can stop him," I scoffed. "I've been fighting him for centuries."

"You were fighting him alone," she whispered. "Right now, you're in one of your colonial care facilities. You're in what your people call a coma state. It," she said jerking her head toward the darkness, "can't control you right now."

"I was always Magpie," I told her. "It couldn't kill Magpie. It just erased my memories. Even now, I can only remember because it's letting me. It's letting me because it knows it tortures me to remember. I was the one who killed your father, Leia. Luke was right all along. Your father was aboard the ships when I destroyed them. You should hate me."

"I've come to terms with that," she replied. "I'm not Luke. I've had a thousand years to get over my daddy issues."

"It made me kill my brothers," I whispered. "It could push me when we wanted the same things. If someone tried to attack me, I would want to live and stop that person, and Yellow Eyes was able to use my will to lash out." I broke open the shot gun, pulled out the shells and slipped two more shells into the breech. I flicked it closed with one hand. "William and his family spent two hundred years looking for me. When they found me, I kept telling William to leave. When he asked why I left the ship, I could only say that I was trying to save the armada. I knew I was infected, and it was getting harder to keep it contained. I was terrified for William. I was begging him to walk away, but he kept coming at me over and over and over again. When I still wouldn't relent, he thrust himself into my mind to learn the truth and Yellow Eyes was waiting."

I felt myself on the verge of tears. "I-I didn't want him dead. I just wanted him to leave, but William saw that I was infected. Brother or not, he was obligated to do the right thing and end me. He tried to kill me. I tried not to die. And Yellow Eyes pushed me and rode my emotions the entire way." Angry tears bled hot from my eyes. "You knew what he was to me! You God damn knew what he was to me, and you used him to punish me!" I shouted at the darkness. The darkness seemed to be laughing.

"In that alley in New Orleans. The levies had broke days before. I had a jug of water with me. Surrounded by all that water, and only the jug I held was drinkable. Those people in the alley, the storm didn't kill them. They didn't want to hurt me. They were just scared and dying of thirst. I wanted to share with them, but I knew if I did, we'd all die. I offered to share it anyway, but that bastard out there thinks only of itself. It slaughtered them so I could survive; so it could survive."

"It's been doing this to me for centuries. I've had half a hundred different names and every name was one I made up after he made me into a murderer and took my memories!" I roared, coming to my feet. I marched up to the door, ripped it open, and fired both barrels into seething sea of corruption without.

The darkness screamed in protest, and the zombies started forward.

"Stop it!" Leia barked, marching toward the darkness, her sword in hand.

"You can't stop him," I spat, going back to the fireplace to sit.

"He's been fighting you for centuries," she told the darkness. "I'm here to fight the battle now," she declared.

The zombies started pouring through the windows and shuffling toward the door. Leia sliced their heads in twain, cut their reaching arms away, sheared through the torsos. "You've been comfortable in here. You've been safe," she told the darkness.

"You can't win," I told her stubbornly.

She ignored me, and instead she addressed the darkness. "He's always been fighting alone, but he's not alone now. You didn't want anyone to find out you were in here." She took a zombie's leg below the knee and whipped her sword across and sliced the top of three skulls off, dropping their owners. "You knew if someone like me came, we would stop you."

"What can you do against two fighters?" Leia asked the darkness, glancing with a smirk at me.

"Or three?" Ailig asked, suddenly appearing in the room beside her. He cut through the mob of putrefied men to reach Leia's side.

"Or four?" Milintart asked, appearing behind them. She raced toward the closest window and started tearing through those who tried to enter.

"Or five?" Xi asked.

"Or six?" Baggam growled.

"Or seven?" Jo snarled.

"Or eight? Or Nine? Or Ten?" Leia asked, and each time she asked, another knight appeared in the cabin around them.

"You cannot win this battle, my friend," Gorjjen announced boldly, appearing at my side. He strode forward through the mass of warriors, and they parted before him. He stopped in the doorway. Leia too stepped aside for him. In Gorjjen's hand, he held the Taurus Judge, and in the other, he held the sword he had given Aaron. "We will destroy you here," Gorjjen promised, issuing his threat with a quiet calm. The zombies seemed to hesitate and none of them approached Gorjjen.

I clutched my head and started to scream behind them. Daggers of pain shot through my skull. Yellow Eyes seemed amused.

"Or, you may kill Daniel," Gorjjen declared. "This one time and this one time only, I give you the chance to live. Leave his body. Leave and I'll make you my prisoner. It is not the end you seek, but you do get to live. That's all you ever wanted. You just wanted to live." The darkness suddenly seemed very unsure of itself.

I was still screaming.

"How do I know you'll keep your word?" the crackling voice of the parasite asked of Gorjjen.

"You face the Baron of Heid!" Gorjjen roared, raising the Judge. "You get what I give you. It is either death here or a chance to exist out there. Choose now because I'm tired of talking," Gorjjen told the faceless apparition. There was a moment of indecision on the part of the parasite, but in that moment, I stopped screaming as the pain disappeared. In the next moment, the darkness was gone. The sun was rising beyond the trees. The zombies, dead and alive, were gone. The moaning stopped. The knights cheered and one-by-one, they vanished from the room till it was only Gorjjen, me, and Leia who remained.

"It is over, my friend," Gorjjen told the man. I looked up, weeping with gratitude. "I look forward to our long talks again," the weapon master murmured softly.

I looked up into the face of the man who had found me aboard the Kye O'Ren, and I knew him at last. I had known him before. I had known him since before we left Cojo.

"Mozzie?" I sobbed, my voice cracking. It was Leia's turn to be surprised. She turned disbelieving eyes upon the man she called her master.

"Hello Magpie," Gorjjen replied with a broad grin. I scrambled to my feet and eagerly embraced my little brother. Gorjjen laughed merrily and pounded my back in welcome. We held ourselves like that for the longest time, neither wanting to let the other go. When I finally started to take stock of Leia, I saw that she was crying too. I held out my arm and rolled her into the hug, kissing her cheek and her face repeatedly.

I held them like that for several long moments, then I staggered forward, suddenly holding empty air. I cast about for them, but they were gone. They were gone. They were gone and I started to sob again. It had not been real. I sobbed fitfully in the silence of my desolate cabin. I knew the truth now, but it was too late. My brother lived and he . . . I suddenly took notice of the paling sky outside and of the glare on the lake beyond the trees. I took notice of the woods outside and realized that the darkness was really gone. That was real. If nothing else was ever real, this was. I marched outside for the first time in centuries and watched as the darkness gave birth to the blue sky.

"I'm free," I whispered. I laughed long and loud, shouting with joy the words I never thought I would say. "I'm—"

"Free!" I whispered hoarsely. I suddenly felt terrible. My eyes were blurry. I could not see. I could smell though. The air smelled of disinfectant and cleaner. There were dark forms hiding behind my cemented lashes.

"He's awake," a familiar voice announced.

"Leia?" I croaked, smacking my dry lips.

"He needs water," Leia blurted, seizing my hand. There was movement, and the shadows shifted to make way for another. A hard thick tube was pressed against my lips and a short splash of cold water struck my tongue and pooled in the back of my mouth.

I swallowed and clutched for the bottle, needing more. Someone used a moist cloth to mop my brow and wipe away the sleep sealing my eyelashes together. I was able to see after that. I felt like Dorothy waking in her own bed, freshly home from Oz.

There was Leia, Ailig, Xi, Baggam, Jo, Milintart, and Gorjjen. Behind them was another squad of knights. I did not know them, but I recognized them from my dream. I really was in a hospital bed on Earth.

"We should have listened to the medical man when he told us to take you here," Leia replied. "They found the parasite in your skull with one of their machines that looks into your head," she explained.

"CAT scan," Tessa supplied. The NSA director looked nervous. I looked past the nurse tending me to Gorjjen.

"It wasn't a dream was it?" I asked. Gorjjen smiled. "You really are Mozzie?" I asked. Gorjjen dipped his head, cutting a warning look to the other knights that this name remain unspoken.

"To you and you alone," Gorjjen replied.

"You shot me," I accused. Gorjjen nodded with a smirk.

"Surgery with a bullet is more like it," Tessa Barnes declared. He put the bullet right above your heart. Half an inch lower or to the left and you would have been worm food. A dozen knights and friends turned menacing eyes on her. Her face paled as she realized how insensitive that sounded in light of what had just happened with the Jujen called Yellow Eyes.

"It seemed like a good idea at the time," Gorjjen replied to my accusation.

"Yellow Eyes?" I asked. Jo stepped forward, holding a cage with an ordinary everyday gutter rat in it.

"Our prisoner," Xi declared.

"Can we kill it instead?" I pleaded. The rat started snarling and hissing in reply. This at least made me smile. Gorjjen shook his head. I sighed and looked to the others.

"It's all worked out then?" I asked.

"No," Leia whispered.

"Luke is in custody for infecting Palasa and killing her. Palasa is dead, her parasite destroyed. Six Earth delegates were killed, twice that many injured. Two dozen dignitaries from the ships were killed. Six times that many were injured. Thirteen bodyguards were killed when Palasa started firing into the crowd. Two knights were killed when you slammed them into the walls, and eighteen were injured by the blast you released when the Baron shot you. All is not well. This Harvest will not take place. Not after this. These people are doomed when the Sylar colonists arrive," Milintart declared. Her nose had been straightened and taped by a doctor.

"Your friend didn't make it," Leia whispered softly. "I'm sorry."

"Aaron?" I asked. Tessa was shaking her head. "The weapon she shot his security with went through them all. He died on the way to the hospital after." This depressed me more than anything else.

"Maybe I could talk to the leaders, before they all leave, and—" Leia was shaking her head.

"That was three rotations ago," Xi explained.

"Three days?" I asked in disbelief. "They're not going to announce the Harvest to the people, are they?"

"It was a resounding no," Tessa declared.

"What about Aaron's daughter?" I asked, grasping for straws. I needed something to go right.

"She'll be notified along with her mother. It'll take some time to create a plausible cover story to explain Aaron's death. He was a very notable personage. It may take some time. As soon as we have a suitable lie to tell, they'll be notified," Tessa replied. This made me smile. This made me laugh. This made Tessa confused. She did not know.

"You couldn't find her after the incident in the stadium, huh?" I asked. Tessa looked confused. "We had more pressing issues. We had . . ." she trailed off as the realization set in. The Director's face drained of blood, paling before my eyes. "You didn't know she was there?" I chortled.

"Aaron's daughter?" Tessa asked, suddenly feeling sick. "She was at the summit?"

"She wasn't just at the summit, Tess. She was at the summit with a camera and sitting ringside to the whole ordeal," I replied joyfully. Tessa threw a folder filled with pictures down on my lap and pulled her phone off her hip. She rushed out into the hall shouldering armored knights aside.

Leia picked up the folder and set it on the pillow beside me so that she could adjust my blanket.

"What now?" she asked.

"I throw dirty pictures in your head till you beg me to stop," I replied. This earned a few chuckles from the other knights.

"We find a way to interrogate our prisoner," Gorjjen replied. "We find a way to stop the insurgent attacks. We try to again to convince these people to come with us. We find the Drifters. We make the Empire whole again, and then, we finish our mission and visit the rest of the colonies." I could not find any problems with anything he said.

"We just have to find a way to reframe our invitation," Ailig declared, chin upraised and chest puffed out.

"You son of a bitch," Tessa cried, rushing back into the room; rushing toward me with her hand outstretched. Gorjjen seized her arm and twisted it up behind her, thinking she was coming to harm me. Tessa cried out in pain, snarled in protest, then reached out for the remote beside me. She used it to turn the television on.

I nodded to Gorjjen, and he released her. The television made small popping sound as it came on. Everyone in the room turned to face it. I could not help but smile. Something had finally gone right. Tessa changed the channel and kept changing, but Sheila was on every channel and the words at the bottom of the screen were all the same.

"World Leaders Meet With Alien Leaders in Secret Summit that Kills Director of Homeland Security."

"There will be repercussions for this," Tessa warned. "You did this."

"I did this," I replied, wincing as Leia threw her arms around me in joy.

You did it, she whispered into my mind. *You saved the Harvest.* I wondered if this were true.

Tessa stormed out, being careful not to abuse the knights like she would her own men. The folder she left behind slipped down between the wall and mattress unobserved. It opened beneath the bed and a single picture spilled out with a name and a hastily scribbled question.

"The Moon Ray: Friend or Foe?"

Printed in Great Britain
by Amazon

17583745R00287